I0674626

The Soul Stone

The Kronicles of Korthlundia

Book 1

Expanded Edition

By: Jamie Marchant

BEWITCHING FABLES PRESS

The final approval for this literary material is granted by the author.

This book was originally published by Black Rose Writing

Cover designed by Lou Harper

ISBN: 978-0-9978624-8-5 print
978-0-9978624-9-2 ebook
PUBLISHED BY BEWITCHING FABLES PRESS
Printed in the United States of America

To Janiece and Reed, my beloved parents,

I lost you both far too soon.

ACKNOWLEDGEMENTS

The author wishes to express her extreme gratitude to the members of the Robrek Steele Conspiracy Writers' Group: Elizabeth Cox, Peg Daniels, and Jim Elston. (I wrote the names in alphabetical order, so don't go quibbling about order of importance.) Peg and Jim, especially, supported me through every stage of the novel and never let up on me until I got it right. Without them, the novel wouldn't be the book it is today. They said they deserved a full paragraph acknowledgement each (and they're right), but they'll have to settle for sharing the same paragraph and sharing that paragraph with Panera Bread who allows us to occupy a booth every Friday.

I wish to thank my husband Tim and son Jesse for their love and patience throughout this process and their willingness to listen to parts of the novel read over and over again. I also owe a debt to my brothers and sisters for the stories they told me as a child and for their support and belief in me.

I am grateful to my sensei, Travis Page, who taught me everything I know about fighting and didn't look askance at me when I asked him the best way to kill someone with a staff.

The songs in the first chapter are adapted from "The Battle of Otterbourne" and "Fair Annie; both can be found in the collection *The Minstrelsy of the Scottish Border*, edited by Sir Walter Scott in 1802, among other places.

CONTENTS

MAP OF KORTHLUNDIA

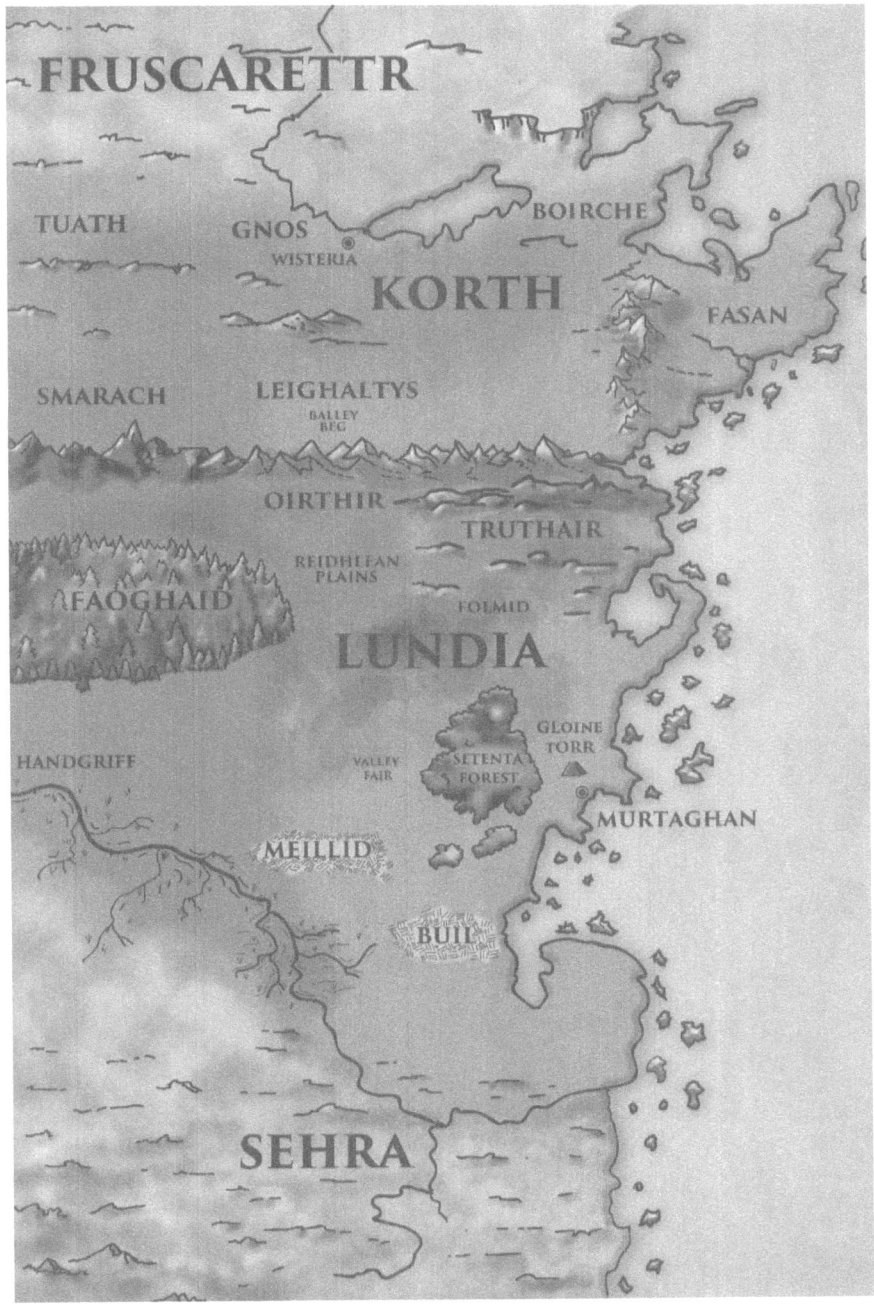

CAST OF CHARACTERS

The Royal Family
Fenella—Solar's third wife; mother of Samantha (deceased)
Robrek—King of Korthlundia
Samantha—Queen of Korthlundia
Solar—Former King of Korthlundia; father of Samantha (deceased)

The King's Council
Arawn—Baron of Buil
Caedmon—Duke of Tuath and Boirche; chancellor
Cadarn—Count
Gwawl—Baron
Nola—Count of Meillid
Pandaran—Count of Fasan
Sheen—Duke of Gnos
Teague—Baron of Smarach
Tierney—Duke of Handgriff
Weylin—Count of Faoghaid
Ultan—Count of Folmid

Royal Guard
Agatone—Lieutenant
Ansgar—Lieutenant
Antain—Member of Royal Guard
Bartle—Member of Royal Guard
Black Giant—Member of Royal Guard
Bearach—Samantha's personal guard
Brendan —Robrek's personal guard
Calvagh—Member of Royal Guard
Cathbad—Robrek's personal guard
Conroy—Captain of Samantha's guard
Crevan—Samantha's personal guard
Eburacon—Captain of Robrek's guard
Findlay—Samantha's personal guard
Geblan—Robrek's personal guard

Gerard—Member of Royal Guard
Iden—Robrek's personal guard
Jarlath—Member of Royal Guard
Hawk—Captain of the Royal Guard
Marcan—Samantha's personal guard
Murdoc—Robrek's personal guard
Ormande—Member of Royal Guard
Rian—Samantha's personal guard
Varney—Member of Royal Guard

Other Nobles

Aislinn—Lady beloved of Lord Devyn
Briallen—Lady of the court
Cedric—Duke Sheen's second son
Crisiant—Lady of the court
Devyn—Duke Sheen's oldest son
Duer—Minor lord, spymaster
Edan—Minor lord
Eira —Lady of the court
Feoras—Morgan's younger brother
Glynnis—Baroness, Gwawl's wife
Morgan—Count of Truthair; traitor
Padrig—Minor lord
Torin—Duke of Oirthir; Lundian, traitor

Palace Servants and Staff

Adalardo—Master of the Horse
Ardra—Samantha's maid
Bedelia—Palace seamstress
Blaine—Samantha's personal secretary
Calum—Royal physician
Daire—Weapons master
Drem—Robrek's personal servant
Druce—chief Librarian
Gael—Duer's servant
Maggie—Chief cook
Malvina—Samantha's maid
Righ—Caedmon's servant
Tuathal—Blaine's assistant

Vaughan—Robrek's squire

Animals
Roberta—Samantha's new horse
Ronan—Cat
Wild Thing—Robrek's Horsetad

The Priesthood
Arabua—Lundian priest
Artan—Lundian novice
Aeronwen—Korthian priestess
Awena—Korthian novice
Bensaggyrt—Korthian High Priestess
Beynon—Lundian novice
Delwin—Korthian priestess
Dorsey—Lundian priest
Eadoin—Father Faolan's assistant
Faolan—Founder and high priest of the True Church of Sulis
Gildas—Priest in Valley Fair
Hafghan—Lundian High Priest
Jenna—Korthian priestess
Leigh Fergalstamm—Lundian priest
Oriana—Korthian novice
Piseag—Lundian priest
Rab—Lundian novice
Venetia—Korthian priestess

Other Characters
Aine—sick child
Alleyn—Angus's farmhand
Alvabane—Sehran Bard
Amergin Kanestamm—Valley farmer
Angus Camlinstamm—Robrek's father; richest farmer in the Valley
Armunn—legendary hero (deceased)
Baakir—Neasarian ambassador
Banagher—innkeeper in Valley Fair; father of Davina
Barris—Mayor of Murtaghan
Beri and Brend Ericstamm—Slathek's bodyguards

Boyden Angusstamm—Angus's oldest son
Brian Brianstamm—Valley farmer
Bree—tavern server
Breasal—Valley resident
Cara—Angus's servant
Chiamaka—Innkeeper of the Traveler's Haven
Chionney —Bard
Cliar—Bard
Davina—Banagher's daughter
Dillion Briacstamm—Cara's husband; Angus's farm hand
Donella, aka Sphrnztegviza, aka Sphry—Robrek's mother; Angus's wife (deceased)
Eolande—Bard
Erick—Alvabane's servant
Slthethkkne, aka Slathek—Robrek's uncle; Donella's brother
Zethar—Mayor of Nios Mo

PROLOGUE

As she braided Awena's hair, Mother Venetia shivered. Their undyed wool robes were not warm enough for the freezing dungeon.

"I'm so cold, Mother!" Awena cried.

"I know, child." Venetia rubbed the young novice's arms to warm her. She and Awena were two of hundreds locked up due to Father Shylah's edict. How the Lundian high priest had got the king to ban and imprison female members of the clergy, Venetia couldn't imagine. Perhaps the rumors were right, and the king had lost his mind.

It was so cold she could see her breath, but Venetia shivered for another reason. Tonight was the night of the new moon, the night all priestesses throughout Korth would perform the ritual to keep the ancient evil contained behind the shield of Armunn's soul. Since her village of Balley Beg was closest to the source of that evil, Mother Venetia's role in the ritual had always been pivotal. This would be the third month in a row she'd been unable to play her part, and because of the mass imprisonment of Korthian priestesses, she was hardly the only one absent. Prophesies spoke of a day when Armunn's shield would fail. She feared the weakened ritual might well bring such a day.

She abruptly stopped braiding as she felt warm tingling through the soles of her shoes.

Awena grabbed Mother Venetia's arm. "What is it, Mother?"

"It's Mother Bensaggyrt. She's sending a call through the earth for all of us to gather."

"Why would she do that? That will only make it easier for the Royal Guard to arrest more of us!"

Mother Venetia shook her head. "I don't know, child." But she could think of only one reason. Had the ancient prophesies come true and evil been loosed to ravage Korthlundia again?

CHAPTER 1

In the palace courtyard, Robrek Angusstamm stirred the cauldron, brewing the potion that would cure Duke Argblutal's former forces of the mass diarrhea caused by the princess's supporters in the palace. Argblutal had attempted to usurp Samantha's throne, and Robrek had just helped her retake it. The potion was ready except for the final ingredient—his magic. Robrek spread his hand over the cauldron and closed his eyes. Pure joy and pleasure flooded his body as his magic flowed out of him. Nothing felt this good. He smiled as he opened his eyes. The potion would provide a nearly instantaneous cure.

Robrek took the ladle from the waiting servant and began ladling out the potion to those waiting. They were bent over from discomfort, and the smell was atrocious. Robrek tried to breathe only through his mouth.

The crowd broke into cries of "Long live Queen Samantha!" He looked up and saw Samantha on the palace balcony. *Holy Sulis, she's beautiful! How can she truly be mine?* It still seemed like a dream that they'd been handfasted the night before and that she had spent the night in his arms.

The man in front of him groaned, reminding Robrek of the task at hand. He filled the stricken soldier's cup. "Thank you, Milord," the soldier said, startling Robrek with the use of his new title.

Robrek filled another cup, then looked back at Samantha. A servant came forward and bowed. "May I, Milord?" The servant reached for the ladle. Robrek relinquished it, but felt awkward doing so. He wasn't used to standing around while others worked. He supposed it was just one of many things he'd have to get used to as consort. *Can I truly be king?* He shook his head at the absurdity of the idea. Only in bards' tales did peasants become kings, but what had his life been if not a bards' tale?

Up on the balcony, Samantha raised a hand, and the crowd fell silent. "My people! Duke Argblutal murdered your king and tried to steal my throne. He has suffered the fate Sulis intended for such betrayal. Let us celebrate this victory, achieved with so little loss of life."

The crowd roared its approval, and Robrek beamed at her. Duke Caedmon stepped onto the balcony beside Samantha, and Robrek frowned slightly. Caedmon disapproved of him, didn't think him worthy of the princess.

Caedmon removed Argblutal's head from the pike. Robrek suspected Darhour, the captain of the princess's personal guard and a former assassin, had put it there. *Where is Darhour?* Robrek would have expected him to be by Samantha's side, but the only two guards with her were Bearach and Conroy.

Caedmon raised his hand for quiet. "Let us remember the fate of those who raise their hands against the goddess's chosen!" Caedmon dropped the head into the midst of the crowd. As the crowd roared and tossed and kicked the duke's head about, Robrek felt a surge of nausea. For what Argblutal had done he'd deserved to die, but did they have to desecrate his remains?

Samantha's eyes sought him out in the crowd, and she smiled down at him. Lost in that smile, he forgot everything else.

The thousands of peasants who had joined Samantha's army as she'd marched on the palace and who now filled the courtyard erupted into dancing and celebration, and Robrek was swept up in the dance. People pounded him on the back and beamed at him, accepting him as he'd never been accepted in the village of his birth.

At the edge of the crowd stood Wild Thing, his Horsetad mare, with Brazen, Fancy Man, and Holy Writ—the magical bronze, silver, and gold horses who had changed his life and helped him win the contest that allowed him to claim Samantha as his bride. Now, the despised youngest son of a peasant farmer would be king. Now, surely, he'd be able to do what he was meant to do and heal in peace. Beyond that he couldn't imagine what his new life would be like.

But having Samantha in it would be enough.

:She liked your moves, didn't she?: came the laughing voice of Fancy Man, who taught him how to dance, among other things. *:Now I've taught you all I know.:*

Holy Writ nodded her head and snorted. *:Thou hast done well.:*

:It is your destiny.:

Robrek laughed as Brazen again said her oft repeated line. Robrek felt happy and at peace. With the horses and Samantha beside him, he had nothing to fear.

Robrek danced over to the horses and gave each one a hug around the neck, ending with Wild Thing. *:Wild Thing and Robbie big heroes.:*

He scratched her neck. "Yes, my girl, I guess we are."

He looked over at the line of soldiers waiting for the remedy and noticed one limping badly. He approached the man as his cup was filled by the servant. "Your foot pains you?" he asked.

The man started and turned to Robrek, eyes widening when he saw who had addressed him. "Er . . . er . . . yes, Milord. I stepped on a nail about a week back, and I'm afraid it's began to fester. I fear I might lose it, Milord."

"Not while I'm here you won't. Drink it down." He pointed to the cup. "Then come with me." After the man drank the remedy, Robrek led him to the nearby mounting blocks and had the man sit and remove his boot. The foot was swollen and red. The nail wound on the bottom was oozing pus and turning green. Red lines of infection travelled up the man's foot. If it weren't for Robrek's skills, it would definitely have to be amputated. Robrek reached out to touch the foot, and the man flinched. "I have to touch you if I'm going to make it better," Robrek said. "It won't hurt."

The man nodded, but he was trembling slightly. Robrek put his hand on the foot, closed his eyes, and went into a healing trance. He gathered the infection and pushed it toward the hole in the foot, so that it streamed out with pus and blood, but after a few moments, the pus stopped flowing, and the foot slowly reduced to normal size. The greenish tinge and the redness disappeared, and finally Robrek closed the small puncture wound.

When Robrek opened his eyes, the man's eyes were wide with awe. The man fell to his knees. "My life for yours! How may I serve you, Milord?"

"You can't," a voice spoke beside Robrek. Robrek turned to Hawk, captain of the Royal Guard, who was looking down at the man with loathing. "His Lordship has no need for traitorous scum. You will depart with the rest after you've sworn your loyalty to Her Highness." He gestured toward the front door of the palace. There stood Samantha, with Bearach and Conroy on either side of her and one of Argblutal's men kneeling before her. A line of men, all who'd fought for Argblutal, waited behind him.

The man whose foot Robrek had healed looked between Captain Hawk and Robrek. "But, Milord, I only served Argblutal for the money. I will give my life for yours."

"Once a traitor, always a traitor," Hawk said, and signaled two Royal Guardsmen over to him. "Escort the traitor to Her Highness."

The Royal Guardsmen took him by the arms. The man was so upset at being taken Robrek thought he should say something, but nothing came to mind. He had no idea how he could make use of the man and no assurance he could be trusted. Hawk called two more Royal Guardsmen over. "You and you are now guarding His Lordship."

"I have no need of guards," Robrek protested.

"Her Highness's orders," Hawk said. "Too many traitors still in the courtyard, not to mention all the peasants." Hawk gestured toward the dancing commoners, all of whom were armed, mostly with makeshift weapons. "Her Highness requests your presence."

Robrek smiled at the thought Samantha wanted him and followed Captain Hawk. The two men Hawk appointed as his guards followed as well and took up station on either side behind him. They were large, imposing men, at least a head taller than Robrek. He felt intimidated rather than protected.

Samantha acknowledged him with a slight smile, but otherwise, her attention was taken up with the men kneeling before her. She held a piece of paper in one hand, and Robrek sensed something was wrong, but he wasn't sure why she wanted him there. She didn't seem to have anything for him to do.

A lot of men had followed Argblutal, and Robrek soon found the oath taking tedious. He scanned the crowd for signs of injury, but couldn't find anything major. Still, wouldn't healing scrapes and bruises be better than doing nothing? He shifted from one foot to the other, wondering if he should go back to ladling out the potion.

Samantha touched his arm. He relaxed at her touch and smiled at her. She smiled in return, but the smile seemed forced somehow and not her true smile. Robrek wondered if he'd done something wrong, but he couldn't imagine what.

When the last of Argblutal's supporters had finally pledged their oaths and been escorted from the palace grounds, Samantha turned to Captain Hawk. "Make sure the palace and grounds are thoroughly searched for any stragglers."

Hawk bowed. "It's being done as we speak."

She turned to Caedmon. "Now, I'll see to my father."

Of course. That's what's wrong. Robrek cursed himself for being so thoughtless. Argblutal had killed her father. Unlike Robrek's relationship with his father, Samantha's with the king had been close.

Still clutching the paper, Samantha took Robrek's hand in her free hand and led him into the palace. Caedmon and their bodyguards followed. The entry hall was overflowing with the nobles who'd sided with her against Argblutal. Although Robrek had been in the entry hall before, he couldn't help staring around like the country peasant he was. Chandeliers full of candles dangled from the ceiling. Robrek wondered how the candles had been lit. Wall sconces provided more light. Between the sconces were brilliant statues of long dead heroes, crossed swords, and suits of armor.

Surrounding him and the princess, the nobles danced and celebrated the nearly bloodless victory. "Long live the queen!" resounded all around them, and the nobles pressed close, congratulating her and reminding her of the part they'd played. She smiled that false smile he found so disconcerting. "Let the wine cellar be breached," she announced. "And all celebrate the joy of our victory!"

Cries of "Hear, hear!" broke out. However, joy seemed to be the last emotion Samantha felt as she moved among the courtiers.

Slowly, they worked their way to the edge of the crowd and down a deserted side corridor. Samantha led him past rich paintings of distinguished looking men and women in gilt frames, bright tapestries of knights and battle, more statuary and suits of armor. The floor was polished flagstone, and large windows provided light. The corridors were wide and the ceilings high. His father's entire farmhouse could have fit in that corridor. *Can I truly be a part of such a world?*

Samantha slowed. She seemed to be in no hurry to reach their destination. She clung tightly to his hand, and he squeezed back to comfort her. But he had no idea what to say. *How can I comfort a queen?*

* * *

Clutching the note Darhour had left pinned to the door above Argblutal's corpse in one hand and Robbie's hand in the other, Samantha approached the room where the king lay dead. *No, Father! You can't truly be gone!* Their steps echoed off the stone floor in the vast emptiness, reminding her of the emptiness of her own life. The air seemed to thicken about them, and she slowed. If she never reached the king's bedroom, maybe she could make his death a lie.

After a few moments and an eternity, she stood before the king's chambers. She hesitated, squared her shoulders, and pushed open the door.

The king lay on his bed, his eyes closed as if merely asleep. His body had been washed and dressed for burial. Seeing him lying there reminded her of when she'd had nightmares as a little girl; she'd come to him and crawl in bed for comfort. He had held her, stroked her hair, and told her stories. She'd snuggled against his long white beard until she fell asleep.

Will I ever feel that safe again?

She was certain she wouldn't. Not when Darhour, too, had deserted her. Darhour had been the captain of her guards, her friend, and as she'd discovered only a few days ago, her true father. Now, according to the note left near Argblutal's body, he'd left her. "My final gift to you," he'd written. "From one unworthy to serve you." *How dare he think of himself that way?*

She forced thoughts of his betrayal out of her mind and looked around the room—everywhere but at the king's body. Above the mantle across from the bed was a portrait of her sitting in her window seat and looking out at the palace grounds. Every two years the king had had a new portrait of her painted to hang in his bedroom. He'd told her he wanted her to be the last thing he saw before he fell asleep.

Maybe it's all a mistake. Praying for life to flow back into him, she knelt beside the bed and took the king's hand. It was freezing and felt more like marble than flesh. Robbie laid his hand on her shoulder. "Can you do something?" she asked him.

To ask anyone else the question would have been absurd, but Robbie was the most powerful sorcerer Korthlundia had seen in centuries. He'd saved Darhour's life when he'd taken an arrow through the heart. Could he not heal her father's heart now, through which Argblutal had thrust his sword?

He shook his head. "I'm sorry, Sam. Maybe if I'd been here at the time. But I can't bring back the dead."

"Holy Sulis, how can I go on without him?" She let go of Solar's lifeless hand and rested her cheek against the coverlet. She wanted to sob, to wail out her grief, but the man who'd always soothed her tears was dead. Robbie knelt beside her and put his arm around her. He didn't tell her the lie that everything would be all right or say any of the trite things people say to comfort those in grief. He just held her.

"Damn Argblutal!" she choked.

Before disappearing, Darhour had done a thorough job of killing the duke—eviscerating, castrating, and decapitating him. Still, she wished Argblutal was alive, so she could kill him with her own sword, rip his heart out of his chest with her bare hands. But nothing she could do to Argblutal could heal the gaping hole in her own chest as she knelt beside the greatest king Korthlundia had ever known and the best father a child could have.

She dropped the note to the floor. Robbie picked it up. His mouth dropped open. "Is this from Darhour?" he asked. "Has he gone?" She nodded and turned away, unwilling to cry over a betrayer. Robbie engulfed her in a hug. "Oh, Sam, I'm so sorry."

She clutched him tightly, grateful for the one thing she hadn't lost.

* * *

His inadequacy in comforting her was like a knife in his heart, Robrek held Samantha and smoothed her auburn hair with his hand. *Why doesn't she weep?* He knew how much she'd loved the king and Darhour, too. The pain in her face was nearly unbearable.

He heard a noise behind him, and Samantha stiffened in his arms. Duke Caedmon was entering the room. "What do I do now, Uncle?" she asked him. "How do I go on?"

Caedmon didn't meet her gaze. "It would seem a celebratory feast is in order. The preparations shouldn't take long, seeing Argblutal had been preparing for a marriage feast that never happened. The people need to celebrate the victory of the rightful queen. Tomorrow you can declare a week of mourning for the king."

She tore away from Robrek and stood. "Are you mad? My father lies dead!" She snatched a gold and gem horse figurine from the mantel. "I gave him this when I was a mere child! He kept it here with my portrait. He loved me! How dare you suggest I celebrate?"

Caedmon held up his hands in a gesture of surrender. "You asked my advice. I have given it."

Samantha glared at Caedmon for a moment more; then the grief flowed off the princess's face and an expressionless mask took its place. The mask made her seem less human somehow. "Very well. Tell Blaine and Maggie to arrange. . . a celebratory feast."

Samantha grabbed Robrek's hand and, without another glance at her father, led him out of the room. She sped through the corridors, her jaw set.

"Where are we going now?" Robrek asked.

"Anywhere but here," she snapped.

They arrived at the edge of the swarming crowd; nearly all the people held glasses or bottles of wine. Glasses were shoved into his and the princess's hands, and the princess halted to propose a toast. "To victory! To another fifty years of unbroken peace!" She drained her goblet, and someone immediately filled it.

The hallways rang with cheers, and when no one seemed to be paying attention, Robrek emptied his glass into a potted plant and set the glass aside. Healers couldn't tolerate alcohol. But before he knew it, someone had shoved another glass into his hand.

Dozens of men Robrek had never seen before pounded him on the back, congratulating him and the princess. They made passage through the corridor slow and difficult. Again, cries of "Long live the queen!" broke out on all sides. The princess smiled at everyone, but the smile didn't reach her eyes. Every time she emptied her glass, it was soon filled again. Robrek merely held his, brimming with wine.

By the time they made it to the banquet hall, where their betrothal had been celebrated two days previously, Samantha's gait was unsteady, and she leaned against him for support.

* * *

"What happens now?" Count Nola asked. "We just sit back and let a bastard reign over us?"

He and the other Lundian members of the Royal Council were sitting at the dining table in his townhouse. Nola, Counts Ultan and Weylin, and Baron Arawn had all sided with Argblutal in his failed attempt to usurp the throne.

Arawn sighed. "Argblutal's accusation about her bastardry was certainly self-serving. Perhaps it isn't even true. Just who is supposed to be her father, anyway?"

Weylin took a large gulp of his wine and waved the matter aside. "Who cares if it's true or not? She has the throne. If Argblutal failed to take it from her, which of us could?"

Ultan's lips tightened. "It is wrong to even speak of it. She gave us our lives when few monarchs would have, and we gave her our sacred oaths of loyalty."

Nola stood. "Words! That's all an oath is. Mere words, spoken under the threat of the axe." The three other men stared at him, mouths hanging open as if the mere thought of breaking their oaths would damn them to the seven hells. "All I want to know is, will she honor Solar's bequests?"

Weylin laughed. "You're concerned about the king's lands?"

Nola turned red. "Shouldn't I be? I have the deed right here." He held up a piece of paper. "Signed by Solar himself. If she's truly the late king's daughter, she won't break her father's word."

Arawn chewed a grape and seemed to consider his words carefully. He spat out the seeds onto a plate before him. "If I were you, I'd figure on kissing those lands goodbye."

"Not while there's still breath in my body. And what about the promises Argblutal made to the rest of you? Are you willing to let them go so causally?" He leaned over the table. "We have to unite on this, or she'll rob us blind."

* * *

Father Faolan knelt before the altar on a plush crimson and gold rug. He fingered the fine silk cloth that had once covered the high priest Shylah's personal altar. The cloth was embroidered with a gold star surrounded by baskets of fruit and roses of the deepest scarlet. He lit the candles on either side of the statue of Sulis. The candlesticks were of gold, inlaid with silver roses and rubies. The statue itself stood two feet tall. Made of pure white alabaster, it depicted Sulis dressed in long, flowing robes. In contrast to most depictions of the Holy Mother, it lacked the curves that differentiated a woman's body from a man's. The goddess's hair, traditionally depicted in long braids interwoven with flowers, was here hidden under a priest's cowl. The statue's face had a strong chin, a pointed nose, and a stern expression. Indeed, it looked far more masculine than feminine. Its sculptor seemed to understand, as very few did, the truth about Sulis, the truth Father Shylah had taught Faolan.

Faolan had taken these things of Shylah's to honor the high priest after his supposed suicide. Faolan, however, wasn't fooled. Shylah had been far too great a man to take his own life. He had been murdered both physically and in reputation. The accusations of child sacrifice were slander of the basest variety, and Faolan knew who was responsible: the bastard who would reign on the great Solar's throne and the abomination she'd taken to her bed.

There was a knock on the door, and Father Eadoin entered. His blonde hair was shaved to a fine buzz, and he had small, beady eyes that avoided looking directly at Faolan. "Am I interrupting?"

Faolan shook his head and got to his feet. "No, I was just praying, asking Sulis for a way to restore the high priest's reputation. What's on your mind?"

Eadoin rubbed his fingers over the silky smoothness of the altar cloth, still not looking at him. "It's the high priesthood, Father. Until the new high priest is chosen, I'm afraid of your flaunting your closeness to Father Shylah. Few believe he was not guilty of the crimes with which he was charged. Your chances of being chosen the next high priest would be greater if you were to repudiate—"

Faolan put his hand on the younger priest's shoulder. "I will not repudiate Korthlundia's greatest high priest merely for worldly ambition. I will find a way to clear his name and trust in Sulis to guide our fellows in the selection of the one most fit to lead the church in these troubled times." Times in which a bastard and an infidel were set to take the throne. Such a travesty must be prevented, and who better than the church to stop it?

* * *

With Samantha laughing somewhat hysterically beside him, Robrek entered the banquet hall. Robrek wondered what was funny. All he'd seen and heard in the entrance hall was nobles boasting of their own feats, when really they had done nothing except ride with him and the princess to the palace. Samantha led him up to the high table, and Robrek felt small as a sea of nobles followed them and sat. As Samantha took her place, she called for music, and soon the hall rang with songs of long-ago battles and bright victories:

> And he marched up to Boirche,
> And rode it round about:
> 'O where's the lord of this castle?
> Or where's the lady of it?'
> But up spoke proud Lord Armunn then,
> And O but he spoke high!
> I am the lord of this castle,
> My wife's the lady gay.
> 'If thou art the lord of this castle,
> So well it pleases me,
> For, ere I cross the Borderlands,
> The enemy's force was nigh.'
> Armunn took a long spear in his hand,
> Shod with the metal free,
> And for to meet the Demons there
> He rode right furiously.

Robrek didn't know who Armunn was or why they'd be singing about him now, but it was obviously a popular song at court; the nobles pounded the tables and sang along with the bard. Samantha merely sipped more wine and leaned her head on his shoulder.

Bard after bard sang until the servants began serving the first course—a leek and chicken soup. Robrek took a spoonful of the soup, remembering to eat in the manner Fancy Man had taught him. But Samantha picked up her goblet instead. Worried about her, Robrek put his hand on hers. "Eat something."

She shook her head, took another sip of wine, and commanded the bard to sing a romantic ballad. Robrek grinned and blushed as the song reminded him of last night in the princess's tent. Hungry from healing, he ate heartily, but he had a hard time getting Samantha to even try the food. All that alcohol on an empty stomach wasn't a good idea.

Midway through the feast, people tapped their forks against their glasses and called for a speech. Samantha rose unsteadily to her feet, her hand on Robrek's shoulder to keep her balance. "Lards and. . . ! I mean Lords and Ladies! Nobles of the land! All of you who helped the rightful queen regain the throne, I thank you! My consort thanks you! If my father were still here, he would thank you! But he was foully murdered." She swayed, but Robrek steadied her. "Argblutal has paid the price for his treachery, and this we celebrate here today!"

Cries of "Long live the queen" broke out again.

"So on with the music!" she said, nearly falling into her chair.

* * *

Duke Sheen watched the princess down goblet after goblet of wine; the wench could hold her own with a sailor. He'd thrown everything he had behind keeping her on the throne; he hoped he hadn't backed a sot. In all the years he'd known Solar, he'd never seen him the worse for drink. Could Argblutal's accusation be true? Was she a bastard? Did it matter if she was?

He frowned at the peasant boy sitting beside the princess, then looked away. "That will never do."

"What won't?" Baron Teague, his fellow Korthian Royal Councilor, asked.

Sheen looked askance at the Baron. He hadn't really intended to speak aloud, but now that he had, he might as well let his opinion be known. "Are you willing to see a peasant, and a mere child at that, in the place you once sought for your own?"

Teague frowned. "Tonight we celebrate our victory against the Lundian scum. Tomorrow's soon enough to worry about who the princess marries."

Next to them, Count Pandaran took a sip of his wine. "His fashion sense is appalling. And look how he positively dotes on her. It's almost putting me off my food."

Sheen grunted. Pandaran's complaints were trivial, as was everything about him, but who cared, if they got him on Sheen's side? The important unknown was Duke Caedmon. Would he support a Lundian peasant on the throne? If Korth united against her, they could force her to realize the absurdity of her peasant lover. Solar had adeptly performed the tricky balancing act between the Korthians and the Lundians on his council, but after the Lundians' betrayal, the princess wouldn't have that recourse. With the Lundian interference out of the way, Korth, not the princess, would direct the course of the joined kingdoms.

Sheen smiled and lifted his goblet. Yes, it was a new day in the joined kingdoms.

* * *

Robrek led the princess through the corridors toward her quarters, the princess leaning against him, giggling, and singing a verse from one of the ballads:

> "But who will bake my bridal bread,
> Or brew my bridal ale?
> And who will welcome my brisk bride,
> That I bring over the dale?"

Her bodyguards had to show him the way; she was in no condition to do so. The two men Captain Hawk had appointed were still following him. Both they, Bearach, and Conroy stopped at the door to Samantha's quarters. Robrek followed Samantha in.

When they were alone in her bedroom, she wrapped her arms around him and kissed him. Gently, he pushed her away. "You're drunk, Sam."

She clung to his shirt. "Please, Robbie, make love to me. Touch me like you did last night in my tent."

Despite himself, his body responded, and he wanted nothing so badly as to give in. But it wouldn't be right. "Sam, I can't take advantage of you when you're like this."

Abruptly, she collapsed sobbing against his shirt. "Robbie, I feel so alone. They're gone! Both of my fathers are gone!"

He led her to the bed. He lay down beside her and let her soak his shirt with her tears. *Holy Sulis, she's lost so much.* At least she was crying now. It seemed inhuman to withstand so much loss with dry eyes. He wouldn't have been able to.

After a long while the sobs subsided and were replaced by a soft snore. She'd fallen asleep on his chest. He gently extricated himself and stood. For the first time, he looked around her room. One entire wall was covered by a painting of a princess, resembling Samantha, riding a Horsetad. Horsetads ran free on the Reidhlean plains, and people said they could never be tamed. Robrek had never known anyone other than himself who had ridden one. He thought of Wild Thing, his Horsetad mare, down in the palace stables, and he reached out to her with his magic. She was sleeping contentedly in the paddock and didn't want to be disturbed.

Besides the painting, the room held two huge wardrobes, carved with horses and stars in intricate detail. He opened them and found them full to bursting with dresses in silk and satin, lace and velvet, so many she could wear a different one every day for an entire year. Robrek shook his head. Although his father had been considered wealthy by those in the Valley, Robrek had never had more than a couple changes of clothes. Figurines of horses in gold, silver, jade, crystal, and precious stones arrayed themselves on the mantle. Ten years' proceeds from his father's crops couldn't have afforded one of them.

Last night the princess had had him leave her tent before dawn— they'd been camped at the base of Gloine Torr waiting for today's battle—so it wouldn't be known they'd slept together. Tonight he didn't know where to go. Robrek left the princess and walked into her reception room. A life-sized horse made of smoked crystal dominated one corner. It had a gold mane, tail, and hooves and wore a gold saddle studded with emeralds. On the wall was a huge tapestry of a white mare at the edge of the forest, helping her newborn foal stand. The mare reminded him of Roberta, the horse he'd helped Samantha choose at the horse fair where they first met. The mantle was covered with more horse figurines. There was enough wealth in this room to support the entire Valley for a hundred years.

What in Sulis's name am I doing here?

Not wanting to wrinkle his bronze silks by sleeping in them, he removed them and placed them over a chair. Then he wrapped himself in a blanket and fell asleep on the rug in front of the fire.

CHAPTER 2

At bedtime, Alvabane sat at her dressing table brushing her long hair. It had once been a bright, rich red, but it had dulled with age and was now mostly grey with only a few strands of color to remind her of what once had been. It seemed a metaphor for her life—small flashes of color to remind her of her once bright purpose.

One of those flashes, Erick, set her nightly goblet of fortified wine next to her hand. She needed the strong alcohol to dull the pain of her joints so she could sleep. Erick had served her for ten years. When her former servant had died, he'd been sent by her people, despite the fact that she'd only been a disappointment to them.

She turned to thank him, but the words died on her lips as she saw the reproach in his eyes. Alvabane turned back to her mirror. Tonight was the night of the new moon. She should have been preparing to perform the rites of the dark gods, not preparing for bed. "They have forgotten us," Alvabane said. "The Soul Stone does not live."

In the mirror, she saw Erick's eyes narrow. He was not yet twenty and still had the optimism of youth. He still believed the Stone would come to life again when the gods willed it. He believed it would again be the weapon it had once been. Created in the far past by magic which had since been lost, it had been used by her people to protect themselves from the barbarians that now ran free over Korth and Lundia.

"I will perform the rites next month," she promised, but so had she promised last month and the month before that. The stairs to the bottom of the East Tower were agony to her knees. Erick made a mewing sound, reminding her what he'd sacrificed to serve her and the dark gods. She herself had cut his tongue from his mouth when he came to her as a ten-year-old child. He had surrendered it stoically. Only the Bards were allowed to sing the rites of the gods. All others who heard them had to be rendered mute so they couldn't repeat music not meant for their tongues.

"Do you think you have sacrificed more than I?" She turned to face him. "I submitted to the brutish duke's bed for years. I gave birth to a child of rape. All so I could remain near the Stone. I performed the rites faithfully every new moon for decades. And for what, I ask you? The power of the Stone remains trapped behind the shield the demon Armunn created from his own soul. That shield can't be destroyed. I have dedicated my life to trying, but it is impossible. The Soul Stone won't live again!"

Erick mewed again and looked toward the tapestry on the wall. It showed the map of the desert of Sehra, to the south of Korthlundia, where her people had lived in exile since Armunn and his hordes had trapped the Stone and then driven them from their homeland. Blinking back tears of despair, she turned from him. "Do you think I have forgotten? Every generation fewer of our children are born. Only by returning to the land of our birthright can we be strong again."

She got up and went to the tapestry, touching it lovingly. "Do you not understand? The dark gods have found me unworthy to be their messenger. I once thought I was the child of the prophecy, the one who would drive the descendants of Armunn's hordes back across the mountains into Korth and reclaim the land they call Lundia as our own. But I was wrong. I'm an unprofitable servant, an unfit vessel."

* * *

Erick left the room of his mistress, fetched the two doves he had caged, and descended the East Tower steps. He couldn't perform the rites of the dark gods, but he could keep their altar bright and their bowls full.

When he reached the bottom, he got the key out he wore under his shirt on a chain and unlocked the door to the small, cold room. Nothing stood in it but the altar: the original altar after which all altars of the exiled were fashioned. It was the size of a banquet table, and set exactly in its center was a large, red stone, one that reached deep beneath the ground to a pool of power—power shut off by Armunn's curse. On top of the Soul Stone sat a silver knife, which he kept polished and sharp. At one end of the altar sat a statue of Balor, the one-eyed god of death. At the other was Fea, the shadowy goddess of war—the dark gods of his people. Before each statue was a bowl, partly filled with blood. Erick knelt at the altar to pray, to beg the gods to accept the sacrifice he was about to make, even though he was no Bard to sing their songs.

As before, he felt their presence descend and heard their voices in his head. *:Armunn's shield grows weak. The campaign against the Korthian demon priestesses has left them unable to perform the rites to keep it strong.:* He'd tried to tell his mistress this, but, without words, he couldn't make her understand. He knew if he could just get her to this room, she'd discover the truth herself. He knew how the stairs pained her, but the dark gods fed on pain. Had not Alvabane told him this herself as she had cut out his tongue? Was this not the reason the animals were tortured before they were killed on the altar, as he would torture the doves before he filled the bowls with their blood?

But as Erick prayed, he suddenly knew the answer. The sacrifice of mere animals was not enough to break the final bonds of Armunn's shield. He stood and stripped off his robe, shivering in the cold. Then, taking the silver knife, he climbed onto the large altar. He started cutting at his toes, planning to give himself as much pain as he could tolerate before plunging the knife into his heart. He wouldn't live to witness his people's triumphant return. Instead, he'd die to make that return possible.

* * *

A terrifying thunderclap jolted Alvabane awake, and a strange buzzing filled her head. Painfully, she tottered to the window and looked at the night sky. It was the night of the new moon, so little light fell, but there were no clouds and no rain. What could have been the source of the thunderclap, and why did her head still buzz?

The buzzing grew stronger; it had, almost, but not quite, a musical quality to it, as if someone was trying to sing through a muffling gag. *What can it be?* It sounded familiar, like a once loved song, almost forgotten.

Her heart began to race. *No, it couldn't be. Not after all this time.* Ignoring the pain in her joints, she rushed out of her chambers and to the East Tower. Agonizingly, she made her way down the hundreds of steps. The closer she came, the louder the buzzing grew until it was indeed a song, one she could almost, but not quite, understand.

When she reached the bottom, she found the door unlocked. It creaked open at her touch. She gasped when she saw what lay on the altar—an altar stained with blood. "Erick, no!" she cried to the one who'd been more like her child than her servant. But he was beyond hearing. "Why did you do this?"

Beneath Erick, a light suddenly burst forth, bathing the entire room in its glow—a light as red as Erick's blood. The Stone beneath him pulsed in time to the music. In awe, she fell to her knees. By Erick's gift of pain and blood, the Soul Stone had broken free at last. She laughed, as she hadn't laughed since she was a small child. The dark gods hadn't deserted her. Perhaps she could be a profitable servant after all.

CHAPTER 3

Robrek stared through the darkness of the cave. Ahead, he saw a pulsing red light. It slid across his vision, forming dim shapes. The air was so thick he could barely breathe, but something beckoned him forward.

He pressed into the next cavern. Suddenly, at his feet lay a blood-red lake whose every motion seemed a riot of joy. Although the odor of rot oozed from its depths, it seemed a thing of perfect beauty. He laughed as desire filled him and pleasure coursed through his body. He bent to bathe his hands in the substance.

Before he could touch it, something grabbed his shoulder. Holy Writ, the golden, magical horse who'd taught him what it meant to forgive, was pulling him back.

:Thou must know it, but thou must not join it.:

Robrek heard a groan and jerked awake. Samantha lay on her bed clutching her head. He could feel the pain in her head and the nausea in her stomach; she needed him. Still, he wanted to close his eyes and get back to that lake. But why? If Holy Writ hadn't wanted him to touch it, it couldn't be a good thing. Besides, it was only a dream.

Clenching his teeth against the desire, he got up from the floor. "Here, let me help."

* * *

Robbie's touch was warm. Instantly, Samantha's hangover lifted, and she felt as if she'd gotten the best sleep in years. Robbie was dressed only in his short clothes, but she was fully dressed. She pulled him down next to her on the bed and wrapped her arms around him. With both her fathers gone, she needed him. All she wanted to do was dissolve into tears as she had the night before while Robbie held her, but she couldn't. She was her father's daughter, and now she had to take his place. Too many problems faced her; she had to put the palace back in order and establish her rule. What will the Lundians do? *Will they keep their vows and be loyal to me?* The two who refused to give their vow—Duke Torin and Count Morgan—were in the dungeon awaiting her judgment. *I'll have to execute them, won't I?* She would begin her rule with blood. She shifted, uncomfortable with the thought, but saw no alternative. Then there was the Korthians to reward, her father's funeral to plan, as well as her own coronation and marriage. She wanted to ask Robbie's advice on what to do next, but knew he'd have nothing useful to say. Despite her love for him, he was a peasant.

Still, he was what she'd never dreamed possible—a man who loved her and not the power he'd gain by being her consort. She snuggled up against him and lightly ran her fingers over his naked chest. He sighed in pleasure and turned to kiss her, but a knock came at the door. A voice called from the other side. "Are you ready to dress, Your Highness?" It was Ardra, her maid.

Samantha wanted to tell Ardra to go away, but knew she couldn't. "In a minute," she said, and kissed Robbie lightly. She drew back from his embrace. "You better get dressed and wait outside."

He got up and went to the chair. "I swear I left my clothes here, but they aren't here anymore." They both searched the floor around the chair and bed and amid the bedclothes, but his bronze silks were nowhere to be found.

"They couldn't have just walked away," Samantha insisted. "Maybe my maids did something with them."

Samantha grabbed the sheet off the bed and handed it to Robbie. He wrapped it around himself and over one shoulder. Samantha called for her maids to come in. They looked between him and Samantha, then back at each other, grinning. Samantha could feel the blood rise in her face.

"These are my maids, Ardra and Malvina," Samantha said. "They have my complete trust." She turned to them. "You will speak of this to no one."

"Speak of what, Your Highness?" Ardra said, with a wink.

"We don't be spreading gossip," Malvina maintained.

Samantha told them Robbie's clothes had gone missing, but the two maids shook their heads. "We didn't be doing anything with them," Malvina said.

"Then who did? My guards wouldn't have allowed anyone else in." She looked to Robbie, who seemed equally nonplussed. "Well, you must have something to wear." She turned to Ardra. "Put Blaine on the problem, and then you two may dress me."

Ardra left. When she returned, Samantha had Robbie step into the reception room.

"He's a handsome one, Your Highness." Ardra giggled.

"Ardra!" Malvina hit Ardra lightly on the shoulder as Samantha felt herself blush.

"That he is," Samantha said, so happy Ardra was alive she couldn't resent the familiarity. Ardra had taken Samantha's place at her wedding to Argblutal, fully believing the duke would kill her for the deception.

"What will you be wearing today, Your Highness?" Malvina asked.

"Something that will make me look particularly royal. Something green. I look good in green."

* * *

While he waited for the princess's secretary to bring him clothes, Robrek reexamined the horse figurines on the mantle. In the light of day, they were even more impressive. He didn't dare touch them, knowing he couldn't replace one in a lifetime. He noticed one made of silver and another of gold. Feeling alone and out of place, he wandered to the window to look out at Wild Thing and the magical horses below in the palace stables. Wild Thing was standing alone by the paddock fence, her head drooping. He reached out to her with his magic. *What's wrong, my girl?*

: No more Fancy Man. Horses gone. Job all done.:

No! His head reeling, Robrek stumbled to a chair and dropped into it. What did Wild Thing mean by "Job all done"? Had they left him? Was that why his bronze silks had disappeared? He'd often been annoyed by the horses' bossiness, but they had become part of him. How would he survive without their guidance? They were supposed to show him how to fit in, to be a royal! Table manners, dancing, and weapons training weren't enough! Not nearly enough!

They hadn't even said good-bye!

The door opened, and in walked two young men close to Robrek's age. The first was tall but slight for a Korthlundian, with blonde hair, a wisp of a beard, and a bad case of acne. The second was shorter but broader, with a fuller beard. They bowed to him. If either of them thought there was anything improper in Robrek being dressed in a sheet in the princess's reception room, they kept their feelings to themselves.

"Good morning, Sir Robrek," the taller one said. "I'm Blaine, Her Highness's secretary, and this is Drem, your personal servant."

"My what?" Robrek shook his head. Too much was happening at once. "I don't need a servant."

Blaine stared at him as if he were speaking a foreign language. "It would hardly be proper for the future king to be unattended." As if that settled everything, Blaine pointed to the clothes Drem was carrying; they seemed composed entirely of ruffles and lace. "Considering your less than commanding size, it wasn't easy, but I've found something that will do. It isn't the latest style, but beggars can't be choosers, so to speak."

Robrek stiffened at the phrase. *Does this man think me unworthy of the princess? How could he not?*

Blaine went on as if nothing were amiss. "I think they'll fit Your Lordship. Drem here will dress you; then I'll show Your Lordship to your new quarters. We're as busy as bees in the springtime, so to speak." Blaine turned his back.

Drem approached. He draped the shirt over the back of the couch and knelt, holding out the trousers for Robrek to step into. Robrek unwrapped the sheet, dropped it, bent, and took the trousers. "I can dress myself." As Drem gaped at him, Robrek put on the trousers and then took up the shirt and put his arm in.

"No, Milord. You're putting it on backwards. The buttons go in back." Drem slipped the shirt off Robrek's arm and turned it around.

"But how will I do them up?"

"That's my job, Milord."

Not seeing a way around it, Robrek accepted Drem's help. From the mirror over the mantle, a stranger gazed back at him. Ruffles protruded from his chest, emphasizing his smallness. He looked like a filly at a horse show. The only familiar thing was the green ribbon tying back his hair. Samantha had given it to him the day they first met. He hadn't known she was crown princess at the time.

When Robrek was dressed, the princess's secretary turned around and scowled as he looked him up and down. "It doesn't seem quite your style, Milord. But if you'll follow me, we'll fix that."

Drem trailing behind him, Robrek followed the secretary into the corridor, his head still reeling from the horses' disappearance. Outside, with Bearach and Conroy, two guards were waiting. They bowed to him. "We've been assigned by Captain Hawk to guard Your Lordship," one of them said.

Robrek responded with a nod of his head. But he would have to talk to Samantha. He didn't need guards, and it made him uncomfortable having men follow him around.

Blaine led him down the hallway and around a corner. He stopped in front of a doorway. "These will be your quarters, Milord. Not too far from Her Highness's." Robrek felt himself redden, but the secretary seemed oblivious to his embarrassment. The guards remained outside the door, and Blaine led Robrek and Drem into a room with large, overstuffed floral couches whose colors clashed badly with the floral rugs. Even worse were the tapestries that covered the walls; they depicted fairies dancing around fountains, winged babies picking flowers, and lambs and puppies frolicking together. Blaine paused. "You'll have to redecorate, of course. These rooms belonged to the old Duchess of Something"—Blaine waved his hand around as if her name didn't matter—"who had as much taste as water from a millpond, so to speak."

Inside the room stood a middle-aged woman. "This is Mistress Bedelia, Milord. She'll be in charge of your wardrobe," Blaine said, and Bedelia curtsied. She held a measuring tape and didn't meet his eyes. "Well, I'll leave you to her. I must return to Her Highness." Blaine bowed his way out of the room.

Drem bowed again. "Would Your Lordship like me to acquire more manly *accoutrements?*" he asked, gesturing around the room.

Robrek wasn't sure what accoutrements were, but he figured they had something to do with the room's furnishings. "By all means," Robrek said.

"Shall I get on it at once, Milord?" Robrek nodded his approval, and Drem started to leave, but stopped and turned around. He bowed again. "Milord, I want you to know it is an honor to serve the hero of Gloine Torr."

Robrek blinked; it was beyond odd to hear himself referred to that way. He didn't know how to respond. Those in the Valley where he'd grown up had considered him a demon. Fortunately, Drem didn't seem to need a response. He bowed his way out, leaving Robrek alone with the woman.

"Shall I be measuring Your Lordship?"

Robrek nodded, though he felt increasingly awkward at the use of the new title. He stood still and let her work, although he had a hard time not fidgeting. The horses were gone! Who would he ask when he didn't know what to do? *Sulis, how could you take them away? If you truly chose me to be king, you must realize I can't do it on my own.* He looked down at the ugly shirt he was wearing. It seemed trivial to worry about his dress in a moment like this, but being improperly clad made him feel even more awkward. "I'd like something with fewer ruffles and ribbons," he told Bedelia.

"I was seamstress of the king, bless his heart. I know my business." Her eyes looked red from weeping.

"And the buttons in the front, please," he added.

She made no response. When she had finally finished taking his measurements, she curtsied. "Will there be anything else, Milord?"

"When will it be ready?"

"We'll have something for you by this evening. The full wardrobe will take weeks, of course." She left in a hurry, as if she must get on the job at once, leaving Robrek wondering just how much clothing she planned to make and knowing neither wardrobe nor accoutrements could replace the horses' presence in his life.

* * *

Samantha sat in her reception room, waiting for Caedmon. Despite her anger with him over yesterday's celebration, she knew he'd been right; the feast had been necessary. Caedmon was a wise man; he'd been her father's chancellor for nearly twenty years. Now, he'd be hers. She squeezed her eyes tight to avoid the threatening tears. Her father was truly gone, and somehow she had to take his place. She was only nineteen years old, but her father had spent her entire life preparing her for this moment. She'd always known she take the throne young. She'd make him proud of her.

When Caedmon arrived, he bowed and settled down beside her. "You did well yesterday, Your Highness."

Samantha looked away. "I got drunk."

Caedmon waved that aside. "The people saw a queen. Today you can declare a mourning period for the king. I don't discount your grief, my dear, but still, you should severely limit the number who see you in tears." He patted her on the arm.

"I understand, Uncle." She vowed that nobody but Robbie would see her cry. "I should hold a council meeting this afternoon."

Caedmon smiled. "Excellent, Your Highness. You need to assert your authority. Let them all know you are in charge now."

She nodded. "See that it's done." Caedmon nodded, but then sighed deeply. Had she forgotten something important? She couldn't let even Caedmon see how unsure she felt. Still, her father had often asked for Caedmon's advice, so it wouldn't weaken her if she did, too. "What is it?" she asked.

Caedmon sighed again. "I know you won't want to hear this, but the peasant sorcerer has served his purpose, Your Highness. Now that the palace and the throne are in your hands, it's time to get rid of him."

Surely he hadn't said what she thought she'd heard. "Excuse me?"

"The boy. The sorcerer. He's a liability now and may become a threat later."

Samantha struggled for words. "Uncle, I will hear nothing against Sir Robrek. He is the goddess's choice. Not only did he win the contest, but the goddess has marked him as her own." She'd already told Caedmon how she'd knelt at Sulis's holy altar and how the goddess herself through her priestess told her she would know without a doubt when the goddess's choice knelt before her. When Robbie had knelt at her feet, his aura had exploded into a halo of blinding white, leaving her no question of the goddess's will. "He is the one I need to help me build my kingdom."

Caedmon patted her arm again. "Your Highness, I realize the boy has charmed you, and you want to believe that. But he brings you no lands, no noble alliances. He hasn't a drop of noble blood in his veins. Worse, his power makes him dangerous. Do you think he'll be content to serve you? At the very least, he'll reduce you to a consort and reign in his own right."

Samantha shook off Caedmon's hand. "He has given me his sacred vow. I trust him with my life."

"My dear," Caedmon said, his tone suggesting she was a stubborn adolescent trying his patience, "your father would never have allowed this marriage to occur."

How dare he! Samantha shot to her feet and jabbed a finger at him. "My father sanctioned this marriage when he knighted Sir Robrek and announced him as my betrothed. My father recognized that the goddess had spoken. I will have your support as well."

Caedmon lurched to his feet and loomed over her. She hated being short. "Now, Samantha, we both know your father intended me to guide you through your early days on the throne. How can I do that if you refuse to listen?"

"Do not fight me on this. I won't ignore Sulis to please you."

"Your Highness—"

She sliced her hand through the air. "The subject is closed."

A knock on the door startled them both. They both turned as Robbie entered. She took a double-take. The shirt he wore was appallingly ugly and made him look like a small boy. Still, he was the man she loved, the one the goddess herself had chosen for her. Glaring at Caedmon, Samantha crossed to Robbie and took his hand. Caedmon's face assumed an expressionless mask.

"I'll see to the council meeting." Caedmon bowed and swept out of the room.

Robbie winced, and she realized how tightly she gripped his hand. She eased up. "What was that about?" he asked.

She dropped his hand and went to the window. "It doesn't matter."

Robbie followed her and dropped a kiss on her shoulder. "If it makes you so angry, it does."

"Caedmon is being difficult. He disapproves of you, says you're dangerous. He thinks you'll lose me the throne or reduce me to your consort."

In the window's reflection, she saw Robbie's face fall. His voice shook. "My power isn't dangerous to you, Sam. I swear it isn't."

"*I* know that! We have to get Caedmon and the rest of the court to see you as you are—the goddess's choice."

Robbie turned away. "And if they will not?"

Samantha grabbed his shoulder and turned him around. "You are Sulis's choice and my own! Nothing will change that! You hear me? Nothing!"

He put his arms around her. "I hope I can be the man you need me to be."

"You already are!" Robbie gave a half-smile but looked devastated. "Don't let Caedmon bother you."

"It's not just that. It's the horses—Brazen, Fancy Man, and Holy Writ. They're gone."

"Stolen?" Samantha grabbed his arm. "But who could have taken them?"

Robbie gave a tiny shrug. "Not stolen. They just left. I guess they figured their job was done."

Samantha's mind flashed to Darhour, who'd probably considered his job done when he killed Argblutal. "How dare they think you no longer needed them!"

Robbie stared at her in surprise. Then his face softened. "I'm sure Darhour had his reasons," he said, hugging her to him. "Maybe he thought *his* presence was a danger to you."

Her hands clenched so tightly her fingernails bit into her palms. "No reason is good enough for what he did. I will never forgive him! Never!"

"Sam, I—"

"I don't want to hear it. Besides, it's not Darhour at issue. It's the horses. Will you be all right?" She touched his shoulder.

"I'll have to be, won't I? I just hope I know enough about how to act. Sam, I'm a peasant."

Her lips tightened. *Robbie mustn't be allowed to think he is nothing more than the son of a farmer.* "And a powerful sorcerer. If you need help, you have me. We'll get through this together."

He nodded. "We will, won't we?" He hesitated and then went on, "Sam, I wanted to talk about the guards you have on me. I really don't need them. I can take care of myself. Healers are very hard to kill."

Samantha shook her head vehemently. "No, I won't risk you. You will have a personal guard identical to mine, dedicated to your protection. We'll see to it before the council meeting." Expecting no argument, she whirled away from him and called in Conroy and Bearach. "Conroy," she said. "You are now captain." She managed to say it without expression, but her insides bled from Darhour's absence.

Conroy blinked. "Surely, you don't think I can replace—"

She cut him off with a look. "Darhour is gone. Someone has to replace him, and that someone is you. I require an additional four members for my guard and six for Sir Robrek. Assemble suitable candidates in the practice arena. I'll be there within half an hour."

Bearach and Conroy bowed their way out, and Robbie turned to her. "Surely these men have better things to do than follow me around. Besides, it makes me uncomfortable having someone watch everything I do."

Samantha was surprised by his resistance; people didn't question her. "Robbie, you are to be my consort. That comes with certain risks. I don't care how hard to kill you are; someone could do it. I will see you protected. You'll get used to the guards. I hardly notice mine."

* * *

Inside the practice arena, more than two dozen guards had paired off, practicing their swordsmanship. When she'd chosen her original guards, her need for men she could trust had enabled her to see their auras. She hoped the same would be true today. As an aurora, Samantha could sometimes see a person's aura—the invisible colors that surround everyone and reveal their characters. But her gift didn't operate reliably and wouldn't until she'd borne a child.

The men were all elite members of the Royal Guard. She knew most of them by name and had trained against many of them. But her gift was stubbornly absent. Not a one glowed with the light blue and white that had announced her guards' loyalty to her.

Fine! Yet another problem! She turned to Robbie. "Do you have a preference?"

"I prefer not to be guarded."

Samantha rolled her eyes. She called Eburacon over to her. He was a tall man of about thirty-five. He was blonde with a full beard and a slight graying at the temples. She'd known him since she was a young child, and he was solid, skilled, and reliable. The other guards respected him. He'd once been one of Solar's guards, but had been dismissed from that position shortly after Argblutal had begun to poison her father, possibly because he would have recognized something was wrong and done something about it. "You will be the captain of His Lordship's personal guard," she ordered.

Eburacon's eyes gleamed. "I'm honored, Your Highness." He bowed to Robbie. "Your Lordship."

She told Eburacon and Conroy to choose the remaining men they would command.

* * *

Robrek sat to Samantha's right in the council chamber. Duke Caedmon sat on her left. Robrek's new guards were behind him. He wasn't sure what he was supposed to do in the council meeting, but Samantha said that as her betrothed and future consort, he should be present. As the Royal Councilors entered the room, Robrek tried to remember their names. The first to come was Duke Skeen, then Baron Teague and Count Pandaran. They all bowed to the princess, and she nodded in acknowledgment. They paid no attention to Robrek. Did they agree with Duke Caedmon that he was unworthy of his place? Did they still scheme to take his place as king? Most of the Royal Councilors or their sons had once courted the princess. Is that why Samantha thought he needed guards? He studied the men's faces for any sign they wanted him dead. Their faces revealed nothing.

Robrek shifted in his chair. Samantha had given him no instructions about what to say or how to act, and Fancy Man, the horse that had taught him what little he knew about court protocol, was gone. He shifted again in his seat, and Samantha put her hand on his leg under the table. She squeezed lightly. Robrek knew she was telling him to be still, and he tried to follow her instruction.

Caedmon cleared his throat. "It's time to discuss the royal funeral."

Samantha raised her eyebrows at Caedmon, and her grip on Robrek's leg told him of her annoyance, but her face revealed as little as the men's did. "Where are the Lundians?" she asked.

Caedmon blinked. "The Lundians betrayed you, Your Highness. You can't trust them."

She released Robrek's leg and put her hands on the table. "If I am going to rule as my father would have, I can't ignore the southern half of my kingdom."

Duke Sheen's face turned red. "You would have traitors, the murderers of the great Solar, sit here with those who loyally came to your rescue? Their titles and lands should all be forfeit to the crown and given to those who stood by you in your hour of need!"

All emotion hidden by that disconcerting mask, Samantha turned to Sheen. "Do you want a civil war? Or do you want the peace my father created and preserved? You have all prospered from the security and low taxes peace has brought you. To keep that peace, Korth and Lundia must be treated equally. I promised Ultan, Arawn, Weylin, and Nola there would be no reprisals if they surrendered and vowed their loyalty to me. They have done so and should be included in this council." She turned to Caedmon. "Have them summoned at once."

Caedmon rose to do as she asked, but Sheen stood. "Your Highness, I will not sit down with regicides and traitors. If you allow them into this room, I will leave." He smirked at her.

"Sheen," Samantha said in a flat tone. "I appreciate your assistance in retaking my throne, but keeping the peace requires the Lundians. They will join the council."

A vein pulsed in Sheen's temple. "You can't rule without me and the other Korthian members of this council. None of us will stand for the presence of the Lundians." He looked to Teague and Pandaran. Robrek followed his gaze. The tension was thick in the room. If only this were an illness he could heal.

Pandaran seemed oblivious, and Teague shifted uneasily in his seat. "The Lundians did betray you," he said, as if Samantha might have forgotten.

Samantha leaned forward. "I'm aware of that, but this is the joined kingdoms. This is my decision and mine alone, and I have spoken."

Sheen leaned across the table toward her. "Your father would have taken their heads, not merely their council seats." He turned to Teague and Pandaran. "Are you going to allow the murderers of the great Solar to share a table with you?" This time they both avoided his gaze. His eyes flashed, first at Samantha, then at the Korthians who failed to support him. He swept out of the room. Caedmon raised an eyebrow at Samantha, but went to the door and sent several of the pages to find the Lundian councilors.

If Samantha was disconcerted by Sheen's departure, she didn't show it. "We must fill the two empty council seats. I propose Count

Kayne's former seat be given to Baron Gwawl." Robrek didn't know who Kayne was or why he'd lost his council seat, but Baron Gwawl was a Korthian and had been a major supporter in her fight to take back her throne. "And Duke Argblutal's former seat should go to Count Tierney. He came to my aid when most of the Lundian nobles rebelled." She leveled a direct gaze at the three remaining Korthians.

They sat in silence for a few moments. Then Baron Teague glanced toward Sheen's empty seat and cleared his throat. "I believe they would make good choices, Your Highness."

"As do I, Your Highness," Caedmon said.

Count Pandaran was looking at his fingernails. He looked up and seemed surprised by the attention. "As Your Highness wills." He bowed his head.

"Good." She turned to Caedmon. "Have them summoned as well." Caedmon stood and obeyed.

Baron Arawn was the first of the Lundians to arrive. "Your Highness is most merciful," he said. He nodded his head toward the Korthian members of the council. Pandaran ignored him, and Teague responded with a tight-lipped nod. Arawn took his seat. He was followed by Weylin and Ultan, the tension in the room increasing with each Lundian that arrived. Robrek shifted uncomfortably in his seat. The hatred the Lundians and Korthians felt for each other was like a living thing. He'd had to raise his shields to protect himself from it.

Baron Gwawl and Count Tierney arrived at almost the same moment. "Your Highness." They bowed.

"You will join this council." Samantha gestured to two of the empty seats.

"I am honored, Your Highness." Gwawl bowed low.

"As am I." Tierney bowed as well, and the two gentlemen took their seats.

Finally, Count Nola puffed into the room. The chair groaned as he settled his vast weight into it. Nola trained his gaze solely on Samantha, ignoring everyone present. "This last-minute summons is most irregular, Your Highness. Why wasn't I informed of this meeting earlier?"

Caedmon cleared his throat and straightened in his chair. "We had not yet decided that after their treachery the Lundians would be still be included in this council."

Some emotion Robrek couldn't read flickered in Samantha's eyes as she glanced at Caedmon, but she said evenly, "We have decided to be merciful."

"Humph!" Nola said, as if he'd forgotten he'd supported Argblutal's attempt to usurp her throne. "I hope this means Your Highness intends to honor His Majesty's bequests." Robrek fixed his gaze on Nola. The count was referring to the king's land, the land where Robrek had grown up. Nola had taken it over with a heavy hand and had beheaded the first person who questioned his right to the lands. He'd placed the head on a pike as a warning to others. Boyden, Robrek's brother, had then been placed in charge in the Valley. The people of the Valley surely hadn't fared any better under Boyden's control.

Samantha blinked. "We all know Argblutal, not my father, gave you the king's lands. They will return to the control of the crown. You will immediately order your men to remove themselves."

"I will do nothing of the kind. I will not be robbed." He looked around at the other council members for support.

Weylin leaned forward slightly. "There were also other promises Argblutal made."

Teague stood. "Sheen was right! These are nothing but traitors to the throne! How dare they think they can keep their hands on the spoils of treachery!" Samantha narrowed her eyes at Teague. He retook his seat.

Samantha faced the Lundians. "As Baron Teague suggests, none of Argblutal's promises hold weight. He gave what wasn't his to give."

Weylin leaned back in his chair, as if admitting defeat. Nola did not. "I speak not of Argblutal's promises, but Solar's bequest. The kings' lands are mine. I have the deed right here, signed by Solar himself." He removed a piece of paper from his pocket.

Samantha ignored it. "Argblutal forced him to sign that. It, therefore, has no legal validity. You will issue orders for your men's removal, or you give lie to the oath of loyalty you swore to me."

Nola looked again at the other Lundians councilors, then back at Samantha. "A true monarch would honor the bequests of her predecessor."

The Lundian Arawn made to speak, but Samantha cut him off with a look. She then trained her gaze on Nola. "Let me make this perfectly clear. Anyone who attempts to hold property not rightfully theirs will join Torin and Morgan. Nola, you will obey my commands or suffer the consequences."

Nola spluttered, "It is no treason to hold onto what was given to me by the king himself." He again turned to the other Lundians for support, but they avoided his gaze.

Without taking her eyes off Nola, Samantha spoke to her guard. "Bearach, have the members of the Royal Guard enter the chamber."

"Yes, Your Highness." Bearach opened the door. Two members of the Royal Guard entered and bowed to Samantha.

She glared at Nola. "This is your last chance." Robrek tensed; would she would really order Nola beheaded with Torin and Morgan?

Nola met her glare. "You wouldn't dare."

"Your will, Your Highness?" Bearach asked

"The guards will escort Count Nola to the dungeon."

Count Nola's mouth fell open. "You can't be serious! You can't have me arrested for objecting to being robbed!"

"I can arrest you for treason, and it is treason to attempt to retain lands that belong rightly to the crown."

Count Nola got to his feet. He looked to his fellow council members for support. "You can't allow this!" The council members either stared at him in stony silence or looked away.

The two guards took Nola by the arms. "Come, Milord."

Nola tried to shake them off. "I will not! Unhand me, you uncivilized louts!"

Bearach drew his sword and pointed it at the count's breast. "You will obey Her Highness, or you will die where you stand." Robrek's eyes shot toward Samantha. Surely she'd tell Bearach to sheathe his sword.

Nola stared at the princess. "You have no right to do this!"

"I have every right. Go with the guards, or die here."

No. She can't mean it. It's a bluff.

Nola continued to struggle against his captors. Samantha didn't call them off, and Bearach's hand tightened on the sword. "Your Highness?" Robrek began, but Samantha ignored him. Instead, she gave Bearach a small nod, and Bearach buried his sword in the count's heart. Nola collapsed.

"Holy Sulis!" Robrek jumped to his feet and started toward Nola. If he was quick, he could probably heal the wound. But Samantha grabbed his arm and pulled him back into his seat. He didn't resist, but stared at her in wide-eyed disbelief. "You killed him!"

Samantha said nothing in reply, but her eyes briefly pleaded with him for understanding before her face resumed an expressionless mask. She kept her hand tightly on his arm as she ordered the guards to clear away the body. She turned back to the councilors. "It seems we have another seat to fill."

As if nothing had happened, the councilors discussed a replacement for the dead man. Robrek felt as if he might vomit. *How can I be the only one present to think life shouldn't be ended so cavalierly?* As if through a fog, he heard Samantha suggest Count Cadarn as the most logical replacement. *Holy Sulis, do I really belong among such people?*

When Cadarn arrived, he said he was honored and took the dead man's chair, which a servant had only just cleansed of blood. The same servant was now busy cleaning up the blood puddle on the floor. Robrek had a strange urge to help, as if he was somehow responsible for the killing. But Samantha's hand on his arm kept him in his chair.

He was barely aware of what went on in the rest of the meeting, but at least he got through it without fainting or vomiting. After discussing the royal funeral and rescinding the edict against female priestesses, Samantha dismissed the council.

* * *

As soon as they were alone in the room, Robrek shook off Sam's restraining hand. He stood, walked to the sideboard, and started to pour himself a glass of water. But he gave it up when he found his hand shaking too badly. He turned back to Samantha. "You killed him. Just ran him through as if he were a boar."

"I had no choice, Robbie. If they see me as weak, the council will tear me apart."

Robrek nodded vaguely. "But death? Just like that?"

Samantha got up and came to him. She took his hand. "Robbie, I don't like it either, but Nola would always have been my enemy. *Our* enemy. After this, other enemies will think twice about defying us."

He pulled his hand from hers and walked to the window. "I guess they will." He leaned his forehead against the window.

"Robbie, you think I wanted to do it? You think life means little to me?" Her voice caught, and Robrek turned to her. "My father trusted me with the throne. I must protect it. The council needed to see what will happen to those who oppose the crown. Can't you understand that? It isn't just me. I have the entire country depending on me. I won't fail my people."

Suddenly, Samantha looked infinitely weary, as if the whole weight of the country truly rested on her shoulders. He should be trying to help her bear the weight, not making things more difficult for her. What did he know about running a country?

He held out his arms to her, and she fell into them. "I love you, Sam. I'll have to trust you."

* * *

Eburacon stood outside the council room door with Geblan, his second in command, and the princess's guards, Bearach and Conroy. Bearach had blood on his uniform from killing the treacherous count. Despite Sir Robrek's obvious disapproval, it was what Solar would have done. Solar had been a great king, and Eburacon knew he had failed him. He'd been so upset for having been dismissed that he hadn't clued in something was wrong with Solar until it was too late. He should have found a way to protect his king from Argblatal's plots. Now, he'd been given another chance to guard a king. He wouldn't fail again.

After the future king had been alone only a few moments with Her Highness, Duke Caedmon came back down the corridor and requested entrance. Sir Robrek and the princess hadn't had half the time enough to work out their differences between them over the count's death. They didn't need to be interrupted now. Eburacon stepped in front of the duke. "Her Highness wishes to be alone with her *consort*."

Caedmon stiffened. "The peasant isn't yet her consort," the duke said, making his feelings toward Sir Robrek evident. This strengthened Eburacon's resolve not to allow Caedmon to interrupt the couple. Rather than repeating himself, Eburacon merely glared at the duke. Caedmon narrowed his eyes. "Do you know who I am?"

"Yes, Your Grace."

A vein in Caedmon's temple throbbed. "Then you should know that I am allowed access to Her Highness." He looked toward Conroy and Bearach. "Tell him."

Conroy technically outranked Eburacon and could order him to stand aside. Eburacon wasn't sure how he'd respond to such an order. When he'd obeyed orders and ceased to guard Solar, the king's mind had been poisoned.

Fortunately, he didn't have to decide. Conroy merely repeated Eburacon's early words. "Her Highness wishes to be alone with her consort." He emphasized the last word. Conroy was a man he could work with.

Caedmon reddened. "None of you have the right to deny me entrance!"

Eburacon merely put his hand on his sword, and Geblan and the princess's guards followed suit.

"Your name?" the duke asked.

"Eburacon, the captain of Sir Robrek's personal guard. His protection is my responsibility." Eburacon added as much menace as he could to his voice.

"Her Highness will hear of this." The duke swept back down the corridor.

"I like the size of your balls," Bearach said. Eburacon nodded in acceptance of the compliment.

* * *

When Robrek left the council chamber, his new guards were waiting for him. They both bowed deeply. Eburacon, said, "We kept Duke Caedmon out. We figured you didn't want to be interrupted."

"Good." Robrek nodded. He hadn't needed the duke interrupting them.

Several pages crept around the corner. Their eyes widened, they giggled and took off running. "What was that about?" Robrek asked.

"They just want to catch sight of the hero of Gloine Torr," Eburacon answered, smiling slightly. "It's all the boys talk about."

"They do?" Robrek shook his head. All his life he'd been the demon child. Now he was the "hero of Gloine Torr." The hero hadn't been much good just now in the council chamber.

* * *

Caedmon stormed along the corridor. Denied entrance to the council chamber! He needed to be in there now. The peasant sorcerer had just proven he didn't have the stomach to rule! He'd have Samantha second-guessing herself at every turn. She trusted the peasant too much, giving him every opportunity to do her harm. And those guards! He'd have them all dismissed. Conroy and Bearach had helped the princess through a tough period, but nothing they had done made up for their insolence today.

* * *

Holding a sheaf of lists, Blaine hurried into the practice arena where the princess was training. She squared off against Bearach, sweat running down her face. She attacked viciously, but Bearach parried with a grace Blaine could only envy. Captain Darhour had tried to teach Blaine the rudiments of sword work, but the sight of an oncoming blade so terrified him that he always ended up closing his eyes. It comforted him to leave the princess's protection to others while he made his nice orderly lists.

The princess bent over panting and waved Bearach away. "That's enough for today." She slammed the practice sword back into its place on the wall with such force Blaine wondered if now was the time to bother her. "I hate to disturb Your Highness, but there are as many details to see to as there are fish in the sea, so to speak."

"What details?" the princess snapped, leaning against the wall and continuing to pant. She was definitely in a mood, but he'd be remiss in his duty if he let things slide.

Blaine looked down at his list. "First, the funeral sermon. Who will preach it? Normally the high priest would, but he hasn't yet been replaced." The former high priest, Father Shylah, had killed himself after committing child sacrifice to create the potion by which Argblutal had controlled the king.

"Ask Father Hafghan."

Blaine nearly dropped the papers, barely catching them before they wafted away. "Hafghan? Are you sure, Your Highness? I know it's not my place to question, but Your Highness, he crowned Argblutal king."

The princess grabbed a towel from a servant and wiped the sweat from her face. "Only under duress. His wedding sermon allowed me to rescue my betrothed and escape."

"I see. It will be as Your Highness wills." Blaine made a check next to the entry. "Next is the funeral music."

"Just do as you deem best."

She headed for the door, and Blaine's legs carried him after her. He forced himself to stop, but he wanted to shout, *Your Highness, you can't leave all this to me. What if I mess it up? What if they say you've not given proper respect to the king?*

"I will try to justify your confidence in me," he yelled as she and her guards disappeared.

* * *

The following morning, Caedmon patted the princess on the shoulder, the cinnamon scent of her shampoo wafting up from her just-washed hair and itching his nostrils. He settled into a seat in her reception room where breakfast was spread on the table. He buttered a piece of toast. "Samantha, I have to talk to you about the guards. I was refused entry into the council chamber yesterday after the meeting. Sir Robrek's guards stopped me, and your Bearach and Conroy backed them up."

She crinkled her forehead. "Did they give a reason?"

Caedmon slammed his toast back on the plate. "What does that matter? They overstepped their bounds. They shall have to be dismissed, of course. All four of them."

Samantha's jaw dropped. "After all they went through with me when Argblutal was poisoning my father, you are not seriously suggesting I dismiss Bearach and Conroy! They are the last remaining members of my guard who stood by me when I had no one else." She shook her head. "No, Caedmon, not even for you would I consider it."

Caedmon threw up his hands. "Now, see here, Your Highness. You do not seem to understand the disrespect they showed me. You can't have guards that won't let me in to see you when it is necessary."

Samantha leaned across the table. "No, Caedmon, it is you who don't understand. They saved my life. I trust them as I can trust few else. They will continue to have my back. Am I understood?"

"You can't mean it, Your Highness. I won't stand for it."

Samantha stood. "You will stand for it if I say you will. Bearach and Conroy's positions are no more open to debate than my marriage."

That infernal peasant! He's poisoning her against me. But she wore the same expression Solar had had when he wouldn't be argued with. "At the very least, they must be disciplined."

"I will hear their side of the story." She turned and called to her maid, who came out of her bedroom. "Tell Bearach and Conroy to come in, please."

Her maid went to the door and called the two men in. They bowed. "Did you keep Duke Caedmon from entering the council chamber yesterday after the meeting?" she asked them.

Does she even doubt my word?

They looked at each other, and then Conroy spoke, "We believed you were having a private conversation with your betrothed and didn't wish to be disturbed."

She nodded to them. "Thank you. That is all." They bowed again and left. Samantha then turned to Caedmon. "They did their duty. Now, why did you need to see me?"

"That's immaterial! It is not their place to make such a decision!"

She shrugged. "It may have been a bit beyond their authority, but they seem to have intuited my wishes. Enough of this, Caedmon. I won't always be available to you."

"You can't be serious!" But he saw that she was. "Well, you at least agree that this Eburacon must go. He had been in his position less than a day, and he somehow thought he could command me."

For a moment, Samantha looked as if she was considering it. "No, he acted correctly, and I feel good about him in that position. What you had to tell me could clearly wait."

"You are missing the point, Your Highness."

"There is no point except your bruised pride, Uncle. Sir Robek's guards and my guards acted as I would have wished them to. What we should discuss is Sheen's disrespect of me. What should I do about him?"

Caedmon stood to tower over her. "I must insist, Your Highness. Those guards—"

"Enough!" To Caedmon's shock, she cut him off. It had been decades since anyone but Solar had dared to interrupt him. Samantha was now his liege, true, but she was still a child. "Sit back down and advise me as I wish to be advised. Don't trouble me with petty matters."

Petty matters! How dare she call me petty? Caedmon could see there was no use pursuing the matter now and breathed slowly to calm himself. He turned his attention to the problem of Sheen. "You will have to reward him, of course."

The princess got up and started pacing. Caedmon wanted to tell her to sit still, but only the king had been able to curb this habit of hers. "Reward him for walking out of the council room?"

"No, for coming to your rescue. Once he feels properly compensated, the other problems will go away."

"Reward him how? You know my father amassed no great wealth to the crown."

Caedmon steepled his fingers under his chin and tried to ignore the princess's movements. "There are a few minor estates under the crown's control in Korth that could be given as rewards, but the true prizes are the estates of the traitors—Argblutal, Morgan, Torin, and Nola."

Samantha dropped into a chair opposite him. "But they're all Lundian estates. I can't give them to a Korthian."

"I'm not sure Sheen would be satisfied with less."

She shook her head and got up again. "My father would have never given a Lundian estate to a Korthian. He taught me that one of the most important things was not to show favoritism."

Caedmon briefly closed his eyes as she spouted Solar's great maxim. But her hold on the throne was nowhere near as secure as Solar's had been, and she might well need to buy loyalty. "What were your plans for the estates?"

"Argblutal's can go to Count Tierney. What about heirs of the others?"

Caedmon nodded; giving Argblutal's lands to Tierney would make him a strong ally, but the heirs? "Torin has no surviving heir. Morgan's heir is his younger brother Lord Feoras, but we don't know how deeply involved he was with his brother's treason. Nola's heir is a five-year-old child. Neither is likely to make you a strong partner. I'd recommend giving Nola's to Sheen, and—"

"No." Caedmon clenched his teeth as she interrupted him again. "I won't show favoritism to Korth, and I see no need to rob a five-year-old of his inheritance. Have Feoras summoned to court, and we can see about his innocence. Torin's can wait." Caedmor moved to object, but she cut him off with a gesture.

The peasant had to be dealt with. This was his doing.

CHAPTER 4

Robrek ran his hand down the naked curves of Samantha's body. Her skin glowed in the firelight, and her auburn hair gleamed like Brazen's coat—the magical bronze horse who'd taught him how to fight. He stroked her cheek, praying he could be the man she needed. Tomorrow was the royal funeral. He prayed for the ability to help her through such a difficult day. He kissed her gently and then, dreading the cold of the palace corridors, slipped from the bed. Samantha stirred. She opened her eyes and reached out to him. "I love you," she whispered.

"I love you, too." He took her hand and leaned in for a kiss. Her lips were soft and supple, and her tongue played with his. He broke the kiss, knowing that if he continued, he'd never be able to leave. But he had to: Samantha had said the court wouldn't tolerate their intimacy until their marriage had been formally solemnized. "I'll see you in the morning."

Robrek dressed quickly and threw on his fur-lined cloak. It was barely warm enough for the freezing corridors. Outside the princess's rooms, he was met by two of the princess's guards and two of his own—Iden and Murdoc, who were on duty during the late night hours. These two escorted him back to his rooms every night, and other than that he never saw them.

"Good evening, Milord," Iden greeted him. The use of his title still made Robrek feel like a fraud.

They reached his quarters quickly. "Good night," he said to his guards, and they nodded politely. What did they think of him and of their job to protect him? Did they consider it an honor to serve him, as Eburacon and Geblan assured him it was? Or did they too think him unworthy? They never gave any sign.

Robrek hurried through his reception room to his bedroom. There, Drem had a fire burning and waited to help him to bed. Drem had cleared out most of the old furnishings but had done little to replace them. A fireplace dominated one wall, and a stand in the corner held the new armor and weapons Samantha had had made to replace those he lost when the magical horses disappeared. The bed was big enough to sleep half a dozen people. A gigantic wardrobe, the dressing table, and a chair took up the other side of the room. Robrek's bedroom and reception room combined were as large as his father's farmhouse. *Why would anyone need this much space?*

Drem rose and took his cloak. "Good evening, Milord. Did you pass a pleasant evening?" Drem spoke with no particular emotion. Although Robrek never told Drem where he'd been, surely the servant knew. Did he think it improper?

"Yes, thank you," Robrek answered, attempting to strip his words of emotion. He didn't want to blush in the servant's presence. Robrek took off his clothes and gave them to Drem. Apparently, it wasn't proper for Robrek to care for them himself. Drem hardly thought it proper for him to use his chamber pot without help.

Robrek accepted a sleep robe from Drem and wrapped it around himself. "Will Your Lordship require any further assistance?" Drem asked.

"No, thank you," Robrek said, and Drem bowed and left the room.

Robrek crouched down by the fire he hadn't made and used the poker to rearrange the logs he hadn't chopped. He found it strange he had no clue who had done these chores. There'd been servants on his father's farm, but he'd always worked alongside them, as hard or harder than any of them. "Sulis," he whispered into the fire, "did you truly chose me for this? If so, I need your guidance now." The fire merely crackled in response.

Robrek sighed, crawled into the bed, and pulled the covers over him. He stretched out his legs, and his foot hit something small and hard. He cried out as something sharp stabbed him.

His guards burst through the door with swords drawn. Laboring for breath, his leg convulsing, Robrek threw off his covers, revealing a narrow segmented tail, arched for attack.

"A deathstalker!" Murdoc swept the scorpion into the fire with his sword.

"It stung him!" Iden cried. "Milord, can you—?"

"In a minute," he wheezed. He closed his eyes and set about neutralizing the venom with his magic. Slowly, his convulsions stopped, and he began to breathe easier. When Robrek opened his eyes, Iden was frantically explaining the scorpion to Eburacon. Robrek's four other guards had arrived, evidently summoned by his cry.

Eburacon knelt and put a hand on Robrek's shoulder. "Will you be all right, Milord?"

"Yes, it's just poison. I can take care of that. How could it have gotten into my bed?"

Eburacon stood. "Someone had to have placed it there, Milord. Deathstalkers aren't native. You can only find them at rare pet merchants down near the docks. Her Highness should be notified immediately." He dispatched Geblan to do so.

"Samantha!" Robrek stumbled to his feet. This might be an attack on her, too!

But before he could make it to the door, Samantha burst into the room, accompanied by her guards. "Robbie, thank Sulis you're all right!" She threw her arms around him. He scanned her with his healing senses and determined she was unhurt. "Oh, Robbie, what would I do if something happened to you?" She trembled in his arms. "Someone will pay for this! I will find them and make them pay!" Samantha disengaged herself and drew herself up, once again becoming more than the woman who loved him: Samantha, the reigning monarch.

* * *

In response to the midnight summons, Caedmon hurried to Samantha's reception room. When the princess's secretary ushered him into the princess's quarters, his heart sank. Righ said it would be tonight, but Sir Robrek, very much alive, sat beside the princess on the sofa. "What's going on, Your Highness?"

Samantha's entire body was rigid with anger. "A deathstalker in Sir Robrek's bed stung him. He could have been killed."

Caedmon's eyebrows shot up, and he turned to the peasant. "Stung? Yet you sit here?"

"Healers can neutralize any poison."

Caedmon sat in a chair across from the couple and drummed his fingers on the arm of the chair. *Damn Righ! He should have thought of that. Just what other tricks does this sorcerer know?* But for now, he had to deflect blame away from himself. "This will not do. They may be after the princess next. Whoever is behind this must be caught! I suggest—"

Samantha rose to her feet, the very power of her presence cutting off his words. At this moment, she was indeed the daughter of the great Solar. "Find me a spymaster. Someone to replace Darhour."

"Someone in The Ghost's league will be hard to come by." The Ghost had been Darhour's nickname when he'd been the chief assassin of the Saloynan king. He was so good at getting into his victims' rooms, it was said he could walk through walls. "However, I'd recommend a man named Righ. He has proven quite useful to me in the past."

"Send for him at once."

* * *

Samantha paced the room. Every few seconds her eyes flicked to Robbie to reassure herself that he was indeed all right. *No one will take him from me! No one!*

When Righ arrived, he was neither particularly handsome nor unhandsome. He was of average height, average build, had very ordinary blond hair and beard and unremarkable blue eyes. In fact, he was one of the most ordinary and completely forgettable men Samantha had ever seen—qualities quite useful in a spy. Darhour had had to resort to make-up and other techniques in order to blend in. Righ would need no such aids.

She had Righ be seated, but she couldn't sit still herself. She briefed Righ on the situation. "I want him caught now so I can roast his entrails over a slow-burning fire."

Righ bowed his head. "I understand, Your Highness."

After Righ and Caedmon left, Samantha turned to Robbie. He put his head in his hands. "Who do you think it is? One of your former suitors?"

She sat beside him and put her hand on his shoulder. "When I find out, they will cease to draw breath."

* * *

Caedmon sat behind his desk in his office and scowled at Righ. "Any other bright ideas?" he demanded. "The throne of Korthlundia must not be polluted with his peasant blood."

Righ pursed his lips. "His being immune to poison is decidedly inconvenient—you know it is my chief weapon. A direct assault would be dangerous and almost certainly doomed to failure. His swordsmanship is said to approach that of Captain Darhour, and his personal guards are all highly skilled."

Caedmon drummed his fingers on the arm of his chair. "Can they be bought? An unexpected sword thrust through the back is difficult to defend against."

Righ glanced at Caedmon's fingers in what appeared to be annoyance. "Doubtful. It would be dangerous to approach them. They seem to worship him. By having Her Highness hire me, you have shown a clear connection between us. Any action on my part will be seen as being directed by you."

Caedmon stopped drumming. "It was necessary. I couldn't afford her employing someone who might trace that scorpion to me." He pounded a fist on the desk. "Sulis curse it! It was supposed to end our problems, not compound them."

"Is there no way to discredit him? Cause her to willingly break off the relationship?"

"Do you think I haven't tried? She's absolutely besotted and won't listen to reason." He leaned forward. "Find me more ammunition. His own villagers hated him enough to want to burn him at the stake. He can't be the simple, ignorant peasant he pretends to be, not with the power he has."

* * *

Alvabane's body ached in every joint and muscle as she bounced around in the coach, but she couldn't afford to ask the driver to slow down. The son of her breast was set to die, and this she couldn't allow.

Despite his being the child of her rapist, Alvabane had always felt some affection for the babe who'd suckled at her breast. But that wasn't the reason she had to stop Torin from dying. He was a descendent of the race of demons who had driven her people out, and so, like all Korthlundians, he deserved nothing but death. But he would help be the means of her people's restoration. She laughed at the irony. For years, she hadn't laughed at all, but since the Soul Stone had started to glow, she'd found many reasons for amusement.

Her servant cowered on the seat across from her, making small mewing sounds. Alvabane glared at her. *Why can't she accept what had to be?* After Erick's sacrifice, there had not been time to send for another of her people to assist in the rites. Alvabane had had to enlist one of Duke Torin's servants. While Erick, as a ten-year-old child, had willingly opened his mouth to the forceps and the knife, Alanna had fought to keep her tongue. It had taken two of Torin's men-at-arms to subdue her. Alvabane hadn't, of course, used her magic to sing the servant to sleep because pain was an important part of the sacrifice. Alanna wasn't yet reconciled to her fate, but her fear was such she would do her duty well enough. She had no family and nowhere else to go.

At last they reached the gates of Murtaghan. Decades had passed since she'd last visited the vast teeming capital of Lundia. Coming from a small tribe of nomads, she'd been disconcerted by the noise and bustle. She still was.

The coach wound through the crowded street to Torin's house. Having quarters in the palace, Torin hadn't used the house in years, and only a single caretaker was in residence. This suited Alvabane. She had little need for servants beyond Alanna, and the fewer prying eyes the better.

* * *

Robrek drank in the scent of the blood-red lake—the delicate perfume of rot and death. He darted a glance behind him, but Holy Writ was nowhere to be seen. This time nothing would stop him from joining with the lake. As he moved his hand to undo the buttons on his shirt, he noticed something he hadn't the last time. Shadows drifted through the lake—hundreds of them, thousands.

"Come to us," a voice whispered. "Be one with us."

The voice was joined by thousands of others, all speaking in unison. The shadows in the lake wanted him as much as he wanted them.

He tore at his buttons. He could wait no longer.

A blinding light rose out of the lake, and Robrek shielded his eyes against it.

"Milord!"

Robrek snapped open his eyes to see Drem standing over him with a lamp. "No, go away!" he cried, bereft of his chance once again.

Drem pursed his lips. "Milord, you don't wish to be late for His Majesty's funeral."

"Samantha," he whispered. He had to be there, be her comfort. But even that knowledge was barely strong enough to tear him away from his desire for the lake.

* * *

Tears streamed down Samantha's cheeks as her maids dressed her in the black dress Korthlundians thought appropriate for mourning. It made her look even paler than usual, almost faint. When her maids were done with her hair, she washed her face and put on a court mask. The court couldn't see a scared, lost, little girl—they had to see their queen.

Robbie arrived, dressed in a black wool tunic and leggings. Unlike her, the black brought out his exotic good looks, especially the emerald brilliance of his eyes. "Sam, I'm so sorry," he said, and put his arms around her. She nearly broke into tears again at the tenderness of his touch, but she swallowed her sobs.

Samantha took Robbie's hand and led him to the palace chapel. The chapel was a sea of black, every noble in the joined kingdoms wanting to show the depths of their grief. Struggling to keep her mask in place, Samantha took her seat in the front pew with Robbie beside her. Solar lay concealed inside a gilt coffin, not five feet from her. She wanted to throw herself on the coffin and wail out her grief, but she sat stiffly and clung tightly to Robbie's hand.

As soon as she was seated, Father Hafghan rose and began the funeral liturgy. Solar's coffin was covered with ivy and laurel to symbolize the continuation of life Beyond the Far Mountain. Father Hafghan sprinkled the coffin with holy water and wafted incense over it to protect the body from demons. Samantha barely listened to Hafghan's sermon as he poured forth the Holy Writ's message of death and life Beyond the Far Mountain and praised Solar as the greatest king in the history of Korth or Lundia. If she thought too much about her father, she'd never be able to maintain her poise. Instead, she concentrated on the calluses on Robbie's hand and on the darkness of his skin next to the lightness of her own. What would a child of theirs look like?

Father Hafghan gave a final prayer for the safe travel of her father's soul, and the service was over. Members of the Royal Council came forward to carry his casket. Sheen was not among them. He'd refused to participate if Arawn, Weylin, and Ultan were allowed to. *How dare he insult my father by his absence?* She didn't know what to do about Sheen and silently cried out to her father for the wisdom he'd had in such abundance.

Still holding Robbie's hand, she followed the coffin out the palace door and onto the cart that would carry it to the Royal Cemetery. The cart moved forward at a slow pace, and she and Robbie followed on foot, the rest of Korthlundia's nobility behind them. They wound through the city streets, lined with black crepe and packed with citizens mourning their king. They called out her and Robbie's names. They seemed to have no problem with Robbie as consort. As she always had, Samantha felt a love from the populace that bordered on idolatry. She was the long awaited heir, not born until her father was in his seventies. *How can I live up to what they expect from me?*

The royal tomb had been opened to receive the body. Father Hafghan drew the star of Sulis over the coffin, blessing Solar on his journey Beyond the Far Mountain. Blaine handed her apples and grain, the traditional offerings for the dead. She lay them on her father's casket. *No, Father, Daddy, don't be dead! Please don't be dead!*

She recited aloud the traditional prayer for the dead. Her voice cracked once, but she got through it dry-eyed. Robbie squeezed her hand as the coffin was placed in the tomb and the tomb sealed shut.

King Solar II, her father, was gone. She must now take his place.

The procession returned to the palace and entered the throne room, where for the first time she sat on her father's throne. Robbie sat to her right in what had been her throne as the heir. One by one, according to rank, the nobles came forward and expressed their condolences and offered the oath of loyalty they had formerly reserved for Solar. Again, Sheen was absent, but his sons Devyn and Cedric were present and gave oaths on his behalf, claiming he was unwell. This, she strongly doubted.

The rest of the day passed in a fog of grief. She attended the funeral banquet, at which she ate nothing, and she listened to bard after bard give tribute to the late king. Finally, she was alone with Robbie in her rooms. Only then did she remove her mask and wail out her grief in his arms.

CHAPTER 5

Robrek cringed as he headed to the practice arena for his usual training session with Vaughan. His guards, Cathbad and Brendan, accompanied him. *What is the point? I'm such a terrible teacher.* When Brazen had taught him how to fight, she hadn't used words or instructions, but had opened his mind and muscles to the skills from the inside. He really didn't know *how* to fight; he simply fought. But Robrek had been told it was a knight's duty to participate in training his squire. Until recently, Vaughan had been a stable boy in the palace stables, but during the contest of Gloine Torr, he'd become Robrek's squire.

"How did this morning's session go?" Robrek asked him, speaking of the time he trained with the other squires.

Vaughan sighed loudly. "Dull and boring, as usual. Master Daire had us practicing stances, parries, and thrusts in front of a mirror again. You never did any of that, did you, Milord?"

"No," Robrek admitted. "A peasant like me could hardly afford a mirror the size of those in the practice arena." As he said that, Cathbad and Brendan lifted their eyebrows. Maybe he shouldn't have called himself a peasant. "But if you're going to be a knight, you should listen to your weapons master." *He has to be a better teacher than I am.* "I often didn't see the sense in what Brazen wanted me to do, but what she taught me saved my life on more than one occasion."

Vaughan wore the look children often wear when their elders are lecturing. "Can't we stop talking, Milord, and fence?"

Robrek could tell his words were having no effect, so he took off his sword belt, hung it on the wall, and picked up a wooden practice sword. Vaughan did likewise. They then squared off against each other, and Robrek gave his squire the signal to attack. Vaughan came at him, but as usual, he was treating it like a child's game, swinging wildly. Robrek had repeatedly tried to tell him that swinging in this manner left him off balance and open to attack, not to mention tiring him quickly. If this had been an actual fight, Robrek could have killed his squire twenty times in the first few minutes. He called a halt and again tried to explain to Vaughan the importance of controlling his movements. But the next time Vaughan came at him, it was with an equal lack of control.

"Milord," Cathbad interrupted. "Might I make a suggestion?"

"Certainly." Robrek was open to anything at this point.

Cathbad nodded to the far corner of the room, and Robrek followed him until they were out of Vaughan's hearing. "Hit the boy."

Robrek looked at the man aghast. "Beat him?" After the number of times his father had forced him to remove his shirt and beat his back raw, Robrek wasn't about to beat a child.

"Not beat him, Milord. Hit him. Show him what would happen in a real fight if he swung like that. My weapons master always said there was nothing like a little pain to drive the point home."

"But what if I hurt him?"

Cathbad shrugged. "You're a healer, aren't you?"

Robrek thought about it, then nodded. "Thank you, Cathbad."

Cathbad bowed and said, "I am at your service, Milord."

Robrek squared off against Vaughan, and Vaughan again attacked with a wild swing to the right, leaving his left side completely unprotected. Robrek countered with a blow to the ribcage.

"Ouch!" Vaughan cried, clutching his left side. "What did you do that for?" Vaughan was clearly struggling to keep his tears back, but Robrek's healing senses told him he had caused no serious damage.

"Cathbad suggested I demonstrate the consequences of ignoring instructions."

"He did, did he?" Vaughan glared resentfully at Cathbad, who didn't look the slightest bit repentant.

"Again," Robrek instructed, and Vaughan raised his sword. This time Vaughan didn't go on the immediate attack, and his movements were much more controlled. It wasn't long, though, before Robrek hit him again and again. Robrek tried to pull his blows so he didn't hurt the boy too badly.

Vaughan was starting to tire, and he made another wild swing, this time for Robrek's legs. Robrek parried, knocking Vaughan off balance and striking Vaughan a stiff blow to the leg. The boy cried out and fell to the ground. He threw the sword across the room. "Sulis curse me! I'll never be a swordsman! A shit shoveler like me doesn't belong with a sword in his hand!"

Robrek stiffened. "Who said that?"

"The other boys." Vaughan again looked as though he was struggling not to cry. "And they're right. They're all better than I am. I should go back to the stables where I belong."

Robrek sat down on the practice mat and indicated that Vaughan should sit beside him. "It isn't easy for peasants like us to fit in with the nobles. They'll continue to think they're better than we are until we prove them otherwise, and that won't make them like us any better. Do you still want to be a knight?"

"Yes, Milord!" Vaughan jumped to his feet. "I want to be like you! It will sure show them when the bards start singing songs about me, too!"

Having bards sing about you is overrated. "Remember, you will be squire to the king, and what will they be? Junior members of the Royal Guard."

A big smile spread across Vaughan's face. "We'll show them, won't we, Milord?"

"Yes, we will. Now go get yourself cleaned up."

* * *

A little over a week had passed since the royal funeral and the attempt on Robbie's life. Samantha squeezed his leg under the table as she sat next to him in council, where the topic of discussion was Argblutal's murder of the Neasarian ambassador and how the resulting tension between the two countries might be eased.

The meeting was interrupted by Captain Hawk and a messenger from Valley Fair. "Your Highness," the messenger said. "Despite Nola's death, his men have refused to leave The Valley. Boyden Angusstamm, who leads them, says he is protecting the lands of his lord's heir."

The councilors erupted in anger. "He shall have to be removed," Baron Gwawl spat. "How many men does he have?"

"About two dozen, Milord," the messenger replied.

Caedmon shifted in his seat. "I suggest we send a force of twice that size. Since Sir Robrek is most familiar with the land and the people, he should lead them."

Samantha grabbed the arm of her chair. She didn't want to let Robbie out of her sight, but saying so would make him appear weak. "The force should be sent as soon as possible," she ordered, trying not to glare at Caedmon.

"I can have my men ready by morning," Captain Hawk declared.

* * *

Mother Venetia stumbled as she came into the light of day, squinting against the sun's brightness. News of Father Shylah's death had reached Wisteria, the capital of Korth, and she and priestesses all over Korth—those who had survived—were being released.

Awena clung tightly to her hand. "What will we do, Mother?"

"I must answer Mother Bensaggyrt's call. There may be danger involved, but with your power, you could be of use. Will you come as well?"

Awena nodded. "There is nothing left for me here. My parents died when I was an infant, and my mentor, Mother Bedelia, was killed trying to prevent me from being taken."

Venetia patted the child's hand. Awena reminded her of her own novice, Oriana. Venetia had seen the child well hidden before she was taken. She prayed the young novice was safe and would be waiting in Balley Beg.

* * *

Oriana opened the door and entered the training arena from the outside. Vaughan was squared off against another boy and didn't look happy to see her.

"Shit shoveler," the other boy hissed, and Vaughan reddened. The other boy attacked, and Vaughan parried. They fought until the other boy scored, hitting Vaughan in the side.

The weapons instructor hurried over. "Can't you even manage the simplest parry?" he asked. "Go over and practice in front of the mirror for the rest of the hour. Why in Sulis's name the princess's betrothed wants a stable boy for a squire is beyond me."

Vaughan passed her on the way to the mirror. "Girls aren't allowed in the practice arena," he said. Oriana stomped out the door. *He's lying, but it's not like I wanted to watch anyway. I just wanted to warm up for a few minutes. I can warm up in my room just as well.*

Oriana entered the palace through a side door, the guard letting her pass without a word. *But where are my father and brothers? They promised to come for me. What can be keeping them?* But that wasn't the only thing bothering her. She'd felt a call through the earth. Someone had summoned all the northern priestesses to gather to Balley Beg. Had something terrible happened? She quickly wiped away her tears before anyone saw them. *Why bother? It isn't like anyone will care I'm crying. Even the princess has forgotten I exist. Maybe she thinks it's my fault the king died. I did my best. Truly, I did.*

While the palace corridors were cold, she couldn't bear the thought of going back to her empty room. She found a page and asked him how to find the palace stillroom. He gave her directions, but the palace was so confusing she had to ask two more pages before she found her way.

A wrinkled old man looked up as she walked in. Three boys about her age were chopping and grinding herbs for the various potions brewing over the fire. "Can I help you?" the old man said, clearly hoping she'd go away.

"I was hoping I could help you," she said. "I'm a novice to a Korthian priestess, and she taught me a lot about potion making."

"We can't have children mucking things up in here," the man said.

Children? I'm as old as any of the boys. "I can use my magic to help enhance your remedies. Mother Venetia said I was quite good at it."

The old man's eyes narrowed. "Magic, is it? Are you, too, going to tell me that magic is necessary for the healing arts? I'll have you know I've been making potions for fifty years, and I don't need a child to come along and tell me how to do it better. Now run along and play with your dolls!"

* * *

Alvabane waited for the guard to open the cell imprisoning the son of her breast. It had taken awhile to get permission to see him, especially since he hadn't been particularly keen to see her. She prayed to the dark gods his stubbornness wouldn't get in the way of their work.

The door creaked open, and she entered with a lamp. The prisoner, sitting on his cot, shielded his eyes against the light. The guard closed the door behind her.

Torin lifted a sardonic eyebrow. "Come to watch me die?"

"I've come to prevent it."

Torin's brow rose higher. "It's a little late for that."

"The bastard is weak. She will still accept your oath, and we will make you king." Alvabane rubbed her hands together in anticipation of victory.

A sneer crossed Torin's face. "*You* would make me king?"

"The Stone of my people lives again." She closed her eyes for an instant, savoring the joy she'd felt since that first moment.

Torin fell back on the cot and barked out a laugh. "You're still obsessed with that thing? Since before I was born you've been—"

"You will not mock what is sacred!" Alvabane put out her hand and sang a note, sending a jolt of pain into Torin. Torin yelped and shot to his feet.

"How dare—?"

Alvabane waved her hand in front of his mouth and sang another note, silencing him. "The Stone that was imprisoned behind Armunn's shield is hidden no more. Its power can be mine, be ours."

Torin reached out as if to catch Alvabane by the throat, but suddenly backed away as if he dared not touch her. "How much power?"

Alvabane drew closer. "Enough to give you the throne. But I require certain items to attune it to my control. Items you can help me find—a life and a soul willingly sacrificed to the will of the dark gods."

Always squeamish where the dark gods were concerned, Torin tried to take a step backward, but his back was already to the wall. "Send for some of your people. They let you cut out their tongues easily enough."

Raised among these blonde demons, he didn't have the proper appreciation for sacrifice or pain. "There is no time. It would take months, perhaps a year for the message to reach my people and appropriate sacrifices found and dispatched. We must act now while the joined kingdoms are still in turmoil."

Torin glanced at her hand, as if afraid what she might do with it, then met her eyes. "How do you expect me to find anyone willing?"

"Look among those whose hate is stronger than their love. The enemies of those who would wear the crown."

"The princess is popular with the people. Her only enemies are among the nobility, who will be missed."

"What of her betrothed?"

Torin rubbed his chin thoughtfully. "A priest from his village tried to burn him at the stake, and rumors suggest his brother tried to help."

Alvabane smiled. "A servant of Sulis and a brother. I can think of none better."

"You're sure of this? If I humiliate myself by bowing to a bastard, you can make me king? You can place the sorcerer dead at my feet and the bastard bitch under me in bed?"

Alvabane's smile widened. "None will be able to stop us"

* * *

Leigh Fergalstamm put his ear to the infant's chest. The baby's breathing was labored and constricted. He closed his eyes and used his healing gift to assess the baby's condition. She had the lung sickness common among the poor in the slums of Murtaghan. She burned with fever, too ill to do anything more than whimper. "How long has the child been sick?" Leigh asked its mother.

"Aine started feeling poorly a week ago. Is she going to be all right?" The mother smoothed the sweat-soaked hair back from the infant's face.

"I'll do my best, but the illness has advanced far into her lungs. Why didn't you bring her sooner?"

The mother's lower lip trembled as Leigh handed the infant back to her. He went to the cauldron hanging over the fireplace, and to the water he added herbs and his magic. "My neighbor only told me this morning you'd see the babe whether or not I could afford to pay," she said. "And I couldn't take her to the temple because I didn't have the donation the priests demanded."

Leigh frowned as he stirred the cauldron. He'd heard this story too often since he opened his shop with the money Robrek's uncle Slathek had given him. Slathek had called it an investment, but the investment promised poor returns for the foreign merchant Only the poorest of the poor came to Leigh, most having nothing at all to give for his services. Some days he didn't collect even enough to eat. His robes were already hanging a little more loosely about him, but that wasn't what worried him. Without proper nourishment, his magic, weak to begin with, couldn't operate, and sick children, like the one nestled in her mother's arms, needed his magic if they were to survive. Without money, he also couldn't buy the herbs he needed to make medicines. It wouldn't be long before his supplies ran out.

He sighed and rolled up the sleeves of the novice robes he still wore even though he'd been defrocked and excommunicated for saving Robrek from being burnt at the stake. *Do I still want to be a priest? The church doesn't serve Sulis and her children the way I want to.*

Leigh took the mixture off the fire and set it in the snow outside his doorway to cool. He then ladled it into a bottle, attached a false teat, and gave the bottle to the mother. At first the baby refused to suck and pushed the bottle away fretfully. But Leigh laid his hands on the baby and entered a healing trance. He worked on easing the tightness of the child's lungs, lowering her fever, and encouraging her to drink. After a while, he was rewarded as the child began to suck.

Leigh emerged from his trance when the baby had sucked down the last of the medicine and fallen into a restful sleep. As he always did after using his gift, Leigh felt light-headed and weak. He struggled not to faint as he refilled the bottle and gave it to the mother. "When she wakes, get her to drink another bottleful. I'll come and check on her in the morning." Leigh gave the mother a few more instructions on properly caring for the baby and said a silent prayer to Sulis for the baby's life.

Leigh grabbed his last loaf of bread and fell onto the tiny cot shoved into a corner of his one-room shop. This bread had been given to him by a baker he'd treated for burns earlier in the day. Despite having saved the man from permanent damage, the baker clearly hadn't paid with his best work, but the bread was the only thing he had to eat. As he ate the dry, tasteless loaf, Leigh closed his eyes and considered his options. He immediately rejected the idea of going to his father. Although Fergal would most likely give him money, Leigh would take no money tainted with the ruin of countless lives: his father was a dealer in paipin leaves. Besides, his father thought him a fool for giving away his talent to the poor rather than selling it to the rich. He could go to Slathek, but his pride prevented him for asking the foreign merchant for a larger investment, knowing he'd never be able to repay it.

Robrek and the princess would surely help. Robrek was a healer himself and would understand the need to heal without regard for profit, and the princess had promised him a reward for saving Robrek's life. But going to them still felt like failure. He wanted to be able to make it on his own.

CHAPTER 6

"You'll be all right, won't you? You know what to do?" Samantha asked Robrek as the procession gathered outside her bedroom window.

Robrek nodded. "Tell them to leave. Arrest them if they won't." Robrek doubted his brother would leave quietly. He wondered how he'd feel bringing Boyden back to Murtaghan in chains. With Holy Writ's help, he'd forgiven his brother for making his childhood a living hell, but he didn't exactly feel brotherly love for the man. "Will you be okay without me?"

Samantha's face hardened. "I'll have to be."

Will I be okay without you? He didn't ask. She had too many problems for him to burden her with his feelings of inadequacy. If he was supposed to be king, why had the horses left him before he felt comfortable in the role? He put his arms around her and breathed in the scent of her hair, a slight cinnamon that must have come from her shampoo. "I'm sorry, Sam. I wish I could bring the king back."

She held him tightly for a moment, then let him go. "The sooner you leave, the sooner you can return."

"I love you," he whispered in her ear, then kissed her.

Robrek and all of his personal guards—Eburacon, Geblan, Brendan, Cathbad, Iden, and Murdoc—made their way to the palace stables. Robrek approached Wild Thing's stall and got out her saddle. She would allow no one but him to handle her, with the occasional exception of Vaughan, his squire.

:Where going?: Wild Thing asked.

"Back to the Valley."

Wild Thing stiffened under his touch. *:Stomp stupid people who try to burn Robbie?:*

"No, we're just going to tell some men to go away."

:What if won't go? Stomp then?:

Robrek laughed. "No, we arrest them. At least that's what Apple Lady says." Apple Lady was Wild Thing's name for the princess. Samantha had given the mare an apple when they first met.

Wild Thing evidently sensed something in his tone. *:Apple Lady not tell truth?:*

Robrek shook his head. "It's not that. What if it isn't that easy? She's used to men like the king and Darhour. For Sulis's sake, Wild Thing, I'm the son of a peasant farmer."

:Robbie is Robbie.:

Robrek wasn't quite sure what she meant, but Wild Thing loved him and, for some time, that had been enough for him. Would it be enough now?

Suddenly, Wild Thing stomped, and Robrek jumped. *:Tell stupid cat go away.:*

"What stupid cat, my girl?" Something rubbed against his leg, and he looked down to see a large gray-striped cat. "Ronan! How did you get here?" He leaned down to pet the cat he'd left half-a-day's ride away in the Valley.

:Found.: the cat purred. *:Hard.:*

"But how could you know where I was?" Ronan merely purred in response. Robrek had never heard anything from Ronan's thoughts to indicate he was anything other than an ordinary cat, but the cat had an uncanny ability to find him.

Wild Thing stomped again. *:Stupid cat go away. Not pet stupid cat.:*

Robrek straightened and put his arms around the mare's neck. "You don't need to worry about the cat. You know you'll always be my best friend."

:Better friend than Apple Lady?:

"She could never replace you." Samantha held his heart and soul, but Wild Thing had been the only friend of his childhood.

Vaughan joined them, leading his horse, a black and white gelding he'd named Thunder Storm. He was wearing one of the ridiculously gaudy outfits he'd worn when Robrek climbed Gloine Torr. The outfit was checkered emerald green and gold. The sleeves were extraordinarily puffy and gathered every six inches so that his arms looked like overstuffed sausages. The cone-shaped hat was gold with a wide brim. From the peaked top flew several emerald streamers. But now that Robrek had seen what nobles wore at court, he guessed Vaughan dressed no more ridiculously than some.

Robrek led Wild Thing out of the stables. Samantha had commanded that a force of fifty men led by Lieutenant Ansgar accompany him. Like most Korthlundian men, Ansgar was almost a head taller than Robrek. Robrek tried not to let it bother him. The officer bowed to him. "Milord, we are ready to depart at your command."

Of all the strange things he's encountered at the palace, the strangest was to have men at his "command." But he swung into the saddle and gave the orders to be off.

Vaughan rode on one side of him, Ansgar on the other. His bodyguards surrounded him in the front and the rear. To protect against the snow swirling through the air, he pulled his cloak tightly around him. It was of finely woven green wool, lined with ermine, and decorated with gold braid. Robrek was sure it cost more than all the clothes he'd ever had in his lifetime and was warmer than any cloak he'd ever worn. Still, he could feel the wind's bitter chill.

Vaughan kept up a near-constant chatter. "We'll show them. Your brother's going to be sorry he ever beat you up, isn't he?"

"I suppose he will." Vaughan knew too much about his past and had too little discretion. Boyden once had almost beaten Robrek to death. Robrek wasn't sure how these men would feel to find out their future king was once the victim of a bully.

Soon, they entered the Setanta forest. The tall trees towered above them. Vaughan, who'd never left Murtaghan, looked around in wonder. "I didn't know trees could grow this big."

Has it truly only been a few months since I first saw them myself? I must be dreaming. Sometime soon I'll wake up and discover that Gloine Torr never happened.

* * *

Just after midday, Robrek and his escort rode into the village square of Valley Fair. The villagers cried out and hid themselves in their homes.

As he looked around, he fought a surge of nausea. Each corner of the square was decorated with a pike topped with a human head. The bitter cold had slowed decay, leaving three of the four recognizable— Banagher, the owner of the village inn; Alleyn, a former hand on Robrek's father's farm; and Amergin Kanestamm, a local farmer. Banagher and Alleyn had been among the few in the Valley who hadn't regarded him as a demon.

Wild Thing stomped a foot, startling him. "People of Valley Fair," he called out to the empty square, "I come from Her Highness, the Princess Samantha, to restore these lands to the control of the crown. You have nothing to fear."

"Nothing but the loss of their immortal souls," a voice sounded behind Robrek. He turned in the saddle to see Father Gildas, the priest who had wanted him dead since his birth, emerging from the shrine. Believing Robrek's dark skin and green eyes marked him as demon-cursed, Gildas had denied Robrek the opportunity to attend school and had made sure Robrek was excluded from any village gathering. Most recently, he'd led the mob that tried to burn Robrek at the stake. "Be gone, thou child of demons! You are not welcome here!"

Before Robrek knew what was happening, Eburacon had drawn his sword and put it at Father Gildas's throat. "You will not address His Lordship in this manner. Get on your knees and apologize."

Gildas glared murderously at Robrek, and Robrek knew Gildas would rather die than kneel to him. Robrek didn't want any bloodshed. He held up a hand. "That's not necessary." Robrek pointed toward the heads. "Who did this?" Gildas stared at him in stony silence.

A woman emerged from the inn. Robrek had difficulty recognizing the innkeeper's daughter. Davina's hair was matted and tangled, and her face and body were covered with bruises. Her gown was stained by what looked like blood, and the bodice had been ripped so that most of her breasts were exposed. She leaned against the side of the inn, a scowl on her face. Robrek rode toward Davina and got down from his horse.

"Mistress, what happened to you?" He reached to touch her so he'd have a better sense of her injuries, but she flinched, and he dropped his hand.

"I'll survive, unlike my father." She waved a listless hand toward Banagher's head.

"Who killed your father and the others?"

"Count Nola had Breasal killed." Her tone was expressionless. "The other three your brother did himself."

Robrek clenched his fists, suddenly fearing he might vomit. "But why?"

Pointing from head to head, she said, "Breasal objected to his land being stolen. My father tried to stop Boyden from making me his whore. Amergin fought to keep his stock from being taken. Alleyn, I believe, said something in your defense."

Robrek shook his head and creased his brow. "And is my brother responsible for your condition?"

Davina shrugged. "He's fond of his sword—both of them. He gave me to his men when he grew tired of me. He said I was lucky he didn't just put my head on a pike as he did my father's."

He'd suspected Boyden was involved in the beheadings, but to hear Davina confess it and worse sickened him. "Were other women so abused?"

People were emerging from the buildings. A farmer strode toward them from the edge of the square. Brian Brianstamm appeared to have aged nearly twenty years in the few months since Robrek had last seen him. His eyes were hollow, and his voice shook as he spoke. "My head should be next to Banagher's. He fought to protect his daughter, but I did nothing while those bastards had their way with mine. She hanged herself when they were through with her." Robrek wondered whether he was talking about Blair or Lavena. Blair had been Boyden's girlfriend at one time.

"How many women were raped?"

"How many women are there in the Valley?" Davina grunted.

Holy Sulis. This was far worse than Samantha had known.

About two dozen of Nola's men, led by Boyden, pounded into the square on horseback. Boyden pulled up short when he saw Robrek. The flicker of fear in his eyes was quickly replaced by rage. "What are you doing here?" Boyden spat.

"What have *you* been doing?" Robrek gestured at the heads and Davina.

"Nothing outside my rights."

"Your rights!"

:Stomp bad brother?:

Robrek wanted nothing more than to turn Wild Thing loose on Boyden. "Nothing gives you the right to rape and murder."

Boyden's eyes narrowed. "Count Nola gave me authority to subdue the people as I saw fit. These are his lands."

Robrek drew himself up. "They are no longer. By order of Her Highness, the Princess Samantha, these lands have been returned to the control of the crown. No armed retainers of any lord are allowed on royal land without royal permission. I was sent by Her Highness to remove you. You will leave immediately."

Suddenly losing her earlier indifference, Davina grabbed Robrek's arm. "You can't allow him to merely ride away! He took everything from me! My father! My property! My honor! Kill him, Robbie! Let me bathe in his blood!"

Boyden's eyes flicked to the fifty men backing Robrek. Then they met Robrek's. "Get out of my village, and crawl on your belly back to where you belong, worm."

Captain Ansgar shouted, "You will not insult His Lordship thus! Attack!" The captain drew his sword and sent his horse barreling toward Boyden.

"No, hold your swords!" Robrek cried, but his voice was lost in the tumult as the Royal Guardsmen bore down on Nola's men. Ansgar's sword cut through Boyden's side, knocking him from the horse. The villagers screamed and ran for the safety of the buildings. Holy Sulis, he had to stop this! He'd never tried to work his magic on this many people before, but he closed his eyes and reached out with his power. He reached into each individual man and froze his muscles, making him unable to move.

Shaking with the effort of his magic, Robrek walked into the midst of them and addressed his men. "There will be no more bloodshed. Guards, you will disarm Nola's men and place them under arrest. Kill no one." But when he released his hold on the Royal Guardsmen, they sat staring at him, their eyes wide with terror.

"Now!" Robrek shouted. He wasn't sure how much longer he could hold Nola's men. His words spurred the guards into action, and they went among the paralyzed men, who sat atop their horses, weapons drawn. The guards removed their weapons, threw their inert bodies to the ground, and tied them up. They were nearly through when Robrek slid into unconsciousness.

* * *

When Robrek awoke, he was lying in a bed in the inn, his bodyguards and Captain Ansgar surrounding him. He noted the blood on their armor. He turned his glare to Ansgar. "Why did you order the attack?"

Ansgar met his eyes without flinching. "Such a vile insult had to be answered."

Eburacon made a noise of agreement. "The goddess's choice shouldn't be addressed thus."

Robrek jabbed a finger at them. "That was for me to decide, not you."

Ansgar didn't look at all sorry. "Then I must apologize, Your Lordship. I should have let the insult stand, perhaps?"

"You do not kill over mere words. I will discuss your actions with Her Highness when we return."

"I'm sure she will approve. She can't want her consort insulted."

Unsure how Samantha would react, Robrek gritted his teeth. "How many causalities?"

"Milord, there are eleven dead. Ten of theirs and one of ours. And another ten wounded. Mostly theirs."

Robrek tried to sit, but his head spun. "How seriously hurt are the wounded?"

"It varies. The most serious is your brother. I wounded the foul-mouthed scum deeply in the left side. He will not recover." Ansgar seemed proud of this.

Robrek tried to sit again and this time managed it. "You are dismissed." He turned to Eburacon. "I need food, then I'll see to the wounded."

Eburacon nodded to Geblan, who left to order food for Robrek. He soon returned, carrying a tray with stew, bread, and a slice of apple pie. Robrek's mouth watered at the sight of the pie. He'd always been particularly fond of sweets. Starting with the pie, Robrek wolfed the food down, feeling it restore the energy he'd expended.

He headed for the temple, where the wounded were being seen to. He'd been inside the temple only once: for his trial. He shivered as he remembered how helpless he'd been. He hadn't learned to access his full power, and if it hadn't been for Leigh, one of Father Gildas's novices, he would never have escaped the flames.

He straightened his shoulders. Now he had his full power and fifty men to protect him.

He entered and found his way to the infirmary where Gildas was leaning over Boyden. The other wounded were laid out on beds. Gildas looked up. "You would defile the goddess's holy place? Be gone from here."

"I will see to the wounded. They need a true healer."

"You dare compare the abomination which flows from your hand with Sulis's holy magic?" Gildas moved in front of him. "No! I will not allow your unclean hands to touch a one of these!"

Eburacon drew his blade. "Remove yourself from His Lordship's path."

Gildas folded his arms and looked defiantly at Eburacon. Eburacon looked to Robrek, and Robrek felt a chill remembering how, in a similar situation, a slight nod from Samantha had led to a man's death. From Eburacon's expression, he knew a nod was all it would take to revenge himself on Gildas.

Robrek put a hand on Eburacon's blade. "There's been enough killing." He reached out with his power and sent Gildas's into a deep sleep. The priest dropped to the ground.

Eburacon nodded at the body. "Simpler."

His guards moved Gildas out of the way, and Robrek approached the wounded. Boyden had his teeth clenched in pain. "Stay away from me!" he cried out. "I'd rather die than be beholden to demons for my life!"

Eburacon made a disgusted noise in his throat. "Don't worry. You'll hang soon enough."

Boyden hissed, "Servant of demons, he'll destroy you as he has destroyed me!"

Eburacon looked toward Robrek, as if again asking for permission to kill. Again, Robrek shook his head, and he sent Boyden to sleep. He approached and put his hand over the wound. The intestines were perforated; Boyden was dying. Robrek closed his eyes and went into a healing trance. He felt a rush of pleasure as he mended his brother's flesh.

* * *

After seeing to the wounded, Robrek, with his six personal guards and ten of the Royal Guardsmen, headed to his father's farm.

Although reluctant to approach the place of his birth, he couldn't take Boyden to what would certainly be his execution without informing his father. Since Boyden had always been their father's favorite, Robrek was unsure how Angus would react.

When Robrek arrived, he was stunned by the signs of neglect. The paddock fence had several broken rails. Farm equipment, left to rust in the weather, littered the yard. The bunkhouse door was missing, and chickens darted in and out. The barn door hung off its hinges, and a pile of refuse lay just outside the kitchen door. Robrek remembered when he'd been beaten for leaving a single pitchfork out overnight. Boyden had actually been responsible, but his brother had blamed him, and his father wouldn't hear otherwise.

:Why messy? Where everybody?: Wild Thing asked.

"I don't know, my girl," he said, patting her neck. "Spread out and look for signs of trouble," he ordered his escort. "Something's wrong." Robrek could feel only a single human life in the farmhouse and none anywhere else. The barn housed only one horse and a horde of rats, mice, and birds.

Feeling as if the entire world was staring at him, Robrek dismounted and knocked on the farmhouse door. No one answered. He went inside, all of his personal bodyguards accompanying him. His father sat at the dining room table, a jug of some kind of homemade brew in front of him. His clothes were torn and filthy, and he smelled like he hadn't bathed in a week. The table was littered with dirty dishes and bits of food. The floor was filthy, and the room was near freezing, the fire in the hearth barely burning. Angus didn't look up when he entered.

Approaching cautiously, Robrek said, "Father."

"The princess throw you out?" Angus slurred into his jug.

His guards couldn't suppress their look of revulsion, and Robrek couldn't blame them. "No, Her Highness and I are to be married soon. I was sent to remove Count Nola's men from the king's lands. Father, I had to arrest Boyden. He's certain to be hanged."

Angus's voice was flat and emotionless. "It's no more than he deserves."

"Let me talk to my father alone," Robrek said to Eburacon.

"I'm afraid we can't do that, Milord. Her Highness's orders are that you are to be guarded at all times." Eburacon had his hand on his sword.

"Follow you even to the privy, do they?"

Robrek took a seat at the table near him. "Father, what has happened here? Where are the servants and farmhands? What happened to all your stock?"

Angus took a long pull on the jug. "Sold it. What's the use any more? I haven't an heir." Angus's farm, once the largest and richest in the Valley, had been a source of pride to him.

"Father, you can't live like this. Come back to Murtaghan with me."

Angus laughed. "I'm certain your princess would be pleased as punch if you brought home your drunken sot of a peasant father, reminding everybody where you came from." Angus looked toward Robrek's bodyguards. "Wouldn't she, boys?" His bodyguards seemed to be doing their best to ignore Angus. "Don't talk much, do they?" He shrugged. "Go back where you belong."

"Father, I can't leave you like this."

Angus staggered to his feet, rage twisting his face. "You both can and will, boy!"

A sword hissed, leaving its sheath. "Back off!" Eburacon said, pointing his sword at Angus's chest.

Angus stumbled back a few steps. "I guess you'll do whatever in the seven hells you please, won't you, Milord?" Angus picked up the jug and staggered down the hall to his bedroom.

Robrek sat staring at his hands. Even knowing his father wouldn't thank him, he couldn't leave him alone in this squalor. "Send for Vaughan," he ordered. His squire soon ran into the room.

"Vaughan, go into the village and see if you can find Dillion and Cara Caerstamm. If they aren't around, find another of my father's former servants." He gave several names. "Take a couple of spare mounts and a couple of guards. If you find the servants, bring them back with you."

"At once, Milord." Vaughan ran out the door.

Robrek told himself he needed to get up and do something about setting the farm to rights, but he couldn't seem to make himself move. What did his escort think now of their future king? He considered seeking his father out, but he didn't know what else he could say to him. It struck him forcibly how right Holy Writ had been when she'd told him he must learn to forgive those who harmed him. Angus hadn't needed Robrek's help to destroy himself. His father's sins had brought their own punishment.

The thought brought Robrek no satisfaction.

* * *

Far quicker than Robrek expected, he heard returning horses. Vaughan burst into the room, followed by Dillion and Cara. "I found them easy, Milord."

"Robbie, what in the seven hells happened here?" Cara asked, taking in the filth and disorder.

Eburacon and Geblan placed themselves between him and his father's former servants. "Sir Robrek is 'His Lordship' to you," Eburacon said.

Cara blanched. "I'm sorry, Milord. I didn't—"

"It's all right," Robrek broke in. "As far as what happened, my father has . . . well, he's . . ."

"Taking Boyden's actions hard, isn't he?" Cara said sympathetically.

"And making it hard on the rest of us," Dillion grunted. "Do you know how many people depended on this farm? A lot of us don't know how we're going to make it through the winter."

"I take that to mean you haven't found another position and are free to accept your old one back?"

Relief spread over Dillion's features. "You mean your father intends to rehire us?"

Robrek shook his head. "As far as I can figure, my father intends to drink himself to death. *I* want to hire you. Dillion, you'll take care of the farm. And Cara, you'll take care of the house. See that he doesn't live in filth and that he at least has decent meals put before him whether he eats them or not. Dillion, send for whoever you need to get this disaster cleaned up. And Cara, please, take stock of the stores and purchase whatever needs to be purchased."

"Of course, Milord." They bowed deeply. Cara stepped forward and pressed Robrek's hand. "We can't thank you enough."

* * *

In his office, Caedmon sat behind his oak desk carved with interlocking chains, symbolizing his chain of office as chancellor. His eyes were focused on the map of Korthlundia on the wall opposite, but he listened attentively to Righ, who he'd had follow the peasant sorcerer to Valley Fair. "Ansgar did what you paid him to do," Righ said. "There were a fair number of causalities." He gave a full report.

"Good, but not good enough." Caedmon then gave Righ an amended version of events in Valley Fair. "See that the story's spread as widely as possible. Call it the Massacre of Valley Fair, and have a crowd on hand to 'greet' the peasant at his return. If an arrow finds him, it would be a bonus."

Righ turned to go, but Caedmon called him back. "Make sure Ansgar can't tell what really happened."

CHAPTER 7

Robrek returned to the capital in a glum mood. A proper consort to the princess would have been able to prevent the previous day's deaths. To make matters worse, his father had refused to speak with him that morning and hadn't eaten or changed into the clean clothes Cara had provided.

When he and his escort neared the city, Murtaghan spread out before him as far as his eyes could see, as massive to him as when he'd first seen it. He'd only been out of the city for a couple of days, but the smell— human and animal waste, rotten garbage, thousands of unwashed bodies, spoiled fish, and the tang of salt water—nearly made his eyes water. He led his men toward the main gate, the guards bowing and nodding him through. Inside the city proper, a crowd was gathered.

"It's him!" somebody shouted.

Someone else cried out, "Murderer," and an overripe peach hit Robrek in the chest. Robrek's personal guards quickly surrounded him.

"Rapist!" Soon the air was full of curses and rotten fruits and vegetables aimed Robrek's way.

Holy Sulis, what is happening now?

Eburacon grabbed hold of his horse's reins. "Milord, we must get you to the palace."

"No!" Robrek closed his eyes and prepared to use his magic to stop the attack. But he heard a dull thud and opened his eyes to see

Captain Ansgar tumble from his horse, an arrow through his heart. A second arrow whistled through the air, hitting one of the horses near Robrek. He could stop the mob on the ground, but he had no idea where the arrows were coming from.

"Now, Milord!" Eburacon cried. As more arrows whizzed nearby, his guards pushed their way through the crowd, batting people aside with the flat of their blades. His other guards crowded in from behind, leaving Robrek little choice but to follow. Soon they were free of the fray and galloping along the city streets.

* * *

"Your Highness, I'm so sorry." Caedmon sat beside Samantha in her reception room and put his hand over hers. "I never should have suggested sending Sir Robrek to Valley Fair. I didn't realize he was still that angry."

Samantha's breath caught. "What's happened?"

"Your betrothed killed over three dozen villagers—men, women, and children. They're calling it the Massacre of Valley Fair."

"Impossible," she declared flatly. "Where did you hear this news?"

"It's all over the streets of Murtaghan, Your Highness. This is a disaster."

"Street rumors, that's all." Samantha shook off Caedmon's hand. "Robbie would never harm a woman or a child. He wouldn't kill *anyone* without good reason."

"Maybe he felt he had good reason—the villagers tried to burn him at the stake, after all." Caedmon touched her on the shoulder. "Samantha, my dear, consider how little you do truly know him."

But truly, she did know him. She'd seen Robbie's aura. "It can't have happened as you say."

She stood and strode to her window. Robbie was riding up to the stables with only his personal guards. Even from this distance, she could tell his guards' armor was splattered with rotten fruits and vegetables. *By Sulis, it couldn't be true.* But it appeared somebody believed it. She sent a page to have Robbie report immediately. He arrived soon after, the smell of rotten fruit heavy in the air. "What happened?" she asked.

He collapsed into a chair and put his head in his hands. "I have no idea, Sam. We were attacked right inside the city gates. The crowd was yelling something about murder and rape. At first they were just throwing rotten fruit, but then an arrow struck Captain Ansgar. Damn it, Sam, I should have stayed! Maybe I could have healed him. My guards practically forced me from the area, and I didn't think fast enough to stop them."

"As well they should have. Your life is too important." Samantha walked over to Robbie and put her hand on his arm. Had Caedmon not been there with a skeptical look in his eye, she would've held Robbie in a long hug. But she contented herself with the touch. He was safe.

Robbie looked up at her, and then looked away. "Things didn't go very well in the Valley."

"What happened?" Samantha seated herself across from him.

Looking down at his hands the entire time, Robbie told her of what he'd found in the village, of Boyden's insult, of Ansgar's order to attack, of the dead and wounded. "I should have figured out how to stop it sooner. I'm sorry, Sam."

Samantha's eyes flicked to Caedmon. He was nodding as if the story were exactly what he expected. She gritted her teeth; she didn't need conflict with Caedmon. "How many of the dead were villagers—women or children?"

Robbie raised his head. "None! One was a Royal Guardsman. The others were Nola's men."

Caedmon made a skeptical noise. "Isn't it convenient that Ansgar is now dead and can't dispute this version of events?"

Robbie jumped to his feet. "You think I'm lying? I'll get my guards. They can tell you what happened."

He headed toward the door, but Samantha caught hold of his arm. "That's not necessary. We believe you." She looked pointedly at Caedmon, and he returned her gaze without flinching.

"Your Highness, the truth of the matter is of little consequence. He was in charge, so the fault is his whatever the circumstances. You have no choice but to repudiate him."

Robbie paled. "Sam, I swear I did my best to stop the fighting."

"I know you did. The fault was Ansgar's, but unfortunately, he isn't around to be disciplined. Go and change now."

As soon as Robbie left, Samantha whirled on Caedmon, her voice tight. "Caedmon, this is the last time we will have this discussion! Sir

Robrek is the goddess's choice and my own. Nothing will change that. Do you hear me? Nothing!"

"Your Highness, I'm only—"

"I am your liege! You will obey me in this, or I may be forced to name another chancellor!"

Caedmon's eyes widened. "Your Highness, you can't be serious. You'd be lost without me."

Inwardly, Samantha knew he was right, or close to it. It would be most difficult to rule without Caedmon's support. "Caedmon, Uncle, don't force me to make that choice. As much as it will hurt me, the choice won't go in your favor. Am I understood?"

Caedmon sighed deeply. "Yes, Your Highness."

She concentrated on Caedmon, but his aura stubbornly refused to reveal itself. Would he continue to fight her? "Now, you will get to the bottom of the attack inside the city gates. I have to know who is trying to kill my betrothed."

* * *

When Robrek entered his quarters, the curtains were drawn, and he stumbled into something. He lit a candle and stared around. *Holy Sulis, no!* The walls were covered with scenes of hunting and war. Dead and dying animals and bloody battles loomed around him. He far preferred the fairies and puppies. The furniture—big, leather, and mahogany—only added to the hyper-masculinity of the tapestries.

Drem entered and bowed. "What have you done with this place?" Robrek demanded.

"I'm glad Your Lordship approves. We couldn't have a man of your stature surrounded by frippery."

"Drem, I'm a healer. Dead things aren't exactly my favorite sight."

Drem frowned. "You do not like battle and the hunt?"

"No, I don't. Give me something alive."

Drem's frown turned into a pout. "If Your Lordship insists."

"I do."

Just then the door opened, and a male servant entered carrying a large tub. He set it in front of the fireplace. He was followed by woman after woman carrying buckets of warm water. Robrek was still astonished at how much work servants went through just to give him a bath. He'd told Samantha he could use the guards' bath house, but apparently, that wasn't proper.

When the tub was full and the last servant had bowed her way out, Drem turned to him and asked, "Shall I assist Your Lordship?" even though Robrek had previously refused Drem's assistance in bathing.

"I think I can manage." Robrek unclasped his cloak and handed it to the servant. "There's some rotten peach on it. I hope it won't be too hard to get out."

Drem blinked. "I know my role, Milord."

Robrek guessed he'd insulted the man. Robrek took off the rest of his clothes and sank into the bath. His thoughts quickly turned to the so-called "Massacre of Valley Fair." He turned his head in the direction of the Far Mountain. *Sulis, if you chose me, why did I handle things so badly?* He pounded his head back against the tub.

But as he sat with his eyes closed reflecting on the scene, an unexpected peace settled over him. Was this the peace the priests claimed came from the goddess? Was she listening after all?

In that moment, he knew that there was nothing he could have done that would have prevented the fight and that the fight had allowed him to demonstrate the power for which Sulis had chosen him. Somehow, he knew his power was the key to his role as consort, and he needed to use it more openly.

* * *

The next morning Samantha secluded herself with Caedmon and Robbie in her reception room. She paced the room while the men sat uneasily across from each other. "Sir Robrek wasn't responsible for what happened," she declared. "We have to get the truth out. I should make a public address."

Once again, as he seemed to always do whenever she mentioned Robbie, Caedmon sighed heavily. "I wouldn't recommend it, Your Highness. It could be seen as you trying to cover for your betrothed's misdeeds."

Samantha halted and put her hands on her hips. "My betrothed has committed no misdeeds!"

Caedmon picked at a stray thread on the arm of his chair. "I apologize, Your Highness. I know the rumors are baseless. But I think it best Sir Robrek himself give the public address, explain how he intends his older brother to hang."

Samantha gaped at him. "You would have him be another assassin's target? I won't stand for it!"

"Your Highness, I only do what is best for you and the crown."

"But not for Sir Robrek?"

"Your Highness, it is his well-being I speak of. As he is the one accused, he should be the one to denounce the accusations."

Samantha growled with impatience and resumed pacing. Caedmon was right, but Robbie had no experience addressing crowds and would likely be ineffective. Is that what Caedmon was counting on?

To her surprise, Robbie spoke up. "There's something else I could do. I could open a clinic. Let the people see me for who I am. I have this power for a reason. I should be using it."

"Robbie, you will be king. Kings don't go around healing peasants' bumps and bruises." She put her hand to her forehead; she was getting a headache.

Robbie got up and walked over to the smoked crystal horse in the corner. He ran a hand across the emerald saddle. "I was thinking of more serious problems."

"Kings have more important duties. I need you at my side."

"Here, let me take care of that." Robbie took her hand and relieved her of her headache. "What duties? Shadow you all the time? Go to meetings where I don't have a voice? Feasts and entertainments? Make sure you don't get headaches?"

"Robbie, nothing like this has ever been done before."

"Was the king ever a healer before?"

"No," she admitted.

Caedmon stiffened in his chair. "It couldn't possibly work. Do you have any idea how many sick and injured there are in a city this size? You couldn't begin treat them all."

Robbie ignored Caedmon and addressed his remarks to Samantha. "That doesn't mean I shouldn't treat some of them."

Samantha shook her head. "But if it were known that the hero of Gloine Torr is healing, the people will swarm the palace."

Robbie walked over to the window and looked out at the palace grounds. "It wouldn't have to be at the palace. Surely, the crown has other properties in Murtaghan that would serve. I could get Leigh and Oriana to help me. They can sort out the trivial cases and hand out potions to those whose problems can be treated that way. The Royal Guard could maintain order."

Samantha paused.

Caedmon shot to his feet. "You aren't seriously considering it, Your Highness? The whole idea is absurd."

She met Caedmon's eyes. They revealed nothing, but his resistance probably

meant that he thought it could work. Still. "It wouldn't be safe. Someone is trying to kill you, remember?"

"You can't lock me in a gilded cage and wrap me in cotton. Sam, please, I've been accused of being a butcher. Let me show the people what I really am."

Samantha breathed deeply, and Caedmon took the chance to interrupt. "Samantha, priests are responsible for healing, not kings. You can't turn your betrothed into a priest."

She turned toward Robbie, who was looking at her pleadingly. "Have Blaine prepare you a list of potential places. If you can find one suitable and Leigh and Oriana agree to assist, I'll consider allowing it."

"Your Highness, don't be too hasty," Caedmon said. "Think of the repercussions."

Samantha marched to him. "You don't want Sir Robrek cleared. Get out of my sight."

Caedmon tried to protest, but Samantha waved him silent and pointed to the door. Caedmon left without another word.

Robbie came forward and put his arms around her. "I don't like coming between you and the duke. I know he was like a second father to you."

Samantha returned his embrace. "He's the one with the problem." She smiled at him. "I have to get out of this palace before I go mad. Come riding with me."

* * *

From Wild Thing's stall, Robrek watched Samantha as she left to fetch Roberta. She was so beautiful he still had difficulty believing she was his.

Wild Thing snorted in annoyance. :*Other horse think pretty. Not. Wild Thing pretty. Other horse ugly:*

"You are beautiful, my girl. Which horse would dare compare herself to you?" He patted her nose fondly.

:*Stupid white horse. Think special. Not. Just stupid. Stupid humans pay her all the attention. Lots of apples. Wild Thing like apples.:*

Robrek laughed. "I'll get you lots of apples, too, my girl, but you don't like other humans touching you. I've told them not to."

:Doesn't matter. Wild Thing show stupid white horse.:

Robrek fetched Wild Thing an apple, and by the time she finished eating it, Samantha arrived with her horse. Roberta tossed her head when she saw Wild Thing. *:Princess's. Beautiful. Shiny coat.:*

Wild Thing bared her teeth at the white mare and reared. *:Wild Thing beautiful. You stupid white horse.:*

Robrek restrained Wild Thing. "Easy, girl. It doesn't matter what she says."

Samantha looked at him in surprise. "What's wrong?"

Robrek couldn't help smiling as he petted and soothed Wild Thing. "Roberta thinks she's the most beautiful horse in the stables, and Wild Thing's jealous."

:Not jealous of stupid white horse.:

Samantha's face lit up as he explained what had passed through the minds of the two horses. She turned and hugged Roberta around the neck. "You are beautiful, my love, but you shouldn't be bragging." She released Roberta and turned back to face Robrek. "They will be able to ride together, won't they?"

Robrek beamed at the woman he loved. "Wild Thing will behave herself. Won't you, my girl?"

:Wild Thing won't hurt stupid white horse. Not worth trouble.: She snorted and tossed her head.

Robrek and Samantha both mounted and, followed by their guards, set off riding toward the king's fields. When they reached the edge of the fields, Samantha turned to him. "Race you to the stream?" She touched Roberta with her heels and took off.

Robrek laughed. "Show them who's fastest, my girl."

Wild Thing didn't need any urging.

* * *

Samantha glanced to see how far behind her she'd left Robbie. To her surprise, he was already even with Roberta's rear. She leaned over Roberta's neck and urged her to a faster speed, but Wild Thing pulled even with them with ease. Robrek straightened, blew her a kiss, and then bent over Wild Thing's neck. Without appearing to strain, the Horsetad sailed past them. Samantha gaped in amazement as Wild Thing's tail disappeared over the rise ahead.

By the time she reached the stream, Robbie had dismounted and was leaning against Wild Thing's side as if he'd been waiting for hours. She wanted to slap the smug smile off of his face. The Horsetad didn't even seem winded. Wild Thing tossed her head and whinnied as if to say, "I told you I was better." Roberta reared and bared her teeth at the other horse. Samantha barely hung on. Robbie ran over and grabbed Roberta's reins.

"It's okay, girl," he whispered to the horse. "Winning isn't everything." He laughed, seemingly at something Roberta said.

"That's easy for you to say," Samantha snapped, more irritably than she intended. She loved Roberta and would have given almost anything to hear her mind as Robbie did.

He looked up at her. "You didn't expect to win, did you? Wild Thing is a Horsetad." Wild Thing walked up behind Robbie and laid her head on his shoulder. Roberta bared her teeth again, but Robbie calmed her with his touch.

"I guess not, but Roberta's never been beaten before. I thought it would be more of a race."

Robbie laughed again and leaned his head against Samantha's thigh. Samantha leaned down to kiss him, and he swept her from the saddle into his arms. He kissed her gently on the lips, and she felt her knees go weak. She held him tightly to her. She wanted him now, but before she could take the thought any further, their bodyguards caught up with them. Robbie looked up at the new arrivals in annoyance. He leaned in and whispered, "We don't need these men following us all the time. I can protect us both if need be."

"I hope we didn't interrupt anything," Bearach said with his usual impertinence.

Robbie snorted, turned away from her, and jumped onto Wild Thing's back. "No, not a thing." He winked at her.

* * *

At Noir Prison, Father Dorsey looked down at the repulsive specimen of humanity he'd been called to treat. This one's odor brought tears to his eyes. Dorsey wondered if the thing had ever bathed. Besides its filth, it had the sunken cheeks, emaciated form, and yellowish skin of a paipin addict. At least it was unconscious, so Dorsey didn't have to talk to it and pretend to care about its fate.

Despite all that, Dorsey couldn't wait to touch the prisoner. He sat next to the creature and put his hand on its arm. Then he felt it—the rush, the ecstasy, the pleasure that nothing else could match, not the finest wine nor the most beautiful woman. Because Dorsey was of mixed blood, Father Faolan refused to acknowledge that Dorsey had magic, but if this wasn't magic, he didn't know what else it could be.

He could do nothing for the creature. Its liver had failed, and neither magic nor potions could repair the damage. Still, he continued to hold onto its arm in order to prolong the pleasure. He took his hand away only when he began to feel light-headed. It wouldn't do to faint on his way back to the temple.

Dorsey knocked on the door to the cell, and a guard opened it. "He's dying, the poor soul," Dorsey said, as he exited the cell and the guard locked it behind him.

"I could have told you that," the guard complained, "but the rules say we have to call a priest every Sulis-cursed time we drag one of these leaf-eaters off the street."

Dorsey held in a smile. He was always the one sent to the prisons because no other priest wanted to treat these creatures. He tried to think of something pious to say, but found he didn't care enough to keep up appearances. The guards never questioned his diagnoses, as Faolan always did. Dorsey didn't know how many times Faolan had killed people Dorsey could have saved. But as long as Dorsey had the opportunity to touch the sick, he didn't really care what happened to them.

On the way back to the Temple of the Mother's Love, Dorsey stopped to look up at the palace. Inside was Dorsey's ticket to a better life. The princess's betrothed was both mixed blood and a healer. If Dorsey could find some way to meet this Sir Robrek, the sorcerer would surely recognize his worth. He longed to see Faolan's face when that day came. And if the sorcerer was as powerful as they said, perhaps he could teach him more about the pleasure.

CHAPTER 8

When Robrek awoke the next morning, something warm was curled up against his leg. Remembering the scorpion, he jumped away.

Ronan, the gray-striped barn cat, meowed in protest at Robrek's abrupt removal of a heat source.

"How did you get in here?" Robrek rubbed Ronan's head, and the cat yawned and stretched, then settled back into a comfortable position. Drem entered. "Do you know how the cat got in?" Robrek asked.

Drem's lip curled. "No, Milord. Should I dispose of it?"

Robrek petted the cat. "Certainly not, but if you could get it food and water, I'd appreciate it."

Drem's lip curled further. "If Your Lordship wills it." Drem got out an outfit that Robrek had never seen before.

"Just how much clothing do I have now?" Every day there seemed to be something new.

"Not enough for Your Lordship's status, but the seamstresses are working on it."

Today's outfit had thick leather pads on the left sleeve and shoulder. "What are these for?"

"For the falcon to perch, Milord."

Robrek groaned. He'd forgotten he was due to go hunting today. He'd wanted to check on locations for the clinic. Besides, he loathed hunting. The first time he'd gone with his father and brother, he'd ended up crying in the bushes and been beaten for his unmanly behavior. But Samantha wanted him to bond with the other nobles, and apparently, nobles hunted.

This time the buttons on his tunic were in the front, so, much to Drem's annoyance, he managed to get dressed without Drem's assistance. Then he went down to the stable. He saddled Wild Thing, and Vaughan joined them, leading Thunder Storm. "How are we going to catch anything without a hawk?" Vaughan asked.

Robrek shrugged. "I don't suppose we will. We're just going along to bond and say knightly things." *Whatever those might happen to be.* Vaughan looked at him askance but didn't question him further.

By the time they led their horses out of the stables, the hunt was beginning to assemble. The nobles, including a number of court ladies, bowed and greeted Robrek. He looked into the faces of the men. How many thought he was a butcher? None of the men gave any obvious signs of their feelings about him; the ladies, on the other hand, giggled and blushed, a disconcerting reaction. The women in the Valley had considered him demon-cursed because of his appearance. But if these thought him a butcher, they obviously didn't mind.

Some of the nobles sported hooded birds on their arms; others were accompanied by underlings who held their birds. As Robrek was about to mount, Count Weylin approached, carrying a magnificent white falcon with two black feathers in its tail. It was the largest bird Robrek had ever seen. "Milord, I'm aware Solar maintained no mews, so I'd like to gift you with my gyrfalcon, Snow Cloud. My men captured her on the borders of Fruscarettr. She has proven an excellent hunter for any man with even *moderate* talent for the sport. A perfect fowl for a beginner." Weylin smiled as he held out the hooded falcon. Robrek couldn't say what, but something was wrong with the smile.

Vaughan smiled broadly. "A fine-looking bird," he said.

Robrek attempted to match his squire's enthusiasm, but was afraid his dismay showed on his face. "Thank you, Milord," he managed.

"Think nothing of it. I'm interested in seeing what a man of your *talents* can do with a bird." Weylin smiled again.

The falcon seemed restless, so Robrek petted her smooth feathers. *:Humans. Hate. Free.:* Robrek snatched back his hand as if it had been burned. He'd never had an animal not like him before.

* * *

Standing at her window, Samantha watched the hunting party ride off. Robbie, with a falcon she'd never seen before, rode at the front. Once she would have led the hunt while her father stayed behind to deal with the endless court matters. She'd never realized how constrained his time had been.

She put her hand on the window pane in a gesture of farewell she knew Robbie wouldn't see. She prayed he'd be safe. At least they were hunting with birds instead of arrows; with arrows, an "accident" was always possible.

Holding another of his endless series of lists, Blaine entered the room. He bowed. "We're busy as beavers today, so to speak. Father Hafghan is due any moment, but there are several matters relating to the royal wedding we need to discuss. First, there is the wedding portrait."

"What about it?" she asked distantly.

"Who is going to paint it? When? How? There are as many 'about its' as there are stars in the heavens, so to speak. First the funeral and now the wedding—the details are endless." Blaine gasped and put his hand over his heart. "I'm sorry, Your Highness. I didn't mean to criticize Your Highness. I wouldn't be in Your Highness's position for all the gems in Neaseria, so to—"

"Enough, Blaine," Samantha interrupted. She smiled inwardly at his overuse of metaphors. "As the court artist, Lord Devyn will paint the portrait. Meanwhile, you need an assistant."

"An assistant?" Blaine croaked, as if the idea were sacrilege.

"To handle some of the lesser matters so that you can focus on the important ones. See to it at once. There are plenty of clerks who could fill the position."

Blaine's eyes narrowed. Then he seemed to shake the annoyance away. "Of course, Your Highness. A brilliant suggestion. May I go on, Your Highness?"

She nodded, but she barely listened as he detailed plans for a brunch to be given by the Guilds in honor of the royal wedding. When Blaine was through with his list, she had him show Father Hafghan in. The priest entered, accompanied by her guards.

"Your Highness." Father Hafghan bowed. "You asked to see me?"

She invited him to be seated and offered him refreshment. He accepted a glass of wine, and she sat across from him. "I want you to perform the wedding ceremony."

He dipped his head. "I'd be honored, Your Highness."

"Also, what you can tell me about how the clergy is responding to the death of Father Shylah? What are they doing about his replacement?"

Father Hafghan took a small sip of wine before replying "An election will be held in seven days, Your Highness. To tell you the truth, it's a right mess. A faction led by one of Shylah's chief assistants, a Father Faolan, refuses to believe any accusations against the high priest. Faolan claims the accusation is a result of your betrothed's malice toward the priesthood."

Sulis curse it all! Robbie's blamed for everyone's troubles? "How could Sir Robrek have been involved?"

"They have heard, of course, of your betrothed's difficulties with one Father Gildas and see the disparagement of Shylah as an act of revenge." Father Hafghan leaned forward. "I will be frank, Your Highness. Father Faolan needs no reason other than your betrothed's mixed blood to see him as a danger."

She tapped her fingers on the arm of her chair. "How strong is Father Faolan's faction?"

The priest sipped more wine. "Hard to say. I'm afraid his feelings about mixed blood are common among the clergy, but considering the seriousness of the accusations against Father Shylah, some want to distance themselves from any who were close to the late high priest."

"Is he the leading contender for Shylah's replacement?"

"At present, it is hard to say whether I or Father Faolan has the most support."

She couldn't afford to have an enemy of her betrothed running the church. "Is there anything the crown can do to tilt the matter in your favor?"

The priest carefully set his glass on the nearby table. "I appreciate the thought, Your Highness. But I think it best if Your Highness did nothing at all—including announcing that I am to perform the royal marriage—until after the vote. Like I said, the prejudice against mixed blood is rather strong among the clergy."

Samantha stiffened. She didn't like being told her help wasn't useful. "There's one other thing. Father Gildas tried to murder my betrothed. I want him charged by the church and tried." She would show them what happened to those who threatened her betrothed. "The church will see him held responsible, or I will."

* * *

"I bet we catch a lot with a bird that big," Vaughan said eagerly, as they rode through the city and out onto the surrounding plains.

Except that it hates me. Sulis curse it, Count Weylin had set him up to look foolish by giving him a difficult bird while publicly announcing it was perfect for a beginner. Robrek had never dealt with birds of prey before, but as he heard the minds of the other birds, he discovered, unlike dogs and horses, not one of them felt any affection for its owner. They served because they'd been trained to see the falconer as the only source of food. Having been wild-caught, Snow Cloud knew better: she saw him not as a food source but as a jailer.

:Stomp stupid bird.: Wild Thing suggested, but Robrek didn't see how that would help.

"There is a wealth of rabbits, grouse, and partridge hereabouts," Weylin informed him. "Shall we place a wager on which of our birds catches the most? Say, fifty drachma?"

Robrek nearly choked. The sum was nearly two and a half times his yearly wages on his father's farm. But turning down the wager would appear cowardly.

Baron Arawn laughed. "Quite the steep bet to place with a beginner, but I'll take that wager. Let's see what the sorcerer can do."

Can it get any worse? While Arawn had saved him from personally accepting the bet, he'd raised the stakes by talking of Robrek's sorcery. The nobles probably thought that, as an amihealer, he could control animals. In truth, he couldn't *make* an animal do anything. What he did was convince animals it was in their best interest to do as he asked. But he couldn't see how hunting for him would in any way serve Snow Cloud's interest or how he could convince her it would.

"Be prepared to launch your bird as soon as the dogs stir something up," Weylin said.

"Launch it?" Robrek asked.

Weylin smiled. "A true novice, I see." Weylin described the process of unhooding the bird and launching it into the air. Robrek thought he understood, but he also thought the most likely result would be for the bird to fly away, never to return. He couldn't accuse the count of lying about the bird, however. Such insults could lead to a duel or worse.

Soon, the dogs stirred up a nest of partridges, and the nobles launched their birds. Not knowing what else to do, Robrek followed suit. Rather than flying away, Snow Cloud struck with shocking savagery, bringing down the largest of the birds. Vaughan gave a whoop of delight. As the partridge's life fled and the gyr celebrated her kill, a dizzying disorientation nearly overcame Robrek.

Before he could get to Snow Cloud, she'd torn into the bird. "Give it here," he said, trying to send reassurance into the gyr. Snow Cloud mantled over the bird, then tore off another piece of flesh. The gyr obviously wasn't going to let him have her catch, and she'd probably rip off his finger if he reached for it.

Weylin was smiling at him. Robrek knew he looked foolish, and the audience watching him was growing. Not knowing how else to handle it, he reached out with his magic. He paralyzed the raptor and took her kill. Vaughan came forward with a large bag for him to put his catch in. "I knew you could do it, Milord." He smiled proudly.

Robrek tried to smile in return, but when he picked up the falcon, it boiled with rage at the loss of its prey.

"That's one to zero," Arawn commented, as Robrek remounted.

"Yes," Weylin said, sounding not at all pleased. "Excellent, Milord. I was sure you had a talent for the sport."

Lord Devyn, one of the youngest of Samantha's former suitors, rode up beside Robrek with another young lord and lady, pushing Vaughan aside. "Well done, Milord," Devyn said. "May I present Lord Padrig, second son of Count Guto, and his sister, Lady Briallen." Robrek had never heard of Count Guto, but he nodded politely.

Lady Briallen had been one of those giggling and blushing earlier. She blushed even more now, and despite the cold, she wore a hunting gown cut so low he could almost see her nipples, which poked against the fabric in the cold morning air. It was hard to keep his eyes off them.

"You were magnificent with that bird, Milord," Padrig gushed, ignoring the fact Robrek was staring at his sister's breasts. "One doesn't often see a gyrfalcon so well handled. They are so temperamental. Do you have gyrs of your own?"

"No, I've never seen one before," Robrek answered. With half of his attention on

Briallen's breast and the other half spent keeping Snow Cloud from attacking him, following the conversation was difficult.

"I do so love the hunt," Lady Briallen said. "It is invigorating to watch the primal savagery, is it not, Milord?" She licked her lips slowly, leaving Robrek wondering just what kind of savagery she was referring to.

:*Mine.*: Snow Cloud suddenly launched herself off his arm. In a blur of white, she skimmed the ground, then slammed into a rabbit and broke its neck. By the time he reached her, she'd already eaten a good portion of the rabbit. :*Not steal again.*: The gyr mantled over the prey again and glared at him.

Feeling like a thief, Robrek again paralyzed the bird and took her prey.

"She's a good hunter, all right," Vaughan said, as he held the bag for Robrek. He was bouncing on the balls of his feet. "You'll win that bet for sure."

Samantha was counting on him to impress these men; Robrek hoped he was doing so—what he was doing to the gyrfalcon was wrong. When he remounted, he was joined by Weylin and Arawn. "Two to zero," Arawn said.

"More like one and a half to zero," Weylin said with a laugh. "Just a little joke between friends, Milord. But you really shouldn't let the bird eat. If it's full, it won't hunt."

I'd like to see you stop her from eating.

He received an image from the falcon of it ripping off his ear. :*Bad. Thief. Mine.*: Nausea rose within Robrek. *It's supposed to be people I have problems with, not animals.* He remembered what his mentor Myst had taught him about the misuse of his power: "If the gift of the goddess is used for evil, it will twist and mangle your soul until nothing of your true self remains." *What I'm doing to the bird is evil.*

"That bird is positively frightening," Briallen gushed. "It looks like it wants to poke your eyes out."

"It does. It is very angry."

"Oh, Milord." Briallen leaned toward him, giving him a view of more cleavage. "Is it true what they say? That you can talk to animals?"

"It isn't talking, exactly. I pick up images, emotions."

"That's so fascinating, Milord," she said, fluttering her eyelashes. Robrek wanted to roll his eyes or ride away, but that would have been rude.

* * *

They hunted throughout the morning, and Robrek grew more and more uneasy taking Snow Cloud's prey. The falcon wanted to be free, and it most certainly did not want to share its kills.

:Not this time.: Snow Cloud launched herself into the sky. She flew far higher than before, and when she went into a dive, it was clear she'd strike some distance from the hunters. "You better hurry after her, or you'll lose the bird," Weylin said.

Robrek took off in the direction of Snow Cloud's dive, Vaughan and his bodyguards thundering after him. He lost sight of the bird, but he could feel where she was, tearing hungrily into her prey. If he gave Wild Thing her head, he could be there in seconds. But if he delayed, maybe the bird could "accidently" get away. It could be free like it wanted to be.

He held Wild Thing to the slower speed of the other horses. "Don't wait for me," Vaughan called, knowing Wild Thing's superior speed. "I'll catch up."

Sulis curse it! Do I have to get her? He outdistanced the others, but took Wild Thing in a roundabout route to the kill. By the time he arrived, Snow Cloud had finished with the bird and taken to the air. She flew toward the tall trees of the Setanta Forest.

"Oh, no!" Vaughan cried, riding up. "Can you still catch her, Milord?"

Robrek didn't answer. She was still close enough he could force her to remain by paralyzing her, but he had no right to hold her prisoner.

The rest of the hunt pounded up to them. "The bird, Milord?" someone asked. He wasn't sure who.

"She's flown off." He gestured vaguely in the direction of the forest.

"That's terrible!" Lady Briallen cried. "You must be devastated, Milord."

Actually, he was relieved, but his relief didn't last long. "I warned you about allowing it to eat," Weylin said. He didn't add, "How could you be so careless?" but it was present in his tone. The other noblemen avoided gazing in his direction, but he could feel their silent censure.

Damn it all to the seven hells, how many prey did the Sulis-cursed bird have to kill before it was all right to let it go?

The master huntsman came forward. "Milord, if you can be more precise in the direction it took, perhaps we can recapture it."

Robrek hesitated. Would it look worse if it was known he let it go on purpose or that it had gotten away from him? The first might be an insult to Count Weylin; the second would call his power into question, the only thing he had to offer Samantha.

He squared his shoulders and spoke what he thought was a king's tone. "The bird wanted its freedom. I let it go."

"L-let it go?" Vaughan stammered. "But, Milord, it's such a good hunter."

"Yes, but it only wants to hunt for itself. Let it alone."

* * *

Samantha sat with Caedmon in her reception room, waiting for Sheen. When the duke arrived and had taken his seat, Samantha said, "You missed the oath of loyalty to your new liege."

Sheen sighed. "Yes, I'm afraid I was unwell, so I sent my sons."

Caedmon leaned forward. "You can offer the oath in open court tomorrow."

Sheen turned a barely concealed glare on Samantha. "Frankly, Your Highness, I'd like to see some sign of your loyalty to those who helped save your kingdom."

What do these people expect of me? Miracles? "You and the others have been decorated, but my father kept taxes low and amassed no great wealth to the crown. There is no more I can do."

"Your Highness, have you forgotten that estates of traitors are generally forfeit to the crown? Argblutal's you have awarded. But Morgan's and Torin's would be especially rich prizes."

"They are Lundian estates, and I cannot give them to a Korthian. That would upset the balance of power between Korth and Lundia."

Sheen's nostrils flared. "What is this talk of balance? Lundia betrayed the crown and does not deserve the same consideration as Korth! If you will not give over the lands, you must take a Korthian, one of my sons, as your consort—the Lundian peasant has no right to the throne."

Samantha stood and pointed a finger at Sheen. "Sir Robrek is not some 'Lundian peasant.' He is the goddess's choice, and I will not defy the goddess to please you."

Sheen waved the matter away. "He knows a few neat tricks, but that doesn't make him the goddess's choice. Marry a Korthian, or be prepared to face the consequences."

Samantha grew still. She forced the tension from her muscles in an effort to appear in control. She placed a cold smile on her lips. "Are you threatening me?"

"I am a loyal subject of the crown. But I will not be disrespected nor will I sit down with regicides!" Sheen got up from his chair and swept from the room without waiting to be dismissed.

"That arrogant bastard!"

Caedmon shook his head. "You'll have to find some way to placate him."

Samantha ran her hand through her hair. "Too bad I can't just have Bearach finish him off as I did Nola. What would you suggest I do, Uncle?"

"If you won't reconsider marrying one of Sheen's sons, you might have a problem on your hands."

No kidding.

* * *

Blaine sat in his neat, orderly office behind his neat, orderly desk. The walls of his office were blank, giving the place an austere appearance. Blaine thought he should soften it with some paintings or tapestries, but he'd been so busy with the princess's business, he hadn't had time for that sort of thing. He turned to his new assistant. "And do you think you can handle arranging with the Temple of the Mother's Love for their boys' chorus to sing at the wedding?"

"Yes, sir," Tuathal said.

Blaine felt odd being called "sir" by an older man, but he was Tuathal's superior. "It should be done right away."

"Yes, sir."

"They will need plenty of time to practice."

"I understand, sir."

Blaine wasn't at all sure Tuathal appreciated the gravity of the situation, and it seemed wrong to trust someone else with a matter of this importance. But Lord Devyn was waiting to see him. He dismissed Tuathal and had him usher the young lord into the room.

"Her Highness wants you to paint the portrait of the royal wedding," Blaine said, waving Devyn into a seat.

Devyn raised his eyebrows. "She does?"

Blaine tightened his lips. "I am merely relaying Her Highness's orders. Personally, I think you should be fed to the fish, so to speak."

Devyn groaned and put his face in his hands. "You're right. If I weren't such a coward, I'd kill myself, like my father wants me to. Tell Her Highness I'm sorry, but I can't paint the portrait, not after what I did."

Blaine had been about to check Devyn off his list. He held his quill in both hands and nearly snapped it in two. "I will do nothing of the sort. This isn't simply a request. Do you intend to defy the commands of your liege?"

"No, I didn't mean—"

"You will paint the portrait. You can kill yourself after the wedding if you wish, but for now, you will get to work. Have initial sketches ready for Her Highness's approval by tomorrow." Blaine waved a hand at Lord Devyn in dismissal. Months back, he would've never dared to treat a noble in such a fashion. But months back, he would've never believed a noble could betray his beloved Princess Samantha.

* * *

Dreading the upcoming ordeal, Robrek, with his bodyguards Brendan and Cathbad, made his way to the lesser banquet hall. Baron Arawn was hosting the hunt banquet, and Samantha was too busy to accompany him.

As Robrek neared, Lord Padrig greeted and fell in beside him. The young lord gestured him aside and complimented him on his hunting skill. "My sister was most impressed."

Robrek made a noncommittal noise in response.

Padrig leaned closer and spoke in a low voice. "Milord, Briallen would like me to let you know our father would have no objections to her becoming the royal mistress."

"The royal mistress?" Robrek spluttered.

"I'm certain Your Lordship has had many fine offers. But Briallen wanted you to be aware of her availability and her assets. She chose her dress for the hunt especially to display them for Your Lordship's benefit."

Robrek gaped at the man. "I am betrothed to Her Highness, the Princess Samantha."

Padrig blinked. "Of course, Milord. My father wouldn't allow Briallen to be just anyone's mistress."

"Holy Sulis, man, I love the princess. I have no need for anyone else."

"I see," Padrig said, as if the thought had never occurred to him. He pondered it a moment longer, then said, "When you change your mind, Briallen will be available." He bowed and gestured for Robrek to precede him into the banquet hall.

All of those gathered stood and bowed. Baron Arawn came forward. "Welcome, Milord. I'm so happy you could attend. Let me show you to your seat."

Arawn led Robrek to the head of the table, to where—*Holy Sulis!*—Briallen sat. She was wearing a pink silk gown cut even lower than the hunting dress. Arawn offered him the seat next to her and took the seat on Robrek's left. Count Weylin sat on the other side of Briallen.

"Well, isn't this lovely, Milord," Briallen said. "I asked Baron Arawn for the seat next to you, and he was good enough to grant my request."

"Her Ladyship can be quite persuasive." Arawn flicked his eyes to Briallen's breasts, and Robrek wished he could be anywhere else. Maybe even back in the cellar, waiting to be burned. At least his dark skin didn't make his embarrassment so apparent.

For a few moments he was relieved of the need to speak by the servants serving the first course—a creamy soup Robrek guessed was pumpkin. But when the servants had withdrawn, Count Weylin turned to him. *Is he angry I let the bird go?* "I hope you don't mind my allowing the falcon to escape," Robrek said. "It truly wanted freedom."

"That's quite all right," Weylin said, but his expression was blank.

"I don't know why anyone would want one of those nasty birds anyway," Briallen said, leaning toward him and giving him another view down the front of her dress. "They'd all just as soon snap your nose off as look at you. Not at all like my sweet Poppet. Poppet is my Bichon puppy. Such a sweet little thing. Do you have a dog, Milord?"

"No," Robrek said, not knowing what else to say.

"That is such a pity. Perhaps when my little angel has puppies, I could give you one."

Count Weylin laughed. "I'm sure His Lordship has no desire for an annoying little lapdog, Briallen. Perhaps Your Lordship would like a pup from Destroyer, my best hunting dog. You should see what she can do to a fox."

"That's evil, Milord. Whatever did the poor fox do to you that you like to watch your dogs rip it apart?"

Weylin gave Robrek a knowing look. "Women. They never can understand the thrill of sport."

While Robrek tried to think of something to say, Weylin and Briallen argued over what kind of dog would most suit him. Under the table, Briallen put her hand on his leg. He jerked his leg away and sat up straighter, struggling not to betray his discomfort. Briallen shifted her leg until her knee was touching his. Robrek tried to move his leg again, but bumped into Arawn's.

"So, Milord, would you rather have a little angel or a huge devil?" Briallen ran her tongue across her lips, and he didn't think she was talking about dogs any more.

CHAPTER 9

When Mother Venetia and Awena arrived in Nios Mo, ten miles east of Balley Beg, the village was a bustle of activity. Priestesses and novices were going from house to house. Venetia didn't know what to make of their activity. She found Mother Bensaggyrt in the temple, praying at the altar. When the old woman raised her head, Venetia asked, "What's happening? I thought the call came from Balley Beg."

Mother Bensaggyrt's face was thin and wan, the wrinkles showing far more prominently than the last time Venetia had seen her. Her hair fell loose around her face rather than in the braids that normally confined it. "My child, Balley Beg is no more."

Venetia sank into a pew. "What do you mean? How can it . . .?"

Mother Bensaggyrt rose and sat beside her. She took Venetia's hand. "A plague. It wiped out all life—both human and animal."

Venetia placed her free hand over her heart. *All those I've served since I was a small child—gone?* "All life? My novice Oriana?"

"The villagers said Oriana was called away in the early stages of the plague by a messenger from the princess. She's probably safe in Murtaghan, but I don't know. Everyone who didn't flee is dead."

Venetia sent up a brief prayer for Oriana's safety. "What kind of plague could do that?"

Mother Bensaggyrt shook her head. "We don't know. Those afflicted weaken and die. It won't respond to any of our treatments, and using healing energy on those stricken leaves a priestess so weak that she too succumbs and dies. I've lost ten priestesses already. I've issued orders forbidding those who remain from using their healing energy. This is like nothing I've ever seen."

"And what is happening here in Nios Mo?"

Mother Bensaggyrt rubbed her forehead, as if troubled by a headache. "The plague has struck here. The villagers are weakening and dying, as they did in Balley Beg."

Dread gripped Mother Venetia's heart. "What if it's not a plague?"

"What else could it be?"

Mother Venetia looked down at her hands, then up to Mother Bensaggyrt's eyes. "What if Armunn's shield has failed?"

The Mother Superior gasped. "The curse! You think it's loose again?"

"The weakening. The ineffectiveness of any treatment. It matches the legend."

Mother Bensaggyrt's eyes went wide. "Holy Sulis, Mother of us all!"

* * *

With her back turned to the room, Samantha ran a hand over the emerald saddle on the smoked crystal horse that had been a gift from Prince Banki and his people. Banki had been a pompous fool, but the horse was gorgeous. Duke Caedmon sat behind her while Blaine stood and recited the plans for the day. "Your Highness, we have yet to discuss the seating arrangements at the wedding banquet. It's a detail as big as Gloine Torr, so to speak. Also, both Count Ultan and Lord Devyn are requesting audiences. I believe Lord Devyn has the sketches you asked for, but Count Ultan wouldn't tell me his reasons for wanting to speak to Your Highness. He said it was business better spoken directly to Your Highness."

"I'll see Lord Devyn first, then the count," she told Blaine. He bowed his way out.

She heard her guards and Lord Devyn enter. She turned from the horse. Devyn bowed but didn't meet her eyes. "I have the sketches Your Highness requested." He held out a small pile of papers to the princess.

Samantha took them and offered Lord Devyn a seat. He sat on the edge of a chair and stared at his hands. The sketches showed her and Robbie in various poses. For rough sketches, they were quite good: Devyn had been able to capture the striking innocence of

Robbie's face. *Holy Sulis, I love him. How can he truly be mine?* "And how is Lady Aislinn?" Samantha asked.

"She is . . . she is well, Your Highness." Devyn looked more resolutely at his fingernails. "We are both grateful for Your Highness's mercy."

She glanced at him, not wanting to give the impression of complete absolution but understanding what people would do for love. Argblutal had threatened to rape and murder Aislinn in front of Devyn's eyes if Devyn didn't cooperate in Argblutal's scheme to marry Samantha. What would she not do if Robbie's life were threatened?

She picked out the pose she liked best: she and Robbie were holding hands and looking into each other's eyes, much like the portrait of her father and his second wife, Britomartus. Roberta and Wild Thing were at their shoulders, and the king's fields spread out behind them. It was the horses that had first brought them together; it seemed fitting they be depicted in the wedding portrait. She touched the sketch lovingly, remembering the day she and Robbie had met. Then she passed it to Lord Devyn. "You will begin at once," she ordered. "My secretary will inform you when Sir Robrek and I have time to pose."

"Of course, Your Highness." Devyn accepted the sketch. "I thought this was the one." He stood and, head kept low, bowed his way out.

Count Ultan was shown in. He bowed. She offered him a seat. "Your Highness, thank you for seeing me. I come on behalf of Duke Torin. He has reconsidered, and he desires another opportunity to swear his loyalty to Your Highness."

Caedmon spoke before she could. "He insulted Her Highness. Why would she give him another chance?"

Ultan faced Caedmon. "He says he's ready to apologize and publicly admit he was wrong about Her Highness being a bastard."

"In return, I assume he expects to retain his head as well as his lands and title," Samantha said.

"He—reluctantly, of course—realizes he may lose his lands and title. I understand Your Highness may doubt his motives, but before I agreed to undertake this intervention, he swore his loyalty to you by the goddess and on his mother's grave. I wouldn't be here if I doubted his sincerity. I'd stake my life on it."

Samantha knew little about Count Ultan and less about his judgment. He'd always been quiet in council meetings, rarely drawing attention to himself. "I'll take the matter under advisement."

"I understand, Your Highness. I simply pray Your Highness does not forget the mercy for which you've become known."

When Ultan was gone, Samantha got up and began pacing. "What would you advise, Uncle?"

"Torin had his opportunity and refused it. Both he and Morgan should die. The sooner the better."

"Will I not be seen as capricious if I deny one the mercy I have allowed others?"

"No, Your Highness, you'll be seen as strong."

"Why? Wasn't I strong enough by having Nola killed?"

Caedmon lifted his hands in a gesture of surrender. "You asked my advice. In one of your youth, mercy will be seen as weakness."

Caedmon seemed bloodthirsty. Again she wished for her absent fathers.

But she did have somebody else whose advice she could seek: Robbie. He would be her consort, and he should start fulfilling that role. She turned to Caedmon. "We'll discuss this later, Uncle." Caedmon started at the abruptness of her dismissal, and she tried to soften it. "Thank you for your advice."

After Caedmon left, she sent a page for Robbie.

When Robbie arrived, he beamed at her, and she couldn't help breaking into a smile. All of her problems seemed lighter when he was around. She kissed him gently. Then she explained the situation to him. "Caedmon wants me to kill them both."

Robbie shrugged. "You killed Nola."

"But I thought you disapproved of that."

Robbie ran his hands through his hair, so silky and curly and long. "I did. I do. But you said it was necessary. You said he'd always be our enemy. Is Torin the same?"

Samantha pulled herself away from thoughts of running her fingers through that hair. "That's just it. I don't know. I wish I could see his aura."

"You can't count on that. It seems to me that by asking me you're looking for a reason not to kill him. I'm a healer, so I'll always be in favor of life."

Samantha smiled. "You're right, Robbie. I don't want to order his execution. I won't allow Caedmon to talk me into being a tyrant."

* * *

Sitting with Crisiant and Eira, Briallen smiled as she bent over her embroidery frame. They were all working on items for Crisiant's trousseau. She thought the banquet with Sir Robrek had gone very well. No one could have missed how often he stared at her breasts, and considering how small the princess's were, who could blame him? Surely it was only a matter of time until he sent for her.

Crisiant looked up from her embroidery and giggled. "And which one of you will be next?" Like all betrothed women, she seemed to think everybody else should follow in her wake.

Eira scowled. Eira was nearly as short as the princess and far more stout. Still, she wouldn't look bad if she had a decent maid and spent more time on her toilet. "I'm sure it will be Briallen."

Briallen laughed. "Not me. I have other plans."

Crisiant pursed her lips. "Still thinking of Sir Robrek?"

Briallen gave a noncommittal shrug. "The mistress of the king will have a great deal of power."

Eira shook her head. "But he's so short."

Briallen winked. "You know what they say about short men."

"That they have large . . ." Crisiant blushed and looked down at her embroidery.

Briallen laughed again. "I don't know about all short men, but it's true about Sir Robrek."

Eira dropped her needle. "And how would you know?"

Briallen pretended to be absorbed in her embroidery. "I told you the pink silk would work."

Both Crisiant and Eira gasped. "You haven't? You didn't?" Crisiant sputtered.

Briallen set down her embroidery. "And what if I have?"

Eira stared at her wide-eyed, shaking her head. "Her Highness won't be happy."

Briallen winked. "And what will she do if she isn't? After all, she insists Sir Robrek is the goddess's choice."

* * *

Samantha sat on her father's throne, Robbie beside her in what had been her throne as the heir. The door to the throne room swung open. Morgan entered, heavily guarded and in chains, Torin beside him. As she'd insisted as a part of his apology, Torin fell to his knees and began the long crawl toward the throne. Morgan looked down at him in disgust and tried to quicken his own pace, but the guards held him to Duke Torin's. When they finally arrived, Torin bowed low, but Morgan merely glared at her.

She held onto the arms of her throne, praying she wasn't about to make a mistake. "Torin, duke of Oirthir, and Morgan, count of Truthair, you stand accused of treason in conspiring in the murder of King Solar and attempting to usurp the throne from his rightful heir. What have you to say?"

"Rot in hell, bastard," Morgan spat.

Torin bowed until his head touched the floor. "Your Highness, I apologize most profusely for repeating Argblutal's lies about your parentage. I am prepared to swear my loyalty to you as the rightful heir."

"Coward!" Morgan pulled against his chains. "We see what happens to your fine principles when faced with losing your head!"

Samantha ignored Morgan and looked down at Torin. His lips were thin, and his teeth clenched. She would have sworn he was furious over her humiliating him. She wavered, unsure if she should go through with the oath after all. Still, she knew her father never ordered an execution when it wasn't absolutely necessary. "I will hear your oath."

Raising his head and looking at her, Torin drew the star of Sulis over his heart. "Your Highness, by the goddess and on my mother's grave, I swear my loyalty to you as Solar's true and rightful heir."

It was the most sacred oath of their culture. Still, she didn't trust him completely. "I will accept your oath on one condition. Until I say otherwise you will remain under house arrest in the palace. Any hint of disobedience will result in your immediate execution."

"I understand, Your Highness. May Sulis guide you in the ways of justice and mercy."

She turned to Morgan. "Count Morgan, for your continued defiance, I sentence you to death by beheading, to be carried out this afternoon. Your head will then be placed on the palace battlement as a warning to those who would defy the rightful heir."

Morgan's nostrils flared. "You may kill me, but you cannot silence the truth. One day, it will destroy you."

* * *

There was a knock on the door, and Leigh groaned. If it was another patient, he hoped it was one who could afford to pay. Because he'd been unable to purchase food for two days, he had little to offer in way of healing energy.

He opened the door to a priest he didn't recognize. The priest looked around in apparent disapproval. "I seek a former novice of a Father Gildas, a man by the name of Leigh Fergalstamm."

Leigh nodded, wondering what this was about. "You've found him." Leigh invited the priest inside and offered him a chair. He collapsed into a second chair across the table from the priest.

"Are you ill?" the priest asked.

Leigh shook his head. "No, I'm merely tired." *And hungry.*

The priest nodded as if this were of no importance. "I've been sent by Father Hafghan to summon you to a church trial on the morrow."

Leigh straightened abruptly. "Of what am I accused?"

The priest laughed humorlessly. "You misunderstand. You're being summoned as a witness against your former master. Father Gildas is being tried for his attempted murder of the princess's betrothed, and we've been told you have knowledge of this matter."

Leigh sagged back into the chair. "Yes, I saved Sir Robrek from being burned at the stake."

After the priest left, Leigh sank onto his cot. Removing Father Gildas would treat one symptom of the illness that afflicted the church but would do little to cure the disease itself—a church that cared more for money and power than the goddess's children.

* * *

Slathek whistled to himself as his servant helped him to dress in his newest outfit. He frowned at his reflection. The tunic was plainer than what he was used to, the blue on the dull side of lapis lazuli and the trim displaying the barest minimum of gold embroidery. But it seemed to be the best these barbarians could do, and he wasn't about to let this land's fashion deficiencies spoil his mood. He was soon to be the uncle of a king! Business had gone swimmingly that morning. Markets that had once been closed to him as a foreign merchant were suddenly open to the uncle of the princess's betrothed. His ships had left in the autumn as he'd ordered when he feared arrest by Duke Argblutal, but they'd return in the spring, and he'd just purchased a cargo that would guarantee him a small fortune when he sold it in Mahngbhayo.

Slathek took one last look at himself in the mirror and then headed down the stairs of the Traveler's Haven. The princess had offered him quarters in the palace, but he'd thought it best to refuse. A foreign merchant would be little assistance to a man trying to prove to nobles he was worthy to be their king. No, Robrek would get on better without him hovering, and Slathek could wait to bask in his kinsman's reflected glory.

When he emerged into the dining room, he saw Chiamaka, the innkeeper and his friend, talking earnestly with two well-armed, tough young barbarians. Like all barbarians, they were ridiculously tall and repulsively ugly, their skin like pasty chalk. Chiamaka's own skin was a deep rich ebony; he didn't look like an animated corpse. Chiamaka signaled for Slathek to join them.

"Slathek, my lad. Allow me to introduce Beri and Brend Ericstamm, the brothers I told you about."

"My friend, I thought I told you I have no need of protection except when I'm handling large sums of money." Slathek put his hand to his own sword. "This has always served me more than well enough in the past."

"Yes, but your nephew was not the princess's betrothed in the past. As you no doubt know, certain elements are less than pleased with the idea of Robrek taking the throne, especially after the Massacre of Valley Fair."

Slathek sighed tiredly. "I've already told you Robrek couldn't possibly be at fault. He is no savage."

Chiamaka jabbed a finger toward his chest. "I know that, but people still think him strange, and there are new rumors about a curse in Korth. Don't go asking me what kind of curse because I haven't the slightest idea. The important thing is, some are blaming your nephew for it. Be reasonable, Slathek. You have more than enough money to pay for a little extra precaution."

Slathek turned to the young men. It irritated him that he had to look up to meet their eyes. "Have you heard any such ridiculous rumors of some curse?"

Beri and Brend looked at him stupidly, and one of them answered, "Some are saying the goddess is angry about the idea of a foreigner on the throne, and she's punishing Korth for it."

"My nephew is no foreigner. His father is as repulsively white and unreasonably tall as the two of you. Sir Robrek grew up less than a day's ride from Murtaghan on the king's lands."

Beri, or perhaps it was Brend, shrugged. "He still looks foreign."

Chiamaka took Slathek by the arm. "Your own life isn't the only thing at stake here. You could be kidnapped and used against Sir Robrek."

Slathek scowled at Chiamaka. He had once before been kidnapped by Argblutal because of his resemblance to his nephew. The innkeeper knew he wouldn't risk being used as a pawn in some political game.

He gave in and hired the two barbarians. He wondered if Robrek had heard rumors of this curse. Perhaps he'd better talk to his nephew.

CHAPTER 10

In the morning light, Leigh made his way through the streets of Murtaghan toward the Temple of the Mother's Love. On his way, he stopped in with a new batch of the medicine for little Aine. The child was worse this morning, and Leigh was deeply concerned, but because he hadn't eaten, he could offer her nothing more than the medicine, which she refused to drink. "Keep trying," Leigh counseled the mother. "I'll return to check on her as soon as I can."

When he arrived at the Temple, he found a priest waiting for him. The priest stared at Leigh's narrow nose that announced him as being of mixed blood. "I'm Father Faolan," the priest informed him. Father Faolan showed him into a small room with benches lining the sides. Leigh took a seat on an uncomfortable bench and settled in to wait. He hoped it wouldn't be long.

* * *

Father Gildas glared at the panel of priests that would dare to sit in judgment on him.

"Father Gildas," Father Hafghan said. "You've been brought here today to answer charges of a most grave nature. You are accused of misusing the power of your office in an attempt to cause the death of a member of your flock in defiance of the laws of both the church and the crown. How plead you?"

"Robrek Angusstamm is not and has never been a member of my flock."

120

"Do you deny you attempted to bring about his death?"

"The Writ is clear that the destruction of demons is an obligation, not a sin. I am innocent of anything contrary to the laws of the land, and my conscience is pure in my upholding of Sulis's holy laws."

Father Hafghan turned to the clerk. "Bring in the first witness."

Father Gildas shivered as the demon child entered the room. He wasn't dressed in the peasant weave he'd worn at his own trial, but rather dared to mimic his betters. *How can anyone who claims to speak for the goddess look at such a monstrosity and not know he is demon-cursed?*

* * *

As Robrek took his seat, he could see the hatred in Father Gildas's eyes. The force of the emotion was so malignant he raised his shields to protect himself.

"Sir Robrek, can you describe your relationship with the accused?" Father Hafghan asked.

"He was the priest in charge of the temple in Valley Fair, which is the closest village to my father's farm. He disapproved of my parents' marriage because my mother was foreign, and because I resemble my mother, he wanted me exposed as an infant."

"I see," Father Hafghan answered. The other priests on the panel looked shocked. Father Hafghan proceeded to question him about the various attempts the priest had made on his life, culminating with the trial last summer.

When Father Hafghan and the other priests on the panel had finished questioning him, Father Hafghan turned to Father Gildas. "Do you desire to ask any questions of this witness?"

"I will not contaminate myself by any more contact with one so cursed."

Father Hafghan nodded. "So be it." He turned to Robrek and bowed. "Sir Robrek, this court thanks you for taking time to speak with us. Unless you have something you would like to add, we have no more call upon your services."

With a sigh of relief, Robrek left the courtroom. He was glad to be out of the presence of Gildas's hatred. He thought he should have felt vindicated or elated about Gildas's coming excommunication, but he'd lost the desire to see Gildas suffer. Mostly, he felt sad things had come to this. As he passed a doorway, he saw Leigh inside a small waiting area. He smiled. "Leigh!"

Leigh jumped to his feet, and they embraced, slapping each other on the back. As Robrek touched his friend, his healing senses became instantly aroused. Leigh was hungry and suffering from the beginning stages of malnourishment.

Before he could question his friend, Father Faolan arrived to summon Leigh to testify. Robrek watched Leigh disappear into the courtroom and decided to wait. He wasn't about to let the man who'd saved his life go hungry.

Father Faolan returned after escorting Leigh inside and looked surprised and none too pleased to find Robrek still in the hallway. He bowed with seeming reluctance. "Sir Robrek, can I be of any assistance?"

"I'd like to wait until Leigh finishes testifying."

"As you wish, Milord. If you wish to wait, I'll show you where you can do so in comfort. I can have you informed as soon as the novice is finished."

Robrek nodded his approval, and Father Faolan ushered him into a dusty, unused office. It had a desk, a single chair, and a few moldering books on a shelf. Eburacon stiffened as he took in the room. "You are being insulted, Milord."

Robrek hadn't thought of the room's significance, but Eburacon was right. He wondered if he should do something about it, but he didn't want to create unnecessary tension. "I'm sure it's just the closest place," he said.

"It is no fit place for Your Lordship. It isn't just you who is being disrespected, but also the princess and the goddess herself." Before Robrek could decide what to do, Eburacon strode to the door and called for the priest. "What is the meaning of this?" he asked, gesturing toward the dusty room.

Faolan looked inside. "Of what?"

Eburacon grabbed the priest and pushed him against the wall. "He is your future king. Surely you have a place that better fits his station."

Robrek put a hand on Eburacon's arm. "Eburacon, it is all right. We won't be here long."

Eburacon ignored him. "Show us to the high priest's office," he ordered Faolan, then pushed the priest toward the door.

Faolan stumbled. When he regained his balance, he glared malevolently, but said, "Right this way."

* * *

Robrek had taken to pacing when Leigh finally arrived. Robrek strode rapidly across the room and grasped his friend's hand. It was trembling, and his face was deathly white. "You aren't well," he said, leading Leigh toward a chair.

"I'll be all right in a minute," Leigh said. "It's just all that hatred. How could you stand to be so close to it?"

"I shielded myself." He put his hand on Leigh's arm, closed his eyes, and infused his friend with his own energy. Soon Leigh stopped shaking, and his color returned. "Leigh, you can't go on like this. How can I help you?"

Leigh looked at him with something akin to desperation. "There's an infant. Very far gone with the lung sickness. I'm not sure I can save her. Will you go with me?"

"Of course," Robrek answered. "But first we must get you something to eat."

"I'm fine." Leigh got to his feet.

"You're not fine. How long has it been since you've eaten a decent meal?"

Leigh looked away. "Two days. Maybe three."

"Come on. There's an inn nearby." Robrek grabbed his cloak, which had a large hood to hide his black hair, dark skin, and green eyes. He led Leigh out of the temple and toward the inn. As they walked, a passerby spat in front of Leigh and muttered, "Cothla."

Eburacon grabbed the man by the shoulder and shoved him against a wall. He drew his knife and put it at the man's throat. "What did you say?"

"Nothing," the man squeaked. "I meant nothing."

"I should carve the tongue out of your mouth for using such a filthy word."

Again, Robrek put his hand on his guard's arm. "Eburacon, what is the problem?"

"This scum insulted your friend and, thereby, you, Milord," Eburacon said.

Robrek raised an eyebrow at Leigh.

"He called me a 'cothla,'" Leigh said. "It's the word they use around here for those with mixed blood like us. It means tainted."

Robrek turned toward the man, and the man saw his face. His eyes widened, and he turned pale. "Don't kill me, Milord," he begged. "Please, I meant no offense."

"Let him go, Eburacon," Robrek commanded.

At first, he thought his guard was going to disobey him, but Eburacon slowly took his knife away from the man's throat. "Go home and wash your mouth out with soap." Eburacon pushed the man away. He stumbled and took off running.

Eburacon turned a glare on Robrek. "The next person who insults Your Lordship in my presence will die. I will defend your honor, as well as your life."

"My honor requires no man's blood," Robrek insisted. He didn't know what else to say, so he turned his back on Eburacon and continued to the inn with Leigh.

When they reached the inn, they were shown to a table. The innkeeper glanced nervously at the two heavily armed guards. Robrek ordered two of the special, and the server brought them dishes of some kind of stew and hunks of only slightly stale bread. It tasted comfortingly familiar. Leigh downed the bowl and ordered a second before Robrek had barely gotten started.

Robrek took out his purse and handed Leigh a fistful of coins. Leigh tried to hand them back. "I can't take this."

"I'm not about to let you go hungry while I use a silver brush on my hair and dine on the best food in the joined kingdoms. Take the money."

"I wouldn't do this if I could continue to serve the poor of Murtaghan without it." He tucked the coins into a pocket of his robes.

"There's something else you can do for me." Robrek said, and told Leigh about the plans for the clinic. "I'll pay you, of course."

Leigh smiled. "I can think of nothing I'd enjoy more."

* * *

After they'd eaten, Leigh led Robrek to a two-story tenement that seemed to remain standing on faith alone. It was constructed of rough unpainted wood that had warped with the weather, leaving substantial gaps between the boards. The entire building listed badly to one side. Climbing up a frigid, rickety staircase, they had to step over puddles caused by leaks in the roof. Leigh stopped at a doorway with only a curtain drawn across.

He knocked on the wall beside the doorway, and a woman pulled the curtain aside. She was weeping and holding an infant Even with his shields up Robrek could tell the baby was near death. The woman held a full bottle in her other hand.

"I haven't been able to get her to drink a drop. She won't even open her eyes." Suddenly, she noticed Leigh wasn't alone. Robrek's features remained hidden by his cloak, but she took in his sword and the two armed men, which announced him as of the upper class. She trembled. "Who have you brought to me?"

"My friend is a stronger healer than I am. If anyone can save Aine, it's he. May we come in?"

The woman nodded nervously and pulled the curtain aside. The room was clean, but nearly bare. The table with two chairs looked about as substantial as the building. Above it was a shelf with various cracked and broken dishes, and a pile of straw and ragged blankets rested in one corner. In the center of the room was a small puddle from the leaking roof, and the woman had stuffed rags into the gaps between the boards. A tiny brazier gave out little heat. Robrek had never seen poverty this abject. *How can anyone live like this? How can a person with a conscience permit it?*

"Please, the child." He reached out for the baby, but its mother hesitated.

Leigh touched her arm reassuringly. "It will be all right."

The mother placed Aine in Robrek's arms. He sat in the rickety chair beside the table, lowered his shields, and drifted into a healing trance. Soon he was one with the suffering infant. A feeling of intense pleasure filled his body as little by little he rid the infant of the disease that threatened her life. He'd almost forgotten how good it felt to heal. He cleaned the mucus from the child's lungs, lowered the fever, and rid her body of all infection. When he emerged from his trance and opened his eyes, the infant was sleeping peacefully in his arms. He felt happier and more at peace with himself than he had since helping the princess retake the palace. *This was what I was meant to do.*

"She'll be fine now." He stood and handed the baby back to her mother. After he released the child, he stumbled from sudden dizziness, and his hood fell from his head.

"Milord." The woman fell to her knees, clinging to the child. "Oh, Milord, they said you were kind, but I never dreamed you would take the time for one sick child." The woman kissed his feet and began washing his boots with her tears and her hair.

"Mistress, I'm a peasant such as yourself. There's no need to honor me in this manner."

The woman resisted his efforts to bring her to her feet. "Please, Milord. I'm not worthy to stand in your presence. My house isn't worthy of such a visitor. Thank you for my Aine's life. Thank you, Milord, but please, don't disgrace yourself by remaining in such a place any longer."

"Mistress, I've spent most of my life in places little better than this." This wasn't entirely true, but he wasn't sure how to handle the woman's complete debasement. He looked at Leigh for help.

"Perhaps we'd better go, Robrek."

* * *

Father Gildas stalked down the steps of the Temple of the Mother's Love. He had nothing but a small packet of his belongings and the coins in his purse. Even his horse had been taken. It belonged not to him, but to the church. *I can't be defrocked and excommunicated! Sulis will not allow it! How dare they find me guilty of holding an illegal trial and attempting to carry out an illegal punishment? The demon had to die! But the princess has been bewitched and betrothed herself to him. Now, any evil is possible, including this gross injustice against* me, *one of the goddess's most devoted servants!*

* * *

Oriana lingered outside the training room where the squires and young nobles took their morning training. *I'm just enjoying the cool morning breeze.* She shivered and wrapped her scarf more fully around her face. *I don't want to see that disgusting boy who dresses like a self-important peacock. Why would I ever want to have anything to do with him? It's just nice out here.* She wrapped her arms more tightly around herself and moved closer to the wall in hopes of finding some warmth. She wouldn't try to go inside the training arena again. It wasn't as if Vaughan was any good. She could tell at once all the other boys were better. *Why would I ever seek out such a loser?*

The door of the practice room opened. Oriana jumped away from the wall and tried to make it look as though she were just casually walking by.

But it was not Vaughan who emerged but her beloved Conroy. "Oriana! What are you doing here?"

She smiled up into his handsome face, trying to forget how flat her chest was. "I'm just taking a walk."

Conroy wrapped his scarf around the lower portion of his face. "It's pretty cold for a walk, isn't it, Little Sis?" She hated when he called her that. He wasn't her brother, and she didn't want him to view her that way. Some day she'd develop enough for him to think of her as something more than a little sister. He'd remember how she'd saved his life.

He looked down at her sympathetically. "If your family doesn't get here soon, you'll never get through the mountain passes before they're blocked by snow. Are you sure you don't want me to arrange an escort to take you home?" He'd offered to do so once before.

"No, they'll be here. They wouldn't forget me."

Conroy paused by the door she knew led to the guards' baths; she'd seen Vaughan go in there before. "I've got to get cleaned up and back to Her Highness. Do you need anything, Little Sis?"

She shook her head. She needed nothing except her family and perhaps a kiss from the lips now hidden by his scarf. But he couldn't give her the first, and it'd never occur to him to give her the second. Well, he had kissed her on the top of her head once, but that was a kiss given to a child, not to a woman. *Who does he give those kind of kisses to?* Oriana had never seen him with a woman. "I'm fine," she said, although she was about as far from fine as she'd ever been.

"Let me know if you need anything, or if you change your mind about being sent home." He ruffled the fur on her hood and then disappeared into the guards' baths.

* * *

As Vaughan exited the training room, he saw Oriana walking away with one of the princess's guards. He hurried in the opposite direction. He didn't need Oriana making comparisons between him and the men who served the princess. He couldn't even compete with boys his own age—a fact which the weapons' master continually pointed out. Sir Robrek had to be regretting his choice of squire.

Vaughan tried to tell himself he was getting better, and indeed, he was, but he seemed so far behind he could never catch up. The only ray of hope was the thought that both Sir Robrek and Captain Darhour had started their training when they were older than he.

* * *

Alvabane approached the cell where the sorcerer's brother was imprisoned. She'd sung the guards to sleep and taken the keys. As a Bard, she could make any audience feel the emotions of her song, in this case lethargy. They'd never remember seeing her.

She opened the door to reveal the young man sitting on his bunk in the darkness. The rage rolled off of him deliciously. "Who are you?" he snapped.

"Such things are immaterial. What matters is whether your hate is stronger than your love. Tell me about your brother."

The sorcerer's brother got to his feet, his hands forming fists. "I have no brother, merely a worm my father claims as a son. What can you know of the depths of my hate?"

"Not enough to set you free."

Boyden laughed bitterly. "No one can set me free. They intend me to hang."

Alvabane jangled the keys in her hand. "The guards sleep. All I have to do is unlock your shackles, and we can walk out of here. Let's start again. Who do you love?"

Boyden tried to lunge for her, but was prevented by his chains. "I love no one," he snarled. "Who ever loved me?"

Alvabane felt pleasure course through her; the man's hate was intoxicating. "What would you give to see the sorcerer dead?"

Rage contorted the man's face. "Everything I have, everything I am."

Alvabane's smile broadened. "You will do nicely." She tossed him the keys. "Unlock your shackles and come with me."

"Why in the seven hells should I?" He clenched his fists.

Alvabane flicked a hand at their surroundings. "Would you prefer to stay here and hang?"

CHAPTER 11

Robrek again entered the cave and walked to the edge of the blood-red lake. Again he saw the shadows swarming beneath the surface. Two of the shadows formed themselves into beautiful women and crawled onto the shore. They were both naked, with large breasts, small waists, and firm thighs. One of them ran her hands over her breasts, her stomach, and down between her legs. Her eyes beckoned him to come and do the same. Despite his better judgment, he wanted to do as she asked. The second woman crawled nearer and held out her hands to him. "Join us. We can give you pleasure the likes of which you have never imagined."

Thinking of Samantha, he wanted to resist, but the first woman leaned back, spread her legs wide, and arched her back, her eyes begging him to fulfill her need and his need as well. He tore off his shirt and began tearing at the buttons of his pants.

"Yes," the second woman hissed. "Come and take our power. The Bard seeks to steal it and make it her own. But it is yours by right."

He tossed aside his pants and moved toward the women. Before he could reach them, someone grabbed his arm. He turned and saw his mother, Donella. "No, my son. You must not."

Robrek pulled his arm free. "I'm a man, not a child."

Donella's eyes were filled with love and fear. "A man can be deceived by his desires. Please, my son, look closely at those who offer themselves to you. Look with your heart and not your eyes."

Robrek turned back to the shadow women. Slowly, the beautiful faces wrinkled in on themselves. The noses lengthened to become beaks. The eyes sank far into their skulls. The well-manicured nails melted into claws. The luxurious hair thickened into snakes.

He drew back in horror, but his manhood still throbbed with desire. He knew they hadn't lied about the pleasure he could find among them. He took another step closer to the lake's edge.

"No!" a voice echoed throughout the cave. "You are our only hope! The ritual restrains no more!"

Robrek jerked awake, startling Ronan, who was curled up next to him. Ronan gave an indignant meow and hopped off the bed. Robrek covered his face with his hands and curled into a fetal position. *What did that voice mean? What ritual? And only hope for what?* All through his childhood, he'd dreamed of his mother, and now she was mixed in with the disturbing dreams of the lake. It had to mean something.

Drem entered the room and opened the curtains, letting in the early morning light, which fell on the battle and hunting tapestries that still decorated his rooms. He'd have to do something about them, but this morning he was too disturbed to bring it up. Besides, today he had more important things to worry about. Today he'd find a place for his clinic.

* * *

Surrounded by his six personal bodyguards and with his hood up so he wouldn't be recognized, Robrek started out from the palace gates to check out the list of properties Blaine had given him. He found the first two places on the list inappropriate—too small or, according to his guards, too hard to secure. The third on the list was City Hall.

When Robrek arrived, he put his hood down. The mayor's secretary's eyes widened, and he jumped to his feet. He bowed, but turned white and seemed unable to find his tongue.

"I'd like to see Mayor Barris," Robrek announced.

"Yes, Your . . . Your Lordship. I'll . . . I'll tell him you're here." He hustled to the door behind him, nearly tripping over his feet in the process. *Why is he afraid of me? Does he see me as the Butcher of Valley Fair? Or is he merely intimidated by my position?*

The secretary entered the mayor's office and closed the door behind him. There was quiet for a few seconds; then Robrek heard a loud voice, not the secretary's, from within. "He's here!"

The secretary came scurrying back out, the mayor close behind. The mayor bowed. "How can I be of service, Your Lordship?"

Robrek explained what he was looking for. "Do you have any place that might do?"

The mayor looked thoughtful. "The old municipal ballroom may be just what you're looking for. It's been gathering dust since the new one was built. Would you like to take a look at it?"

Robrek nodded, and the mayor led him down a corridor and through a large double doorway at the end. Robrek sneezed as he entered. A thin layer of dust covered everything. "It will need to be cleaned, of course," the mayor said.

The room was large, and possessed another doorway to the outside. The doorway opened onto a quiet back street. The room seemed perfect. He turned to Eburacon. "Is it defensible?"

Eburacon insisted on walking around the building and up and down the street. Finally, he pronounced himself satisfied.

* * *

That night in bed, Robrek told Samantha about the ballroom at City Hall. "But what about when I need you?" she asked.

"There's plenty of time when you don't need me. The clinic wouldn't have to operate every day. Let's say twice a week to start with." Samantha hesitated and looked away. He took her shoulder and turned her back to face him. "Sam, this is something I need to do. Healing that child convinced me of that. Besides, it can't help but improve my reputation. The people will see me giving life, not taking it."

"But Robbie . . ." She threw her arms around him.

He returned her embrace. "Don't worry, Sam. I'll be safe."

* * *

The next day Robrek had Leigh meet him at the palace. With Oriana, they headed to the palace stillroom to make a wide variety of potions needed at the clinic. "The old man wouldn't let me help before," Oriana informed him. "He said I should run off and play with my dolls. As if I still played with dolls." Oriana snorted.

"Why didn't he want your help?" Robrek asked.

"He didn't think magic was necessary for making potions."

"Well, he might not like the three of us interfering today," Robrek said.

In the stillroom, Calum, the palace physician, and his apprentices were busy making potions. They froze as Robrek entered followed by his guards, Leigh, and Oriana. Then, they all bowed.

"May I be of assistance, Your Lordship?" Calum asked stiffly, his words clipped and harsh. The boys stared at him wide-eyed. Robrek didn't know whether it was because they viewed him as the Hero of Gloine Torr or the Butcher of Valley Fair.

Robrek acknowledged the bows with a nod of his head. "Yes, we'd like to make a variety of potions and could use the assistance of you and your apprentices."

"I see." Calum's eyes narrowed. "If Your Lordship could tell me what kind of potions you desire, we could prepare them for you. There is no need to bother yourself with the matter."

"Actually, there is. The three of us,"—he pointed to himself, Leigh, and Oriana—"all have magic, so we can make the potions more powerful than you could on your own." Oriana smiled in satisfaction.

Calum's lips tightened. "Then I guess you have no use for me," he said, and walked toward the door.

Eburacon stood in his way. "His Lordship said he required your assistance."

A vein throbbed in Calum's temple, and he clenched his fists. "I have been making potions for over thirty years. I won't be reduced to the status of an apprentice by a boy just out of grammar school, no matter whose betrothed he is."

"Let him go," Robrek ordered. Eburacon hesitated, but stepped aside. Calum stormed out of the room.

The four boys stared after their master. Robrek met their eyes. "I could really use your assistance, but I won't force you to remain."

The boys looked at each other, and the largest stepped forward. "It would be an honor to assist the Hero of Gloine Torr."

* * *

The next morning, surrounded by Robrek's personal guard, by an additional twenty members of the Royal Guard, and by about a dozen servants carrying potions, Robrek, Leigh, and Oriana arrived at City Hall; people were lined up for blocks. Many had camped on the streets.

The sickness and misery weighed on Robrek, and he could tell it was affecting Leigh and Oriana, too—they were both pale. They took up positions near the door; Robrek's examination table lay farther into the room.

The first in line was a father carrying a six-year-old boy with a twisted leg. Leigh touched the boy, shook his head, and sent him on to Robrek. His guards stopped the man and searched both him and the boy for weapons. They even took away the man's eating knife. The father bowed repeatedly. "My boy can't walk right no more, and his leg always pains him. It was broke awhile back, and it didn't never heal right." He looked at the ground while he talked, and Robrek had to lean forward to hear him.

Robrek had the man set the boy on the examination table. The boy tried to cling to his father. "Got to be brave," the father told the boy, as he backed away.

Robrek smiled at the boy, trying to calm his nervousness. "It will be all right," he promised. "I won't hurt you, but I have to touch you if I'm going to make your leg better. Is that all right?"

The boy looked fearfully at his father, and the man nodded. The boy looked back at Robrek and nodded as well. Robrek touched the injured leg, closed his eyes, and went into a healing trance. The boy's leg had been badly set. He could rebreak the leg, set it properly, splint it, and allow it to heal, or he could use his healing power to straighten the bone. The first would take a minimal amount of energy; the second would tire him significantly, but would certainly be more spectacular. Robrek decided that with all the people waiting to see him, he'd better do the former.

He came out of his trance and explained the problem to the boy's father. The man trembled slightly as if he wasn't sure it would work, but he said, "Do it, please, Milord."

With his healing energy, Robrek created a block in the boy's upper leg so he wouldn't feel the pain, broke the leg, and reset it. As he did, pleasure flooded him. His skin tingled, and his heart swelled with joy. *Holy Sulis, what did I ever do to deserve such a gift?* The only way to repay the goddess for the pleasure was to continue to heal her children. He smiled broadly as he splinted the leg and had a waiting servant fetch a pain potion. "Give the boy two spoonfuls of this if his leg pains him, and don't take the splints off for six weeks. If he isn't better by then, bring him back to me."

The man took the potion, picked up the boy, and went on his way. Robrek had already done more good today than in his entire time in the palace.

Next, a young woman led a blind old man toward him. The young woman bowed and turned to the old man. "Bow, father. It's his Lordship."

The old man bowed. "The Hero of Gloine Torr, is it? My daughter said there would be nothing you could do, but I told her that if His Lordship can climb Gloine Torr, an old man's eyes would be a snap."

Robrek laughed. "Gloine Torr was surely not an easy feat, but I'll see if there's anything I can do about your eyes." Robrek had the old man sit on the table and close his eyes. He put his hands over the man's eyes and closed his own. Robrek smiled when he determined the old man's problem. The eyes had become cloudy. It was a relatively simple matter to make them clear again. He did so and took his hands away from the man's eyes.

The man opened his eyes and looked around in wonder. "It's a miracle! Holy Sulis, it's a miracle!" he shouted. "I can see! See as plain as day!"

Robrek smiled broadly. "It isn't a miracle, merely magic."

The man ignored him and continued to proclaim a miracle as he was escorted out of the ballroom.

* * *

By midday, Robrek had seen dozens of patients. Suddenly, a commotion near the front door drew Robrek's attention. Leigh called out, and Robrek hurried over to find several men carrying an injured man between them. The man's leg had a large gash and was bleeding profusely. Leigh had his hands on the man's leg. Although the bleeding was slowing, Leigh probably couldn't heal it before the man bled out. Robrek dropped down beside him to add his healing power to Leigh's, but the injured man grabbed hold of Robrek's arm. "Milord, I can't feel my legs. Don't save me if I'm not going to be able to walk no more. I don't want to be a burden to my family."

"You'll walk," Robrek promised, and helped Leigh close the wound. The gash in the leg closed, leaving a pink scar behind. The immediate problem solved, Robrek turned his attention to the man's back. Robrek put his hands on the man's torso, and he felt the aching numbness in his own legs. The back was broken, the spinal cord severed. If Robrek didn't heal it, the man wouldn't be able to walk. If he did heal it, he'd be too exhausted to do anything else for the day.

"What happened?" Robrek asked, and he was told that the man was a carpenter who'd fallen from the roof of a house onto a saw. "Your back's broken," Robrek said, and the man's eyes flashed with desperation. "But I can fix it." Robrek looked up at Leigh. "This will be my last patient. You and Oriana can close up or carry on as you wish."

"I'm about drained," Leigh said. He looked happy, but fatigued.

Oriana nodded. "I'm so tired I couldn't do much more than hand out potions, but although we've seen what seems like a hundred patients, the line's still down the street."

"They have to come back next time. There's only so much we can do." Robrek issued orders to close the clinic and told the people they could return in two days' time. The crowd groaned and murmured that they'd been waiting for hours. "I'm sorry" was all Robrek could think to say.

He ordered the doors to the clinic closed and returned his attention to the injured man. Robrek put his hands over the break and went into a healing trance. Slowly, he wove the spinal cord back together and healed the break in the bone. When he was done, he came out of the trance and dropped to the floor in exhaustion. A servant came scurrying forward. "A chair, Milord." Robrek was so tired he wanted to just stay on the floor, but decided it probably wasn't proper for the future king. He allowed the servant to help him into the chair.

* * *

Samantha was sitting in her reception room with Blaine discussing wedding plans when Robbie burst through the door, grinning wider than she'd ever seen him. He plopped down on the coach beside her and gave her an enthusiastic kiss on the lips. "It was wonderful!" he crowed. "I've never felt so good in my life!"

She couldn't help grinning in return. "It went well, then?"

"Fantastic. They can't see me as a butcher now, not after what I did today. The people kept talking of miracles. I tried to tell them it was simply magic, but I don't think they believed me." He lay his head back on the sofa. "I'm exhausted and starving, but by Sulis, it was worth it."

Samantha turned to Blaine. "We'll discuss the wedding later. Try to get some idea how the people are talking about the clinic and have the kitchen send up some food."

"Something sweet, please," Robbie piped in. When they were alone, Robbie went into an enthusiastic description of all the people he'd healed. "And Leigh and Oriana took care of a host of lesser problems. Sam, you have no idea how good it feels. There's nothing like it."

"Not even my touch." She ran her hand up his thigh.

He caught her hand before it reached his groin. "Your touch is pretty damned good, but I couldn't now. At least not until I rest a bit and eat something."

CHAPTER 12

Samantha sat with Caedmon in her reception room. He was going on about the planned arrival of the Neasarian ambassador. She barely paid attention, her mind on Robbie and his clinic. Blaine had taken care of the ambassador's arrival. Caedmon cleared his throat, and Samantha turned to him. "On another matter, there are rumors, Your Highness."

"What kind of rumors?" she asked.

"Rumors linking Sir Robrek with Lady Briallen."

Samantha laughed. "They are lies."

Caedmon shifted in his chair and scowled. "They may be, Your Highness, but it seems the rumors have started with Briallen herself. She is a very attractive woman, and . . ."

She waved him silent. "I will hear no more of this. I'm as sure of Sir Robrek as I am that the sun will rise in the east."

"Your Highness, at least consider it for a moment. Briallen has been publicly seen throwing herself at Sir Robrek, and well, men have certain needs."

She stood. "Sir Robrek's needs are being met."

Caedmon gaped at her. "What do you mean?"

Before Samantha could respond, Blaine scooted in and announced that Captain Hawk requested an audience.

"Your Highness, we should finish—" Caedmon tried to protest.

But Samantha waved him silent again. "Enough. I will not dignify such rumors." She turned to her secretary. "Have Captain Hawk shown in."

Hawk entered, bowed to the princess, and nodded toward Caedmon. "Your Highness, Your Grace, the prisoner Boyden Angusstamm has escaped."

The princess grabbed the back of a chair. "How is this possible?"

Hawk shifted his feet and didn't meet the princess's gaze. "I don't know, Your Highness. He was there last night for his evening meal. He was missing this morning when the guards came with his breakfast. I don't see how it could have happened without help from the inside."

"Darhour could have done it," Samantha said.

Hawk paled. "Surely, there's only one Ghost. I can think of no other that could have accomplished it. I have detained the guards on duty last night, but so far, they are professing innocence. I wouldn't have expected it of either of them, but I guess anyone can be bought if the price is right. Should I proceed to more intense interrogation?"

Samantha paused briefly. *Is this a danger to Robbie?* Boyden had nearly killed Robbie when they were younger, and he'd only grown more angry since. He was an ideal pawn to use against his brother. Still—torture? She gritted her teeth and turned to Hawk. "Be as harsh as you believe necessary."

Hawk bowed and was dismissed, but before Caedmon could turn the conversation back to Briallen, a page interrupted them to inform Samantha that Count Morgan's heir, Lord Feoras, had arrived as ordered and was ready to present himself at court.

* * *

Samantha sat on the throne, with Caedmon standing beside her. At the entrance to the throne room, Feoras and his men fell to their knees and trekked across the throne room as the entire court watched in silence. When he reached the dais, Feoras bowed to the floor. "Your Highness, I arrive in answer to your summons. I humbly submit myself to your mercy."

Samantha looked down at Feoras with all the royal dignity she could summon. "Your brother plotted treason against my throne and refused to offer me an oath of loyalty. What do you know of this?"

His voice trembled as he spoke. "Nothing, Your Highness, I swear. I mean, my brother and I have never been on the best of terms, and he considered me a child. I mean, he is ten years my senior. His treason is a disgrace to our house. I mean, our father was always a loyal subject of the crown, and so he raised me to be."

He was so deathly pale she feared he'd faint. She'd forgotten how young he was. His face was covered with acne, which his scant beard did little to hide. He reminded her of Blaine, which made her feel instant sympathy for him. She wished her gift would work when she needed it.

Suddenly, the entire room burst into glowing colors—reds, oranges, yellows, blues, greens, and whites in all shades and intensities bombarded her. Her head spun, and her stomach threatened rebellion. *What's happening?* She barely prevented herself from thrusting out a hand to protect herself from the light; she needed to get out of there and fast. In the midst of the swirling colors, it was hard to determine which aura was Feoras's, but she fought off the bombardment and focused intensely on him. He glowed with white. He meant every word he said.

"Will you so swear?" she asked hastily.

"I swear by the goddess and on my mother's grave my loyalty to you and your heirs." Feoras rolled up his left sleeve and drew a small knife. Samantha sent a prayer of thanks to Sulis. The blood oath was part of the old ways, fallen out of favor during her father's reign. His willingness to give it without being asked would increase others' belief she was right in trusting him. He made a small cut on his forearm, then used his finger to draw Sulis's star on his forehead with his blood. "I seal this vow with my blood. May any who breaks a vow so sworn be tortured for eternities in the deepest of the seven hells."

She rose, and he offered his bleeding forearm to her. Her stomach heaved at the scent of blood, but she managed to dip her finger in it and drew Sulis's star on her own forehead. "By your blood, I accept your oath." She drew her sword and touched him on both shoulders. "Arise, Feoras, Count of Truthair."

"Count, Your Highness?"

"You are your brother's heir, are you not? You're welcome among us and needn't fear retribution for actions in which you had no part."

He bowed low to the ground before rising. "Thank you, Your Highness. Your Highness is most merciful."

Feoras backed out of the throne room. He bowed at the door, then turned and left. Samantha barely made into a private reception room before she fell to her knees and began vomiting.

Bearach knelt down beside her. "Are you okay, Your Highness?"

She opened her eyes to see Bearach's aura blazing light blue and white. "No." She shut her eyes tightly.

As if from a great distance, she heard her guards sending a page for Sir Robrek. Robbie was in the city healing. Bearach was beside her, helping her to her feet. She fought her way through the colors to a couch and lay down. Bearach and Conroy hovered over her.

After what seemed like an eternity, Robbie swirled into the room out of breath, his aura blazing silver, gold, and bronze. She grasped his hand. "I'm ill, terribly ill. Everyone's glowing like a Solstice bonfire. Make it stop!"

Robbie ordered the other men out of the room. The colors were more tolerable now that only the single aura was glowing, but she still felt terrible.

Robbie touched her shoulder, and she felt the warmth of his power. Instantly, the nausea went away, but not the colors. "Robbie, you're still glowing. What's wrong with me?"

Robbie looked away from her, down at his hands. "Sam, I don't know how to tell you this. You're . . ."

"I'm what?" she said. *By Sulis, I'm not dying, am I? I can't be dying. My people need me.*

"You might be . . . er . . . Sam, you're going to be angry."

Samantha grabbed Robbie's arm. "Tell me!"

He disengaged and walked to the window. "You're pregnant."

"No! You said the tea you've been giving me would prevent it."

He didn't face her. "I said it should help. I'm sorry, Sam. I didn't mean this to happen."

"No! You're wrong!" She shook her head vigorously. "I can't be pregnant now!"

Robbie approached and knelt next to her. "I wish I could make it not true for you."

She wanted to slap him, to insist that he was mistaken, but he was too powerful to be wrong. "Help me! The colors are driving me mad!"

He sat on the couch with her. "The nausea I can take care of with a daily tea, but I don't know what to do about the glowing colors. Except . . ."

"Except what? Robbie, I can't face nine months of this."

"Perhaps shielding would work—I'd go mad if I couldn't shield. I nearly did the first time I accessed my full power."

"How do you do it?" She grasped his arm again, desperate for relief.

His voice sounded hopeful. "Your gift—can you feel it? Do you know where it is inside you?"

She shook her head. "I don't know what you mean."

"Here, let me hold you."

Robbie wrapped his arms around her, and she felt the warmth of his power pouring into her. For a long time, he said nothing. *What if this doesn't work? Oh, Sulis, make this not true! Make me not be pregnant!* She willed Robbie to discover he'd been wrong. But finally, he said, "There. Do you see that?"

His mind directed her deep inside herself, and she gasped. Centered in her womb was a small, pulsing power—a light that radiated heat and life. Awe overcame her. "Holy Sulis, it's there, isn't it?" she whispered.

"Can you grab onto it? Touch it?" Robbie's mind guided her mind toward it.

She reached out to it, and she convulsed as the spark of her power sent waves of bliss through her body and her mind. She now understood a little about Robbie's pleasure from magic. It was glorious. "I didn't realize my power could be touched."

"It's okay. I won't let anything happen," Robbie whispered. "Now, form it into a bubble."

"How do I do that?" It was heat and light.

Images flowed from Robbie's mind into hers. At first, they made no sense. "Breathe into it," Robbie told her. But how could she breathe into a pulsing light? How could her lungs form a bubble in her womb? "Relax! Magic can't be forced. Relax, and the bubble will form." His power poured into her stronger than ever, releasing her tension and relaxing her muscles. Finally, she saw what he meant. The power was more than heat and light. It was matter, too. She centered on its substance and breathed. She smiled as a small bubble of energy appeared to her mind's eye. She felt Robbie's approval in her mind. "Good. Now, expand the bubble until it covers your entire body." She tried and tried, but nothing happened. She grew frustrated and tried to force more air into the bubble, but Robbie's grip on her arms tightened. "No, don't force it! Breathe into it. Allow it to expand." Samantha breathed deeply, and the bubble grew larger and larger. She wanted to laugh with delight. She had power. She had magic! Maybe it was different than Robbie's, but it was strong, and it felt wonderful. "Good," he said. "Now, allow the bubble to flow outside of you and form a barrier between you and the rest of the world." He showed her with his mind how it worked for him. With a sudden jolt, the bubble snapped into place around her.

Her eyes flew open, and she turned back to look at Robbie. He wasn't glowing any more. "It worked!" she shouted and kissed him deeply.

After a few moments, Robbie broke the kiss. "Well done! As Holy Writ said, a total shield isn't too difficult. It's subtlety that's hard to achieve. How do you feel?"

"I've never felt this good, and you're not glowing any more."

"Forming a shield will get easier with practice. I do it without thinking now. I'll teach you how to raise and lower the strength of your shields later. It's much more difficult." He wrapped his arms around her abdomen. "Sam, I swear I didn't mean it to happen. Can you ever forgive me?"

He'd made her feel better than she ever had in her life. What did she have to forgive him for? She stiffened, as she remembered a baby grew within her. "We aren't officially married yet. I can't be pregnant!"

Robbie met her eyes. "I know, but please, Sam, don't ask me to flush our daughter from your womb."

"Our daughter?" she asked. "You can tell?" Robbie nodded. "Robbie, it's too soon. Let me think about it."

* * *

Artan sat in the schoolroom with the other novices, carefully copying a letter Father Faolan had written. The other boys were copying similar documents while the priest sat at a desk at the head of the room doing more writing that they would copy later. Artan's hand ached from holding the quill. Most boys only did an hour or so of copying a day, but because he was a worthless cothla, Artan had to spend most of the day at it. No one wanted a cothla healer. He'd been told so all of his twelve long years, and he'd always believed the priests, but he wasn't so sure any more. The princess was about to marry a cothla healer, and Artan had heard the stories of miraculous healings at his clinic. If a cothla could be good enough to marry the princess, couldn't Artan be good enough to learn how to make potions or do anything other than endless copying?

Nearly finished with the document, Artan dipped his quill into the ink. But he pulled the quill to him before it was free of the jar. The ink spilled. He quickly righted the bottle, but it was too late. "No!" he cried, pulling the document and his copy out of the spreading ink.

Father Faolan's head jerked up. He got to his feet and stalked to Artan's desk. "What have you done, you clumsy oaf?" The priest slapped Artan so hard he staggered. Faolan snatched the two pieces of paper out of the novice's hands. "Do you have any idea how much time your clumsiness has cost me? How long that letter took me to compose?"

"I'm sorry, sir. I didn't mean to, sir. Most of it is still readable, sir." Artan trembled, struggling not to cry in front of the other boys.

"You know what this means, boy!"

"No, sir. Please, not again, sir." Artan wrung his robes with his hands. *Please, Sulis, no!*

But of course, Sulis didn't listen to a filthy cothla. The priest smiled, and Artan felt sick to his stomach. "Go and prepare yourself. I'll be there momentarily."

Artan opened his mouth to beg, but Faolan cut him off. "Any more whining out of you, and I'll add five lashes to the ten you've already earned."

Artan ran from the room, hoping none of the boys noticed the tears coursing down his cheeks. *Ten! Please, Sulis, no!* But Faolan never gave fewer lashes than he threatened. Artan kept his head down as he hurried down the hall to the punishment room, but despite himself he couldn't stop a sob from escaping.

"Hold on, there, son!" A priest grabbed his arm, and Artan looked into Father Dorsey's face. Artan shivered as he met Father Dorsey's eyes, though he wasn't sure why. Father Dorsey was a cothla like Artan, and the only priest who took any interest in him. "He isn't punishing you again, is he?" Artan nodded, not trusting his voice. Father Dorsey made a disgusted sound. "This will be the third time in a month. What did you do this time? Forget to shine his shoes?" Artan wiped his tears away and told the priest what had happened. Father Dorsey hissed in a way that reminded Artan of a snake. "Sulis curse the bastard! I'll be by later with some salve." Father Dorsey patted him on the shoulder and walked off.

Artan hurried down the hallway toward the punishment room. If he wasn't in position by the time Father Faolan came, the priest would double his punishment. Sometimes Father Faolan came quickly, and sometimes he kept him waiting for hours. He hoped today would be one of the quick times.

When Artan reached the room, he got the flail down from the wall. His hands trembled as he looked at the knots and bits of glass embedded in the lash. Ten would leave him covered in blood. He put the flail on the table. He untied his robes and bared himself from the waist up. He stood on tiptoes to put his hands in the manacles. Still, it was hard to reach them and clasp them around his wrists.

Stretched uncomfortably, he waited. *Please, Sulis, let him come quickly.* When the priest kept him waiting, he ached and trembled from exhaustion before he was even beaten.

* * *

"What is your determination?" Father Faolan asked Father Eadoin, his chief assistant.

Eadoin shook his head. "It will be close, but I think Hafghan will win by a narrow margin."

Faolan clenched his fists. "That cothla-loving fool cannot lead the church along the paths it needs to go. How could he possibly be favored over me?"

"Your relationship with Father Shylah and your refusal to denounce him seem the decisive factors."

Appalled at the ignorance of his fellow clergy, Faolan made his way to the punishment room. At least he had a target for his rage. He'd do to another cothla what he was unable to do to the one who truly deserved it, the cothla who threatened the entire joined kingdoms.

The cothla's naked back with its too-dark skin faced the doorway. He picked up the flail that lay ready for him. The boy's back was covered with healing wounds, wounds that should be far worse than they were. Like some cothlas, this boy healed far faster than was natural, preventing him from properly learning his lesson. Faolan whipped the lash down with all of his strength. The boy screamed, and the blood began to flow.

* * *

Anticipating another chance to heal, Father Dorsey smiled as he made his way to the novice's dormitory. No one cared if the cothla novices were healthy, so Dorsey had them all to himself. Despite the pleasure healing would give him, he raged at the sight of the bloody back of the twelve-year-old boy. It reminded him too much of the hundreds of times Faolan had reduced Dorsey's back to ribbons. Thankfully, since he'd made his vows and become a priest, Faolan was no longer able to flog him. But young Artan had many years to go before he could hope for that kind of reprieve.

"I'm here, son," he whispered to the half-dead boy. "It will feel better soon."

* * *

Grateful that Father Dorsey had arrived at last, Artan looked up at the priest, but he quickly turned away. He didn't like the expression on the priest's face, the same one he always wore when he came to heal him—a greediness, almost a hunger, as if Dorsey reveled in Artan's pain.

Artan bit into the pillow as Dorsey washed the blood from his back, but then came the blessed relief as Dorsey rubbed in the salve. A tingling coldness spread wherever the priest touched, freezing the pain away. Still, his stomach heaved, and he nearly vomited. The salve seemed like the foulest slime. He felt somehow used and unclean.

* * *

Staring at the shackle on his foot, Boyden fumed. He'd been taken from the palace dungeon to a house a short distance away. There he'd been chained to a bedpost. That was yesterday, and he hadn't seen or heard anyone since. The chain was fairly lengthy, and he could pace the small bedroom. He could even go to the door and open it, but no one brought him any ale or food. *How is this any better than the prison?*

The door opened into an anteroom that held nothing but a mahogany altar covered with a crimson cloth. A book and a blood-stained knife occupied the center. Grotesque statues stood at either end next to a bowl. Boyden couldn't see what was in the bowls from the doorway, but it smelled like blood. Just looking at the bowls made him sick, so he kept the door shut.

A door opened somewhere nearby, and footsteps sounded. An unattractive young woman entered, carrying a tray of food. She set it on the small table and went to remove the chamber pot from under the bed. He grabbed her by the arm. "Where's Alvabane? I'll not be locked up like a criminal."

The woman made a mewing sound and opened her mouth. Boyden gagged as he saw her tongue had been cut off. He let her go, and she hurried away.

The pathetic meal didn't contain any meat or ale. He'd give the old woman a piece of his mind when he saw her again. If she wanted his help, she had better start treating him with more respect.

Noise sounded again inside the anteroom. He opened the door a crack. Alvabane was clearing the book off the center of the altar, and the tongueless woman was dragging an unconscious man wearing the livery of a servant into the room.

"Put him on the altar," Alvabane said. "The blood of the gods runs low." Together they heaved the servant onto the altar.

Alvabane caressed the ceremonial knife as if it were a babe. She lit black candles at the head and the feet of the servant and began chanting in some strange language. She lifted one of the bowls toward one of the grotesque statues, then placed the bowl on the floor under the servant's dangling right arm. As her chanting built to a crescendo, shivers ran up Boyden's spine. He wrapped his arms around himself against the sudden chill. Alvabane knelt and made a quick slice across the wrist, nearly severing the hand. She allowed the blood to pour into the bowl.

Boyden stared, fascinated. The flowing blood reminded him of how much blood there'd been when he'd chopped off the men's heads. The tongueless woman cowered back from the altar. Alvabane continued chanting, lifting the second bowl toward the second statue. She placed it on the back side of the altar and slit the servant's dangling left wrist. She knelt at the altar and, for several moments, seemed to pray.

"Did you enjoy the show?" she asked without turning.

"Is that what you intend to do to me?"

The old woman turned. He couldn't meet her blank, dark eyes. "No, I have a special purpose for you. You will help me destroy the one who would wear the crown."

"You don't have to chain me up to get me to help you. There's nothing I wouldn't do if it harmed the worm."

"I wouldn't want you to wander in search of drink or entertainment, only to be recaptured and hanged. You are too important to waste." Alvabane stood and caressed one of the statues.

"Your *concern* is touching, but I can take care of myself."

Alvabane laughed, causing his stomach to heave. "I very much doubt it. Besides, you will be richly rewarded for this small inconvenience when the time comes. The dark gods take care of those who serve them."

Boyden put his hands on his hips. "Rewarded? How?"

"Beyond your wildest dream."

Boyden snorted. "I can dream pretty big. What about the king's lands? Can you give me those?"

To Boyden's surprise, Alvabane nodded. "Can you not dream bigger than that?"

"Bigger? A dukedom, perhaps?"

Alvabane nodded. "Perhaps."

* * *

Robrek awoke with a cry that brought Drem running. "Is there a problem, Milord?"

"I'm fine," Robrek snapped. But he wasn't. He'd dreamed of the lake again. He'd had repetitive dreams before, but none that disturbed him quite so much. *What does it mean? What do those women want from me? And why do I want them so badly?* It was his own desire that disturbed him most of all. Samantha was the only woman he'd ever wanted, and when he looked at his dreams in an objective light, there was nothing desirable about them. The lake was a putrid thing, and he knew the women weren't as they appeared. But he shook with a desire more powerful than any he'd ever felt. *Where is that lake? Does it truly exist?* When he'd dreamed of his mother, she had been real. Could he dare hope the lake was nothing but a product of his imagination?

Trying to shake off his desire, he rose and began preparing Samantha a tea that would help with the morning sickness. *I'm going to be a father!* As he added the herbs to the pot over the fire, he thought of his own father and vowed he'd be nothing like him. His child would know she was loved, and he'd never raise a hand against her.

* * *

Samantha awoke to find her maids hovering over her, glowing with colors that burned through to the back of her head. She shut her eyes. "Go away!" she groaned. She needed peace so she could concentrate on shielding.

"But Your Highness, Sir Robrek said we were to be giving you this tea the moment you woke," Ardra protested.

As the colors pushed through her closed eyelids, the princess felt nausea rising. "Leave the tea and go!" she commanded.

She heard the clink of a teacup on the table next to her bed. "Make sure you be drinking that," Ardra said. "I didn't be saving you from His Evil Dukeship to be having you die of some disease."

Her maids left, and a vast weight of misery pressed down on her. She picked up the cup and sipped the hot brew. It tasted awful, but almost immediately her nausea went away. *Please, Holy Sulis, don't let me be pregnant! How will the court react to a pregnancy before the formal marriage?* They wouldn't know she and Robbie had been handfasted, and even if she did announce it, they wouldn't care—handfasting was a custom only among the peasants. As well as being a personal inconvenience, was this pregnancy a threat to her crown and the joined kingdoms? She wished there was someone she could ask, but she couldn't tell Caedmon.

She put her hand on her belly and considered having Robbie make her miscarry. But as she thought of the life stirring within, she knew she couldn't do it. Somehow, she'd make it through this, as she'd made it through the loss of her two fathers.

For now, she needed to shield. She repeated the process Robbie had shown her yesterday. It took awhile, but eventually, her shields snapped into place.

A timid knock came at the door, and Ardra said, "Your Highness, Blaine is about to go into hysterics. Should I tell him to go jump in the ocean to cool himself off?"

She wished she could, but a queen didn't have the time to indulge herself. She called out that she was ready to dress. When her maids entered the room, she apologized, "I'm sorry I snapped. I haven't been feeling well."

"It's okay, Your Highness," Malvina said. "Did Sir Robrek be knowing what ails you?"

"Yes." Samantha felt the blood rising in her face.

"Oh!" Ardra smiled and nodded knowingly.

"What do you be 'ohing' about?" Malvina asked.

"Don't be thick, sweet cakes," Ardra chided. "Her Highness be feeling sick in the morning times."

"She was sick in the afternoon yesterday as well. She stayed sick until Sir Robrek came."

Ardra rolled her eyes. "And hasn't Sir Robrek been here a lot lately." Ardra nudged and winked at Malvina.

"Yes, but—" A look of startled comprehension came over Malvina's face. "Oh, you don't be saying. . . Her Highness is not . . . You aren't, are you, Your Highness? Sir Robrek said the tea would be stopping such things."

"It didn't work." The princess turned away from her maids and looked at the picture of the Princess Danu that dominated the wall of her bedroom and the suitors she'd turned to toads hopping about her feet. Danu never had problems like this.

Then again, Danu never had a man like Robbie in her bed.

* * *

Blaine entered to find the princess looking not at all ill, which was good, because things were piling up. "Your Highness, you look like a lark at the break of day, so to speak. Are you better?"

"Yes, Sir Robrek has taken care of the problem."

Blaine smiled widely; the healer had proven himself useful yet again. "Well, that's certainly good news. The next thing we must discuss is the entertainment."

A knock came on her door, and Sir Robrek entered. Blaine threw up his hands. Sir Robrek was supposed to be being fitted, and his seamstress was desperately behind schedule. Was Blaine the only one who cared about such things? He wondered how he could broach the subject delicately. "Milord, isn't there something you're supposed to be doing? I mean . . . I wouldn't presume . . ." Blaine paused. Sir Robrek looked like he'd spent the night fighting monsters. "Are you all right?"

Sir Robrek shook himself. "I'm fine. I promise I'll go straight back to Bedelia," he said, which was a relief. "I just wanted to check on Her Highness." Sir Robrek touched the princess on the shoulder. Blaine supposed it was sweet, but he drummed his fingers on the papers he was holding, hoping the princess and Sir Robrek would get the message that more important matters were at issue here than sweetness. "How are you feeling, Sam? Did the tea I made you help?"

"Yes," the princess said. "Are you sure you're all right?"

Sir Robrek nodded. "Call me if you have any more problems." He kissed her and left the room.

Blaine finally had the princess's attention for ten whole minutes before

Captain Hawk arrived.

* * *

Samantha told Blaine to show Hawk in. The captain of the Royal Guard had bags under his eyes, his hair was disheveled, and he looked to be in danger of vomiting. Specks of what looked like blood dotted his uniform.

"They won't speak, Your Highness," Captain Hawk reported, his voice hoarse as if from yelling. "I'm beginning to wonder if somehow they weren't involved. Money doesn't buy this level of loyalty."

Samantha put her hand to her stomach, and she felt faint. *Just what did I permit Hawk to do to the men? Holy Sulis, now I can know if they're telling the truth.* "Take me to the prisoners," she commanded.

* * *

Samantha stared at the two men hanging by their wrists from the torture chamber wall. They were naked, and their backs were ripped to ribbons, blood pooling at their feet. A hot brand lay in a fire nearby, and the scent of roasted flesh told her it had been used. Their fingers were bent into odd positions. One of them had a bone protruding from his leg. Her stomach heaved at the sight.

Turning away, she took a moment to lower her shields. The auras of all the men in the room pulsed against her eyes, causing her to wince, but she needed to know the truth.

Hawk brandished the bloody whip. "Who paid you to help the prisoner escape?" he asked for probably the hundredth time.

"Tell me what you want me to say, and I'll say it," one of them cried out.

"What I want is the truth." Samantha moved into the man's line of sight. "Did you help Boyden Angusstamm escape?"

"Your Highness, I swear I didn't." To her horror, his aura glowed white.

"We didn't, Your Highness," the other protested. "He just disappeared." He, too, glowed white. *Holy Sulis, they are innocent.* She shut her eyes and tried to raise her shields, but her horror and shame at what she'd done made the necessary concentration impossible.

"Release them," she said to Hawk. "And send a page for my betrothed." At least Robbie's skills would assure they wouldn't be permanently maimed.

Hawk gave a sigh of relief and ordered the men to be carried to cots in a nearby cell.

* * *

Robbie arrived out of breath, his face lined with concern. He touched Samantha's arm, and she felt the pleasant buzz of his magic. "Are you all right, Sam?"

Trembling and unable to speak, she nodded and pointed toward the cell. *What will he think of me?*

Robbie entered the cell that held the brutalized men. His face contorted, as if he were in great pain, and he clenched the bars as if to steady himself. "How did they sustain these injuries?"

"During interrogation, Milord," Hawk answered.

Robbie's head whipped toward Hawk, his eyes widening. "You did this? Why?"

Bile rose in Samantha's throat, and she wished she could deny responsibility. But the truth forced her to speak. "It was done on my orders." Robbie's eyes widened further, and Samantha had to look away. "I'll explain later. Can you heal them?"

Robbie looked back toward the torture victims—*her* victims. *How can I make it up to them? Will Robbie ever look at me the same again?*

"Yes," Robbie answered. He touched both men, who instantly lapsed into unconsciousness. She had to turn away as he straightened the bone in one of the guard's leg, pulling it back inside the damaged flesh.

* * *

Father Gildas sat at a table in a cheap inn with a half-full mug of ale in front of him. Soon his money would be gone. *How can the goddess have forgotten me after all I've done in her service?*

The door to the inn opened, and an old woman entered. Gildas shivered as she looked around the room with eerie, blank eyes. They fixed on him, and she crossed the room to his table. "You are Gildas," she stated. A strange accent made her words clipped and harsh.

"Who wants to know?" he stammered, unable to look into her eyes. There was something wild there, something evil.

"I am Alvabane, and we have much in common. May I join you?"

Not seeing what he could have in common with the strange woman, Gildas hesitated, but the woman sat without waiting for his permission. The innkeeper came over, and the old woman ordered a bottle of cheap wine. When the innkeeper brought it, she didn't offer to share.

"Tell me about the one you attempted to cleanse with fire."

Surprised by the question, Father Gildas snarled. "He's an abomination! A demon child born of an unholy union! The very soul of the joined kingdoms is at risk if he takes the throne."

Alvabane poured herself a glass of wine. "And what would you do to prevent this travesty?"

"Any true child of the goddess would give his very soul to prevent it."

Alvabane smiled. "If your hate is strong enough, for the small price of your soul, I can promise he will not reign."

Father Gildas leaned forward. "He has destroyed all that I hold holy. None hates him more than I."

"And what of your love? Who do you love?"

"None save the goddess is worthy of love." And he'd even begun to question that.

CHAPTER 13

Robrek came awake in his own bed. Apparently, he'd passed out after the healing and been carried to his rooms. The late afternoon sun found its way through the window. Ronan butted against his arm, and with a shaking hand, he petted the cat. Perhaps if he were a proper consort, torture wouldn't faze him. *How could Samantha have authorized that?*

He got up and headed to the practice arena to work off some of his disgust.

Two nobles sparred inside the arena. Both were shorter and slighter than average, and neither was better than adequate with a blade. One of them noticed him watching and motioned to the other. They stopped and bowed to him. "Care for a bout, Milord?" one of them asked with what appeared to be genuine friendliness. The other turned bright red. His friend's remark was probably improper. "I've heard you're quite good, so perhaps you wouldn't find either of us enough of a challenge."

"My weapons master taught me a different style of fighting than that typical of the Royal Guard. Perhaps we could learn from each other."

"Milord, we'd be. . ." the one who had blushed began. "I mean, Milord certainly has more pressing. . . I mean, we aren't. . . I mean, we'd love—"

"Shut up, Feoras!" the first noble said. "Please forgive my friend's babbling. I am Lord Edan. I believe you know my sister, Lady

Aislinn, and the babbler is Lord—no, it's Count now—Feoras. If Your Lordship wishes, I'd be most honored to go a round with you."

Why not? It will keep my mind off Samantha. Robrek picked up a practice sword, and Feoras withdrew to the edge of the sparring area. As they fenced, Edan frequently stopped Robrek to ask how he performed a particular move. At one point, Feoras exclaimed from the sidelines, "You avoid the blow if you can, rather than counter it. You don't have to parry as much. You simply aren't there."

Robrek pressed an attack. "It's a style well suited to one who is usually smaller than his opponents."

Edan parried. "I knew size couldn't be everything. It's what the ladies keep telling me." Robrek didn't know whether to laugh or blush. But he found himself liking Edan. After awhile, Feoras took Edan's place. He was less skilled, but very eager to learn. Given Feoras's size and timidity, Robrek would have bet Feoras had often been the victim of bullying.

After awhile, Edan called from the sidelines, "You could take both of us at once. Except for Captain Darhour, you're the best I've ever seen."

Robrek shrugged, knowing it was true but not wanting to sound arrogant. "Shall we see?"

With both of them against him, Robrek had to use more of his skills, and the match became fun. He whirled and struck, avoiding their blows and "killing" the two men repeatedly. But he got overconfident and left his right side open as he attacked Edan. Feoras took advantage of the opening and struck him in the ribs. "I scored one!" he shouted. "I scored one! Did you see that, Edan! I got him!"

Robrek stopped, panting and rubbing his side. "Good one," Robrek acknowledged.

"You just got lucky," Edan slammed his practice sword back into the rack.

"I didn't see you getting lucky," Feoras said. He turned back to Robrek and bowed. "Thanks for the lesson, Milord. I'm beat. Will you come and have a drink with us?" Immediately, he turned bright red. "I'm sorry, Milord. I forgot my place. I mean, I'm sure. . . It's just that. . . "

Robrek hesitated. He'd been invited to a musical reception tonight given by Duke Tierney. Although Samantha had told him she wouldn't attend herself, she expected him to go so he could win the nobles' goodwill. Feoras and Edan weren't as important as Duke Tierney. But except for Samantha, these were the first people at court to treat him like a normal person.

And Samantha had just had two men tortured nearly to death.

That memory decided him. "I'd like that," he said. He grabbed his cloak and found a page to send his apology to the evening's entertainment, saying he had a headache and was retiring early.

"Milord." Eburacon stepped in front of him and spoke in a low voice. "Her Highness will certainly not approve of your exposing yourself like this."

No, Her Highness approves of breaking every bone in a man's hands. Robrek ignored him and joined the two young nobles, giving Eburacon and Geblan no choice but to follow.

* * *

The two nobles led Robrek to The Thirsty Knight—an inn not far from the palace. "Will this do, Milord?" Count Feoras asked.

Though Robrek knew nothing about the place, he nodded. Eburacon insisted on leading the way inside, leaving Geblan with Robrek and the two lords. When Robrek came in, all noise in the tavern stopped, and the patrons got to their feet and bowed. The innkeeper hurried forward. "Milord, I'm honored by your presence. How can I be of service?"

"We'd like a private room, a bottle of your best wine, and whatever the special is for tonight," Count Feoras answered. "That is, if that meets Your Lordship's approval."

Robrek nodded. "That and an urn of *bhat*, please."

"Of course, Milords. Right this way, Milords." The tavern keeper led them toward a room with a table and large comfortable chairs. After a moment's hesitation, Robrek sat at the head of the table, and Count Feoras and Lord Edan took the seats on either side of him. Eburacon and Geblan stood behind him.

Edan grinned at Feoras. "Remember how long we had to wait last time to get a table? I could get used to this."

There was a knock on the door, and Geblan opened it to admit a serving girl carrying a tray laden with wine, food, and *bhat*.

"Bree!" Robrek called out in surprise.

She smiled and bowed, setting the tray on the table. "I'm honored Milord remembers me. I wasn't sure you would after all this time. I see you're wearing the ribbon in your hair now instead of underneath your shirt."

To Robrek's embarrassment, he found himself blushing at the mention of the ribbon Samantha had given him on the day they'd first met. Bree had found it around his neck when she'd bathed him at the Silk Curtain on his first day in the capital. At the time, he'd been unconscious from healing a horse.

"So you've met this pretty lass, Milord," Edan said, giving Bree a slap on the rump and winking.

Robrek abruptly put down the mug of *bhat* he'd been about to drink. Bree smiled down at Edan, but Robrek didn't need to lower his shields to feel her discomfort.

Edan seemed to misinterpret Robrek's expression. "Sir Robrek, there's no need to feel embarrassed about having fulfilled your natural urges with a sweet thing like this." Edan pulled Bree down on his lap.

Bree tried to push herself away. "Let her go," Robrek commanded in the manner he'd so often witnessed Samantha use, and like Samantha, he was instantly obeyed.

"I'm sorry, Milord," Edan said, allowing Bree to escape. "I didn't realize she was yours. I meant no offense."

"She isn't mine. She's her own. Touch her only if she invites it."

Edan picked up his goblet of wine and took a quick gulp. "Again, I'm sorry, Milord," he stammered. Bree finished serving and hurried from the room.

Feoras shifted uncomfortably in his seat. "You must forgive Lord Edan, Milord. He acts before he thinks, but he really isn't a bad sort. He stood up for me to the other boys when I first came to court. Protected me from more than one beating. He'd make some obnoxious comment, and they'd decide to go after him instead."

Edan cleared his throat. "Like you said, I act before I think, and I can run faster than you. They never could catch me. Still, I don't know why I didn't let them pound your snotty nose into the dirt. I don't know what I hoped to gain from the second son of a mere count." Edan's eyes brightened. "But now that *you've* become a count, maybe I can come up with some way to remind you what you owe me." They both laughed, and Robrek found himself joining them. It was hard not to like Edan when he spoke with such unabashed bluntness.

"Is she a whore?" Robrek asked, hoping Bree hadn't sunk to that level. She had worked at a higher class inn where she hadn't had to put up with such behavior.

Edan scratched his head, then comprehension dawned. "Oh, the pretty lass! Whore, server, there's little difference at the Thirsty Knight. They have rooms upstairs if you want her."

"I most certainly do not. I have the only woman I could ever desire." At least, he thought he did. *Surely, she had a good reason for ordering torture. But is any reason good enough?*

"Her Highness is that good, is she?" Edan winked.

"Edan, you are talking about your liege!" Feoras objected. "Show some delicacy, for Sulis's sake!"

Edan, turning a brilliant shade of red, picked up his wine and took a quick drink. "I'm sorry, Milord. I often talk before I think, too. Caused my father to toss me out when I was fourteen, which I found better than the beatings he usually gave me for mouthing off. Still, it was fortunate my sister Aislinn could get me into the Royal Guard, or I don't know what would have happened to me."

"Nobles beat their children?" Robrek asked.

"Holy Sulis, did mine ever. Nearly lamed me a time or two. And my older brothers! How do you think I learned to run so fast? Had to outrun those two, or I'd have ended up at the bottom of some canyon." Edan paused and took a sip of wine. "You see, I'm the third son, and my father's nearly bankrupted himself. Bairre thought there might be more left to inherit if there were fewer of us, and I think Eber still might be planning to knock Bairre off when the time is right and get it all. I'm well shut of the lot, I tell you." He paused and emptied his wine goblet in one gulp.

"Your father and brothers seem a lot like mine." Robrek picked up his mug of *bhat*. "Here's to short men and all the fathers, brothers, and bullies we've left behind."

"Hear, hear!" Feoras touched his wine goblet to the mug.

"May they rot in the seven hells!" Edan grinned, as he refilled his goblet and did the same.

The two men emptied their goblets, and Feoras moved to refill them. Edan picked up his and studied the liquid inside. "The wine's really quite good, Milord. Did Her Highness warn you not to come home drunk? Although it's never affected me that way, I hear wine can cause some to have problems meeting the demands of a woman." Edan winked at him.

Robrek laughed. "No, it's just that healers can't tolerate alcohol. Our bodies are too sensitive to its effects."

Lord Edan put down his goblet. "Really? I never knew that, but, of course, I've spent little time hanging around priests. You mean to say you've never had any alcohol? Not even once in your entire life?"

Robrek felt himself reddening. "I was stupid enough to indulge twice, and it's not an experience I'd like to repeat."

Edan laughed. "That's what I said the first time I indulged. I remember it like it was yesterday. Or rather I don't remember it. I was fourteen at the time, and I can remember nothing between the time my brother gave me the first mug and the morning where I woke up naked in a haystack with one killer of a headache. I never did find out what happened to my clothes. What about you, Milord? Is your story worse than that?"

"Depends on what you mean by worse. I never lost my clothes."

"Come on, Sir Robrek," Feoras urged. "Tell us, or Edan will be telling his stories all night, and I've already heard them all."

"Well, I was. . . To tell the truth, I was longing for Her Highness. It was after the second time we met. I didn't even know who she was then. I thought I'd feel better if I got drunk."

Edan shook his head. "Women! They'll drive any man to drink."

"Shh, Edan! Let him talk."

"I went to the village inn." As he told of his two mugs of ale and the card game, the two noblemen laughed riotously.

"You had a full house, Milord," Edan said, trying to catch his breath. "I'd have loved to have seen the arrogant bastard's face when you showed your cards. I bet it was a sight." Feoras nodded in eager agreement.

Robrek was surprised at how fully the two men were on his side. "I couldn't say, really. I wasn't seeing very straight at the time." The two men laughed again. They stopped laughing when he told how the three men had taken him out back. "They would've hurt me pretty badly if my Horsetad hadn't driven them off."

"Bastards! We should give them a lesson." Edan patted his sword. "But you, my friend, passed out from two mugs of ale? I guess it shall remain *bhat* for you. I'd hate to have to carry you back to the palace. It might look rather bad."

Feoras nodded. "I doubt Her Highness would be terribly pleased with us." Count Feoras turned to him with a suddenly serious expression. "Please tell Her Highness I won't forget her mercy. She is a queen more than worthy of loyalty."

Robrek pursed his lips. "I'd be happy to convey your regard to Her Highness," he said tonelessly.

* * *

Samantha kept herself busy throughout the day, knowing she was doing it to avoid Robbie's recriminations over the tortured men. But when evening came, she decided she needed to face the inevitable.

When she reached Duke Tierney's reception, the nobles were just finishing off a rather delicious looking cake. Too bad she had no appetite.

Talk ceased, and everyone rose to greet her. Tierney smiled. "Welcome, Your Highness. It's so good of you to join us. We were disappointed your betrothed's headache prevented his attending."

Samantha barely maintained her court mask. *Healers don't get headaches!* "Yes, I know he looked forward to hearing the bard you arranged for this evening. His disappointment was such I decided to come myself. If the bard lives up to your description, we may arrange another opportunity for Sir Robrek to hear him."

"Of course, Your Highness, and I do not believe you will be disappointed. The bard is one of the few female bards in the joined kingdoms. She has written the best rendition of your betrothed's feats I have yet to hear. May I offer you some cake or brandy?"

Samantha refused the cake, but accepted the brandy, despite it being a bad idea on an empty stomach. When she was settled, Tierney signaled for the bard to enter. "Your Highness, may I present Eolande of the Ten Thousand Songs." A woman came forward Her dress was made of a fabric that rippled and wavered from blue to green like the ocean on a sunny day. Samantha could almost hear the sound of the waves. The dress was covered with artfully made cuts that flashed dazzling colors—vibrant purple, blood red, vivid yellow, and luminous orange. To her back, she had attached wings of the same brilliant colors, and on her head, she wore a cone-shaped hat of the same blue-green of her dress; trailing from it were streamers of purple and red. Surely no other woman could have dressed that way without looking ridiculous, but the outfit's outlandishness seemed to suit Eolande.

Samantha tore her eyes away from the woman's dress. She had more important matters to consider. She motioned to Crevan, one of her guards. "Find him immediately," she whispered. Crevan slipped off to summon a page.

* * *

When Robrek returned to his rooms late that night, he found Samantha waiting for him. She sat in one of his chairs, her arms crossed. "Where have you been?"

Robrek stiffened at her tone; she sounded just like his father, chiding him for some imagined fault. "Out," he snapped. He took off his cloak and threw it over a chair. He wasn't the one who reduced men to so much meat.

She stood. "The guards at the palace gates reported seeing you leave in the company of Count Feoras and Lord Edan. You went drinking with them, didn't you?"

"If you knew where I was, why did you bother asking?" he asked with pretended indifference.

She stormed across the room. "Robbie, what were you thinking?"

"You told me to make friends with the nobles. That's exactly what I was doing."

She put her hands on her hips. "I told you to earn their respect. Royalty don't have 'friends.' And going out drinking with two minor members of the court earns nobody's respect."

"Would the court respect me more if I broke every finger in a man's hand and lashed his back to ribbons? I'm sorry, Your Highness"—somehow he couldn't call her Sam—"but I heal things, not destroy them."

Samantha clutched at her stomach as if he'd kicked her in the gut. His daughter lay there, the daughter she was unhappy about bearing. "You have no idea why I thought it was necessary."

He turned away from her. "Why don't you enlighten me?"

"Your brother has escaped. It can mean no good for you."

He rounded on her. "Don't say you did it to protect me! I'd risk the danger of my brother a thousand times over before I'd do something like that. Do you have any idea how much pain those men were in?"

"How was I supposed to know they were innocent? How could your brother have gotten past the guards—by magic?" she sneered. "You said he doesn't have magic! So who could have gotten him out? Don't you see—I had to know? It's a danger to my throne, too." She waved the matter away impatiently. "Enough of this! *My* actions aren't the issue here!"

"Of course not!"

But she continued to speak over him. "Did you never think Tierney might find out where you were? What if he's offended by your stunt?"

Robrek blinked; he hadn't thought of that. But he wasn't about to admit he'd been irresponsible. He'd had fun. He would never have had fun with all those stuffy nobles looking down their noses at him. "I needed to get away. Sulis curse it, Sam! I've never seen that much damage to any one man, let alone two of them."

"Damn it, Robbie! You can't go hurrying off whenever you disapprove of my actions! You acted like a. . . like a. . ."

"Like a peasant. That's what I am, you know. I didn't ask to be king. Those horses just showed up." *Holy Sulis! Why can't I just be a healer? Why do I have to deal with all this other crap? Why are these stupid death tapestries still all over my rooms?* "Maybe Caedmon's right. Maybe I should just go back where I belong."

Samantha came forward and jabbed a finger at his chest. "Maybe you should. I need a man to rule beside me, not a boy."

"Boy." His father always called him that. "So you want me to prove my manhood?" Robrek snapped. "I suppose real men break others' jaws and yank their arms out of their sockets. Should I be proving my manhood to the women as well?"

Samantha's eyes narrowed. "What are you talking about?"

"Lady Briallen has been shoving her breasts in my face, and they are rather large ones." He glanced down at her smaller ones. "Her brother assures me Count Guto would have no objection to her becoming my mistress."

Samantha clenched her fists. "Damn you! I thought you loved me! I thought you'd at least try to understand things from my perspective!" Samantha's expression turned cold, that inhuman mask he'd seen her put on, but never before with him. "I'll instruct your guards to keep you within the palace, but I'll tell them to give you free access to any woman with large breasts." She whirled from the room, slamming the door in his face.

"Damn it!" He hit the door jamb with his fist. "Why did I say that?" Part of him wanted to run after her, but a bigger part still couldn't forgive what she'd done to those men.

* * *

Eolande sat alone at a table in the Pied Piper, trying to figure out where she'd gone wrong. She fingered her lute. *"The Ballad of Gloine Torr" is my best work. I know it is. It has romance. It has adventure. Sir Robrek comes across as heroically as any man could wish himself to be. Sulis curse him! If only he'd shown up to hear the damned thing!*

The door opened, and Eolande groaned as Chionney and Cliar walked in. Her fellow bards were the last people she wanted to see at the moment.

"Well, if it isn't Eolande of the Ten Thousand Songs," Chionney said, giving her a mocking bow. "Performer for kings and future kings." They sat across from her. "So tell us, Mistress Eolande, did the king swoon with pleasure at the sound of thy dulcet tones? Did he get down on his knees and beg to give thee patronage?"

They'd hear it from someone; it might as well be her. "He didn't show. He excused himself because of a headache."

Both Chionney and Cliar burst out laughing. "He just didn't want to hear you."

That was exactly what Eolande was afraid of. "The princess said he was longing to hear me and most disappointed to miss out."

"Sure he was," Chionney said. "And I'd be 'most disappointed' if I missed my own execution."

"Why would the princess lie?" she asked. *Because she didn't have a clue where he was herself.* Eolande knew the look of a woman whose man wasn't where he was supposed to be.

"Still, performing for Her Highness isn't at all bad," Cliar said. "What did she think of the ballad?"

"She was most appreciative."

"Most appreciative!" Chionney laughed, and he and Cliar exchanged a glance.

Eolande bit her lip. "If you want to know the truth, I don't think she was listening. She obviously expected Sir Robrek to be there and was furious he wasn't." Eolande had the magic that allowed her to make her audience feel the emotions of her songs, making her a Bard in the true sense of the word. She had used her talent to the best of her ability. But it hadn't been enough to influence the crown princess.

Cliar reached across and patted her arm. "Tough luck, Landy." He knew she hated that nickname. "Maybe you'll get another chance at the royal wedding."

More than she'd ever admit, Eolande hoped so. The wandering life of a bard had suited her well in her adolescence and early twenties, but now as she neared thirty, she feared for the future. She wanted some place she could settle, some income she could count on. Patronage was hard to come by for a female bard because prospective patrons wanted her services in the bedroom as well as the banquet hall. She might be the daughter of a whore, but she refused to become one herself. It was said that Sir Robrek would marry out of love, and so she thought he'd be the perfect patron, but his absence tonight made her wonder if he was just like every other bastard noble she'd met.

"It is a good piece," Cliar admitted, referring to "The Ballad of Gloine Torr." "You practically make Sir Robrek into Armunn." Armunn was the greatest hero of Korthlundian legend. Some thousand years previously he had saved Korth from a race of demons who'd inhabited Lundia and driven them into the desert. "You have everything but the swearing of the swords."

"Hey, maybe you should put that in," Chionney observed.

Eolande leveled a glare at her fellow bards. "Sir Robrek would never do that, and Her Highness would be none too pleased if he did. You know how angry Armunn's king was said to have been. Nearly had him executed, if the legends are true."

Cliar nodded. "Made their loyalty to Armunn come before their loyalty to the king. But Her Highness is said to be deeply in love. Surely she wouldn't execute Sir Robrek."

"She might execute *me* for singing of such things."

* * *

Boyden waited until the tongueless girl had put down his meal and grabbed her wrist. She wasn't pretty, and she had tits barely bigger than a child's, but Boyden had gone without long enough.

The girl tried to pull away, but he knew how to handle an unwilling bitch. He slapped her hard, dragged her across the room, and threw her onto the bed. He climbed on top of her and pinned both her hands above her head in one of his. "Lie still, you slut." He used the other hand to slap her half a dozen more times. He used his knee to spread her legs apart and stuck his free hand down the front of her dress, grabbing and pinching her nipples.

The bitch cried and made whimpering noises. They were even more exciting than the pleas of others he'd forced himself on.

* * *

Alvabane entered the house and went to her altar. She heard the rhythmic creaking of the bed from the room of the sorcerer's brother. That noise could mean only one thing. She rushed to the room and flung open the door. The peasant was rutting like a swine between her servant's thighs. "How dare you!"

"Get out!" the peasant shouted, not pausing in his rhythm.

Alvabane had felt filthy hands on her breasts and a man's hard thing pounding inside of her. But as she started to sing him to sleep, she felt the dark gods' pleasure. The girl's pain and fear were sweet incense to the gods; they reveled in it. She closed the door and went to kneel at her altar. She closed her eyes and focused on the fear, rage, hatred, and pain coming from the other side of the door. She'd been thinking too small; these were precious gifts to be savored.

Sometime later, the noise from the room stopped, and the chambermaid stumbled out. Her dress was torn, and she bled from a cut to her lip. She ran from the room, and Alvabane didn't try to stop her. The girl had nowhere to go.

Alvabane turned, and the peasant was standing in the doorway. "Keeping me chained to a bed, what did you expect?" He smiled.

"The gods are pleased, so how can I object?" She smiled despite her anger.

The peasant threw back his head and laughed. "I think I like these gods of yours. Tell them I'd be happy to entertain them anytime."

CHAPTER 14

Robrek tore off his clothing as the women beckoned him. Despite knowing what lay hidden behind their beautiful façade, he ached with desire.

"No! This you cannot do!" yelled the shadowy figure of a man, rising from the middle of the lake. "Don't let them take you as they have taken me!"

"Who are you?" Robrek asked, but the figure answered only with a shriek of pain.

Robrek awoke clutching his pillow tightly in both hands. *Holy Sulis, what does it mean?* The beautiful women hid an ugly truth. Wasn't that also true of Samantha? He couldn't shake the image of the tortured men and wondered if there was any connection between them and the dream. *Just what am I getting into?* He needed advice, and he knew of only one person who could help him.

He dressed without Drem's help, but the servant stood there watching with a disapproving frown. Apparently asking him to go away wouldn't be proper. Robrek looked at the tapestries and paintings of battle and the hunt that still lined the walls. "I thought I asked you to replace these."

"Yes, Milord. I still haven't found any fit for Your Lordship's status."

"Any with living things in them will do."

Drem nodded, but Robrek realized Drem probably wouldn't do a thing about the tapestries. Apparently, these were the ones *he* thought proper, and he no doubt figured if he left them long enough, they'd grow on Robrek.

Robrek grabbed his cloak and headed for the door. When he exited his rooms, Eburacon and Geblan bowed to him. "Where are you going, Milord?" Eburacon asked. "Her Highness has ordered you to stay in the palace unless she says otherwise."

And she says I need to act like a man? Real men don't let people imprison them in their own rooms! "I know what Her Highness has ordered. If you'd rather stay and explain to Her Highness how I got past you, it's fine by me. I never thought I needed guards anyway."

Eburacon stood in his way. "We have our orders."

Leaving would probably only make Samantha angrier, but he had to talk to his uncle. He reached with his mind, paralyzing Eburacon. He stepped around him, then released the guard. "Don't try that again, or I'll put you to sleep. Now do you want to come with me or not?"

Geblan glanced at Eburacon uncertainly. "Hadn't we better go with him?"

Eburacon nodded curtly, and Robrek started down the corridor, his guards following.

* * *

"You're sure of this," Samantha asked her spymaster. *No, don't let it be true! Robbie wouldn't do that!* Robbie hadn't sent her any tea that morning, and she'd vomited repeatedly. But she wasn't about to call for him, especially now.

"I personally witnessed Lady Briallen enter Sir Robrek's rooms," Righ said. "Two hours later, she left, looking somewhat disheveled."

Caedmon clicked his tongue sympathetically. "I know you don't want to believe it, Your Highness, but you've only known the boy for a short time, and I did inform you of those rumors."

To hide her tears, she went to her window. *I thought you were different from the rest, Robbie. I thought you loved me.* "I never expected to marry for love. My father taught me that."

"But Your Highness, after this, surely you can't still plan on marrying the boy."

It's a little late to change my mind. But she wasn't about to tell Caedmon about the pregnancy. "I don't have a choice!" she cried. "Sulis has chosen him." She couldn't see through the blur of her tears.

"Samantha, my dear, isn't it time you gave up that absurd belief?"

"I won't hear it, Caedmon! Leave me!"

"Of course, Your Highness. You've suffered a nasty shock. We'll discuss it later."

After Caedmon and Righ left, Samantha collapsed onto her window seat. She wept until her face was raw and her throat hurt. Then she washed her face and put on a court mask. She'd never let him know how much he'd hurt her.

* * *

When Robrek reached the Traveler's Haven, Eburacon insisted on preceding him inside. When he himself entered, the patrons stood and gave a cheer. "Long live the consort!" they yelled, and Robrek felt instantly at home as he looked over a sea of faces ranging from pale yellows through the darkest of blacks, but none with the pale Korthlundian whiteness. These people accepted him without fear or awe. Most of them had known his uncle and grandfather.

The innkeeper, Chiamaka, hurried forward. "Welcome, welcome, Sir Robrek. It's so good to see you again." He turned to a boy. "Hurry, tell Master Slathek his nephew is here." He turned back toward Robrek. "Come this way, Milord, to my finest table."

Trailed by his bodyguards, Robrek followed the innkeeper to a quiet table in the back of the inn. All along the way, men and women greeted him; some pounded him on the back. With their hands on their swords, his guards glared at the crowd that was getting too close to Robrek for their comfort.

Robrek sat down at the table, and Chiamaka hovered over him. "I'll get you an urn of *bhat* right away, Milord. Would you care for anything else? The specials today are lamb with curry and Chicken Trkari, a dish of your homeland." In other words, it was a Mahngbhayon dish, the homeland of his mother. The Traveler's Haven served cuisine reflective of the many different peoples who frequented it, dishes found nowhere else in Murtaghan.

"I'll have some Chicken Trkari," he told the innkeeper.

Chiamaka beamed. "At once, Milord."

Chiamaka had scarcely left when Slathek entered the room followed by two well-armed Korthlundians. Robrek stood to greet his uncle, but before Slathek could reach him, Robrek's guards stepped in front of him with their hands on their swords.

Slathek stopped abruptly. "What is the meaning of this?"

"Eburacon, he's my uncle."

Eburacon nodded. "Yes, but who are they?" He gestured toward the Korthlundians following Slathek. The two young men also had their hands on their swords.

Slathek looked behind him and seemed embarrassed to see the men there. "Oh, them. They're, well, they're merely the guards I've hired."

Eburacon narrowed his eyes. "You may approach His Lordship, but they will keep their distance."

"Yes, of course, you can't be too cautious with the princess's betrothed." Slathek grinned. He turned to his guards and waved them away. They moved to the far side of the inn's dining room, and Robrek's guards moved aside and allowed Slathek to approach.

Slathek grasped him by the shoulders and gave him a kiss on each cheek. They sat at the table.

"You have bodyguards now?" Robrek asked.

Slathek rolled his eyes. "It's rather a pain, but I had to employ them to keep Chiamaka happy."

"You never did know what was good for you." Chiamaka appeared and set the *bhat* and food down on the table. "I brought you some Wobra bread as well. It goes well with the Chicken Trkari."

Robrek thanked the innkeeper and turned back to his uncle. "And why does Chiamaka think you need protection?"

"I'm sure he's merely being a mother hen. But I did want to mention his fears to you, though there was no need for you to come to me. It would have been far more proper to have me summoned to the palace."

"I'm sick of proper." Robrek stabbed the chicken with his fork.

Slathek raised an eyebrow. "Is something wrong, kinsman?"

"Samantha and I had a fight." Robrek told his uncle everything that had happened between them, but couldn't bring up the dreams. Just having such dreams made him feel soiled. "I don't know what to do. You should have seen the injuries those men sustained."

"It isn't easy to be a ruler and make that kind of decision. Do you still want to go through with the wedding?"

"How can I love a woman who would do something like that?"

"The question isn't how can you, but do you? Do you love her, my kinsman? What would you do if you were in her place and you thought someone threatened her?"

Robrek tossed his fork onto the plate. "Boyden's no threat."

"That's not the point. I daresay you'd do whatever you thought necessary. Love tends to . . . cloud our judgments on such occasions."

Robrek put his head in his hands. *What would I do if something threatened Sam? And my daughter? How could I not protect her?* Still, he shivered at the memory of the tortured men. "But, Uncle, the men had been brutalized. If it weren't for my skills, they would have been permanently maimed."

Slathek cleared his throat and looked away. "I must admit I have no stomach for such things, especially after having been through a bout of torture myself. But you didn't answer the question. Do you love her?"

Robrek looked up. He couldn't imagine living without her. It would be far worse than amputating his right arm. "With all my heart and my soul."

"Then forgive her and move on. Kinsman, she's spent her entire life learning how to run a country. You've only been at it a very short time. She's also human and is bound to make mistakes. Is not the same true for you?"

"Yes," he admitted. "And I did say some hurtful things last night."

"Apologize. First, we will go to the flower sellers and buy the biggest, most gorgeous combination of flowers we can devise. Flowers are ridiculously expensive this time of year, but fortunately, you can afford it. Write a simple note, saying you're sorry. Everything will work out. You'll see."

"You'll have to leave your guards behind," Eburacon spoke up, startling Robrek. He'd forgotten his guards were there. Could he already be getting used to such things?

"Why did Chiamaka think you need guards anyway?" Robrek asked.

"I feel silly when I have nothing more to offer than vague rumors," Slathek said. "But rumors speak of a curse of some kind, causing death in Korth. Some of those who believe in this curse are blaming you for it."

Robrek paused, a forkful of food halfway to his mouth. "What curse? And what could I have to do with it? I've never even set foot in Korth."

Slathek laughed uneasily. "There's no sense behind it, clearly, but they're saying it's a punishment for Korth's support of you as the princess's consort. Chiamaka feared that because we resemble each other so strongly, some might take it out on me. Thus the guards."

Robrek ran his fingers through his hair in frustration. Why must he always be blamed for things that weren't his fault?

Robrek questioned Slathek further as he ate, but his uncle could give him no more information. He had a vague memory of Oriana saying something about a curse affecting her home village. He'd been so distracted he hadn't followed up on it. Maybe he'd better.

* * *

Mother Venetia leaned against the shrine in the village of Mor Fos. They'd had to fall back to escape the curse again. They were now twenty miles from Balley Beg, and nothing lay between it and Mor Fos but death.

The sound of weeping drew her around the corner. Awena knelt in the dirt. The priestess put her hand on the novice's shoulder. "What's wrong, my child?"

"Those people, the ones in Nios Mo who refused to leave? They'll die, won't they?"

"Yes, child. Nothing survives in the Dead Lands." The Dead Lands were what they had come to call the area affected by the curse, the lands where nothing—not even the vegetation—still lived.

"But we told them! Why wouldn't they go?"

Mother Venetia shook her head. "Sometimes the ways of others are hard to understand, but the goddess has given everyone their freedom to choose. We couldn't force them to leave."

Awena doubled over as if she'd been slugged. "Where will it stop? Will the curse keep growing until it consumes all the joined kingdoms?"

Venetia knelt down beside her. "Mother Bensaggyrt has an idea that might work. Mother Delwin and Mother Jenna are going into the Dead Lands, to Balley Beg. They are the strongest among us. Perhaps they can stop this thing at its source." *Armunn had, but just how strong had the legendary hero been? Did Delwin and Jenna have his power?* "They should reach the village in two days. The rest of us will perform the ritual of the new moon. Perhaps we can lend them our strength. In the meantime, we must evacuate Mor Fos in case they fail."

* * *

As Samantha sat on the throne, she dropped her shields, and the entire room burst into colors. She reeled under the onslaught and nearly vomited again, but there was nothing left in her stomach. Sweat beaded on her forehead, but she wasn't about to make another mistake in judgment. The one she'd already made about torturing innocent men had cost her the man she loved. With auras blazing in front of her, it was easy to tell who was lying. In under an hour, she dispatched the cases that would normally have taken her all afternoon.

As soon as possible, she escaped to the smaller reception room, hoping to relax enough to bring up her shields. To her chagrin, Caedmon followed. "Are you quite all right, Your Highness?"

"No, I'm not all right," she snapped. "I'm pregnant, and everyone's glowing like a Solstice bonfire." To her horror, when her gaze swept over her guards, she realized she had two of her new guards with her—Crevan and Findlay, and not Conroy and Bearach. Worse, Crevan's aura was crackling with black. She couldn't trust him. She'd been so distracted she'd made another unforgivable mistake.

Her face must have shown her horror because Crevan took one look at her and bolted for the door. "Stop him!" she commanded.

But Findlay hesitated. "I shouldn't leave Your Highness without protection. Captain Conroy would never approve."

"Now!" she snapped. "Before he gets away!"

Findlay jumped into action, but Crevan now had a head start.

"What has your guard to do with this irresponsible act of yours?" Caedmon asked. He was shaking with fury. *Damn it all! Why couldn't I have kept my mouth closed?*

But she'd opened it, and Caedmon needed to know about Crevan. She told him everything about the glowing colors and what she'd just seen on her guard. Caedmon glowed with blue, similar to the color that announced her guards' loyalty, but darker, murkier somehow. She was sure he was loyal to her, but something was wrong with his aura.

Caedmon's fists were clenched as if he wanted to hit her. She found herself taking a defensive stance. "This is nothing short of a disaster, Your Highness. You realize you have only one choice, don't you?"

"Kill him?" she asked, clutching at her stomach, which had chosen that moment to act up again. It was one thing to condemn a man to death for a treason he had committed and another for a treason he might commit. She had no evidence Crevan had acted against her, merely that he might, but he now knew a secret that could ruin her.

Findlay came back into the room. "He got away from me, Your Highness. But I've set the Guard looking for him. He shouldn't be able to get out of the palace."

"See that he doesn't." Caedmon growled, and nodded a dismissal to Findlay, but the guard ignored it and took a step closer to the princess.

Caedmon's eyes glowed with so much anger that the last thing she wanted was to talk to him alone. What good could come from such a conversation? He'd want her to end the pregnancy, but despite Robbie's betrayal, that was something she wasn't going to do.

Caedmon glared at Findlay, but Findlay didn't so much as flinch. "Your Highness, we need to discuss the ramifications—" Caedmon said.

"No, we don't. What's done is done. Crevan will be caught, and that will be the end of it." She turned her back on Caedmon and swept out of the room.

* * *

Samantha struggled to read Robbie's atrocious handwriting. The note was simple. "I'm sorry, Sam. I love you." She picked up the vase and threw it against the wall, shattering it. How dare he apologize for Briallen and think everything would be okay? He'd ruined everything. He'd gotten her pregnant; then he hadn't had the decency to remain faithful. He'd ripped her only support and comfort out from under her, right when she needed it the most. *Damn him to the seven hells!*

Malvina informed her Robbie was without, asking to see her. She wanted to pick up the largest piece of glass and carve the heart out of his chest as he'd done to her. But she needed to get a few things straight between them.

As Robbie was ushered into her quarters, he gaped at the broken pieces of glass strewn amid the hothouse flowers. She covered her face in a court mask. She'd be as hard and cold as he thought she was. "From now on, if you have something to say to me, make an appointment with my secretary like everyone else."

Robbie's face fell; he had the audacity to look hurt. "Sam, I'm sorry. I don't agree with what you did, but I love you. We can work this out."

"You bastard! I did what I did to protect you and my throne! Thousands of lives weigh in the balance! How can you compare that with what you did merely for the pleasure of your bed?" She strode across the room and slapped his face hard.

Robbie's hand flew to his cheek. "What in the seven hells are you talking about?"

"I won't be played the fool! Briallen was seen entering your rooms last night and leaving two hours later!" Robbie's forehead creased as if she were speaking Saloynan. *How dare he pretend to be confused!*

"Holy Sulis, I wouldn't have Briallen in my room if she were the last woman alive in all of Korthlundia."

Samantha snorted. "My spymaster was perhaps having hallucinations?"

His face clouded with confusion again. "Righ told you Briallen came to my rooms?"

She snorted again. *How dare he look so innocent?*

He pressed his hand over his heart as if in pain. "Holy Sulis! How could he. . . ? Why would he. . . ? Sam, he's lying. I swear by the goddess and on my mother's grave that no one came to my room after you left last night. You can ask my guards. You're the only woman I've ever been with, and the only one I've ever wanted."

"Don't blaspheme!" she said, but Robbie had never lied to her before. "Why would Righ lie?"

Robbie ran his fingers through his hair. "I don't know, Sam. Look, it was stupid to say what I did about Briallen, but I was angry." He dropped his hand from his hair. "Sam, I would never do you wrong. I love you."

"I thought you did." To her fury, tears formed in her eyes. "My father told me to trust no one, and I made the mistake of trusting you."

Robbie grabbed her shoulder. "No! I won't have you believe this! Condemn me as a peasant! Damn me for being weak and unmanly! Hate me for my poor judgment! You have plenty of reasons for thinking you're mistaken about me being the goddess's choice, but I won't have you doubt my love or my faithfulness! What do I have to say? What can I do to convince you it is a lie?"

Samantha shook off his hand and went to her window seat. If Robbie wasn't lying, her spymaster was, and only one person could have put him up to it.

She had to know. She dropped her shields and turned to Robbie. His aura swirled with bronze, silver, and gold, as bright and clear as ever.

He was telling her the truth. "Caedmon hates you," she whispered.

Robbie grabbed her shoulders again. "He can hate me all he likes, but I didn't sleep with Briallen."

She threw her arms around him. "I love you, Robbie. Holy Sulis, I thought I lost you." His lips met hers, and she wanted nothing but to join with him.

But a knock on the door interrupted them. Bearach and Conroy tumbled inside. Robbie and she broke apart. "What is it?" she snapped.

"It's Crevan," Conroy reported. "He appears to have gotten away. What did he do, Your Highness?"

"He's a spy," Samantha said. "I just don't know whose." She told them about Crevan's aura.

Conroy didn't meet her eyes. "He was employed on my recommendation. The captain wouldn't have made such a mistake."

Samantha felt cold inside. "No, Darhour made a much bigger one. He left me. You two remained."

Conroy and Bearach shifted uncomfortably. Darhour was a hero in their eyes.

"What of Findlay?" Conroy asked.

"Findlay is loyal," she said. "I saw his aura, but I don't know about Guthrie and Hamish." Doubting Caedmon felt like a raw wound. She needed to confide in those she knew she could trust.

Samantha settled onto a sofa with Robbie beside her. She didn't want to let go of his hand. Not now. Not ever. She gestured at the seats across from her. "Have a seat."

Bearach and Conroy looked at each other and then sat. This kind of intimacy had been common during the crisis over Argblutal, but things with her guards had stood on a more formal basis since they'd retaken the palace.

"The first thing I need you to know is that I'm pregnant."

Bearach burst into a smile. "Your Highness, that's—" He trailed off and looked at his hands. "That's. . . that's a . . ."

"Disaster could be the word you're looking for." She smiled sadly. "It's too soon for me to have a child, but what's done is done, and it does have its advantages." She told them how it affected to her ability to see auras.

Conroy's face brightened. "So we can bring Guthrie and Hamish to you, and you can tell us if they're loyal?"

Samantha nodded. "After we speak, I'll train. Have them brought to me then. Sir Robrek's guards as well."

"Of course, Your Highness." Conroy looked like a vast weight had been taken off his shoulders.

"Who else knows about the pregnancy?" Bearach asked.

"Sir Robrek, of course. My maids and Duke Caedmon. I told him in a moment of weakness."

"Is His Grace a traitor, too?" Bearach asked, with his usual insight and lack of tact.

"I don't know." She told them what she'd seen in his aura and the lies about Robbie. "I'm sure he's loyal to me, but he may see an attack against Sir Robrek as an act of loyalty. His Grace doesn't trust my betrothed." She paused. "He may even be the one who started the rumors of a massacre in Valley Fair."

"The captain would have known," Conroy said.

"Yes, but he's not here, is he?" she snapped. "If I can't trust Righ, I need someone else to take on that role."

Again Bearach and Conroy exchanged a glance. Conroy said, "We're simple guards, Your Highness. Point us to the enemy, and we'll take care of it for you." A light came into Conroy's eyes. "There's an informant the captain used. His name is Lord Duer, a minor lord from west Lundia."

Samantha said, "Have him brought to me at once."

* * *

Alvabane watched the peasant rape on the altar of the dark gods the peasant woman she'd lured into the house with the promise of bread. Blood flowed from her mouth and her nose and dozens of small cuts. Alvabane had given the peasant the ceremonial knife with which to enhance the pain and fear of the act. When he was done, he would slit the woman's throat, and Alvabane stood ready to fill the bowls with her blood. Alvabane could feel the dark gods' revel in the pain and humiliation as much as they would in the blood.

She'd been weak before, refusing to give the dark gods what they craved. The peasant had taught her better. She would be weak no longer.

* * *

"You have something for me?" Father Faolan asked Crevan, his spy among Her Highness's guards.

Crevan dropped into the chair across the desk from him. "Yes, but it'll cost me my life, if I'm found."

"Whatever do you mean?"

"I have evidence you could use to bring down the princess."

Faolan relaxed back in his seat and steepled his fingers. "Go on."

"I need money to get out of town."

Faolan narrowed his eyes. Greed wasn't pleasing to Sulis, but if the information could bring down the crown, it would be well worth it. He opened a drawer in his desk, took out a purse, and threw it to Crevan. The princess's guard caught it, opened it, and looked inside.

He nodded in satisfaction. "Her Highness is pregnant."

Faolan sat up straighter. "Before the marriage has been solemnized?" Faolan drummed his fingers on his desk top; this he could certainly use.

"She also made a strange comment about everyone glowing like a 'Solstice bonfire,' and she looked at me like she knew exactly what I was up to."

"Her Highness sees auras? Damn her! Argblutal was right. She is a bastard!"

* * *

Blaine announced Lord Duer and, accompanied by Conroy and Bearach, one of the ugliest men the princess had ever seen entered the room. He looked to be in his forties. He was short for a Korthlundian and rather on the plump side. He was going bald but tried to disguise this fact by growing what little hair he had long on one side and then combing it over the top. He had a wide, flat nose, and a single eyebrow over both eyes. He went down on one knee before her in an overly dramatic bow. "Your Highness, how may I be of service?" he asked.

"I understand you were an informant for my former spymaster."

Duer chuckled. "Your Highness, I was much more than a mere informant. Captain Darhour would have been lost without my aid. May I tell you something about myself?"

Yuck! What arrogance! But his aura glowed light blue and white with none of Caedmon's murkiness. Duer would be loyal to her. She nodded, and he began his story.

He was a younger son with no hope of inheriting more than a pittance. His older brother, Count Guto, had inherited the title and the land. Duer seemed to have a rather low opinion of his brother. "He's loyal to the crown, mind you," Duer assured her. "His judgment is just lacking at times, especially in regards to his children." He didn't elaborate, but she thought of his willingness for BriaLen to be Robbie's mistress.

Duer's tale of his exploits was lengthy, filled with all kinds of irrelevant details aimed at showing himself in a heroic light. But he did have the experience she needed. Before spying for Darhour, he'd spent time in the service of the king of Neaseria, during which he'd uncovered a plot on that monarch's life. He'd worked in tandem with his valet, a man who had served him faithfully for over twenty years and was an expert at worming information out of servants. "Servants usually know more than nobles give them credit for," Duer concluded. Samantha felt a pang of sadness; Darhour had said much the same thing. "I assume you'll want to meet my valet. He's outside awaiting Your Highness's pleasure."

Gael was about as different from his master as possible. He looked to be in his mid-twenties. If Duer was telling the truth about how long Gael had served him, Gael had been a mere child when he had begun his work as a spy. He had thick golden hair, a neatly trimmed beard, and eyes as blue as the sky at midday. Apart from Robbie, he was the most gorgeous man Samantha had ever seen. Like his master, Gael went down on one knee before her. He glowed with an aura identical to his master's. "At your service, Your Highness."

"And how have you assisted your master?" Samantha asked, after he rose to his feet.

"Your Highness undoubtedly knows what gossips servants are. I'm especially good at getting the females to *bare* all their masters' and mistresses' secrets," he said with a wink. He gave examples of the manner in which his information had been of assistance to his master, chuckling at the way the stupid women betrayed secrets. Despite his looks, Samantha liked him even less than Duer. She wanted to throw the pair of them not only out of her presence, but out of the palace itself. But despite how personally distasteful they might be, she knew she could trust them both.

"I'm satisfied as to your capabilities. You will begin at once."

Duer bowed again. "You have merely to command, Your Highness."

"The number of those whose loyalty is beyond question is low— these two guards, my betrothed, my secretary, and my maids. Everyone else is suspect, and no one else is to know you're working for me." She confided in them her concerns about Duke Caedmon and his spy. "Blaine will arrange for your allowance, and you'll let him know of any resources you need."

Duer bowed. "We will justify the faith Your Highness has shown in us."

* * *

In the practice arena, several members of the Royal Guard were training. They stopped and bowed to Samantha as she entered. She instructed them to resume. She picked up two practice swords—one she tossed to Hamish, the other she kept for herself. She got into a ready stance. "Shall we dance?" she asked.

Hamish grinned. "If Your Highness wills it."

She went in for a quick attack to probe his defenses. He batted her blade aside easily. They fought around the room, neither one able to get an advantage. She saw an opening and thought she had him, but she lost control of her shields, and the entire room burst into colors. The distraction allowed Hamish to take her in the side. He didn't pull his blow well, and the force of it knocked her sideways. Losing the bout didn't upset her—she'd never beaten any of her guards—but his aura did. He didn't have the black of Crevan, but a rich purple that shone of gold and gems. He could be bought. She glanced at Guthrie, and he shone with pure blue and white. She glanced around the room at the guards training, and two of the others glowed with the colors that announced their absolute loyalty.

She called to them. They lowered their weapons and approached bowing. "How may we serve you, Your Highness?" one of them asked.

"What are your names?" she asked.

"I'm Marcan, and this is Rian."

"Marcan and Rian, I hereby appoint you as members of my personal guard. Captain Conroy will brief you on your duties."

"We're honored, Your Highness," Marcan sputtered.

"We'll see that you never regret your choice," Rian said. She nodded her dismissal, and they went off with Conroy.

Bearach came up beside her. "Neither Marcan nor Rian is bad with a blade, but they aren't the best either," he said.

"I realize that, but they are unquestionably loyal. I can't have a guard who might stab me in the back." She grimaced at the dark joke. She turned back to Hamish, who was still grinning at her. "Hamish, your services as a member of my personal guard are no longer required. Report to Captain Hawk for reassignment." Hamish's face fell. "Your Highness, what have I done to displease you? I thought you didn't want us to let you win."

"That isn't why you will no longer serve me," she said. Hamish threw down his practice sword and left the arena.

"You've made yourself an enemy, Your Highness," Bearach said.

Soon, Robbie and all of his guards entered. Fortunately, all of their auras passed inspection.

* * *

Duer smiled at Gael when they were alone in Duer's dingy quarters, a room in his brother's house near the palace. "My lad, we are back in the game!" They had worked in concert for so long that, when they were alone, differences of rank disappeared.

"With an allowance that is none too shabby," Gael added.

Duer pursed his lips. "You think I do this for the money? It is an honor to serve the rightful queen." He crossed to the sideboard and poured himself a glass of wine. It was cheap, foul-tasting stuff, and his face must have shown it because Gael grinned at him.

"Shall I head for the market and buy something better?" Gael looked around at their shabby furnishings. "And perhaps some new rugs and drapes?"

Duer laughed. "Soon enough, lad, soon enough. We need to find Her Highness something to justify our keep as soon as possible. I don't think she liked us much."

"She *did* seem impervious to my charm. But there's plenty of fish in the sea."

"The time has come for you to catch a few." Duer winked lewdly.

* * *

"You allowed him to rape and murder that woman?" Father Gildas clenched his fists and towered over Alvabane. In the confines of the small house, it had been impossible to hide the sacrifice from him.

Nearly bursting with power, Alvabane closed her eyes. No power she'd ever before obtained from the dark gods had been as strong and delicious as this. "It was necessary," she said. "The gods must be pleased   if   we   are   to   succeed." Gildas gasped. "Gods? What heresy is this you speak? Sulis is the Mother of us all!"

"If Sulis is the mother, who is the father? Besides, did you not want to be rid of the demon child regardless of the cost?"

Gildas folded his arms and glared at her. "I will neither commit nor approve heresy!"

"Sulis's church will need a new leader when we are through. Who better than you?"

Gildas relaxed his arms.

"*You* would make me high priest?"

"Once the power of the Soul Stone is mine, there is nothing I can't do."

The priest dropped all objections.

CHAPTER 15

I can handle this. It isn't like I have to do any killing myself.

The Neasarian ambassador had arrived the day before and expressed a desire to hunt boar. Since the relationship was a bit dicey between Neaseria and Korthlundia—what with Argblutal's murder of the former Neasarian ambassador—Samantha had immediately agreed and said Robrek should accompany him.

As the hunt assembled, Robrek pulled his cloak tightly around him. It was a cold morning with a hint of snow in the air. They would be going deep within the Setanta Forest and staying overnight. Vaughan was by his side, mounted on Thunder Storm. In addition to the ambassador and the huntsmen, Count Weylin, Baron Arawn, and several minor nobles would accompany them. Boar was evidently considered too dangerous for ladies. Robrek breathed a sigh of relief. *No Briallen.*

Samantha had also assigned twenty-five members of the Royal Guard as well as all of Robrek's personal guards to accompany them. There were some problems with bandits in the forest, and Samantha wanted to be sure the group was large enough to discourage them. Huge boarhounds stood nearby, slobbering and anxious for a kill.

Baakir, the Neasarian ambassador, yawned widely as his horse trotted up beside Wild Thing. "The only problem with the hunt is leaving at such a blessedly early hour. All gods-fearing mortals are still safely tucked up in their beds."

Robrek wasn't sure what to say to this, so he shrugged. "My uncle always says the sunrise is a pleasure the gods intended only for themselves."

Baakir clapped Robrek on the shoulder. "That they did, Milord. That they did."

Robrek allowed his eyes to wander over the growing group. He smiled when he saw Lord Edan and Count Feoras among the Royal Guard. The two he was coming to consider his friends smiled and waved. Sitting on a huge horse behind them was the largest man Robrek had ever seen. His beard was matted and the right side of his face was covered by an enormous black mole. He was glaring at Robrek as if he wanted to lop his head off and eat it. Robrek shuddered, wondering what he'd done to make the man hate him. Probably the same thing he'd done to make people hate him all his life—nothing.

Robrek gave the signal to move out. They passed through the city and out onto the plains surrounding Gloine Torr. The ambassador stared at the monument. "It would take powerful magic to build such a thing. Is it true you managed to ride a horse up its side?"

Robrek nodded. "It wasn't an ordinary horse."

"So I heard, Milord. You'll have to tell me the story sometime. If there hadn't been so many witnesses, I wouldn't credit such a tale."

"It is a rather fantastic story." Robrek wondered how he could tell it without sounding like he was bragging.

When they reached the edge of the forest, the hounds and the beaters went in first to flush their quarry. They took a few deer in the morning hours, but it was mid-afternoon before the hounds flushed the object of their hunt.

"Let us, Milord." Baakir's eyes shone. "We must be in on the kill." The ambassador touched his heels to his horse and was off. Robrek thought about hanging back, but he was afraid doing so might insult the ambassador.

The boar led them on a good chase, the hounds at its heels and the men on horseback struggling to keep up as they dodged the limbs and branches of the tall trees. At last Robrek and the ambassador burst into a clearing. The dogs had trapped a boar against an escarpment. The animal was enormous, at least eight hundred pounds and seven feet long; huge tusks protruded from its mouth. It was panting, and its small beady eyes were fixed on its tormentors.

Robrek could feel the rage and fear rolling off the animal. It wanted to tear everything in its path to ribbons, and its tusks made it capable of doing so.

Robrek wanted to let the animal go, but he couldn't deny Baakir the kill without political repercussions. Baakir readied his boar spear, and a huntsman cried out, "Here, Milord," and tossed a spear to Robrek.

"Together, Milord." Baakir edged toward the line of slobbering hounds. Struggling to conceal his dismay, Robrek accompanied him.

In a split second, the boar made its decision and charged. Before Robrek could react, its tusk speared Wild Thing in the side, and the Horsetad collapsed under him, Robrek jumping free just in time to avoid being crushed. Confused shouts echoed through the clearing, and the boar gave out an enraged scream.

Eburacon was instantly at Robrek's side. "Milord, are you hurt?"

Robrek scrambled to his feet. "Wild Thing!" The boar was readying another charge, and Robrek feared it would gut the mare. He'd lost his spear in the fall, so he drew his sword, but Eburacon and Geblan jumped in front of him with spears. Both his guards and Baakir threw, catching the boar in its head and heart.

:Big Hurt!: Wild Thing cried, blood flowing from her wound.

Robrek sheathed his sword and dropped to her side. He put one hand above the wound and sent calming energy into her. "It will be all right, my girl. Robrek will fix that." It was bad, but not beyond his power. Robrek put his other hand below the wound, closed his eyes, and went into a healing trance. He stopped the bleeding and slowly closed the wound.

When he opened his eyes, the clearing was quiet, and all eyes were upon him. Although the men had surely heard of his abilities, few of them had seen him in action. Dizzy, Robrek stood, Vaughan helping him upright. Wild Thing shuddered and rolled to her feet.

Baakir let out a breath. "Truly marvelous, Milord. Truly marvelous. I would have wagered the animal would have needed to be put down. I thought the stories about you were exaggerations, but it turns out they don't approach the truth."

* * *

Vaughan watched as the men set about butchering the wild boar to roast over the evening fires. The thing was unbelievably huge.

When it had charged Sir Robrek earlier, Vaughan had almost peed his pants.

"He *is* good with a horse," said a voice behind Vaughan. He turned. A man Vaughan didn't know was talking to Black Giant. Black Giant was one scary looking man. He was a head taller than the man next to him, who was no shorty. And that mole! The two men hadn't noticed Vaughan. "And didn't you see him heal his horse earlier?"

"Well, hurray, hurray, we get a stable groom for a king," Black Giant said. "What good is such magic in battle? Did you see his guards jump in front of him today? He can't handle real danger. The midget can hold the horses while the real men charge the enemy."

Vaughan clenched his fists. "If you think Sir Robrek's not a real man, you've never seen him fight!"

Black Giant snorted. "I heard Her Highness had to rescue *him* from Argblutal's dungeon. His commonness disgraces her. He should have stuck with shoveling shit as he was born to do."

"Take that back!" Vaughan launched himself at Black Giant and drove his fist into the soldier's belly with all the strength of his thirteen-year-old arm. Black Giant didn't even budge.

"Why, you!" Black Giant roared. He jerked Vaughan off his feet and dangled him over a rather large pile of manure.

* * *

Robrek sat by the fire eating, restoring the energy he'd expended healing. The ambassador sat beside him, making small talk Robrek only half heard. A commotion sounded behind him, and he turned to see his squire hanging by his ankles in the grip of the huge guard he'd noticed earlier.

Robrek stood. "Just what do you think you doing with my squire?" he demanded. His guards fanned out and surrounded the big man.

The man glared at Robrek, but he set Vaughan on his feet. "Forgive me, Milord," he sneered. "I didn't know who he was."

Vaughan straightened his coat and glared at the big man. "Black Giant insulted you, Milord. He said you disgraced Her Highness and you were better off shoveling shit." The immediate area went silent, as whispers spread the word.

"That's a damned lie!" Black Giant swore. "There's no one more pleased about Your Lordship's marriage. Ask anyone." He looked at his fellow guards for support, but most refused to meet his eyes. Robrek groaned inwardly. He was being challenged yet again.

Vaughan stamped his foot. "You know *I* don't lie, Milord. He said Your Lordship wasn't man enough to handle a fight. He said Your Lordship was a midget only good for holding horses."

The ambassador gasped, and Robrek wanted to strangle his squire.

Lord Edan laughed from the edge of the growing circle of watchers. "Black Giant, you never did have any sense in that oversized head of yours. He could take any five of us without working up a sweat."

Oh, great! Now what in the seven hells am I supposed to do? Sulis, if you want me to be king, you better tell me. If I don't handle this right, I'll be a laughingstock.

Suddenly, the same peace he'd felt in the tub the day after the so-called Massacre of Valley Fair settled over him, and he knew the answer. He snorted. "I might sweat a little." A few of the watchers laughed nervously. "Choose four other men, arm yourselves and prepare a circle. If I win, you will fall at my feet and apologize. You will then personally ensure that every member of the Royal Guard hears of my victory."

Black Giant's jaw tightened. "And if you lose, Milord?"

"I will admit in front of everyone present that I should have stayed shoveling shit." Robrek turned his back on the big man and left to arm himself.

When they had distanced themselves from the crowd, Eburacon stepped in front of him. "Milord, you can't do this! Her Highness would never allow it."

"I can't let an insult like that stand. You've told me so yourself."

Eburacon glared at Black Giant. "I'll fight them for you."

"That would only prove Black Giant's words." Robrek turned away from Eburacon. "Vaughan, find me a staff." A staff would give him more leeway to fight without the risk of killing someone.

At his command, Vaughan ran off, but Eburacon turned his glare on Robrek. "Do you have any idea what Her Highness will do to us if you are injured or killed?"

Robrek swore under his breath. *Why can't anything ever be easy?* He tried to look down at Eburacon in the manner of a king, but he was too damned short. Still, he put on the voice of command. "And what will happen to Her Highness's throne if I allow myself to be insulted?"

Eburacon shifted uncomfortably. "I will not bring Her Highness news of your death. If you allow them to kill you, I will kill them all and then fall on my sword."

"Then you'd better pray I win."

Just as Vaughan returned, Edan popped up beside Robrek. "Should be an interesting bout." Edan was smiling, and Robrek felt an urge to strangle the man.

"What in the seven hells were you thinking?" he snapped. "Five! And one of them the size of a house! Why couldn't you have said three?"

Edan shrugged. "I thought five sounded better. You're not worried, are you?"

With a groan, Robrek turned to the captain of his guard. "Eburacon, if I die, put Lord Edan first on your list of people to kill."

"With pleasure, Milord." Eburacon glared at Edan. Edan blanched. But he evidently decided Robrek was kidding and laughed, if a bit nervously.

Robrek took the staff Vaughan had found for him and strode to a circular area that had been cleared. Five men stood in the center. A light snow was falling, and it was bitter cold.

Robrek closed his eyes to calm both his breathing and his heart rate. He opened his eyes and stepped into the circle. His five challengers approached. Black Giant introduced the other four: Bartle, Jarlath, Gerard, and Ormande. They looked disdainfully at his staff.

Robrek smiled in what he hoped was a kingly way. "I'd rather not kill anyone. Digging graves would be a Sulis-cursed job in the frozen earth." Soldiers behind him laughed, and doubt crept into his challengers' eyes, telling Robrek he'd struck the right note. Baakir smiled slightly; Robrek could tell the ambassador was sizing him up every bit as much as the Royal Guard was. He tried to project indifference. "Shall we get on with it? I'm rather hungry."

"As Your Lordship wishes." Black Giant bowed with his hands held wide. The other men followed suit. They fanned out in front of him, drew their swords, and looked hesitantly toward Black Giant. Robrek's confidence seemed to have unnerved them.

Black Giant bellowed an ear-shattering roar and ran toward Robrek well ahead of the others. Black Giant lifted his sword for a quick overhead strike. Even if Black Giant turned his blade to the side, it would still crush Robrek's skull. It seemed the man really meant to kill him.

Robrek stepped to the side and rammed the staff between the giant's legs with all of his strength. Black Giant's roar turned into a shriek of pain, and he dropped, barely missing Robrek on the way down.

The other four moved closer. Bartle and Jarlath split off from the right and the left, trying to encircle him. He feinted toward Bartle and then whirled left. Jarlath was caught off guard and before he could block, Robrek smashed the staff down onto Jarlath's right wrist. Jarlath cried out and dropped his sword in the snow.

Again Robrek whirled away from the others. *I can do this. It might even be fun.* But he forgot to allow for the slickness of the ground. His foot hit a patch of ice, and he fell, landing on his side, his staff landing under him. Bartle's sword came swinging for his head. He'd never get his staff out from under him in time, so he launched himself at Bartle's feet, bowling him over backwards. Bartle's sword slipped from his grasp, and Robrek rolled to his feet with Bartle's sword in his hand.

Gerard and Ormande were closing on him, Black Giant struggling to his feet behind them. Bartle had picked up Robrek's staff, and Jarlath was holding his sword with his left hand. Robrek gritted his teeth. None of them were out, and he had a sword now, so he'd have to be more careful.

Robrek moved to the left to avoid Gerard and Ormande, the closest two, only to discover how fast Bartle was. Bartle greeted him with a blow aimed at his sword arm. Fortunately, Bartle wasn't as good with a staff as a sword. Robrek stepped to the side and brought the sword up to block, trying to turn the sword sideways to avoid giving serious injury, but Bartle was so fast, Robrek didn't quite manage. Bartle screamed as the sword cut into his wrist. He dropped the staff and fell into the snow. Robrek snatched up his staff as Gerard and Ormande rushed him. But when Gerard, out in front, flicked his eyes to Bartle, Robrek took advantage and swung his staff into Gerard's head. Gerard dropped so suddenly Robrek feared he'd killed him. Ormande took advantage of his inattention, swinging his blade. Robrek barely got his staff around in time to block it. The sword hit the staff with a resounding crack. Robrek then struck a hard blow to Ormande's kneecap. Ormande dropped to the ground, his knee bent behind him at a grotesque angle.

Robrek heard a bellow behind him and whirled. Black Giant charged toward him, although slower than before. Again, the huge man lifted his sword for a quick blow to Robrek's head. It seemed Black Giant knew no other attack. Robrek rammed his staff into the giant's groin a second time. Black Giant's scream resembled that of a little girl as he dropped at Robrek's feet.

Robrek turned to face the remaining man. But Jarlath knelt before him. "I yield, Milord. You are the finest fighter the joined kingdoms has ever known. Certainly the goddess has chosen you. I will blaspheme her no further by raising my hand against you."

With intense relief, Robrek dropped his arm to his side, struggling to remain on his feet. The peace he'd felt earlier descended on him with even greater force, and he knew without a doubt he was truly the goddess's choice. Despite his exhaustion from the fight and his earlier healing, he pitched his voice as loudly as he could. "I never asked to be king. I sought only a place where I could heal animals without disturbance. I would have been content as the stable groom this man named me." He pointed to Black Giant, who was still on the ground in a fetal position. "But the goddess had other plans. She sent me her faithful steeds, who shone like bronze, silver, and gold. Together the horses taught me what I needed to know to take my place beside the Princess Samantha. Why Sulis chose me, I don't know. But I have learned not to question the goddess's will."

As he finished speaking, Robrek noticed Black Giant crawling toward him, dragging his sword. *Surely he doesn't intend to continue the fight.* The huge man stopped at Robrek's feet and looked up. Tears flowed down his disfigured face, as Black Giant raised both arms with his sword lain across them. "I believed it dishonored our queen to mate with one of such low birth, but you have shown me it was I who dishonored Her Highness, the goddess, and Sulis's choice. For my heresy, I offer you my sword or my life." Black Giant thrust the hilt of his sword toward Robrek's hand, and Robrek dropped the staff he carried and took it. His arms were so tired he could barely hold its weight. "With my sword, remove my head from my body, and all will proclaim you have done a just deed. But if Your Lordship will have mercy, return my sword to me, and I, Vercingetorix, known as Black Giant, do hereby swear it to thy service."

The camp fell utterly silent, and even the wind seemed to calm as Black Giant put his hand to his heart, "I shall become thy liege man. In Sulis's holy name and on my mother's grave, I promise in matters of life and limb and of earthly honor that I will maintain faith and loyalty to King Robrek and his queen, Her Majesty, Queen Samantha. May my sword ever be stained bright with the blood of thine enemies."

A gasp went up from many of those watching as Black Giant bent and kissed Robrek's feet. The huge man exposed his neck and awaited Robrek's decision. Robrek stared down at him. Fancy Man's teaching hadn't covered such a situation. He glanced at Lord Edan for help. The young nobleman leaned toward him and whispered, "He does you high honor. If you would accept his oath, take his sword and touch him on both shoulders. Or chop off his head. Your choice."

The entire camp watched in utter silence as Robrek lifted Black Giant's sword. "I accept your sword and your oath. Live long in service to the crown." Robrek touched the kneeling man on both shoulders.

Black Giant kissed Robrek's feet again. "Your Lordship is most merciful. You shall never have cause to regret this decision." Black Giant straightened, and Robrek returned the huge man's sword, happy he was able to do so without dropping it. Sheathing his sword, Black Giant crawled away.

Ormande crawled toward him, dragging his injured leg behind him. His face white and his voice trembling with pain, he too offered Robrek his sword and his oath. The clouds parted, and the moon shone full on the scene, seeming to demonstrate Sulis's blessing of the proceedings. Feeling truly like a king for the first time, Robrek touched the kneeling man on both shoulders and repeated the words. Jarlath came next. Gerard still wasn't moving, and Bartle knelt in the snow, staring at the bloody bandage wrapped around his wrist. Robrek's arm trembled as he accepted Jarlath's oath. To Robrek's surprise, another man knelt at his feet and offered his sword. "I,

Calvagh, do hereby swear my sword to thy service." The man bowed and repeated the words of the oath.

Varney followed, then Antain, and over a dozen more. By the time the last man had finished kissing Robrek's feet and taking back his sword, Robrek swayed on his feet. He leaned toward Eburacon. "Is he dead?" he whispered, gesturing toward Gerard. *Holy Sulis, let me not have killed a man.*

Eburacon nodded toward Cathbad, and Cathbad went to the unmoving man. He bent down and felt the man's neck. "He's alive, Milord." Robrek gave a sigh of relief.

Vaughan appeared by his elbow. "Are you all right, Milord?"

"I will be," Robrek said. "Fetch my healing supplies."

Robrek knelt down beside Gerard. He put his hands on the man's head and entered a light trance. He quickly determined that although Gerard would wake with a terrible headache, there was no permanent injury. "Have him put to bed, and see that he's warm," he ordered. Two men stepped up to carry Gerard away.

Jarlath and Bartle staggered forward, cradling their injured wrists. Bartle's bled shockingly. Robrek unwound the bandage. Holy Sulis, he'd nearly severed Bartle's hand. He touched Bartle's forearm and slowed the bleeding. "Why didn't you tell me at once it was this bad?"

Bartle shrugged. "You might as well chop it off or kill me. What good is a swordsman who can't manage a sword?"

"Certainly not!" Robrek tried to go into a healing trance, but he was far too tired to weave the injured tissue back together. He could do no more than stop the bleeding. He trembled as he opened his eyes. "We'll have to bandage it for now. I need rest before I can do more, but I promise you in Sulis's holy name and on my mother's grave, you will have full use of your hand again."

Bartle stared at him in awe. "What you claim would seem impossible, but I trust your word, Sir Robrek." He fell to his knees and drew his sword with his left hand. He held it up to Robrek. "I didn't pledge earlier because I believed my sword would be useless to you, but if you give me back the use of it, I vow it to your service." He repeated the oath the others had sworn before him.

Robrek accepted Bartle's vow. He then set the bones in Jarlath's wrist and Ormande's leg and promised further healing after he'd rested. He staggered to a seat by the fire.

One of the guards who'd sworn his sword to Robrek approached with a bowl of stew, a hunk of bread, and a mug of cider. The man bowed deeply. "I've heard a healer such as yourself can't drink alcohol, Milord."

Robrek gratefully accepted the food and drink. "Thank you, Varney."

Varney smiled, seemingly pleased Robrek remembered his name. Robrek looked around the fire, trying to name all those who had given their oaths. A king remembered the names of those who served him.

"Ha!" Lord Edan said, sitting down beside him. "So, you are a hero of legend now."

Robrek nearly choked on his food. "What are you talking about?"

"The swearing of the sword hasn't been done for centuries. Black Giant's words come from a bard's tale about Armunn, Korthlundia's greatest hero. Perhaps you're the next Armunn. They say Armunn too was the son of a farmer." Robrek didn't know who Armunn was or what bard's tale Edan was talking about, and he was too tired to care. Lord Edan clinked together a handful of coins. "You've made me a tidy bundle today, Milord."

"You bet on me?" Robrek asked.

"Of course, Milord. I must admit I was a bit nervous when I saw Jarlath and Bartle in the group, but I still thought you could take them."

The Neasarian ambassador sat down beside him. "Most impressive, Milord. You almost had *me* ready to swear my sword. What does the swearing of the sword mean?"

Robrek looked at Edan for help, but Eburacon answered solemnly. "It is the most sacred of our oaths. It is an ancient ceremony which was believed to link the soul of the sworn one to that of his liege lord. Whatever act you command them to do with their swords, they will do without hesitation, even if you ask them to fall upon them." Neither Eburacon, nor any of his personal guards, had sworn.

"Not that you'd ever do that," Edan, who had sworn, added from Robrek's other side.

Robrek shivered. *No one should have that much power over another.*

Baakir's eyes gleamed. "I think this is the beginning of a great friendship between our two countries. The taking of such a large boar was surely an auspicious sign."

Robrek nodded politely, but his eyes lit on Count Weylin and Baron Arawn. They were staring straight ahead, avoiding looking in his direction. What had they thought of the proceedings?

When Robrek finished his stew, Lieutenant Loach approached him, bowing deeply. "Milord, the men have all heard various bards' tales about how you acquired the magical horses on which you climbed Gloine Torr. If you don't mind, Milord, they would very much like to hear the truth from Your Lordship."

Robrek groaned inwardly. He was so tired he could hardly keep his eyes open. But as he looked around the fire and saw the men— no, *his* men—staring back at him with the eagerness of children, he knew he had no choice. He was discovering a king rarely did. So he told the story of Brazen, Fancy Man, and Holy Writ destroying his father's crops and teaching him the skills to become king. As he finished, the men stared at him in awe.

Afterwards, Antain was asked to sing to the group. He smiled nervously at Robrek, and Robrek knew he couldn't refuse to listen to at least one song. Robrek nodded, and Antain fetched his lute. He tuned the strings and began to sing. Drifting in and out of sleep, Robrek vaguely heard the tale of Armunn fighting demons.

* * *

"Your Highness, I'm happy to report I have been chosen as the next high priest." Father Hafghan seated himself across from Samantha in her reception room. "It was a close vote, but in the end, Father Faolan's ties to Father Shylah doomed him."

Samantha inwardly sighed in relief, but she maintained a court mask. "I am pleased." The high priest wasn't meeting her eyes. "Is there something else?"

"I'm afraid there is, Your Highness. Rumors are being spread about you through the clergy. I don't know where they began, but few haven't heard them. I've done my best to put a stop to it, but I'm afraid that many, especially among Father Faolan's faction, believe them, or at least find it convenient to do so."

Samantha tried to keep her face expressionless. "What rumors?"

"That Your Highness is both an aurora and pregnant."

Samantha barely avoided putting her hand on her abdomen. If the news had spread beyond the palace, soon every citizen in the joined kingdoms would hear it. *Damn you, Caedmon. I should have told the people the truth to begin with.* She remembered Morgan's words: "A bastard sits uneasily on the throne."

"The rumors and your betrothed's clinic have ignited a growing discontent among the clergy. Offerings to the church have dropped off precipitously since he began healing for free."

She kept her tone free of emotion. "Thank you for bringing this to my attention. I would appreciate any efforts on your part to prevent any unseemliness."

"Of course, Your Highness." The high priest bowed his way out.

Samantha got up and went to her window. Alone now, she put her hand on her abdomen. A profound loneliness swept over her. *It will not be this way for you, my daughter. You will not be thrust alone into a position for those far above your age. How did my mother feel about giving birth to the heir of a seventy-year-old king? Did she even think about what this would mean for me?*

On sudden impulse, she headed for the Royal Gallery, Bearach and Conroy joining her as she left the room. As she neared the gallery, she heard the sound of soft weeping. A figure sat on the bench in front of her mother's picture. The clanking of her guards' armor announced their arrival, and the woman jumped up from the bench. Baroness Glynnis, Baron Gwawl's wife, bowed to her. The baroness had only accompanied her husband to court on rare occasions, so Samantha didn't know her well.

"Excuse me, Your Highness. If this is a private place, I didn't mean to intrude." The baroness wiped her eyes with a handkerchief, but their red puffiness revealed she'd been crying for some time.

"There's no need to apologize. The galleries are for all who want to enjoy them." She added a note of concern to her voice. "I don't mean to pry, but enjoying them doesn't seem to be what you were doing."

The baroness waved the princess's words away with her handkerchief. "Pay me no mind, Your Highness. I'm being maudlin. Crying about a childhood friend, dead these twenty years."

"You were sitting in front of my mother's picture."

The baroness looked fondly back at the painting and tenderly touched the plaque underneath it. "Your mother was my dearest friend."

Samantha drew closer to the baroness. "I didn't know that. I know little of my mother."

"My parents died when I was young, and your mother's parents became my guardians. Your mother and I grew up together. We were closer than many true sisters I've known. I came with her when she married the king. It wasn't until after she died that I married the baron." Glynnis cleaned an imaginary speck from the plaque with her handkerchief. "I was touched to see Fenella's name had been placed here since my last visit. It used to be labeled only as 'The Mother of the Heir.'"

Samantha approached her mother's portrait. "I had her name placed there. The painting seemed incomplete without it."

The baroness nodded. "I've always thought so. She was thrilled about becoming a mother, but that was only one part of her, and a part she never really got to play."

"Please, tell me about her. The only thing my father ever said was that she was a good girl. I think he felt guilty about her death." Samantha sat down on the bench and patted the place beside her. "Please."

Glynnis took the offered seat. "Where to begin?" The baroness paused a moment. Then she laughed. "She had quite a streak of mischief in her. Oh, the tricks she'd come up with for us to play! Now mind you, I never hesitated to follow along with her harebrained schemes, but I didn't have the imagination she did. There was one time when Duke Torin was visiting her folks. He'd just buried his latest wife—you know how he goes through them— and Fenella was worried he'd come to talk about making her his third wife, or maybe it was his fourth. Who can keep track? Anyway, Fenella wanted none of that, but she knew going to her father would do no good. He was a strict one, your grandfather. He didn't think a girl had any business choosing her own husband. Well, you know how Torin has that mole on the side of his neck, the one with the hairs growing out of it?"

Samantha smiled. "I always had the urge to pluck them when he was courting me." It seemed strange she could have shared a suitor with her mother.

Glynnis laughed. "That's exactly what your mother said. She sent me into the village to buy as many tweezers as I could find and had servants search the keep for every pair they could come up with. She placed them all on strings and had every servant attending the duke wear a pair around his neck. The duke asked her at dinner if tweezers were some new symbol for her house." Glynnis laughed again. "Your mother smiled just as sweet and innocent as could be and said that she had had the servants wear them in honor of our guest. Torin's hand flew straight to the mole, and he left the next morning in a huff. Your grandfather was furious. He'd wanted his daughter to be a duchess. Of course, he readily forgave her when she became queen instead."

Samantha glanced over at the wedding portrait of her parents. Solar was seated on his throne, his long white hair and beard flowing around his head. Next to the throne stood her child mother. It seemed a picture of grandfather and grandchild, not husband and wife. "How did she feel about marrying a man so much older than she?"

Glynnis lost her smile, and she suddenly became interested in the painting of Samantha as a baby. "You were such a beautiful child. She would have been proud of the woman you've grown into."

Samantha placed her hand on Glynnis's arm. "Please, I'd like to know the truth, even if it isn't pleasant."

Glynnis shuddered. "It was the ugliest scene I've ever witnessed. When her father announced the betrothal, Fenella flatly refused. Your grandfather was still furious about the trick she'd played on Duke Torin. He went out and found the ugliest, filthiest, most repulsive of his peasants and gave your mother a choice. Either she'd be a good girl and marry the king, or he'd marry her to the peasant and let him take her home with him that day. He was so angry he would have done it. He had two sons, so your mother was merely a liability if she didn't do as she was told. Fenella saw the anger in his eyes, to say nothing of the lust of the peasant. She married the king, of course, but she cursed her father on her wedding day. Since then I've always wondered if she'd had a bit of witch in her. Within a year every male member of his household died—his two sons, his younger brother, his nephews. On your parents' first anniversary, your grandfather himself suffered a hunting accident and died. His father's house died with him. Fenella claimed her curse had nothing to do with all the accidents, but I can't help wondering if there is power in a curse uttered with so much anger."

Samantha looked back at the portrait of her parents and felt some of her nausea returning. Glynnis touched her gently. "Forgive me, Your Highness. I shouldn't have told you such stories. It's not a thing a girl needs to know about her mother, and a woman in your condition should be treated with more delicacy."

"My condition?" Without thinking, Samantha put her hand on her stomach.

Glynnis patted her arm. Samantha knew she should have resented Glynnis's familiarity in touching her, but she didn't. It felt warm and comforting, like the mothering she'd never had. "I've always been able to tell. A woman just gets that look about her. Don't worry, Your Highness. Your secret's safe with me."

Samantha stared at Glynnis and concentrated on dropping her shields. It was becoming easier with practice. The baroness's aura burst into colors, and Samantha could tell the love Glynnis had felt for Samantha's mother extended to her. The baroness wouldn't betray her.

Samantha looked back at the picture of her pregnant mother. "How did my mother feel about being pregnant?"

Glynnis smiled. "At first, she was delighted. The king had promised once she gave him an heir, he'd make no more demands on her."

"'At first.' But later. . ."

"The pregnancy was hard on her. Even past the normal time, she couldn't keep a thing down. That color in her cheeks"—Glynnis gestured towards the painting—"the artist added that. Fenella was white as a ghost by that time. Toward the end, she was certain she wouldn't survive, and she was so miserable she was ready to die."

Samantha pressed her hand to her belly. "Did she blame me?"

"Blame you?" Glynnis gaped. "Not for an instant, Your Highness. She was proud her child would rule. She grew up a lot near the end, and she became reconciled with the king. She understood the gift she was giving her people and was delighted you were a girl. One of the last things she said to me was that her daughter would show the world the power of women. She believed you'd change things. 'My precious gift,' she called you before she died."

As Glynnis finished speaking, all the sadness and longing Samantha had long felt in relationship to her mother welled up inside her, and before she could stop herself, she found herself sobbing. "Oh, my poor mother! I never knew any of this!"

Glynnis put her arms around her, and the princess sobbed onto her shoulder. The baroness rubbed her back softly and made soothing noises.

"There, there, child. Don't worry. A girl should have her mother at a time like this, but since Fenella can't play a mother's role, I promise you I'll stay with you through it, if you'll let me."

For the first time in her life, the princess felt as if she were being held in a mother's arms. Samantha rested in the older woman's comfort until she gained control of her tears, then pulled away. "Oh, baroness, I don't know what to do. Ugly rumors are being spread about me. They are calling my baby a bastard's bastard."

"My poor child. Never mind such lies."

"What if they aren't lies?" Samantha said, and the baroness's eyes widened. She, however, did not look truly surprised. "You know, don't you? My mother told you of her lover."

The baroness's lips pursed. "I swore to Fenella I'd never speak of it. But are you telling me the rumors are true? You are an aurora?"

The princess nodded. "It's how I know I can trust you. I know Solar wasn't truly my father, and so do these guards." She gestured to Conroy and Bearach. "Darhour, my former chief bodyguard, told me of his relationship with my mother. Tell me, baroness, what do I do? I have no one I can trust to guide me. I can't admit the truth, but how can I live a lie?"

"You have no choice, Your Highness. Don't dignify such slander with a response. The people love you. They will not be turned against you by rumors which cannot be proven." The baroness put her hand under the princess's chin and lifted her face. "You are their queen. Don't let them ever doubt it. And more importantly, don't let yourself doubt it."

"Thank you, baroness." The princess fell into the older woman's hug.

CHAPTER 16

"Samantha, this time you can't fail to listen." Caedmon's face was red, and a vein was pounding in his temple.

Samantha looked away. *What can it be this time? Another complaint against Robbie, no doubt.* She settled into a chair in her reception room. "Calm down, Caedmon. You'll rupture something." She didn't ask Caedmon to be seated.

"Your Highness, this is no petty matter. An outrider has arrived, informing us that your *Robbie* and his party will arrive within the hour." His fists were clenched, his body shaking with his anger.

Samantha narrowed her eyes. "Sir Robrek is Robbie to me and to me alone. You will refer to him as Sir Robrek or His Lordship. He will be your king."

Caedmon stalked toward her and loomed over her chair. "You can't possibly plan on going through with this absurd marriage after you hear what he's done!"

She stood, forcing Caedmon to back up. "You have more lies to tell me about my betrothed?"

"Lies?" he sputtered. "How can you possibly doubt my word?"

"Briallen," Samantha breathed. "Do you think I don't know you arranged that?" Caedmon sighed loudly and settled into a chair. "I admit, that was a rather low tactic."

"Is that all you have to say for yourself? How do you expect me to ever trust you again? You tried to break my heart!"

Caedmon opened his mouth as if to deny any such thing, but closed it again. Finally he said in a patronizing tone, "Samantha, my dear, everything I've done, everything I've said, has been for you. You know I love you like a daughter. I don't want to see you hurt! What the peasant has done now isn't some dalliance. It's treason."

Samantha's blood boiled at Caedmon's use of that word. "Watch what you accuse my betrothed of, Uncle. Is it not treason to lie to your liege?"

Caedmon threw up his hands. "If you weren't so besotted as to ignore all sound council, I wouldn't have had to resort to such tactics. But this time I don't even need to embellish the truth. That peasant has made himself into Armunn! He's sworn the swords of two dozen members of the Royal Guard to him, using an oath straight out of one of the Armunn ballads."

Samantha laughed without humor. "Impossible! With his background, he probably doesn't even know Armunn's tales."

"If Sir Robrek has the temerity to deny it, I can bring more than enough witnesses. He is corrupting the Royal Guard, getting them to put their loyalty to him above their loyalty to Your Highness. There is only one reason to do that. He wants your throne, something he has made clear to anyone with eyes to see. I won't back down this time, Samantha. You must have him dealt with before it's too late!"

At that moment, Robbie walked in the door with his face beaming. His smile faltered a bit when he noticed the obvious tension between her and Caedmon. He bowed formally. "Your Highness, Your Grace."

Samantha longed to take him in her arms, to again assure herself that all Caedmon's objections were unfounded lies.

"If you don't believe me, ask him!" Caedmon shouted, pointing at Robbie. "Tell her you've made yourself into Armunn and sworn the swords of two dozen members of the Royal Guard to you!"

"Enough, Caedmon!" She approached Robbie and took his hand. "You have no need to answer such absurd lies."

Robbie paled slightly. "It's not a lie, Sam. Members of the Royal Guard did swear their swords to me."

Samantha dropped Robbie's hand and stood there gaping at him. Caedmon pointed again at Robbie. "You see? He wants your throne! And the Royal Guard will help give it to him! What other motive could he have for making himself into Armunn?"

Samantha struggled for words. "Robbie, what have you done?"

"What I had to do." Robbie met her eyes and spoke with more authority than she'd ever heard in his voice before. He told her of the insult, the fight against the men challenging his right to be king, Black Giant's offer of his loyalty or his life, and the oaths of the other men. "Would you have had me cut off Black Giant's head? Refuse to accept the vows of the others? I swear I didn't understand the significance of the ceremony until after it was over. Edan and Eburacon explained it to me." Robrek turned to Caedmon. "Still, I did the right thing. The Royal Guard respects me now." He turned back to Samantha. "Isn't that what you wanted?"

Caedmon stalked between them. "Not like this, she didn't! Your Highness, he admits his treason! You must have him arrested and tried before he gains any more power over the people!"

Robbie turned cold eyes on the duke. "I wasn't talking to you." Robbie pushed past him and went down on one knee before her. "Sam, you know I'd never be disloyal to you. I don't care about being king! It's always been you I've wanted! *Only* you." His eyes shown with fervor. "I'll prove it. I'll swear my sword to you right now."

Caedmon snorted. "As if a private gesture could make up for your public treason! Your Highness, you must arrest him!"

Samantha glared at Caedmon. What Robbie had done was politically dangerous, but he'd meant no disloyalty. Still, it would need careful handling. Before she could determine what to say, Robbie stood and faced Caedmon, and despite the difference in their height, it was Caedmon who flinched. "I'll swear to Her Highness any time, any place of her choosing, but this is between her and me."

Samantha stepped beside Robbie and took his hand. "He's right, Uncle." She turned to Robbie. "Swear at our wedding."

Caedmon swelled to the point she feared his head would explode. "You *can't* forgive this, Your Highness! You *have* to take his head!"

"Leave us," she commanded.

Caedmon folded his arms as if he would refuse, then he turned his glare on Robbie. "Know this, Robrek Angusstamm! You will marry the daughter of my liege over my dead body!" He stormed from the room.

* * *

When Leigh arrived at the Temple of the Mother's Love in answer to a summons from the high priest, he found Father Faolan waiting for him. The priest's lip curled as he looked at Leigh's narrow nose inherited from his Saloynan mother. "Father Hafghan is expecting you," Faolan snapped. The priest led him to the high priest's office.

Father Hafghan was sitting behind a wide desk covered with parchment, books, ink, and pens. He smiled and got to his feet when he saw Leigh. "My son, come in, come in." The high priest gestured toward a chair. "We have much to discuss." Father Hafghan nodded his dismissal to Faolan.

The sideboard contained a large tray of sausage rolls and breakfast pastries and an urn of *bhat*. The high priest picked up the tray and brought it to Leigh. "May I offer you some refreshments?"

Why in Sulis's name would he serve me? Until he understood what the high priest wanted, Leigh was tempted to refuse, but politeness won out. Leigh filled a plate with pastries and sausage rolls and began to eat.

The high priest again sat at his desk and observed Leigh without speaking until Leigh began to feel uncomfortable. Finally, he said, "You have refused to rejoin the priesthood, but still you wear the robes of a novice. May I ask why?"

"I seek to serve the goddess."

"But not the church?"

"The church serves itself, not the goddess. Those who come to me have often been turned away by the priests because they lacked the proper donation."

"Well, yes, that has been a common practice." The high priest shifted in his chair. "But such men don't belong in the priesthood. Under my predecessor, the poor of the joined kingdoms have been neglected. I'd like to remedy this. I propose to open several small shrines in the poorest sections of Murtaghan." He paused, evidently waiting for a reaction. Leigh gave none. "As a start, I'd like to reopen an abandoned shrine near your present location. The shrine would be supported from central church funds and accept donations only as high as the parishioners can afford. I'd like to anoint you as a priest and have you run this shrine. The compensation would be small, of course. But you would tend to the needs of your flock's souls as well as their bodies."

Leigh looked at the priest suspiciously; what Father Hafghan was offering was exactly what Leigh had long wanted. The high priest seemed to guess his suspicions. "You will be free to run the shrine as you see fit, my son. Sir Robrek tells me you're one of the goddess's most faithful servants."

Leigh locked eyes with the priest. "I won't stop helping Sir Robrek with his clinics, if that's what you're after."

Father Hafghan lifted an eyebrow. "You think I'm doing this to sabotage Sir Robrek's efforts?"

"I know the church isn't happy with him healing for free."

The high priest's lips tightened into a thin line. He sighed, and his face relaxed. "I guess I deserved that."

He got up from his seat and went to the window. He was silent for so long that Leigh wondered if Father Hafghan was waiting for Sulis herself to appear. Eventually, he turned and faced Leigh.

"I haven't always been the ambitious man you see before you. In my youth, the goddess and her children meant everything to me. They are why I entered the clergy." He waved his hand in a dismissive gesture, walked back to his seat, and sat down. "Somewhere I lost my way. I began to care more for the approval of those in this world than for the goddess. I guess it could be said I'm trying to use you to reclaim a portion of my youth. Also, my power within the church is limited. Although Her Highness has accepted my reasons, some hold my coronation of Argblutal against me. Others. . . well, it doesn't really matter what others say." Father Hafghan shuddered. "However, if I begin to meddle overly much with their privileges, they won't keep quiet long. I want to use you to lead the church back to what Sulis intended it to be. I want to use you to attract a new generation of men into the clergy who will truly serve Sulis. I want to use you to begin reclaiming the soul of the church and perhaps a piece of my own soul in the process. Will you allow yourself to be so used?"

Shocked by priest's apparent sincerity, Leigh was unable to say anything for several moments. "I wouldn't turn anyone away," he warned, "even if they can afford no donation at all."

"I would expect no less of you."

"The shrine would not be profitable."

"I don't expect it to be.

A slow smile spread over Leigh's face. "Then how could I refuse?"

Chuckling in relief, the priest fingered the figurine of the goddess on his necklace. "Shall we arrange for your ordination to be held on the next holy day?"

Leigh nodded. "I'd like that."

"Good." Father Hafghan took out a piece of paper and a quill and began to write. "You will present this to Father Duane, the treasurer. It authorizes the release to you the keys to the shrine in your neighborhood and whatever funds you immediately require. Once you've been ordained and have had time to assess the condition of the shrine, we'll make permanent financial arrangements."

* * *

On the way to Duke Torin's estates, Alvabane gloated. Torin would follow soon, slipping away in the confusion of the royal wedding. He had enough loyal men that those who guarded his quarters could be either bought or otherwise dealt with. He was no longer completely necessary to her plan, but, despite herself, she still felt affection for him.

Alongside her rode the sorcerer's brother. The defrocked priest trailed behind them. Their hatred was so strong it couldn't help but please the dark gods. "When do we do another ritual?" the peasant asked.

"As soon as we get to Duke Torin's estates. The dark gods are pleased with you," she said. "But perhaps next time, you could make the sacrifice last a little longer."

"With pleasure." He leered; Alvabane would not be loathe to part with him when the time came.

"And how long until I get my dukedom?"

Alvabane smiled. "Not long. The night of the new moon, we will claim the power that will destroy the sorcerer king." She turned to Father Gildas. "And what will you do with the high priesthood?" The priest had been a harder sell than the sorcerer's brother, but the promise of the high priesthood seemed to have sealed the deal.

Father Gildas stiffened. "That is not something I intend to discuss with heathens."

* * *

Mor Fos had been evacuated, but the curse had crept yet onward, and the priestesses were forced to evacuate another village. As they walked, Venetia looked sadly at the mother with her newborn babe who would likely not make it to safety.

Awena turned to Mother Venetia. "Can I lend them my energy, Mother? Can I help them survive?"

"No, my child. If you do, you will die, and we need every one of us with magic to fight this curse." Their numbers had dwindled to no more than a dozen.

"But what good are we doing, Mother?"

Venetia closed her eyes, wishing she had an answer. For now, they could only move these people to safety.

They travelled on, and when they had reached the next village outside the Dead Lands, Mother Bensaggyrt called a meeting of those who remained. "Mother Delwin and Mother Jenna have not returned. We can only surmise they have failed and have fallen victim themselves."

"If Delwin and Jenna have failed, what hope do we have?" Awena's eyes were swollen from crying, and her cheeks were blotchy. This much death was hard on the young ones. It was hard enough on the old ones.

"We are truly desperate. I fear none of us have enough personal power to make it through the Dead Lands alive." Mother Bensaggyrt said. "Therefore, I have an idea. It has not been tried in centuries. I will again ask for a volunteer to go into the Dead Lands, but she will not go in with her power alone. I will give her mine as well. She who agrees would permanently gain all my power, and I will be left without. Then, maybe she will have enough power to make it through and confront the evil at its source."

All those present gaped at Mother Bensaggyrt. She was talking about tinkering with the forces of life itself!

Mother Venetia rose to her feet. "Legends speak of those who have taken the power of others. The results are almost uniformly disastrous. The goddess knows how much magic our bodies are capable of bearing and has given us only this amount and no more. Trying to add to our natural magic risks both life and sanity. It is not the way of a true child of the goddess."

Bensaggyrt's lips tightened. "It is a terrible risk, and I would never have proposed it if I thought any of us could get through alive without the power of another."

Mother Aeronwen fiddled with the beads in her hair; it was a nervous habit of hers. She was young, not yet twenty-five. "What about these rumors we have heard about the princess's betrothed? He is said to be a powerful sorcerer and to have ridden a horse up the side of Gloine Torr. Perhaps he is the one who can save us."

"Perhaps. But even if he's willing to come and risk his own life, fetching him will take time we do not have." Mother Bensaggyrt said.

"We should not attempt your mad idea," Mother Venetia insisted. "The shock of the power loss might kill you."

Bensaggyrt nodded. "It might. Given I'm nearly ninety, it probably will. It is only because of my magic that I have lived such a long life, but it is a sacrifice I'm willing to make. A life without magic would be, in many ways, worse than death."

Venetia shook her head. "We cannot! We dare not!"

Bensaggyrt met Venetia's eyes. "If you have another idea, I'm willing to entertain it."

Aeronwen raised her hand. "I'll do it. I don't want to see any more death."

Venetia wanted to argue more, but perhaps Mother Bensaggyrt was right. Perhaps it was the only way.

* * *

Bensaggyrt and Aeronwen sat facing each other, holding hands. "Now, you have to find the source of my power and sever it," Bensaggyrt said. "I will help guide you. Once you have severed it, you must open yourself up to it and allow it to flow to you. Do you understand?"

Aeronwen nodded. Venetia held her breath as the two linked shields. She watched with her magic as Bensaggyrt guided Aeronwen to the very center of her being, the place the goddess had stored her power and her love. When Aeronwen's magic invaded this place, a darkness spread over them both. Aeronwen's magic became like a knife and flayed Bensaggyrt's very soul, shredding the cord that connected Bensaggyrt to her magic. With nothing left to sustain its vitality, Bensaggyrt's soul collapsed within her. It was a vile thing to witness. Venetia wished she'd sent Awena out of the room.

As Bensaggyrt's magic flowed into Aeronwen, the younger priestess's face burst into a smile of pure ecstasy. "Oh, this is wonderful! I feel so alive!" Aeronwen's face glowed with unnatural power, but her heart beat at nearly twice the normal speed, and her breathing was rapid. Venetia feared her heart and lungs would burst and that Mother Bensaggyrt's would stand still. The color had gone from the old priestess's face; her breathing was shallow and her heart rate slow. Venetia doubted she'd live long.

Goddess bless this sacrifice and make it worth it.

* * *

Duke Caedmon looked into the faces of the men he'd gathered to his quarters—Count Pandaran, Baron Gwawl, Baron Teague, Duke Sheen, and Duke Tierney. With the help of these men, he hoped to prevent a disaster. He couldn't have been happier with Gwawl's change of heart. It was the swearing of the swords that finally brought him over, as it had Teague.

"So we agree we will face her united?" Caedmon asked. "Demand she give up the peasant?"

"By all means," Sheen agreed. "I will not bow to a Lundian and a commoner at that."

"Sir Robrek is no mere commoner," Pandaran objected. "He's a dangerous sorcerer. How do you propose dealing with him?"

Caedmon stared at Pandaran. He was surprised the count had shown political insight. He'd never seemed concerned with anything other than his appearance. "If he tries to cause problems, he can be taken care of," Caedmon said. He'd thought of a way to deal with the matter. It was risky, but he believed it would work.

"But who will get the prize if we succeed in stripping it from him?" Pandaran asked.

Caedmon had anticipated this question. "I suggest we draw lots."

"It is the only way." Duke Sheen nodded, and Caedmon suppressed a sigh of relief. He'd been afraid Sheen would insist on one of his sons.

With Sheen's support, the other men agreed. It took all of them a step closer to the throne. Only Caedmon didn't have a personal stake, his sons all being married already. "The wedding is less than a week away, so we have little time. A council meeting is scheduled for tomorrow. I propose we address the matter then."

* * *

Gael brushed a hand over Jenna's hair. Duke Caedmon's servant wasn't pretty and had the figure of a ten-year-old boy. He wanted to leave immediately, but he hadn't yet got what he'd come for. Duke Caedmon had met with several members of the Royal Council earlier, and Gael needed to know what had gone on in that meeting. Jenna had served the refreshments and had no doubt eavesdropped when she'd been dismissed.

Jenna sighed. "Do you think Sir Robrek truly loves the princess?"

"Absolutely."

Jenna sighed more loudly. "That's what I thought. It's all too sad, really."

"What's sad about two people in love getting married?"

"Maybe they won't be able to marry, that's all."

"Why wouldn't they?"

Jenna sighed yet again. "I really shouldn't say anything."

Praying for patience, Gael closed his eyes. Jenna always protested endlessly before divulging what she knew. Gael nuzzled Jenna's neck and kissed her ear. "I can keep a secret."

Gael expected more protests and maybe the need to bed her all over again, but Jenna must have been upset because, after another sigh, she said, "His Grace is trying to stop the marriage." Jenna told Gael what had gone on in the meeting. "I know Sir Robrek is really a peasant, but sometimes His Grace can be just plain mean. Shouldn't Her Highness get to marry the man she loves?"

"Certainly she should." Abruptly, Gael slipped from the bed. "I need to get back to my master before he misses me." Her Highness needed this information immediately.

* * *

In her reception room with Sir Robrek beside her, Samantha listened to Duer's report with alarm. "They plan to withdraw all support from Your Highness, financial and otherwise, if you refuse to comply."

"No," she breathed. If she lost the support of all of the Korthian members of her council and the one Lundian who hadn't betrayed her, she couldn't rule. *How can Caedmon do this to me? How can he see this as loyalty?* She slipped a ring from her finger and gave it to Lord Duer. "Present this to Gael. He has done well."

Duer bowed deeply. "We only seek to serve the Your Highness." He bowed again and left.

Robbie took her hand. "What will you do?"

She squeezed his hand tightly. "I will not give you up."

"What if we preempted them?" Robbie said. "You wanted me to swear my sword publicly. What if I did it tomorrow at court? Would that not prove that I'm not after power for myself?"

Samantha stared at Robbie. He'd shown no ability for political maneuvering before. Every day brought her one more reason to love him. "That has possibilities. But I doubt it will be enough."

"What if those who swore their swords to me swore to you as well?"

"Will they do that?"

"Yes," Robbie answered, with complete assurance.

Samantha was less certain, so she sent a page for Captain Hawk; she knew he was loyal to her, but did that make him loyal to Robbie as well?

Hawk bowed as he was ushered into the room. "How may I serve, Your Highness?"

"You have heard of the recent swearing of the swords to my betrothed?"

Hawk looked nervously between her and Robbie. "I have heard, Your Highness. I hope Your Highness does not take it amiss. I assure you they meant no disloyalty to Your Highness."

"Some among my council see things differently. They see it as an attempt by Sir Robrek to usurp my power. He assures me it is not and, on the morrow, plans to swear his sword to me and have those sworn to him do so as well."

Hawk's face cleared. "An excellent idea, Your Highness, but if I might make a suggestion?"

She nodded her permission.

"Might not the gesture be more powerful if more than the two dozen sworn to Sir Robrek also swear to you? I know it would take a while, but why not the entire Royal Guard, starting with me and my officers? It would demonstrate the Royal Guard's support for Your Highness and your betrothed."

Samantha could hardly stop herself from jumping for joy. "Would they be willing to?"

"The Royal Guard stands behind the throne."

CHAPTER 17

"And where is Sir Robrek today?" Caedmon whispered, as he stood beside Samantha's throne in the throne room. Other members of the Royal Council stood in groups throughout the crowded room.

"He'll be here," she said.

Caedmon made a noise in his throat. "Late."

Samantha wanted to round on him. *How dare he criticize Robbie when he plans to betray me so thoroughly?*

She quickly ruled on the first two matters brought before her. Suddenly, the doors of the throne room were thrown open, and a trumpet sounded. All heads turned to the door, and Robbie, backed by those who had sworn to him, stepped into the room. The herald announced, "Sir Robrek."

Robbie strode across the throne room, dressed in his armor and looking every inch a prince despite being far shorter than the men who followed him. Robbie stopped in front of her, turned and faced the crowd, and extended a hand in her direction. "Some have questioned my motives and my loyalty to my betrothed." His voice carried throughout the large room, which had fallen silent. "They see me as seeking power that is not mine to have. But I never sought to be king. When I rode to the top of Gloine Torr and won the contest, I swore an oath that I would faithfully serve Her Highness, the Princess Samantha, as her consort and never attempt to usurp her power as the reigning monarch. I repeat this oath and more here today." He drew his sword and went down on one knee before her.

"I, Sir Robrek, do hereby swear my sword and all the swords at my command to thy service." A soft rustling passed through the room as Robbie continued, "I shall forever be thy consort and liege man. On Sulis's holy name and on my mother's grave, I promise in matters of life and limb and of earthly honor that I will maintain faith and loyalty to thee, Princess Samantha. May my sword be ever feared by thine enemies." A gasp went up from those gathered.

Samantha accepted Robbie's sword. "I accept your sword and your oath. Long may you live and rule at my side." Samantha touched Robbie on both shoulders. She took Robbie's hand and lifted him to his feet. He sheathed his sword and stood by her side.

Black Giant stumbled forward, his face streaming with tears. He drew his sword, fell at her feet, and repeated the oath he had previously given Robbie, although this time with her name first. One by one all the sworn ones came forward. Except for the men kneeling and speaking the oath, there wasn't a sound throughout the room.

After the sworn ones, Captain Hawk came forward. "After today, let there be no question wherein lies the loyalty of the Royal Guard. We firmly stand behind Her Highness, the Princess Samantha, and Sulis's choice for her consort, Sir Robrek of Mahngbhayo." He drew his sword and went down on one knee. "I, Hawk, captain of the Royal Guard, do hereby swear my sword to thy service. I shall become thy liege man. In Sulis's holy name and on my mother's grave, I promise in matters of life and limb and of earthly honor that I will maintain faith and loyalty to Her Highness, Princess Samantha and her consort, Sir Robrek of Mahngbhayo. May my sword ever be stained bright with the blood of thine enemies."

As Samantha accepted Hawk's oath, she felt a surge of triumph. *The Royal Guard is mine! Let anyone try to stop me now!* Behind Hawk came every one of his officers, and behind them, a line of Royal Guardsmen stretched out the door.

It took over an hour to accept the oaths of all those who presented themselves. When she accepted the sword of the last man in line, her arm was trembling with exhaustion.

* * *

In the council chamber, Samantha sat with Caedmon alone, except for her guards. Court had gone on so long that the council meeting had been delayed until tomorrow. "Caedmon, I thought you were my oldest friend, my most loyal supporter," Samantha said.

He somehow managed to look offended. "You thought? How can you doubt it?"

Samantha closed her eyes briefly, trying to contain her anger. She hoped to talk sense into him, something she could do only if she remained calm. "I am no fool, Caedmon. I know of your meeting with the other Korthian councilors. You're trying to undermine my rule, and if that isn't treason, I don't know what is."

Caedmon threw up his hands. "I'm trying to save you from the foolishness of youth! That peasant will doom you!"

"You refuse to believe in my power as an aurora, to believe I know when the goddess has revealed her choice to me, as she promised. But further, can you not see what assembling the council against me will do to me? How much it will weaken me? Soon, my every decision will have to be approved by a council of men at each other's throats. At best, I will become a mere puppet."

Caedmon leaned forward in his chair. "I would never allow that to happen, Your Highness. But for your own good, this peasant must go."

"Don't turn against me, Uncle! I need you." She held out a hand to him, hoping to soften him.

He didn't take it. "Samantha, you know I love you like a daughter, but I can't allow this sorcerer to become king."

"Uncle, as much as it pains me, if you refuse to give me your sacred vow that you will abandon this plan, I must have you arrested for treason. Uncle, don't make me execute you." She again reached out to him.

Caedmon pushed to his feet, his face blanching. "How can you hope to rule without my guidance? And do you think eliminating me will stop the others?" *Please, don't make me do this.* "Yes, I do. As you have seen, the Royal Guard is mine. The others will give up if you are no longer leading them. Respect my choice and the goddess's. Give this up."

He stared at her for a few moments, and a resolution she didn't like passed over his face. But he sighed deeply. "Your Highness, I'll back down this time. I'll inform the others we won't go through with it."

Samantha leaned toward him. "Can I have your sacred oath on that?"

His eyes narrowed, but he drew the star of Sulis over his breast. "I swear by the goddess and on my mother's grave, I won't lead the council against Sir Robrek."

"Thank you, Uncle." She reached again, and this time he took her hand. "You don't know how much this means to me."

* * *

Caedmon stormed away, wondering how Samantha had learned of his plans. When he entered his quarters, Righ was waiting for him, drinking his finest brandy. Caedmon stiffened but didn't say anything. Caedmon crossed to the sideboard and poured some for himself. "Find out who leaked the information, so I can gut them." Caedmon tossed down the glass and poured another. "There seems to be no way to get her to willingly separate from the accursed peasant. We'll have to proceed with the alternate plan."

* * *

In her chamber at her windowsill, Oriana rested her head on her hands and glumly contemplated the snow swirling around the palace. *Why didn't they come?* Snow this thick in Murtaghan certainly meant the mountain passes were blocked now, and they would be until spring. Oriana was so homesick she didn't think she could stand it any longer. Sometimes her brothers had been annoying, always trying to boss her around because they were older. But they'd loved her.

She started at a knock on the door and jumped up to answer it. That irritating boy Vaughan stood there, dressed in another ridiculous outfit. "What do you want?" she snapped.

"He was kind enough to escort me to you," said a man, stepping out from behind the door.

"Quinn!" Oriana squealed and launched herself into her brother's arms.

Quinn hugged her tightly. "Oh, little Rosemary, at least you're safe." As her healing talent had become evident, her brothers had taken to calling her by the names of various herbs, a habit which had once irritated her but which she now found comforting. "I couldn't bear it if you'd come to harm, too."

Her brother's face was wet with tears. She pulled away from him. "Where's Father? Where's Arlen?"

Quinn shook his head. "I don't know how to tell you this, Burdock Root, but they're gone. Both of them."

"What do you mean, 'gone'?" She pulled him into her chamber and shut the door in Vaughan's face.

"The curse got them." Oriana trembled at the grim despair in her brother's voice. "It's not just the sick anymore—everything and everybody is dying. It got father first and then Arlen. I tried to care for them, but when Arlen died, I knew I needed to get out of there quickly or it'd get me, too. Masterly was our only horse still alive, so I saddled him, packed everything I could, and headed east as fast as possible. I guess I outran it. Probably no one in our village is alive now."

Oriana remembered those who'd weakened and died under her hands after Mother Venetia was taken. How could she have let even the princess take her away from her people when they had so badly needed her? "It's my fault," Oriana sobbed. "If only I'd been there, none of this would have happened."

"Sweet Thyme, you couldn't have done anything. The curse is too strong. Nobody can stop such a thing."

Oriana wiped her face viciously and grabbed Quinn's hand. "Sir Robrek can."

* * *

"Milord." Drem's voice jarred Robrek out of his dream of the blood red lake. "I didn't want to wake you, but Duke Caedmon has invited you to breakfast."

Robrek sat up in bed and read the note Drem handed him.

Sir Robrek,

In light of my recent conversation with Her Highness, I'd like to resolve our differences. Please, accept my invitation to breakfast.

Her Highness's faithful servant,
Caedmon, Duke of Tuath and Boirche

Robrek jumped up and dressed quickly. If the duke was serious, this would be a tremendous relief to Samantha.

Followed by Eburacon and Geblan, Robrek entered the duke's rooms. Tapestries of the battle and the hunt, similar to those Drem had found appropriate for Robrek's rooms, lined the walls, making Robrek instantly wary. Caedmon rose to greet him. "Welcome, Sir Robrek," he said. "I've been wanting to have a little chat with you. Have a seat. What may I offer you to drink? I have fresh cider and *bhat*." A large breakfast table set with only two plates stood in the middle of the reception room. The table was covered with meats and cheeses, breads and fruits—enough food for at least a dozen people. Robrek still had a hard time stomaching the elaborate palace meals at such an early hour.

Glancing at Caedmon's guards, Robrek accepted the *bhat* and took a seat. At Samantha's insistence, Robrek was always accompanied by his guards, but it wasn't usual for Caedmon to be. "You feel the need to have protection from me?"

"Let's just say they are here to ensure there are no misunderstandings." Caedmon narrowed his eyes at Robrek's guards, who stood behind his chair. He picked up a sausage and took a bite. "Let's get straight to the point. What is it you're after—the money or the power? I can provide you both. I can send you anywhere you want to go and make sure you never have to work a day in your life." He leaned closer. "What will it take to get you to go away? Name your price."

Robrek tightened his hands into fists. "Your question is an insult. I crave neither wealth nor position. I love the princess."

Caedmon's eyes narrowed further. "You don't know the meaning of the word. If you truly loved her, you would see you aren't fit to be her stable groom, let alone her consort."

Robrek rose. "I won't stay to be insulted."

Caedmon slipped his knife from his belt. "You'll marry her over my dead body."

Robrek's guards drew their swords. "Drop the knife, Your Grace," Eburacon said.

"I will not live to see the end of Solar's dream!" With that cry, Caedmon plunged the knife straight into his own heart.

"No!" Robrek vaulted over the table and lowered Caedmon to the ground. He pulled out the knife, pulled his hands over the wound, and went into a healing trance.

* * *

While her maids were doing her hair, Samantha received a message that Oriana and a young male peasant were asking to see her. She had them shown in. Oriana's face was red and stained with tears. The princess got to her feet. "Oriana, what's wrong?"

Oriana bowed to her, and the peasant followed suit. "Please, Your Highness, this is my brother Quinn, and he's brought terrible news. My father and brother are dead."

Samantha squeezed her eyes shut at the mention of a dead father. She pushed the grief away. "Oriana, I'm so sorry. How did it happen?"

Oriana came forward and grasped the princess's hand. "It's the curse. It's getting much, much worse." The young girl repeated what her brother had told her.

An entire village wiped out by plague! Even the animals! The vegetation! Samantha's gut churned at the news of yet another problem. She sat on a sofa, pulling Oriana down beside her. "I know you said that healing had become more difficult in your village, but you never indicated it was anywhere near as bad as this."

Oriana's eyes filled with tears. "It wasn't, Your Highness. The curse got stronger."

Samantha patted Oriana's shoulder. "Sir Robrek should hear of this."

Oriana wiped her eyes. "I tried to tell him, but he wasn't in his quarters. His servant said he was breakfasting with Duke Caedmon."

Samantha felt her heart drop into her stomach. *No! Caedmon gave me his sacred vow!* But she remembered the resolution that had passed over Caedmon's face, and his oath had only mentioned not leading the council.

"Stay put!" Samantha ordered Oriana and her brother. She grabbed her sword and, with her guards beside her, hurried out of her rooms. She gathered every guard they passed to accompany her.

Caedmon's door was locked. She knocked. Voices shouted from the other side of the door:

"Do it now! Before it's too late!"

"He isn't finished yet!"

"There's no more time! Kill him now!"

No! Samantha whirled toward her guards. "Break it open! Stop them!"

Conroy and Bearach crashed through the door. Swords clanged. Samantha hurried inside. At first her mind refused to register what she saw. Eburacon and Geblan lay on the floor with knives through their throats. Righ and another of Caedmon's men lay dead. Blood dripped from Bearach and Conroy's swords. And in the center of the room, Duke Caedmon and Robbie lay covered in blood, and Robbie had a sword sticking out of his back.

"No!" she screamed. "No, Robbie, no! Please, Sulis, he can't be dead!"

Bearach touched the side of his neck. "He has a pulse, Your Highness."

She grabbed the nearest guard. "Fetch Oriana from my quarters! *Run!*"

She knelt next to Robbie and took hold of his hand. She wanted to wrench the sword out of Robbie's back, but she knew she had to wait for a healer. "Don't you dare die," she whispered. "Don't you dare!" Blood bubbled around the sword.

The guard sprinted in with Oriana. The young healer gasped. "Sir Robrek! No!" She fell to her knees and put her hands on either side of the sword and closed her eyes. When she opened them, her eyes were wide. "It's missed his heart, but it's punctured his lung. Your Highness, I can't do this alone."

"Leigh!" the princess cried, and sent a messenger to fetch the healer. "Keep him alive!" Samantha commanded Oriana.

Oriana's face went blank, and Samantha knew she was entering a healing trance. *Oh, Sulis, Mother of us all! You chose him! Make him live! I beg you! Make him live!* She felt Robbie's pulse in his wrist; it was slow and weak. Bubbles continued to appear around the sword's hilt.

She looked at the man she'd called uncle all of her life. "Is he dead?"

"No, Your Highness," someone answered. Samantha didn't know who and didn't care. "His pulse is strong and steady. It looks as if Sir Robrek had been healing him when he was stabbed."

"Take him to the dungeon," she commanded, unable to tolerate the sight of the man who'd done this to the one she loved. If Robbie died, nothing mattered. She didn't want to be queen if it meant this much pain. Samantha blinked to clear her eyes, but the world blurred in front of her. Savagely she wiped her eyes on her sleeve.

After an eternity, Leigh arrived. He pulled Oriana out of her trance. Even though all she'd been doing was sustaining Robbie's life, she was shaking with exhaustion. The two healers had a rapid discussion, and then Oriana and Leigh put their hands on either side of the sword sticking from Robbie's back. Iden, one of Robbie's guards, held the sword. "On the count of three," Leigh said. On three, Iden yanked the sword free. Both healers put their palms over the wound and closed their eyes. Blood poured over their hands. The blood slowed, but the two healers reeled and passed out.

Holy Sulis! Samantha knelt and wiped the blood off Robbie's back with the sleeve of her gown. The bleeding hadn't stopped completely, and bubbles of air continued to appear at the wound. "No! No!"

She grabbed his wrist and felt his pulse. It was stronger, but still slow. She tried to shake the healers awake, but got no response. Panicking, she sent for Calum, the royal physician. When he arrived, he cleaned and bound the wound. "He may live an hour or two," he said. "But men don't recover from blood-filled lungs."

"He will!" she said, willing it to be true.

* * *

Struggling to breathe, Robrek drifted in a world of pain until he came to the blood-red lake. Beautiful women rose from the depths. They bared their breasts and beckoned to him, "Come to us. Be one with us. We will heal your pain."

Already naked, Robrek started toward the lake.

"Stop!" a voice called from behind him. He turned. Brazen, Fancy Man, and Holy Writ stood at the mouth of the cave. "The lake is like sweet paipin to one of your power."

Pain raged in his chest, and paipin sounded like blessed relief.

"Come!" the women beckoned again. Robrek forgot about the horses and started forward, but a man with ragged holes where his eyes should have been rose out of the depths.

"Do not let them take you as they took me."

Shocked at the implication, Robrek woke with a start, pain tearing at the center of his chest. He cried out, and someone grasped tightly to his hand. "Robbie, you must live!" Samantha said. "Don't die! Don't you dare die!"

He tried to speak, but he couldn't form words around the pain. He drifted inward and found the hole made by the sword. He tried to heal it, but he was too weak, so weak . . .

* * *

Alvabane knelt at the altar at the bottom of the east tower and stroked the Soul Stone. Over a thousand years ago, the greatest sorcerers of her people had created the Stone by magic long since lost, and it had nearly run the northern invaders back into Korth until the demon Armunn had trapped it behind his soul. In a few days, it would again be the night of the new moon, and she could perform the ceremony which would attune the Stone to her control. It would again do what it was created to do.

The base of the Stone was deep within the earth, resting in an underground lake. The lake was the source of the Stone's power; it fed on the souls sacrificed to its hunger, and hungry it was. For nearly a thousand years it had been unable to feed upon new life; now it fed without restraint. It drew life after life into the lake surrounding its base, and Alvabane laughed at its rapacity. The infidels who drove her people out were already paying for their crime, and they would pay much more once the Stone was hers.

CHAPTER 18

Samantha sat by Robbie's bedside alternately praying for his life and damning Caedmon to the deepest of the seven hells, the place she'd soon send him. From now on, she would be cold, as her father had been cold to all except her. She would care for no one but Robbie; no death would hurt her ever again. If Robbie died, she'd care for no one at all, least of all herself.

Robbie stirred and opened his eyes. "Water," he moaned.

"Oh, Robbie!" She wanted to launch herself onto the bed and cover him with kisses, but she wouldn't risk hurting him. She quickly filled a glass and helped him lift his head. He winced but got most of the water down before he pushed her hand away and lay back.

"What happened?" he rasped. "I tried to stop Caedmon from killing himself. . ."

"It wasn't suicide. It was a plot to assassinate you." She told him everything that had happened, including the deaths of Eburacon and Geblan.

"Holy Sulis!" He blinked back tears, and his face paled as if he was going to be sick. "They were too good to die like that. Had they any family?"

Samantha shook her head. "I don't know."

"If they did, I want to be sure they're cared for. And what else? What's the proper response when someone sacrifices his life for yours?"

"I'll have Blaine see to their families. But don't torture yourself over it. They knew the risks when they signed on to be your protectors." Robbie snorted, as if he didn't believe they'd envisioned dying in so cowardly an attack. "They will get justice, I assure you."

He took her hand. "So you mean to execute Caedmon?" His eyes were full of concern, which she didn't need. She wouldn't mourn someone who'd betrayed her.

"He tried to kill you. No other punishment fits his crime. My love, no one will stop me from marrying you! No one!"

A smile lit the corners of his mouth. "What day is it?"

"Three days before our wedding. If you're not strong enough—"

"I'll be strong enough." He winked.

* * *

Samantha stood before the entrance to Duke Caedmon's cell. She'd passed sentence against Duke Caedmon without hesitation, but a part of her heart had turned to stone as she'd done so. The duke had asked to see her before his execution, and she'd nearly denied him. Nothing he could say could excuse his actions, but she couldn't ignore the last request of the man she'd once loved as her uncle

She nodded to the guard, and he unlocked Caedmon's cell. Bearach entered first, and Caedmon rose to his feet. "Samantha, surely you don't believe you need protection against me."

Samantha narrowed her eyes. "You will not address me familiarly. You lost that right when you betrayed me."

Caedmon put his hand over his heart. "Your Highness, you can't believe I would ever work against your interests. I love you like the daughter I never had."

Samantha stepped forward and slapped Caedmon's face. "How dare you talk of love when you tried to kill my betrothed? If he hadn't been so powerful, you would have succeeded!"

Caedmon threw up his hands, and Samantha wanted to order them chained to the wall. "Your Highness, you have to know it was a last resort. I did everything in my power to make you see reason."

"You were behind the rumors of a massacre in Valley Fair, weren't you?" Caedmon stared at her defiantly. "And the scorpion attack? How could my father have been so wrong about you? From the beginning, you have never been my advisor. Instead, you've attempted to take the power out of my hand and rule yourself. It is not Sir Robrek but *you* who has attempted to reduced me to a consort!"

"No, Samantha— Your Highness, surely you don't believe that. Everything I did, I did for you. You have to rid yourself of him before it is too late. He's—"

Samantha slapped him again, harder this time, and swept from the room. She should have known better than to come.

* * *

Shivering from a cold that wasn't physical, Samantha stood on the execution platform with the members of the Royal Council arrayed behind her—all except Duke Sheen. She had let it be known attendance wasn't optional, but Sheen had again pleaded illness. The duke was a problem she had no idea how to solve, and her most important advisor and her oldest friend would die today. She struggled to keep her court mask in place. She would shed no tears over the death of a traitor.

The crowd jeered and threw filth at the condemned as he was led toward the platform, but Caedmon held his head high. When Caedmon neared, his eyes sought hers, but she avoided them and stared steadfastly at the executioner's block. A masked executioner stood next to it with his axe.

When the condemned was in position, Samantha spoke, keeping all emotion out of her voice and pitching it to be heard throughout the square. "My people, let it be known that Caedmon, duke of Tuath and Boirche, has been found guilty of treason in plotting the assassination of my betrothed, Sir Robrek." The crowd booed and threw more filth. Public opinion was such a fickle thing. She raised her hand for silence. When she had it, she turned to Caedmon. "For your crimes, you have been sentenced to death by beheading. Your head will then be placed on the palace battlements as a warning to any others who would plot against the crown. Tradition allows the condemned to speak. You may do so now if you so desire."

Caedmon thrust out his chest. "I make no apologies. I did what any man who truly loves his country would have. The peasant sorcerer, Robrek *Angusstamm*, must be removed at any cost." The crowd hissed, as Caedmon gave Robrek no title and emphasized the surname that marked his peasant birth. "If he becomes your king, there is no hope." He turned to the princess. "Samantha, Your

222

Highness, with pride and pleasure, I watched you growing from a delightful young child to a mature woman I willingly honor as my liege. Sometime in the future you will look back on this day and weep bitter tears that you refused to heed my counsel. I'm sorry your actions will prevent me for helping you pick up the pieces of your kingdom. I can merely pray that you come to your senses before any more damage is done." He looked away from her and addressed the rest of those gathered. "As I go to my death today, my only regret is I didn't succeed. I ask all of you who love your country as I do, to ask yourselves—"

"Enough!" Samantha's voice rang out.

Caedmon bowed to her. "As Your Highness wills."

The guards grabbed Caedmon, but the duke shook off their hands. "I will face my death with honor." He calmly walked to the executioner's block, knelt, and placed his head on the block. The executioner bowed before Father Hafghan and traced the star of Sulis over his breast. The high priest placed his hand on the executioner's head, absolving him of the sin of taking life. The executioner stood and looked toward the princess. "Proceed," she ordered.

The axe rose and fell, and Caedmon's head fell into the waiting basket.

* * *

Baron Gwawl avoided Duke Sheen's eyes as he met with the other Korthian councilors. He looked instead toward the empty chair that should have been occupied by Duke Caedmon. Korthlundia wouldn't be the same without him. When Gwawl had watched Caedmon die, he'd longed to do something to stop the executioner's axe, to take Caedmon's place even. But unfortunately, Caedmon had crossed a line that Gwawl could have told him was sacrosanct.

Sheen opened the meeting. "What do we do now? How do we stop this wedding? It is only two days away. We came to her rescue. We deserve something more than to be shunted aside for a mere peasant!"

Gwawl took his eyes off the empty chair and faced Sheen. "She has shown she won't back down. She won't become the puppet of this council. She is her father's daughter after all."

"Are you sure about that?" Sheen said. "What if Argblutal's accusation is true? What if she is a bastard?"

Gwawl gasped, and Teague rose to his feet. "I agreed something needed to be done about Sir Robrek, but I won't listen to treason."

Pandaran looked up from examining his nails. "Nor I. I, at least, look better with my head attached."

Sheen rose. "If we unite, we have enough men to challenge the Royal Guard and force Her Highness into a more appropriate marriage." Sheen wouldn't be truly satisfied unless Her Highness married one of his sons.

Baron Teague laughed. "It would be a bloodbath at best, and you won't have *my* men."

Gwawl leaned forward. "I won't countenance such treason."

Sheen puffed up, then turned and stormed from the room.

* * *

Robrek woke to find Ronan curled up next to his feet, purring, and Oriana sitting next to his bedside. The young novice's face was red from weeping. "What's the matter?" he asked, trying to raise himself. "I'll be all right." But would he really? Physically, he'd heal, but he was tired of people wanting him dead. *And Eburacon and Geblan are dead because of me.*

Oriana helped him into a sitting position. It hurt to move, but not more than he could handle. "I know, Milord. That isn't the problem. It's my family." Oriana told him what she'd learned from her brother. "I know Her Highness has forgotten in her worry over you, but, Milord, something is terribly, terribly wrong. It doesn't seem to spare even the cockroaches."

"Cockroaches?" Robrek repeated. He'd never heard of a disease that affected cockroaches. "What are the symptoms?" he asked.

Oriana shook her head. "There are none, Milord."

That didn't seem possible; Oriana must not have understood. "Send for your brother."

After a brief while, Oriana's brother appeared. He bowed repeatedly as he was led into the room by Robrek's guards. They were new ones—Varney and Bartle. The two were among the sworn ones, but would he ever get used to Eburacon and Geblan being gone?

Oriana's brother stared at his feet as Robrek asked him about the disease. "Everything just weakens and dies, Milord. Nothing else."

"No fever? No breathing difficulties? No rash or swellings?"

"There's never a mark on them, Milord. I felt myself start to weaken and ran for the only horse we had still alive and rode out of there as fast as he could take me. As I got farther away from our village, I began to feel stronger again. My horse did, too. Whatever it was, we escaped it."

"If the disease had already started to affect you, distance shouldn't make any difference," Robrek protested.

Quinn shrugged, still staring at his feet. "Milord, I don't believe it's a disease. It's magic, a curse."

Remembering his conversation with his uncle, Robrek nodded. Was this the problem he was blamed for? He didn't really believe in magical curses, but certainly this disease was acting like none he'd ever heard of. "If you don't mind, I'd like to touch you."

Quinn approached the bed, and Robrek touched him. He closed his eyes and went into a healer's trance. But he found nothing wrong with Oriana's brother.

Samantha entered the room, and he smiled at the sight of her. The entire world seemed brighter in her presence. But the smile quickly left his face as he contemplated the problem. "Have you heard of this curse?" he asked her.

Samantha sighed and collapsed into a chair next to the bed. "I didn't want you bothered until you were stronger." Her eyes narrowed at Oriana and Quinn.

"I'm strong enough." He took her hand and drew her back to face him. "Do you think this is why the goddess chose me as your consort?"

Samantha brushed the hair back from his head. "Maybe, but you need to recover your own strength before you worry about such things."

Samantha and the others left him to rest and recover, but he tossed and turned. Hundreds wiped out by a curse, and what if it spread to other villages? This had to be the reason he was chosen, but how could he stop something like this? *I can't just lie here when hundreds, thousands of lives may be at risk.* He needed more information, and there was only one place he knew of to get it.

Sam would be angry if he got out of bed, but he rang for Drem anyway and, for once, had the servant help him get dressed. Drem seemed so satisfied that Robrek was allowing him to be a proper servant he didn't question Robrek's reasons for being out of bed. Robrek exited his rooms and asked his guards to show him to the palace library.

Entering the library, he gaped like the country peasant he was. The room was as vast as the shrine in Valley Fair and carpeted with a thick ruby red carpet interwoven with gold to form interlocking triangles. The walls were lined with bookcases that reached from the floor to at least five feet above his head. Windows equally tall stood between the bookcases, offering a view of snow whirling around the palace. More bookcases stood row upon row in the center of the room. A staircase led up to a second floor which was also lined with books. He had never imagined so many books existed in the entire joined kingdoms. There had to be at least ten thousand volumes. If the answer to the curse was here, Robrek couldn't imagine how he'd find it.

Robrek shivered, and not simply at the sheer number of books. The library was freezing cold. Off in one corner, a fire burned in a small grate, but each of vast fireplaces on the side walls were empty.

Dressed in scholar's robes and with his white hair sticking out in tufts, an old man scurried forward to greet him, bowing repeatedly. "Milord, I am Druce, the chief librarian. How may we be of service?" The man's hand twitched as if he wanted to draw Sulis's star but didn't dare.

Robrek ignored Druce's hand. He walked to the table near the fire, directed Druce to a chair, and sat across from him. "Can I trust your complete discretion?"

Druce beamed. "Of course, Milord. Her Highness can vouch for my loyalty. I can be absolutely discrete."

Robrek somehow doubted that, but the library was simply too big for him to hope to find anything on his own. He leaned toward Druce so that the half-dozen under-librarians wouldn't hear and told him all he had learned from Oriana's brother.

Druce nodded. "And you fear it won't stop its deadly work with this one village?"

Robrek blew out a breath. "Sulis bless that it might, but we can't count on it."

Druce's eyes gleamed with excitement. "This is certainly a most interesting problem, one that will take a great deal of research. We could make more rapid progress if you'd allow me to enlist the aid of a couple of my assistants. I assure you they too will be most discrete."

Considering the size of the library, Robrek agreed, and Druce called over two of his assistants, who he introduced as Garran and Garrett. The two men were in their mid-twenties and identical to the last freckle. They both had their hair shaved to a fine stubble, large noses, and eyebrows so pale they might as well have had none. They even dressed in identical scholars' robes of rough, undyed wool. They seemed as excited as Druce by the prospect of such an unusual problem. Robrek found their excitement ghoulish, but he couldn't fault the enthusiasm with which they set about finding an answer.

Within minutes, the small table near the fire was groaning under weighty volumes, and the four of them crowded uncomfortably around it. Robrek looked toward the much larger table near the huge fireplace. "Is it possible we could have a fire lit in the big fireplace? We could do our research in greater comfort and convenience."

"Of course, Milord. I'll see to at once." Druce sent Garran or Garrett—Robrek couldn't tell which—to fetch a servant. Soon they were immersed in research in front of a roaring fire. Garran, Garrett, and the other library assistants looked at him as if with that single act he'd earned their undying loyalty.

The first book Robrek opened was a thick volume bound with rich, dark brown leather. The gold lettering on the spine read *Strange Diseases and Unusual Curses* "by a faithful servant of the Goddess." The first section was devoted to curses to "prevent the most foul and dishonorable practice of the thievery of books." The person was to take the volume to be protected outside in the woods on the night of a full moon, sacrifice a rabbit, and sprinkle the blood in a circle surrounding the book. He was then to chant the following words:

> He who steals this book
> May he be frizzled in a pan
> May his hair fall out
> May his bowels run red
> May his Manhood wilt . . .

The curse went on in like manner for two full pages, calling down increasingly terrible punishments upon the would-be book thief. Robrek flipped quickly to the end of the section.

But the next section was devoted to something even more bizarre: "Curses to protect thy crops from the demons that rise from beneath." Under the section title was a drawing of a strange bat-like human rising from the ground in a field of grain. Next came a section on causing madness in your enemy, and section after section on causing a number of repulsive illnesses, mostly involving the genitals or bowels, including a puzzling one inducing "the fate of Ned's cock on the most foul wooer of thy wife." Robrek couldn't help wondering what had happened to poor Ned's cock.

"Nonsense," he muttered under his breath, further convinced there were no such things as curses. He shut the book with a sigh. The next one looked more promising. The gold lettering on its spine read *The History of Plague in the Land of the Goddess*. Fortunately, the book didn't discuss any nonexistent curses; instead, it described various epidemics that included symptoms such as lumps in the armpits and neck, fever, chills, abdominal pain, bleeding into skin and other organs, coughing, difficulty breathing, rotting of the flesh, blackening of the skin, foul odor, paralysis, and spasms. But there was nothing from which the victim simply weakened and died.

* * *

Samantha sat in her window seat and watched the snow swirling around the palace. From here, she couldn't see the palace battlements where Caedmon's head was mounted, but she was aware of its presence. Or rather, she was aware of Caedmon's absence.

She cursed him for making his death necessary. She leaned against the window. "Father, how am I supposed to make it alone? Why didn't you see what he was? Who is going to guide me now?"

She thought she should cry, but she had no tears left. Except for the part that belonged to Robbie, her heart was stone. A monarch had no use for emotion; her father had taught her that, but she never truly understood what he meant until now. She never understood how lonely her father must have been all those long years he'd been king. At least, she had Robbie. She touched her stomach. Soon she would have a child. She wasn't sure there was enough of her heart left to love a child, like her father had loved her. She certainly wouldn't make the mistake of loving anyone else, not ever again.

There was a knock on the door, and Robbie entered. She got to her feet. "What are you doing out of bed?"

"I'm fine, Sam. I couldn't lie still any longer, not with so many problems surrounding us." He crossed the room and took her in his arms.

"Are you sure you're fine?" She touched his chest where the sword had so recently been.

He released her and pulled up his shirt. A thin white line outlined the wound, but there was no other sign of the injury. "Yes, I'm sure. You don't need to worry about me anymore. How are you?"

"What could be wrong with me since you are alive?" she said, and tried to smile, but she knew the smile didn't reach her eyes.

"It's Duke Caedmon, isn't it? You're mourning your friend."

She turned away. "Of course not. A friend doesn't murder the one you love. Do not speak of him."

He put his hand on her shoulder. "It's okay to feel bad. You've loved him since you were a child."

She stepped forward, so his hand no longer touched her. "The man I thought I loved would never have done what he did. I never knew the *real* Caedmon."

"Sam—"

She whirled to face him. "No, I forbid it!"

Another knock on the door disturbed them, and Robbie's Uncle Slathek came in, followed by their guards. He bowed to her and pounded Robbie on the back. "Kinsman, are you ready?"

Robbie looked uncertainly toward her. "I don't think I should go." Samantha wasn't sure what they were talking about.

"Nonsense. A marriage can't take place if the bridegroom hasn't been properly feted beforehand. It simply isn't done. Not even in this backwards country." He blushed. "Forgive me, Your Highness. I meant no disrespect."

"None taken," she said, as she remembered the bachelor party planned for this evening. "But maybe Sir Robrek is right. I'm unsure he's sufficiently recovered for that kind of thing."

Robbie shook his head. "It's not that." He looked at her tenderly. "I just think I should stay."

Samantha let the coldness seize her heart. "Go with your uncle."

He stepped forward and touched her. "Are you sure, Sam? I don't want to leave you to mourn alone."

"You are alive. I have no loss to mourn."

"Of course she doesn't!" Slathek said. "The scum tried to murder you. Besides, tonight we must prepare you to wed your lady love. Come, Kinsman." He clapped Robbie on the shoulder again and began directing him toward the door.

Robbie let himself be led, but looked back at her. She tried smiling again, and said, "Go!"

* * *

Not certain he was doing the right thing, Robrek followed his uncle through the palace corridors. Outside the palace doors, they were met by Count Feoras, Lords Devyn and Edan, and all of the original sworn ones. The party proceeded to The Thirsty Knight. The sworn ones formed a perimeter around the building, and Robrek's personal guards preceded him inside. The outside looked the same as he remembered it, but when he went inside, there were flowers everywhere—a display that must have cost a fortune in the chill of winter. The crowd greeted his arrival with bows and cheers. The room was full of the young nobles of the court as well as the many friends of his uncle he'd met at the Traveler's Haven.

"Here, here, we have brought the bee," Lord Edan called out. "Let the party begin!"

"Bee?" Robrek asked.

"Ah, yes, my friend. Are you not the bee? Is not Her Highness the flower?" Edan winked lewdly and gestured to the flowers on the table. Robrek blushed, and the room exploded in laughter.

"Strike up the music! Bring on the mead and honey cakes!" Edan ordered. "We must prepare our bee to make honey with his lady love!"

"Hear! Hear!" The men laughed and cheered, as waitresses wearing low-cut gowns brought out huge trays of drink and food, most made with honey to celebrate the occasion. To the cheers and catcalls of the audience, the musicians played, and a singer sang a bawdy ballad about the wedding nights of long-dead heroes. Robrek blushed as one bawdy song followed another.

"Does Your Lordship think you could go for four full days and nights like Lord Bearnard of old?" someone called out.

"Marriage is not all about what happens between the sheets," Lord Devyn objected. "Sing of love and romance."

Devyn's comment was greeted with a chorus of both boos and cheers, and the singer bowed to Robrek. "With Your Lordship's permission, I will sing a song written especially for this occasion."

Robrek nodded, and the musicians began to play a calmer melody. Soon the singer's voice joined in. Robrek nearly choked on his honeyed tea when he realized the song was about him. It was a highly romanticized tale about his courtship with the princess. The magical horses had apparently come merely to see that true love would prevail. When the singer finished, he was greeted with riotous approval, but Robrek felt subdued. He hadn't believed Myst's claims that someday bards would sing of him.

The men around him cheered and patted him on the back, and the singer immediately launched into another bawdy song. The mead and honeyed tea flowed, and the singer continued to vary between romantic and bawdy music. After awhile, Slathek got up.

"Shall we not have dancing?"

"I don't think there are enough women to go around," Edan said.

"Bah!" Slathek waved the objection away. "Who needs women to dance?" He nodded to some of his friends and said something in his strange language without vowels. Chiamaka joined him, and others approached the musicians for their instruments. They yielded them reluctantly.

A wild, haunting song began that sounded to Robrek like an ocean storm breaking against the rocks. Slathek and Chiamaka began the dance by stomping their feet. The dance started slowly and built up momentum. They whirled and leaped, high-kicked and stomped, moving faster and faster until they were little more than a moving blur. Then they came to an abrupt halt with Slathek and Chiamaka shouting a strange, harsh word. Slathek paused and gestured to Robrek. "Will you join us, kinsman?"

Robrek smiled and joined his uncle, as did several other young noblemen. The music started slowly, and Robrek and the other Korthlundians followed the foreigners' movements as best they could. The dance was wild and freeing. Robrek felt as if he were becoming a part of the ocean itself. The music built, louder and faster, and Robrek swirled in the midst of the others as more and more joined in the dance. By the time the music came to a close, sweat streaked Robrek's face, and he panted heavily. Robrek laughed, collapsed into a chair, grabbed a passing pint of cider, and drained it.

CHAPTER 19

Blaine glanced at the lightening sky. It was nearly dawn. He'd spent all night going over his lists. *What have I forgotten? There must be something. A princess's wedding day should be perfect in every detail, and she gave me so little time to plan. Why in Sulis's name couldn't she have had the wedding in the spring or even at Solstice? Solstice would be an excellent time for a wedding. It isn't as if she isn't already enjoying the favors of Sir Robrek's bed.* Blaine gasped in horror that he'd even entertained such a thought. She was his queen, not some brazen hussy.

Blaine looked over his schedule for the day's events, trying to spot any potential difficulties. The morning started with the ceremony itself. The dressmakers had assured him the princess's and Sir Robrek's wedding finery were ready. Father Hafghan had promised he would be there to perform the ceremony. Blaine had already checked on the chapel decorations, and all was in readiness. The boys' chorus from the Temple of the Mother's Love would sing.

Blaine froze. *Holy Sulis, will they sing?* His notation on the list of ceremony plans indicated he'd delegated this task to Tuathal, and he'd had no confirmation that Tuathal had completed it. Blaine frantically searched through his piles of lists for any indication the boys' chorus had indeed been contacted. He found nothing. *Why did I ever trust anything of this importance to someone else? Her Highness can't walk down the aisle in silence!*

Blaine hurriedly rang for a page; when a sleepy young boy responded, Blaine sent him at once to fetch Tuathal. "And tell him I don't care what time it is! I need him immediately!"

When the page left, Blaine tried to make sure no other disaster lurked. The crowns for the coronation were in Captain Hawk's keeping; he insisted his men would have them in place beside the altar. After the ceremony, the new royal couple and the court were to set out in procession to greet the people. Tuathal had been responsible for seeing that the ceremonial trappings for Roberta and Wild Thing were ready. Blaine bit back a scream as he saw the notation that confirmed Tuathal's completion of the task. *Where I am going to get a chorus at this late date?*

Blaine tried to calm his breathing as he looked over the plans for the brunch sponsored by the Guilds in honor of the royal marriage. *Damn him to the seven hells. Where is Tuathal? How could I ever have thought he was fit for the princess's staff?* Blaine closed his eyes and counted to ten. He opened his eyes and looked over the brunch, which was the easiest event of the day because the Guilds had taken care of all of the arrangements themselves. He merely had to make sure the procession made it to the Guild Hall on time.

"Merely?" Blaine laughed, and he blushed at the hysterical note in his laughter. So many things could make them late. Father Hafghan could draw out the ceremony for the pleasure of listening to himself talk. The boys' chorus could sing more songs than they'd been asked to. *That is, if they're even singing at all. Please, everything should be for her as it is for the princesses in the bards' tales!* The princess had made only one mistake—appointing him to be her personal secretary.

Tuathal entered Blaine's office, looking as if he'd been dragged out of the deepest sleep. Blaine didn't understand how anyone responsible for the princess's affairs could sleep, and he barely resisted the urge to shake the man. "The boys' chorus! Did you make the arrangements or didn't you?"

"The boys' chorus?" Tuathal repeated, as if he were having difficulty understanding the concept of boys singing. "I talked to the chorus master. He wanted to know what songs the princess wanted sung. I'm sure I sent him the list, but I can't remember doing it."

"It is Her Highness's wedding day, and she is going to walk down the aisle in silence because you can't remember doing it!"

Tuathal put up his hands as if to ward off a blow. "Calm down, sir. I'm pretty sure I took care of it."

"'Pretty sure' may have been good enough when you were in the clerks' office! But 'pretty sure' is not good enough for any member of Her Highness's staff, especially today! You will go immediately to the Temple of the Mother's Love and make *absolutely* sure, and if there are no boys singing Her Highness down the aisle, I will rend you limb from limb, so to speak! Am I understood?"

"Perfectly. I'll go at once, sir." Tuathal hurried toward the door. Blaine sank into his chair, wondering if Tuathal's screams while being dismembered would be a proper substitute for the music of the boys' chorus. *What am I going to do?*

After the Guilds' reception, the royal couple would progress through the merchants' district to the city square, where the mayor, the chief magistrate, representatives of the merchant committee, and as many of the populace as could fit would greet them. Blaine didn't see what could go wrong with that. He'd personally coached Sir Robrek on what to say, and the princess had, of course, never needed coaching.

Then, back to the palace for the wedding banquet. Blaine groaned as he thought of the banquet and went over his list of the preparations. Maggie, the palace's chief cook, had guaranteed all would be prepared on time, but what if it wasn't? Wasn't the wedding feast the most important part of the occasion next to the ceremony itself?

Blaine got up, intending to go down to the kitchen to check, but stopped himself. Maggie had been in charge of royal banquets longer than he'd been alive. If he couldn't trust Maggie to get it right, who could he trust? He sat back down and looked over the seating arrangements, which had cost him dozens of agonizing hours. The princess had approved his arrangements and told him not to worry. He was still certain somebody would be offended by them. He could never live with himself if a mistake in the seating arrangement cost her the throne and led to civil war. As he stared at the arrangements, he could see no way to improve them, and the palace staff had already set out name cards.

He grabbed his hair as he looked over the portion of the day that was virtually a guaranteed disaster: the entertainment at the wedding banquet. Every bard, musician, actor, juggler, mime, dancer, acrobat, and entertainer of any variety in the entire joined kingdoms had petitioned for one of the slots on the program. It had been a difficult job, but Blaine had finally settled on a variety of acts. The princess had given it her approval, but she hadn't really been paying attention when he'd tried to describe the acts for her. She'd made the mistake of trusting him to make the appropriate choices, and she was sure to be mortified. He looked over the list again. How could he have thought a juggler would be appropriate? Blaine grabbed his hair tightly and pulled. He had no idea what he could do about the program now. Should he hang himself now and spare the populace from demanding his head? No, suicide was the coward's way out. He'd face his humiliation and make sure all of the blame for the fiasco fell on him in order to spare the princess.

As the sun rose in glorious brilliance, Tuathal returned, his face red, and he was panting as if he had run all the way to the Temple of the Mother's Love and back. Blaine jumped to his feet and grabbed the older man by the arm. "Will Her Highness be the first princess in the history of the joined kingdoms to be married without music?"

"No, sir," Tuathal panted, "it was as I told you. Everything's arranged. When I arrived at the Temple, the boys were busy getting into their formal robes. They're making their way to the palace as we speak."

"Thank you, Sulis, Mother of us all," Blaine sighed. He sent Tuathal to check on the preparations for the wedding feast and hurried to the chapel himself to make sure no unforeseen disasters had occurred with the decorations. Then he'd make sure the bride and the groom were dressing.

* * *

Ardra and Malvina fluttered around Samantha. Malvina beamed, "Your Highness, you're going to be the most gorgeous bride imaginable."

"And both of us be dressing you for your real wedding day, after all," Ardra said, helping the princess on with one of the many slips that would go under her gown.

Samantha felt a tightness in her chest and grabbed Ardra's hand. "I don't think I can ever thank you properly for what you did at Mabon."

Ardra blushed and turned away. "Let's not be talking about that again. Seeing you on the throne is thanks enough, Your Highness— although I don't think I'd mind taking your place today, either. Sir Robrek is a right handsome one." She winked lewdly.

Samantha couldn't help grinning. "He is, isn't he?"

* * *

Blaine had thought things couldn't get worse. It was just over half an hour before the ceremony was set to begin, and he'd just finished overseeing fixing the decorations in the chapel. Several of the flowers were positively wilted. Those who had been in charge of the decorations hadn't been able to understand his objections. They claimed things looked perfectly fine, as if a princess could get married surrounded by wilted flowers! He'd set things to right at last, but it'd been a close call. The boys' chorus and Father Hafghan had arrived, the crowns were in place, and the courtiers had begun lining the hallways down which the princess and Sir Robrek would pass on their way to the chapel. But he hadn't heard a word from the bride and groom. *Holy Sulis, are they still asleep?*

* * *

Robrek stood stiffly as Drem buttoned the buttons on the back of his tunic.

Slathek was all but bouncing around the room. He stopped suddenly, facing Robrek. "You're the very image of your mother. How proud she would be if she could see you today."

Robrek looked at himself in the mirror. He did look good. Samantha had chosen the cloth for his wedding finery to match her gown. He wore trews and an undertunic of creamy satin that brought out the richness of his skin color. The overtunic was emerald green silk with gold, silver, and bronze braid. Drem fastened a gold medallion of a horse around his neck, and his hair was braided and tied with the green ribbon Samantha had given him.

A commotion sounded from the doorway, and Blaine scurried in, his hair sticking out in all directions. Even through his shields, Robrek could feel his panic. Robrek clutched Blaine's arm. "What's wrong? Has something happened to Samantha?"

Blaine grabbed at his hair. "What isn't wrong? You seem nearly ready, so I guess that isn't wrong. But there are probably more wilted flowers I have yet to find. Holy Sulis, for all I know the princess is still in bed!" He fled the room.

* * *

Blaine stopped short at the doorway of the princess's dressing room, stunned by her beauty. Decorated with bronze, silver, and gold braid, her dress was a brilliant emerald green with slits to reveal a cream-colored underdress. But the dress wasn't what made the princess so beautiful today. Her smile set her entire face aglow. It was the smile of a woman about to marry the man she loved. For that smile alone, Sir Robrek earned Blaine's undying loyalty. Blaine had loved the princess ever since she'd smiled at him when he was five years old. He been sitting on his father's shoulders, watching the king's procession at the time. But over the time he'd served as her secretary, he'd seen too few of her smiles. She'd had far more difficulties before she'd even reached twenty years of age than most people faced in a lifetime. But now the difficulties were surely over.

The princess's maids were making the final touches to the flowers in her hair and her wedding veil. She turned to face him. "What is it, Blaine?"

"I. . ." Blaine bit back his litany of impending catastrophes. "I just wanted to inform Your Highness that everything is in readiness."

"Thank you, Blaine. I can't thank you enough for all you have done. I don't know anyone else who could have pulled it off on such short notice."

Blaine nearly swooned with panic. "Your Highness, I merely hope you won't have cause to withdraw your thanks before the end of the day."

The princess laughed, and her face sparkled even more brightly. "Oh, there's little danger of that."

Holy Sulis, she'll have my head on the chopping block!

* * *

When the formal knock came, the princess rose, and her bodyguards opened the door to admit several of the unmarried women of the court. They all held large baskets of flower petals.

Ardra drew her veil over her face and leaned in close to whisper, "Sulis bless you, Your Highness."

Malvina nodded and smiled. As soon as Samantha was gone, her maids would run to the servants' galleries above the chapel. It struck the princess as unfair that two of the people she cared most about had to watch from afar while the floor of the chapel would be littered with many for who she cared little. She squeezed her maids' hands and followed the unmarried women of the court out of her chambers.

She walked down the corridors as the women of the court sang the traditional bridal song, those accompanying her strewing flower petals in her path. After she passed, the women lining the corridors fell in behind her, escorting her to the chapel with their song. From some distance away, she could hear the sound of male voices singing to Robbie.

* * *

Robrek followed his uncle, Lord Edan, Lord Devyn, and other unmarried men of the court as they sprinkled flower petals in his path. The sound of so many voices singing the traditional groom's chorus sent shivers up his spine. Today he was to marry the princess. His heart sped up, and he had a brief fear he might faint. As he neared the chapel, he saw the princess approaching from the other direction.

All fear of fainting vanished. She was stunning, and Sulis help him, she would be his wife in only a few moments.

They met at the chapel's entrance, and heat filled his veins as he joined hands with the woman he loved. He squeezed her hand gently, and she responded in kind. Still singing, the men and women filed past them into the chapel. Once the courtiers were seated, they concluded the song, and the chapel filled with the sweet sound of the boys' chorus, signaling it was time for Robrek and Samantha to enter. Holding hands, they went through the doors and headed down the aisle. Father Hafghan stood solemnly before the altar. Beside the altar Robrek saw the crown he'd wear. Part of him still didn't believe he was about to be crowned king. Most of him wished a crown didn't have to accompany marriage to the woman he loved.

When they reached the altar, the chorus finished, and the high priest came forward. "We have come together here to celebrate of the joining of Her Highness, the crown Princess Samantha, and Sir Robrek Angusstamm. Sulis is the goddess of healing, of life, and of love. It is pleasing to the Holy Mother that we knit our hearts in love, one with another, as she has knit all of our hearts to her. We are blessed today to unite not merely a couple, but a kingdom. Let Sulis heal the wounds that have divided us and unite us again as one people as she unites the Princess Samantha and Sir Robrek this day."

Father Hafghan turned to the bridal couple. "Your Highness, Sir Robrek, always remember the vows you make before this people and the Holy Mother today. You are truly blessed that yours is a marriage of love, and not merely an affair of state. Always remember the love that flows through your hearts at this moment and allow it to flow outward until it encompasses all of the joined kingdoms. As your union thrives, so thrives the life and health of this kingdom and this people. Let your people bask in your love as you bask in the love of each other. Now, please, take each other by both hands, as a symbol that you will be united in both body and soul."

Father Hafghan turned to Samantha. "Do you, Samantha, Crown Princess and Heir to the throne of the Joined Kingdoms, take Sir Robrek Angusstamm as your husband under the eyes of the goddess from this day forward as you journey the path through this life and Beyond the Far Mountain?"

Robrek saw tears of joy streaming down Samantha's face as she answered. "Yes."

Father Hafghan turned to Robrek. "Do you, Sir Robrek Angusstamm, take Her Highness, the Crown Princess Samantha and heir to the throne of the joined kingdoms, as your wife under the eyes of the goddess from this day forward as you journey the path through this life and Beyond the Far Mountain?"

Robrek beamed at Samantha. "Yes, with all of my heart and all of my soul."

* * *

Pure joy flowed through Samantha as the priest turned back to her. "Repeat after me. I, Princess Samantha, in the name of Sulis, the Holy Mother of us all, by the life that courses within my blood and the love that resides within my heart, take thee, Sir Robrek Angusstamm, to my hand, my heart, and my soul, to be my chosen one."

As Samantha repeated the high priest's words, she thought for the first time about what they really meant. *Robbie is my hand, my heart, my soul. My chosen one.* Joy soared through her as she heard Robbie repeat the high priest's words.

"I, Sir Robrek Angusstamm, in the name of Sulis, the Holy Mother of us all, by the life that courses within my blood and the love that resides within my heart, take thee, Princess Samantha, to my hand, my heart, and my soul, to be my chosen one."

Father Hafghan took the traditional chalice from an assistant. Normally, the chalice was filled with the finest wine, but because of Robbie's intolerance for alcohol, today it held pure grape juice. "May you drink your fill from the cup of love."

The high priest handed the cup to Samantha. She held it to Robbie's lips for him to drink. He then took the cup from her, lifted her veil, and held it to her lips. He handed the empty chalice back to Father Hafghan.

Father Hafghan handed the chalice to his assistant and traced the star of Sulis high in the air. "By the power vested in me by the Holy Mother, I pronounce you wife and husband, Princess and Prince of the realm. Seal your love and this holy vow with a kiss."

Samantha felt her heart would burst from happiness as Robbie met her lips with his. The assembled courtiers cheered.

When quiet had been restored, the High Priest again addressed the assembled audience. "Today is a great day in the joined kingdoms. Not only do we unite Princess Samantha and Prince Robrek to each other, but we unite them with all of us, as we crown them our queen and our king. Let the love they share for one another fill our hearts today and bind us to our liege and to each other in love and harmony." He turned to Samantha. "Your Highness, please kneel before the altar of the Holy Mother."

Trembling, Samantha took her place before the altar. *Oh, Father, I miss you! How can I ever hope to reign as you did?* Father Hafghan set the crown that would now be hers upon the altar. "In the name of the High and Holy Sulis, Mother of us all, I anoint you, Samantha, as Queen of all Korthlundia, giver of justice, guardian of the peace, and protector of the weak." The High Priest sprinkled her head with holy water and then lifted the crown. "By the will of the goddess, I place this crown upon your head. Arise, Queen Samantha the First, and bow again to no man."

The crown weighed heavily on Samantha's head as she stood and faced the audience. She felt the burden of her awesome responsibility as she heard "Long live the Queen!" echo throughout the chapel.

Father Hafghan then turned to Robbie. "Your Highness, please kneel before the altar of the Holy Mother."

For a moment Robbie looked at her in confusion, not realizing the priest was addressing him. Then he seemed to recall who he now was, and he looked every bit a king as he bowed before the altar.

Father Hafghan picked up the lesser crown that would now be Robbie's and set it upon the altar. "In the name of the High and Holy Sulis, Mother of us all, I anoint you, Robrek, as King Consort, giver of justice, guardian of the peace, and protector of the weak." The High Priest sprinkled Robbie's head with holy water and lifted the crown. "By the will of the goddess, I place this crown upon your head. Arise, King Robrek, and bow again to no man." As he stood, again the chapel was filled, this time with "Long live the King!"

* * *

Robrek felt as if he were walking in a dream. He never imagined he could be so happy. Samantha was his now in the eyes of the goddess and the people. Surely, the worst was now behind them.

Holding hands, they exited the palace doors where horses stood saddled and ready. At the front, Roberta, with her tail and mane braided with ribbons, stood next to Wild Thing, who was similarly bedecked. Robrek had only gotten Wild Thing to agree to the treatment by hinting that he might have to ride another horse. She still wasn't happy about it. :*See, look silly with ribbons. Ribbons for sissy horses, like stupid white horse.*:

Wild Thing's comment broke his feelings of unreality, and he laughed as he patted her and swung into the saddle. Robrek had to admit he preferred her without the ribbons, and he whispered to assure her that he would never ask her to wear them again.

They rode out of the palace gates, surrounded by their bodyguards and trailed by the nobles and merchants who had attended the royal wedding. Soon the streets were lined with people, chanting, "Long live the Queen! Long live the King!"

* * *

The procession and the Guild Hall reception passed without incident, and Samantha thought the day was going to proceed without any difficulties. Then they reached the city square. To one side of the dais, several priests were gathered. They weren't smiling or cheering for the long lives of their new queen and king; a group of about a hundred similarly unsmiling peasants stood with them. She and Robbie dismounted and climbed up on the raised square to address the people. She raised her hand for silence, and the cheering crowd quieted.

Suddenly, the priests and their followers called out in unison: "Queen's bastard! Cothla's whore!"

The Royal Guards grabbed their weapons, but it was the reaction of the populace that surprised her. A cry of "Get them" rose from the crowd, and people surged toward the disrupters, grabbing and beating them. The queen's and king's bodyguards tried to move the royal couple toward the other side of the platform.

"No!" Samantha yelled and grabbed for Robbie's hand. He seemed to know what she wanted because when she next spoke, her voice rang out above the riot. "Stop!" she called. "Let not this day be marred with violence!"

The crowd attacking the priests stopped to look at her. They still held onto the priests, who were bleeding, as were a number of the other peasants.

"However misguided these priests may be, they have a right to speak without fear for their lives. Never let it be said that Solar's heir can be hurt with mere words. Let them go, and do not prevent them from departing in peace." The crowd released the priests, and glaring at her, the priests and their supporters turned and pushed through the crowd. They were jostled and spat upon, but they made it to the edge of the square without further injury.

Samantha continued to speak, "Although their language was foul, it is clear for all to see that my consort is of mixed blood. It is to that he owes the power of his magic, and for that he is chosen of Sulis. It is also true that the day before the battle with the usurper, my consort and I were handfasted in the tradition of the people. I now carry his child. The people will not have to wait decades for the birth of my heir, as they had to wait for the heir of my father."

The crowd burst into cheers of delight, and cries of "Long Live the heir!" rang out. It was quite awhile before the cheers quieted and she and Robbie gave their prepared speeches.

* * *

Even in his worst nightmares, Blaine had never imagined things could go this badly. While it was true the Queen, King, the court, and the entire population of the joined kingdoms, with the exception of a few rabble rousers, seemed to be enjoying themselves, the royal procession was only just now riding back through the palace gates—nearly two hours behind schedule! Blaine was certain Maggie must be near hysteria, trying to keep the food edible in the face of such a delay. Some of the acts scheduled for entertainment would have to be cancelled. Blaine wondered how everyone else seemed able to maintain calm in a catastrophe of these proportions. Although he'd clearly told Her Majesty just how late they were running, she didn't seem terribly concerned, and His Majesty couldn't keep his eyes off the queen long enough for a coherent thought to pass through his head. He'd heard several bystanders comment on how sweet it was, but Blaine knew there was a time for being sweet, and that time wasn't when a wedding feast was congealing into an inedible mess.

* * *

Robrek reentered the palace with Samantha holding tightly to his arm. It had been a very long day already, and all he wanted to do was to take Samantha to their room and participate in the act that would complete their wedding in the eyes of Sulis. But hours remained until they could be alone. The feast, entertainment, and dancing lay ahead of them. At least Blaine had promised him there would be no ballads sung about him, and he'd mentioned a rather interesting juggler. Robrek had developed a fascination for jugglers since the first day he'd come to Murtaghan and seen one performing on the streets.

* * *

Samantha laid her head briefly against Robbie's shoulder as they walked toward their places at the front of the banquet hall. He was hers now, and the crowds in the streets had seemed to have no difficulty with this fact. Cries of "Long live the King!" had rung out along with "Long live the Queen!"

Soon, she and Robbie stood before their seats at the top of the hall as the rest of the court filed to their places. The queen was amazed at how smoothly everything had run. Blaine was truly a master of organization. She caught sight of him across the room and sent him a smile of appreciation. He looked as if he were about to faint.

When all the court had taken their places, the new queen welcomed them and took her seat, signaling the servants to begin serving the feast.

* * *

As the court began to eat, Blaine gave a sigh of relief that at least Maggie had been prepared for such a contingency. Blaine had been flabbergasted by her complete lack of panic. She seemed to be under the impression that royal feasts rarely started on time, and Blaine had to admit that the feast both looked and smelled delicious. Unfortunately, he was certain if he tried to eat a single bite of it, he would disgrace himself by vomiting all over the banquet hall. The worst was yet to come. He'd cancelled a comedy and the juggler that had never been appropriate anyway and a few of the purely musical numbers; King Robrek wasn't fond of music. The disappointment on the entertainers' faces had been almost more than Blaine could bear, but he'd had absolutely no choice.

He kept his eyes fixed on the princess, and as soon as the first course was served, she signaled him, and he announced the first entertainment of the evening—a troop of dancers who performed a celebration of the seasons to the accompaniment of lute, harp, and tabor. When Blaine had seen it performed in audition, he'd been mesmerized by the beauty of their movement and the manner in which they'd been able to convey the essence of every season.

* * *

The feast and entertainment seemed to be progressing with no new catastrophes. Blaine was just congratulating himself on how well he'd overcome the disasters when he looked down to see a page at his side, the one who'd been waiting behind the queen and king.

"Master Blaine, His Majesty asks when the juggler is set to perform. He's been looking forward to it ever since you mentioned it to him."

"The juggler?" Blaine squeaked, and he felt the blood drain from his head. How could he have forgotten how much King Robrek liked jugglers? Of all the acts to cancel, why had he had the stupidity to cancel that one? He hoped it wasn't too late to repair this terrible mistake. Since all the performers were being treated to the feast, he didn't think any of them had left. "Tell His Majesty that I have scheduled him in a few moments."

Blaine grabbed Tuathal by the arm. "Find that juggler and tell him he's on next. The king himself has requested it." Tuathal ran from the room. *He better find that Sulis-cursed juggler, and the juggler better not have indulged too heavily in the wine, or I will be forced to offer the new king my head on a platter.*

* * *

Samantha saw Robbie laugh as the juggler performed his tricks. Robbie looked gorgeous, and the spark of excitement in his eyes reminded her of how different her and his lives had been.

As she watched him watch the juggler, she felt a wave of increased tenderness for Robbie. His smile grew wide, and he gasped. Samantha turned back to the juggler, and even she was impressed. The juggler was juggling an apple, an egg, and a mace. Samantha was sure that the egg was hard boiled, but still the differences in weight between the three objects would make it a most difficult task. Then the juggler did something truly amazing. He took bites out of the apple while keeping the three objects spinning in the air around his head. When he'd eaten the apple down to the core, he caught it in his left hand while catching the mace in his right. To the laughter of the crowd, he allowed the egg to fall on his head. It broke, and yolk ran down his face.

* * *

At long last the entertainment was over, and courtiers escorted the bridal couple to the queen's rooms. Robrek was happy to finally be alone with the one he loved. "I love you, Sam," he whispered, meeting her lips with his. Her lips parted, inviting his tongue inside.

He played with her tongue and broke the kiss. "Holy Sulis, I love you." He trailed kisses along her cheek and nibbled at her ear. He was in no hurry, wanting this time to last now that he could truly claim her as his in the eyes of the goddess.

"Thank the goddess you're finally mine," Samantha whispered back, rubbing her hands up and down his back.

Slowly, they undressed each, kissing each new piece of skin as it was revealed to glisten in the firelight. When her breasts were finally free, he took them in his hands, feeling their round firmness. He took her nipples in his mouth one after the other, feeling them hardened with desire.

He rolled her over so that he was on top; he pulled off the last of her petticoats. He felt more alive than he'd ever been as he sheathed himself inside her, moving slowly to make her pleasure mount. She begged him for more, and he thrust faster and deeper. He felt her release and spilled himself inside of her.

She laughed as he rolled off of her. She propped herself up on her elbow and looked down at his nakedness. "You're beautiful," she breathed. "As long as I have you, I know everything else will be alright."

He pulled her down for a kiss. "I'm not leaving," he promised.

* * *

In his chambers at last, Blaine sat in a chair by the fire. He wanted to go to bed, but he was too tired to move. A slight smile played at the corners of his mouth. He'd done it. Their Majesties were married! And although the day had not gone perfectly, the new queen and king seemed happy with the occasion. He could relax for a few moments before facing the next catastrophe, which, no doubt, lurked just over the horizon.

CHAPTER 20

With Father Gildas behind him, Boyden followed the old witch down the tower stairs. At last, the worm would get what he deserved. Alvabane had promised that the ritual they were about to perform would give her power the worm couldn't rival. All Boyden had to do was dedicate his life to the worm's destruction. Then he would receive the reward the old witch had promised, the reward he deserved. *Duke Boyden. Your Grace. I like the sound of that.*

As they reached the room at the bottom of the stairs, Boyden shivered in the freezing cold. In the center of the room was a stone altar with a large red stone set in the middle. Boyden smiled at the altar; he'd pleased the witch's dark gods there before, and today, she'd assured him, he'd do the same. But for some reason no woman was present.

"Who are these pagan gods?" Father Gildas complained. Evidently, it was the first time he'd seen the altar.

Alvabane stroked one of the statues lovingly. "They are the ones who will destroy the one who would be king. What is your Sulis doing to stop him?"

Father Gildas folded his arms across his chest. "I won't participate in a pagan rite."

Boyden had had enough of the priest's whining. He grabbed the ceremonial knife off the altar and pushed Gildas back against the altar, the knife to Gildas's throat. "You'll do as the old witch says. I can hate him enough for both of us."

Father Gildas attempted to push the knife away, and Alvabane put her hand on Boyden's arm. "We shall not use force here. The ritual will not work with an unwilling participant." She turned to Gildas. "Would you allow the demon child to be king? You said he'd destroy all you hold holy. Would your Sulis want this?"

The priest gritted his teeth. "Get on with it. The demon child must be stopped, and once I'm high priest, we'll discuss the sanctity of your rituals."

Alvabane nodded at Boyden, and he backed away from the priest and replaced the knife on the altar. Alvabane had him stand to the right side of the Stone, Gildas to the left.

The room seemed to grow colder still as the old witch began to sing in some odd language. The air became thick with burning incense. "Remember, there will be some pain," she said "But once we are through, none will be able to stop us, and you will both receive the rewards you so richly deserve. Give me your hand, Boyden, son of Angus." Boyden held out his hand, and she made a quick slice across it. He took a quick breath, the pain surprising him, despite the witch's warning.

"Now wait a minute!" He'd always done the cutting before.

"Place your hand on the stone, and remember your hatred." Boyden shrugged off the pain. What was a little cut next to a dukedom? He placed his hand on the stone. It was warm to the touch, and his blood sizzled against it, although his flesh didn't burn.

Alvabane turned to the priest. "Now, you." Gildas held out his hand, and the witch cut it. He put his hand on the other side of the Stone.

The old witch smiled her creepy smile. "Good. Now, both of you repeat after me. I, and then your name . . ."

"I, Boyden. . ." Boyden said. Father Gildas echoed with his own name.

"Son of Angus. . ." She nodded to Gildas. "Priest of Sulis. . ."

"Son of Angus. . ." Boyden felt his arm jerk, and when he tried to pull it back from the Stone, it wouldn't move.

Gildas must have felt the same thing because he said, "What's going on here?"

The witch closed her eyes. "Relax, and remember your rewards." She opened her eyes and continued the words of the ritual. "By my blood and the hate that lodges in my heart. . ."

"By my blood and the hate that lodges in my heart. . ." Boyden and the priest said in unison. The Stone sparked. *The dukedom,* Boyden told himself, as the Stone became uncomfortably hot.

The witch nodded at Boyden. "Willingly dedicate my life. . ." She nodded at Gildas. "My soul. . ."

"Willingly dedicate my life. . ." A loud crash thundered from the Stone, and Boyden cried out. It felt like every bone in his hand had been broken. *Oh, she'll pay for this. When this is over, I'll make her pay.*

The witch spoke the final words of the ritual. "To the Soul Stone and the cause of Alvabane."

Boyden gritted his teeth against the pain. "To the Soul Stone and the cause of Alvabane," he and the priest repeated. The Stone burst forth with blood-red light, and a jolt of sheer agony shot up Boyden's arm. He tried to scream, but found he had no voice. The stone flared sizzling hot, and he tried again to jerk his hand back but was unable to do so. The old witch smiled at him and nodded. *No!* he screamed silently. *You tricked me!*

Alvabane laughed triumphantly. "Yes, I tricked you. The reward you deserve is nothing other than your death." *No! Holy Sulis, mother of us all, help me!*

"Your goddess has no power here," the old witch said. "This is a place of old magic and the dark gods. Balor and Fea have accepted your sacrifice, and now we will feed them your blood." In terror Boyden watched as the witch cut off the sleeve of his shirt, baring his arm. He struggled, but was unable to move. She began to sing again in what had to be a demon language and made deep cuts at his wrist, elbow, shoulder, and armpit. Boyden screamed silently and watched his blood flowing down his arm and into the Stone, which seemed to absorb it and began to glow even more brightly. He grew faint. *No!* He wrenched at his arm, but still he couldn't move. The room grew dark around him.

* * *

Father Gildas couldn't keep his eyes off the blood as it poured down Boyden's arm, the Stone absorbing his blood and his life. The priest silently called out to the goddess to save him, but the goddess didn't hear his cries. Since he'd consented to paganism, it seemed the goddess had deserted him. He tried to pull away from the Stone, but he couldn't move.

Alvabane came toward him with the bloody knife. She sang as she touched it to him on the forehead, each breast, and his loins, smearing him with Boyden's blood. Boyden stood grotesquely on the other side of the Stone, dead and held up by the magic alone. Gildas looked desperately at his unmoving arm, fearing to be cut as Boyden had been.

Seeming to read his mind, the demon witch said, "No, my priest, the gods took the peasant's life, but you have offered your soul." The priest screamed, although no sound came out, feeling as if his body were being ripped apart. But no, his soul was being ripped from his body. He shook and trembled as bit by bit, his soul flowed into the Stone. Gildas became blind and deaf and knew nothing but pain.

* * *

The Soul Stone burst into blinding light, and a thunderous crash filled the room, throwing Alvabane against the wall. Despite the pain, Alvabane cried out in triumph. She crept back to the Stone. Eagerly, she touched it, and its power flowed into her. "It is mine! *Mine!* Nothing can stop me!"

* * *

Robrek again stood outside the mouth of the cave. Again he heard the voices calling to him, promising him indescribable pleasure. He strode forward, following the voices, but a hand grabbed his arm. He turned and saw his mother.

"No, my son, you must not go there. Ever."

But he wouldn't let a mere dream hold him back. He shook off her hand. "You are not real! You have never been real!" He entered the cave.

Inside, he saw the blood-red lake. He still couldn't tell what it was made of, but he knew the promised pleasure lay within it. He began to strip off his clothes.

Suddenly, howls of anguish and despair clawed through the air. They echoed off the cavern walls, and Robrek clamped his hands over his ears. Again a shadowy form emerged from the depths of the lake, and Robrek saw the man more clearly this time. He was naked, and his back was to Robrek. Robrek noticed he was missing parts of his body—an ear, three fingers on the left hand, two on the right. Wounds covered the rest of his shadowy form, and more of the blood-red fluid poured forth from these.

He turned toward Robrek. He had no nose, and his eyes were ragged holes. His body bucked and writhed as if in excruciating torment.

Shadows by the hundreds separated themselves from the form of the man and flitted through the lake toward Robrek. As the shadows left the man, he grew more and more still until he wasn't moving at all. The howling ceased. The others had become aware of Robrek. He still had no idea what they were, but they were the source of the voices that promised pleasure. They wanted him.

Faces in the throes of ecstasy appeared and disappeared in the lake as the shadows approached. "Come to us. We have been set free. Join us."

"Who are you?" he asked.

"Those Who Were."

"Those who were what? What do you want with me?"

"To share with you. To let you feel the power. Bathe in it. Imagine the pleasure of having it surround you forever. Who else can offer you this?"

He could already feel a tingling passing over his skin. He gasped. If it felt this good now, how much better would it feel once he joined the shadows in the lake? He needed to plunge into that lake more than he'd ever needed anything. He felt his manhood stiffen. He tore off his trousers, and a woman's arm appeared from the lake.

"Yes," the voices whispered as the woman's hand reached toward him. "We want you as much as you desire us. The Bard wants to master us, but we belong to you."

He shook with anticipation as the woman's hand neared his groin. Nothing mattered but joining her and the others in the lake.

A bellow rent the air. "No! You are our only hope! Stop, or we are all lost!"

Robrek jerked his head up; the shadowy man was yelling at him.

"Who are you?" he stammered.

"Armunn!" the man screamed as he was pulled back under the lake.

Robrek jolted awake. He felt as if a thousand knives were being thrust into him. He gasped for breath and clutched at his heart. A sensation of cold evil crawled over him.

Samantha knelt over him, her eyes wide with fear. "Robbie! You cried out! What's wrong?"

"I don't know." He shuddered, as the pain slowly eased. "Something has happened. Something terrible." He lowered his shields slightly. He and Samantha were alone in the room. Although the pain had faded, he felt sick, and cold sweat beaded on his forehead. He leaned over the chamber pot and vomited.

"Robbie, are you ill? Is it your wound?" Samantha clutched at his arm.

"I'm all right," he said, still shaking. "Leave me alone for a minute. Let me figure out what happened." He closed his eyes and drifted into a healing trance. He slowly lowered his shields and reached outward with his healing senses for the source of the problem; he had gotten proficient at letting in only a few sensations at a time. His own and Samantha's guards stood outside the room. He reached further out. Somewhere above, a couple was in the throes of sexual ecstasy. Robrek felt his own groin tighten as the sensations brought back his pleasure in Samantha's arms. He hurriedly shut out the feelings. As he searched onward, he felt an old man who was unable to sleep; his joints ached and sharp jolts of pain passed through them. He found others suffering from overindulgence, and his stomach heaved with their nausea. He found people with slight illnesses; servants suffering from fatigue. He caught the sense of guards—some alert, some drowsing. But mostly he found people sleeping peacefully in their beds.

At last, in a distant part of the palace, he felt a child cowering in intense fear, and then another, a woman this time. The child was Oriana. He'd never met the woman.

He opened his eyes. Samantha was staring at him. "Are you all right?"

"Something has happened. I need to go check on it." He grabbed his trousers from the pile of clothes that Samantha had taken off him and pulled them on.

Samantha tried to get loose from the bed coverings. "You're scaring me. What is it, Robbie?"

He sat beside her on the bed. "I don't know, Sam. You stay in bed where it's warm. There's nothing you can do to help. I'll take Iden and Murdoc with me."

"Are you sure?" she asked. "Should I summon more guards?"

Robrek shook his head. "Whatever happened, there's no immediate threat, and it isn't close."

Robrek kissed her, pulled on a shirt, wrapped his fur-lined cloak around him, and headed for the door. Iden, Murdoc, and Samantha's guards all jumped to attention as he opened the door.

"Your Majesty!" Iden said. "Is anything wrong?"

Robrek looked in confusion at his guard. Then he realized Iden was using his new title. "There's something I need to check on." He started down the corridor, and Murdoc and Iden fell in behind him.

He focused his healing senses on the two people whose fear he'd sensed. Oriana was closer. He followed her fear through the corridors and up and down staircases. Having been built and added onto for centuries, the palace was a maze, but the sensation of fear drew him unerringly. Finally, he stopped in front of Oriana's room and knocked.

He heard movement on the other side of the door, and Oriana's brother called out. "Who is it?"

"It's Sir Robrek," he said, remembering too late that he should have used his new title.

"Your Majesty," Quinn gasped in surprise. He pulled back the bolt, opened the door, and fell to one knee. He was dressed only in his trousers. "Forgive me for appearing before you in this state. How can we serve you?"

Now that the door was open, he could feel Oriana's fear even more intensely. "Is Oriana okay?"

"Sir Robrek!" Oriana squealed from behind Quinn and launched herself into his arms, sobbing.

"Oriana!" Quinn scolded. "That is no proper way to greet the king!"

Robrek ignored the kneeling man and put his arms around Oriana. "What's wrong? What's happened?"

"Something terrible," she sobbed into his shoulder. "Quinn wouldn't let me come to you, but I knew you could help me. I'm sorry I called you, 'Sir Robrek,' Your Majesty, but please believe me. Something's wrong."

"Hush!" he whispered. "Let's get out of the hallway, and you can tell me all about it."

Quinn scrambled out of the way, and Murdoc pushed into the room ahead of Robrek. Robrek followed with Oriana still clinging to him, and Iden waited outside the door. Robrek took a chair, and Quinn stirred up the fire. "Can I offer you anything, Your Majesty?" Robrek shook his head.

Oriana collapsed to her knees, sobbing into his lap. He touched her and used his energy to calm and soothe her. "Something woke me. It hurt—it hurt so badly! It felt like some kind of horrible insect was spreading its filth all over me. It wasn't just a nightmare. Something has happened. You believe me, don't you?"

Robrek nodded. "I felt it, too." They talked for a while about what they both had felt, and Robrek wondered if Leigh or any of the priests at the Temple of the Mother's Love had felt something as well.

"I need to go check on someone else who may have felt it. I'll summon you to my quarters when I'm ready to talk more."

Oriana's eyes went wide, her hands trembled against his legs "No, please, don't leave me! Let me come with you." Understanding the child's fear too well, he readily consented.

* * *

Eolande cowered in the corner of the small room she'd been given, the male performers that had entertained at the wedding sharing a common room. At least, she'd been scheduled to entertain. *How in the name of Sulis's creation could they have put a damned juggler in my place? The princess's Sulis-cursed secretary raved about my music! He said it was as "beautiful as the larks at daybreak, so to speak." And when I was set to go on, he'd sent his stupid assistant to tell the juggler to perform instead. I should have drugged the damned apple eater's wine!*

She pushed those thoughts away; missing out on entertaining the royal couple seemed trivial. Something terrible had happened. She'd never felt anything like it, but she was certain it was no mere nightmare.

She jumped when someone knocked on her door. "Who. . . who is it?"

"King Robrek," a voice answered.

If she hadn't have been so terrified, she would have laughed at the pathetic attempt to imitate the king's country accent. "Go away, Chionney. I'm not in the mood for your games." Her fellow bard had been trying to sleep with her for years and wouldn't take no for an answer.

"I am not this Chionney. I really am the king, and I need to speak with you."

Eolande got up and whipped open the door. "I told you—"

She found herself looking into the eyes of the king. He had a child at his side and was backed by two fierce-looking guards.

"You felt something that frightened you," the king said.

"H-how could you know?" she said. Far too late, she thought to bow.

"May I come in?"

"Of course, Your Majesty." Eolande backed away from the doorway and hurriedly cleared a chair of her clothing. The king sat in the chair, the child clinging to him. She remained standing until the king motioned for her to sit on the bed. One of the guards followed the king into the room, making the tight space very crowded.

"Tell me about what you felt."

"Your Majesty, I felt evil, pain, and, and. . ." She struggled to find words to describe it.

"Like being coated in blood and filth?"

Eolande leaned forward. "Yes! Exactly! What was it, Your Majesty?"

Looking very young, the king put his head in his hands. "I wish I knew. But Oriana and I felt it, too." The king shook himself and looked at her piercingly. "You are different. You aren't a healer, but I sense magic around you. What are you?"

"My mother called me a Bard, but she didn't mean simply a singer of tales. She scraped up every dram she could to find someone to teach me to play and to sing, but she could never find anyone who could teach me a Bard's magic. She wanted to find a way for me to go to her homeland and find a mentor, but it wasn't meant to be."

The king nodded, suddenly looking years older. "I must report to the queen. Will you come with me?"

* * *

As if pursued by a demon, Leigh ran through the city darkness. Dawn was hours away, but he couldn't wait until morning. He knew of only one person who could explain what he'd felt. He was stopped by the guards in front of the palace. "I must see His Majesty immediately. It's an emergency. Tell His Majesty it's Leigh Fergalstamm. He'll see me. He'll want to."

* * *

Awena woke with a scream. Something terrible had happened. She hurried to Mother Venetia, who was staring at her with open-mouthed horror. "What is it, Mother? What has happened?"

Mother Venetia gathered her in her arms. "I don't know, my child."

Awena felt a sudden burst of lifelessness under her feet. "Holy Sulis, Mother, the Dead Lands! They've grown again! We have to move now, or we're all dead!"

* * *

Almost immediately after Robbie, Oriana, and the Bard filed into Samantha's reception room, a knock came at the door. Bearach entered. "Your Majesties, Captain Hawk saying he must see Her Majesty."

She wanted to tell Captain Hawk to take himself to the seven hells until she got to the bottom of what Robbie and the others had felt. But she didn't know what she could do to help them, and she had the responsibilities of a queen. She turned to Robbie. "Take Oriana and Eolande to your quarters to see if you can figure out what happened. I'll see to Hawk."

Robbie kissed her on the cheek and left with the others. Her guards showed Captain Hawk in. "Your Majesty, Duke Torin slipped away some time during yesterday's celebration. His guards were poisoned. His remaining servants believe he is headed for his estates, although they don't know what he hopes to accomplish."

Samantha creased her brow. *Why would he have done such a thing? He has to know it will result in his execution.* "Take one hundred men and retrieve him. His estates are lightly fortified, and he has few men-at-arms. Bring him back alive if you can, but dead will suffice."

"I'll see to it at once, Your Majesty."

* * *

A page arrived and handed Robrek a note. Leigh was at the front gates asking to see him. "Have him shown to my rooms immediately," Robrek ordered

When Leigh arrived, Robrek clapped Leigh on the back. He was pale and trembling. Robrek led the priest toward a chair.

"What *was* that evil?" Leigh asked as he dropped into the chair. Robrek sat across from him. "It felt old. Ancient."

Eolande's eyes widened.

"What is it?" Robrek asked.

"They always refer to Armunn's evil as the ancient evil. And. . . what I felt. It does seems to correspond to some of the ballads?"

Armunn was the tortured man from his dreams. "Who is Armunn?"

Eolande leaned back. "Do you not know Korthlundia's greatest hero? Shall I sing his ballads to you?"

"Please."

As Eolande began to sing, Robrek leaned forward, intent on what the song could teach him.

* * *

Armunn rode through the corpse-strewn streets of the village. In all the villages he'd ridden through, from the small village of Reidhlean to the once-bustling town of Byge, the sight was always the same—many dead and the rest dying, the very life being sucked out of them. He was the most powerful sorcerer alive, yet his magic did nothing to stop the deaths. He had killed hundreds of demons on the field of battle, but against this weapon, his sword was as useless as his magic. He'd killed the demon Bard, but that had only made the threat worse, the death escalating. There was no enemy left to kill, and soon the death curse would reach his very door. His own family was at risk.

He entered the small shrine on his estates and knelt at the altar. "Please, Sulis! Please, oh goddess! You are the Mother of us all. Help me stop this curse! Help me end the dying!"

The goddess's voice pounded in his heart and his mind: "To win against such evil, you must be willing to sacrifice all!"

"To end this, there is nothing I wouldn't give!" he cried, and the goddess showed him the way.

He returned to his home. Knowing he'd never see either again, he kissed his wife goodbye and laid his hand upon the head of his infant daughter. Tears streamed down their faces, but his wife didn't beg him not to go. They both knew this was his destiny, the very reason Sulis had provided for the birth of such a powerful sorcerer.

To make it through the Dead Lands, he would need a fast horse, far faster than his own. He captured a Horstad on the Reidhlean Plains, and together they rode forth with nothing but his heart, his soul, his magic, and the goddess at his side. Even though the Horstad flew over the Dead Lands, Armunn was trembling with weakness by the time he reached the cave. He stumbled down the passageway searching for the cavern where the Stone dwelt. "Please,

Sulis! Let me have the energy to do this! Don't let me die until I've ended this!"

With the last of his energy, he reached the cavern and knelt at the base of the Stone and put his hands on it. An evil as vast as the seven hells pulsed against his palms. To save his people he must sacrifice his very soul to this evil. He prayed to the goddess to give him strength.

* * *

Armunn fell to his knees. But it was Robrek who clutched at his chest and wept, unable to control his tears. *Surely, the goddess can't expect a sacrifice like this from me! Is the goddess so cruel as to give me everything only to take it away again?* "No!" he cried out. "No! No!"

The room spun around him, and he came back to his surroundings with a jolt. Eolande was backed against the wall with Brendan's sword at her throat. "Brendan, no!" Robrek managed to shout.

Tears streaking his face, Brendan pressed his sword against the Bard's throat. "Your Majesty, this witch has bespelled you, bespelled all of us! You can't trust her!"

Eolande's eyes pleaded with him. "Please, Your Majesty! I meant no harm!"

His voice strong again, Robrek commanded, "Brendan, sheathe your sword! Now!"

Brendan sheathed his sword. "Sing another note," he hissed, "and I won't hesitate to slit your throat."

Robrek looked at Leigh and Oriana, both of whom were sobbing. He wiped his eyes and fought to regain his composure. He'd never felt such despair in his life—not even when he'd been trapped in the temple's cellar waiting to be burned at the stake.

Robrek motioned Eolande back to her seat. "So that is the power of the Bard—to make your audience feel the emotions of your songs?"

"It's never happened that strongly before, Your Majesty! I swear it!"

Robrek shook his head. "It's a powerful effect, but I don't care to feel it again, at least not unless it's a much happier song."

Eolande smoothed her skirt. "The Armunn ballads are tragic, Your Majesty."

"There's more than one?"

"Oh, yes, Your Majesty, I know at least two dozen."

"Your Majesty," Oriana broke in. "Armunn's cave is said to be in my village, underneath the altar in the shrine. Some say it's only a legend, but Mother Venetia believed it." The child was shaking. "Every new moon the priestesses perform a ritual to renew the seal Armunn put on the evil, but after Father Shylah's edict, there weren't enough priestesses to do it. The evil is loose again, isn't it? That's what happened to my village."

Still trembling, Robrek fell into a chair. "But what's happening to your village has been going on for months. What we all felt last night was new. Who was supposed to be behind Armunn's evil?"

"Demons, Your Majesty," Eolande answered. "Before Armunn drove them out, Lundia was supposedly inhabited by demons."

Robrek made a noise in his throat. "Korthlundians think everyone who doesn't look like them is a demon."

Eolande nodded. "You're right. I'm sure they were just a different race of people—but legends say that they practiced human sacrifice to fuel their magic and worshipped dark gods, who fed on pain and fear. They may have had cause to attack our ancestors, though."

"How so?" Robrek asked.

"It is said Korth became crowded, and there was unused land in Lundia, so groups of our people began to settle and till the land. Over the years, they took more and more land, and the demons, for lack of a better word, demanded we worship their gods and provide sacrifices if we were going to stay. One child in ten was required."

"That's terrible," Oriana blurted out. "Our ancestors didn't do it, did they?"

Eolande shook her head. "No, Sulis is the Mother of us all and has a special fondness for children. Not only did they refuse, but they armed themselves and sent to their king for protection. The king sent troops led by Armunn, a powerful sorcerer and mighty warrior. When the demons came to claim their human sacrifices, they were defeated and driven back. Emboldened by their success against the demons, more and more of our ancestors moved into Lundia and gobbled up the land, and Armunn continued to push the demons farther and farther back."

"So Lundia doesn't rightfully belong to us," Robrek said. "We took it from them? How does the ancient evil fit in?"

"After some years, our ancestors had taken over a good portion of Lundia, and the demon king sent a message to Armunn. At first, it seemed an absurd ultimatum: that all our people withdraw to Korth immediately, or they would die. Armunn merely laughed, confident he could defeat any army sent against him. But one by one, the towns and villages started to die, and not just the people either—all life, both animal and plant. The very earth itself became lifeless. At first, Armunn thought the people had just fallen victim to some new disease, but our healers could find nothing wrong with those who died. It seemed as if the life were being simply sucked out of them."

Oriana gasped. "And it was, wasn't it? That's what was happening to the people of my village. That's why I couldn't save them."

Eolande looked at the child and smiled sadly. "Most likely, yes. Armunn discovered the demons had created a terrible weapon they called the Soul Stone. All of their greatest sorcerers—Bards, healers, magic-users of any type—had assembled in a castle on the border between Korth and Lundia. Together they had poured their magic, even their lives into a blood red stone that reached from a room at the base of the castle down deep into the earth until it rested in a cave. Untold hundreds gave their lives, or were sacrificed, during its creation, their souls trapped in a lake at the base of the Stone, fueling its power. Only a single Bard among them survived, but that was enough. With the Soul Stone attuned to his control, the Bard merely had to sing, and the souls of those in the area he targeted were sucked into the lake, making it even stronger. Thousands of our people died before Armunn could find the Stone."

Eolande paused and looked lost in thought.

Robrek leaned forward, intent on the story. "Go on."

"Armunn killed the Bard. Using his magic, he sneaked into the castle, found the Bard, and killed him with his sword. He tried to destroy the Stone, but all of his efforts didn't even crack it. Still, our ancestors celebrated, thinking they had won. Without a Bard to control the Stone, surely, it was no threat.

"But they were wrong. Without a Bard to control and direct its power, the Stone fed unrestrained. The demons had shielded their homeland from just such a threat, but Korth had no protection. Starting in what is today Balley Beg and spreading outward in an ever widening semicircle, the people and the earth began to die, their souls sucked into the lake at the base of the Stone so they couldn't travel Beyond the Far Mountain."

"And they're still there." Leigh broke in. "That's the horror of it. After a thousand years, their souls are still trapped."

Eolande nodded. "So they say. Armunn's solution was far from perfect. He couldn't figure out how to destroy the Stone and release the souls. He could only prevent further death. He entered the cave and created a shield out of his own soul that blocked the power of the Stone."

"And that's what the ritual's for, isn't it?" Oriana asked. "The one the Korthian priestesses do every new moon? It strengthens the shield Armunn created."

Robrek got to his feet, unable to sit still any longer. "So, when the priestesses were locked up by Father Shylah's decree, the shields failed, and it began to feed unrestrained again. But last night, something new happened. Has a Bard grabbed the power for himself again?"

Eolande looked down at her feet. "That's what I suspect, but I have no proof."

Robrek moved a chair and sat closer to Eolande. "How did Armunn create the shield?"

Eolande shook her head. "The legends don't say."

A part of Robrek was relieved. If he didn't know how, he couldn't be expected to give his life as Armunn had. *No, Sulis! You didn't chose me only to die. You couldn't have.* "I need to learn more of this Armunn. I want you to write out the lyrics to every Armunn ballad you know and check with the other bards to see if they know any you don't. What else can you tell me about Bards?"

"Not much, Your Majesty. Like I said, I never had a proper teacher."

"Perhaps we can find something in the palace library." But Robrek knew he didn't have time to deal with Druce and his disorganization. Robrek dismissed Oriana and Leigh and brought Eolande with him to Blaine's office.

Blaine's hair was standing on end, like he'd repeatedly run his fingers through it, which he probably had. "Blaine," Robrek said. "I need information from the library, and I'm afraid Druce won't be able to find it for me in time."

"Druce." Blaine closed his eyes, as if praying for patience. "You're right, Your Majesty. That library is as disorganized as a leaf pile after a big storm, so to speak, and Druce's mind is just as bad. But the library at the Temple of the Mother's Love, run by a Father Loman, is as orderly as a rack full of freshly polished swords. Perhaps you should try there first."

CHAPTER 21

Arriving at the front gates of his estates, Torin found the guards pale and trembling. "What's wrong with you?" he demanded.

A guard pointed a shaking finger in the direction of Alvabane's quarters. "She's different, Your Grace."

Torin knew his men had never liked Alvabane, but they'd never reacted this way. He waved disdainfully at the guards and proceeded to her chambers where he found a beautiful young woman with striking red hair and eerie blank eyes. "Who are you?" he demanded, his eyes trailing down her body, coming to rest on her breasts.

The woman laughed. "Ah, son of my breast, you do not recognize your old nurse?"

"Alvabane?" he breathed, feeling the blood drain from his face. "How is this possible?"

Alvabane poured a glass of wine and brought it to her lips. She drank as if savoring the moment. "The Soul Stone is now mine. It has given me back the youth your father and your people stole from me."

Trembling, Torin sank into a chair. "How is that going to help? The Royal Guard is right behind me. You said the Stone would give us the power to combat them."

"As it has." She laughed again, and her eyes shone. "Oh, how it has."

* * *

Captain Hawk led his men toward Duke Torin's estates. Hawk hated unnecessary bloodshed, and he hoped the traitorous duke would surrender without a fight, a fight Torin couldn't win. When they arrived, Hawk had his men spread out in front of the main gate. The walls were not high nor was the gate particularly strong. The duke's flight here was a pointless gesture.

He rode forward, flanked by two of his officers and carrying a white flag. "Duke Torin!" Captain Hawk called out to the men on the walls. The duke stood among them. "You cannot stand against the forces of the crown! Surrender now, and save the lives of your men!"

"I'd like to discuss terms of surrender," Torin called down. "Come inside, and I will guarantee your safety."

Hawk nodded in approval. The gate opened in front of him, and he rode inside. The guards who greeted him made him surrender his sword, promising its return when the parley was finished. They led him to the top of the wall where Torin awaited him. The duke looked pale and slightly ill. With him was a striking young woman with freakish eyes, the irises so black they looked at one with the pupils. Hawk shuddered.

The captain bowed ever so slightly to Torin. "Your Grace, Her Highness offers no terms for your surrender except the safety of your men."

The woman moved forward. "We are not talking of our surrender, but that of your bastard queen."

Hawk stiffened at the insult to his liege, but he ignored the woman's absurd comments. He focused his remarks toward Torin. "We both know you don't have enough men to hold this fortress against me."

Torin said nothing, and again the woman spoke. "He needs no men, just one woman." The woman turned from him and walked to the edge of the walls. She spread her arms out toward his men and began to sing in what had to be the demons' own tongue.

The power of her song pulling against his very soul, Hawk dragged himself forward to look down at his men. The two officers he'd left by the gate tumbled from their horses. The horses themselves fell beside them; none of them moved.

Hawk whirled toward Torin. "What is happening?"

Behind Torin's smile, his eyes were wide. "They die. Alvabane sings their souls from their bodies."

"That's impossible!" Hawk cried. But more men and horses fell. "Holy Sulis, no!" He reached for his sword, but his scabbard was empty. No matter! He surged forward to wrap his hands around the woman's throat, but the points of a dozen swords prevented him. In panic, he glanced back at his men. They toppled from their horses like dominos. *No! I have to stop her!* But her song clutched at him, making both movement and thought difficult. "Stop her!" he bellowed at Torin.

Torin laughed with a tinge of hysteria. "I guaranteed your safety only, not that of your men. You will live to tell Her Majesty the tale."

Hawk gripped the edge of the wall as below, more and more of his men died—young men just starting out in life, men with families, men whose wives and children he knew, new recruits, veterans seasoned by years under his command. How could he look their families or the queen in the eye when he did nothing as their lives were taken? *No, I will stop this now! I will fight this to my last breath!* He ignored the swords and surged toward the woman whose lips poured forth evil and death. Before he could reach her, he was tackled from behind and wrestled to the ground. He fought fiercely, but he was unarmed and outnumbered.

The woman brought the song to a crescendo. Abruptly, the song died away, and the woman dropped unconscious to the ground. Hawk prayed she too was dead, but as Torin's men allowed him to get to his feet, he saw the rise and fall of her chest. Below, all one hundred of his men and their horses lay still. He turned to Torin. "By the goddess, what have you done? What is this evil you have let loose upon good men?"

Torin didn't meet his eyes. "You will carry this message to Her Majesty. She will repudiate her new consort and send me his head in a box. She will agree to marry me and surrender the regency to me. She has ten days to comply before Alvabane sings the death of the village of Reidhlean, here on my estates. If she refuses, Alvabane will sing the death of every village from here to the capital, and then the capital itself!"

* * *

Robrek entered the temple library with his entourage. Brendan insisted on preceding him, as if he feared attack from the books on the shelves. Father Hafghan and Eolande followed him, and the rest of Robrek's guards brought up the rear.

"I hope you don't find it too warm in here, Your Majesty. Father Loman is the oldest member of our community and takes chill easily," Father Hafghan informed Robrek. The old librarian didn't look up as they entered. "Father Loman!" the high priest said in a loud voice. The librarian still didn't respond. "His hearing is poor, Your Majesty," Hafghan said and pitched his voice even louder. "Father Loman, His Majesty has honored us with a visit!"

"His Majesty!" The old librarian's head shot up. "Well, bless my soul! So it is!" Father Loman wore his long white hair in braids. He was clean-shaven, and the skin of his face was heavily wrinkled and as translucent as old parchment. It bore a sickly yellow hue. Bent over with age, Father Loman rose shakily from a chair and looked as if he were trying to go down on one knee.

Robrek rushed forward to prevent it. He grabbed the priest's arm and was nearly overwhelmed with a stabbing pain in all of his joints. "Please, Father, one of your age should kneel to no one."

"Thank you, Your Majesty. If I got down, I'm not sure I'd ever get up." Father Loman's voice was strong and steady and betrayed no hint of his age, except for the tendency those hard of hearing often had to talk loudly.

"Sit down, Father. You're in great pain." Robrek used his magic to make certain the priest had no difficulty hearing him.

Father Loman laughed a strong, hearty belly laugh, and again Robrek was surprised to hear the contrast between the man's voice and the condition of his body. "You have no idea, Your Majesty. Father Hafghan wanted me to retire, but I told him no one but Sulis takes me away from my books." He glared a mock challenge at the high priest.

Hafghan laughed the false, grating laugh of a courtier and continued speaking loudly. "His Majesty has expressed the need for your assistance, Father Loman."

"A newly married young buck needs the assistance of an old man? Well, there's a book or two around here that might give him some hints." The old priest winked at Robrek and broke into peals of his hearty belly laugh. Robrek blushed deeply, but couldn't help laughing himself. Eolande stood to the side, trying not to laugh as well.

Father Hafghan looked scandalized. "Your Majesty, please, forgive Father Loman's manners. He is truly a very old man. But he and the library are at your disposal, Your Majesty. How else may I be of assistance?"

"I need nothing else presently. I'll let you know if something arises." He nodded a dismissal.

Hafghan blinked in surprise. "Well, then. . . well, then, I'll have a novice stationed outside the door, Your Majesty. Send him for your least need." The high priest bowed and left.

"Your Majesty Young Buck and this pretty young lady, what secret can I help you uncover and hide from Father Sneaky Eyes?"

"You don't trust the high priest?"

"About as much as Your Majesty does, I reckon, seeing as you sent him from the room with his tail between his legs." The old priest laughed again, and Robrek found himself liking the librarian a great deal. "I trust Father Hafghan to think of himself first, last, and only."

Robrek took a seat across from the priest. "This is Eolande, the Bard." He gestured her to the seat next to his. "Her Majesty's secretary, Blaine, speaks very highly of you."

"Now there's a young pup with a head on his shoulders. Still a little wet behind the ears, if you know what I mean, but there's nothing wrong with that one's brain." The librarian tapped a finger to his temple and burst out laughing. "Of course, I'd say that of anyone who speaks highly of me. Old Sneaky Eyes thinks I'm losing my marbles because I can hardly walk and the hearing's none too good, but I assure Your Majesty, all the marbles are secure."

"I hope so, Father, because I don't want what I'm about to tell you to spread beyond this room, and I need answers."

The old librarian nodded. "Does it have anything to do with an evil, an ancient one, perhaps?"

"How did you know?" Eolande asked.

"Not too much gets past this old man, lass. Another young buck, Father Dorsey, came to me in terror the night before last. Said he felt something evil. Wondered if there was something about it in one of my books. I didn't think much of it until I saw Your Majesty walk through the door. Dorsey's a little high strung, if you know what I mean. Has an exaggerated sense of his own importance, but I suppose he was right this time. You felt something as well, Your Majesty?"

Robrek answered, "Yes, and so did Eolande and two other healers I'm aware of. Where is this Father Dorsey? I'd like to talk to him."

"I think Father Faolan has him kneeling on the stone floor in the altar room doing penance." Father Loman leaned in closer and whispered loudly. "I heard he refuses to say he imagined everything. He's a stubborn one. Young Artan recanted pretty quickly when Faolan—he's in charge of discipline—took the scourge to the boy. Now the boy says he felt nothing at all."

At the news of a child being whipped, Robrek's shoulders tightened in remembrance of the times his father had whipped him across the back. "I take it Artan is a novice."

Father Loman nodded. "The boy likes to help me out from time to time. He's had it pretty rough, that young 'un. Left on the temple steps as a baby, and the other kids have never accepted him. You see, he's like Your Majesty—a cothla. So is Father Dorsey, for that matter." Though Robrek cringed inwardly, he could tell Father Loman meant no offense. "Now that I'm thinking about it, I believe Dorsey was abandoned on the temple stairs as well. Lots of cothlas are. The port, you know. Sailors come in, find a local girl, and then sail off again without thinking of the damage they might have done. A single woman with a cothla child doesn't stand much of a chance, now does she?"

"No, she doesn't," Eolande said with such vehemence Robrek wondered if she were a child of such a union. She was obviously of mixed blood.

But Eolande's background wasn't at issue at the moment. Robrek told Brendan to fetch the novice stationed outside. A very scared looking young man of about fifteen entered the room. Like almost all Korthlundians, he was tall, blond, and blue-eyed. He bowed repeatedly to Robrek.

Robrek put on a kindly expression. "Could you inform Father Hafghan I'd like to talk to Father Dorsey and the novice Artan as soon as it is convenient?"

"Yes, Your Majesty, at once, Your Majesty." The novice backed to the door, turned, and fled.

As soon as the door closed on the novice's heels, Father Loman said, "Well now, would Your Majesty like to wait until they get here to tell me exactly what you felt that night, or can you give me a little hint to soothe my curiosity?"

Robrek got up from the table and crossed to Father Loman. "What I'd like to do is see what I can do for the pain in your joints and your hearing loss."

Father Loman looked at him thoughtfully. "You think you can do something, King Young Buck, do you? The healers around here say there isn't a thing in the world that can help. Then again, none of them rode up Gloine Torr, either. I certainly won't stand in your way of trying."

Robrek knelt in front of the old librarian and placed his hands on the man's ankles. He closed his eyes and entered a healing trance. The old priest had lost most of the cushioning tissue in his joints, causing them to become inflamed and terribly painful. Robrek couldn't rebuild the tissue, but he could lessen the inflammation and the pain. He moved his hands up the old priest's body, treating his other joints. Finally, he rested them on the librarian's ears. Age had destroyed much of the sensory tissue; there was nothing Robrek could do, except slow the deterioration of what remained. Father Loman's liver was also not working properly. Robrek knew just the herbs for a potion that would help stimulate the liver function.

When he dropped out of his trance, Father Loman wore an expression of surprised relief. "Your Majesty, whatever did you do? I haven't felt this good in ten years."

"Unfortunately, what I did is only temporary. I can't heal the effects of age, but if I have time, I'll make you a cream that will prevent your joints from giving you quite so much pain, and a tonic that will help your liver. There's nothing I can do for your hearing loss."

"And some people doubt you're the goddess's choice?" Father Loman shook his head, as if such a doubt were beyond comprehension. "Who are we to say the goddess couldn't choose a cothla?"

Robrek squirmed slightly in his seat, but said nothing. People seemed to regard him as demon or divine. Never normal.

There was a knock on the door, and Cathbad opened it to announce the priests and novice were here to see the king. Robrek wondered at the mention of "priests." He'd only asked for one. He got to his feet as two men and a boy filed into the room. Eolande rose as well. The boy's skin had a slight hint of brown to it, and his nose was broader than typical for Korthlundians. His hair was a very dark brown. While the novice was darker than normal, one of the priests was the exact opposite. Robrek hadn't thought it possible, but his skin was even whiter than a typical Korthlundian. His eyes were the palest blue and his hair so blonde it was almost white. He looked like an ice statue come to life. He also looked so tired he could barely stand.

The second priest was Father Faolan; he bowed to Robrek, attempting to hide the fear and malice in his eyes behind a false smile. Robrek's guards stiffened at the appearance of the priest behind the protest at the royal wedding. Robrek wondered at his gall, appearing without being asked for. "Your Majesty, it's so nice to see you. I hope Father Loman hasn't been troubling you with ridiculous rumors."

"There was no need to bother yourself, Father, unless you, too, felt something." He gestured toward the door.

Father Faolan frowned at Father Loman. "You must forgive Father Loman, Your Majesty. He is a very old man and subject to bouts of superstition. I assure Your Majesty there is no truth to these rumors, and Father Dorsey and the novice have been properly punished for spreading lies."

Robrek formed his hands into fists. "So if I told you I too felt something, you would call me a liar." He felt his guards tense.

Faolan's jaw dropped. "But Your Majesty, I would never. . ."

"In calling them liars, you have so called me. Did you even once entertain the idea they might be telling the truth?"

"But Your Majesty, the claim was absurd and upsetting to others. Besides, if it was true, others closer to the goddess would have felt it as well. After all, they are both only—" Faolan broke off abruptly.

"Cothlas? Like your king?"

Faolan started to take a step backward, but stopped himself. "I was merely going to mention that neither of them has been noted for piety. And when Artan himself admitted he was lying in order to get attention, how could I not assume Father Dorsey was doing likewise?"

Robrek lowered his shields slightly. The novice's back was in far worse condition than his own had ever been. Robrek's father had used a leather strap. It had hurt like the seven hells, but it'd never broken the skin. Whatever Artan had been beaten with had left gouges and open sores. "Tearing someone's back apart has the tendency to get him to say whatever you want him to. I'm certain you wish to offer Father Dorsey and Artan your sincerest apology."

A flash of hatred briefly appeared in Father Faolan's eyes, but he quickly quenched it and smiled that false smile again. He nodded toward the young priest and the novice. "I ask your forgiveness. I am sorry for doubting your word."

What about for beating the boy's back raw? Robrek wanted to strangle the priest or use on him whatever he'd used on the boy, but he held his anger in check and dismissed the older priest.

As soon as the door closed behind Father Faolan, Father Dorsey bowed. "You've made yourself an enemy, Your Majesty." The priest looked as if he wanted to spit on the ground where Father Faolan had recently stood.

"Faolan already was my enemy."

Eolande hurried forward and put her arm around the boy's shoulders. "Come sit down. You look like you're ready to drop."

Instead, Artan trembled and fell at Robrek's feet. His words came tumbling out. "It was awful, Your Majesty. The worst thing ever. I thought a demon was trying to steal my soul. *Everyone's* soul. I've never been that scared before, not even when Father Faolan's standing over me with the flail. It's evil, Your Majesty!"

Robrek repressed a shudder. "It certainly felt evil. It seems every *true* healer felt it."

"And don't forget us Bards," Eolande said, and Robrek nodded toward her.

Dorsey smiled smugly, but Artan spluttered. "But. . . but. . . but surely Your Majesty doesn't think I'm anything like you? I've heard the most amazing stories of the things you can do."

Robrek crouched down by the child. "Surely you've noticed you're different from others? You heal faster, don't you? And you're never ill?" Father Dorsey and Artan exchanged glances, and they both nodded. Robrek held out his hand. "May I touch you?" The boy flinched. "It won't hurt. I promise."

At Artan's nod, Robrek laid his hand on the novice's shoulder. When he closed his eyes and opened his shields fully between himself and Artan, he nearly cried out from the pain. While the gouges on the boy's back had begun to heal, they had been extremely deep, cutting into the muscle and in some places even near the bone. Artan's back would have been covered with blood after the beating. The damage was severe enough to maim or even kill an ungifted child. Robrek shook with anger. *Calm yourself! The priest will suffer for his own sins. Your anger isn't necessary to protect the child, and a clear head is.* He breathed quietly for a few moments, letting go of the anger. As the anger drifted away, he felt the surge of his power. He healed the boy's flesh and closed his wounds. As he did so, he felt the boy's power cooperating with his own.

When he opened his eyes, Artan was staring at him in awe. "You fixed my back. It doesn't hurt anymore."

"Did you feel your own magic working with mine?"

"I think. . . I think so," the child nodded uncertainly. "It felt. . . it felt good."

Robrek smiled, standing. "Yes, with healing magic, the goddess has given us a two-fold blessing. The one being healed is relieved of pain, and the healer feels intense pleasure. With proper training, you will come to know this well. I'll have you sent to my friend, Father Leigh, for training—he, too, is of mixed blood. I'll talk to Father Hafghan to make sure nothing like this is ever done to you again. Is Father Faolan that harsh with all the children?"

"Only the cothlas," Father Dorsey hissed. "I've seen my own blood puddle at my feet often enough, and more than one child has died at his hands."

Robrek clenched his fists. "And nothing has been done about this?"

Dorsey snorted. "Father Shylah would hardly have wept at the death of a cothla. He considered us less than animals."

"And Father Hafghan?" Robrek tried to relax, but letting go of the anger was becoming difficult.

Dorsey shrugged. "He is new to the job, and so far, he's chosen not to notice anything Faolan does."

"I will see he takes notice." Dorsey shrugged as if what Robrek did was nothing to him. Robrek creased his brow at the priest's apparent callousness, but didn't pursue it. "Now, can I touch you to better gauge the strength of your magic?"

Father Dorsey bowed. "Certainly, Your Majesty."

Robrek placed his hand on Father Dorsey's shoulder. He had to reach up to do so. Father Dorsey was slimmer than the average Korthlundian, but he was every bit as tall. The man's exhaustion and the pain in his knees beat at the king. But underneath that, Robrek felt Dorsey's magic. It wasn't as strong as his own, but it was stronger than any other healer he'd met. Far stronger than Leigh's. Stronger even than Myst's.

He opened his eyes. "You are very powerful." At his words, Robrek saw a gleam in the priest's eyes. Robrek felt compelled to repeat to Dorsey the words his old mentor had once spoken to him. "You must be cautious and remember that with great power comes great responsibility. If the gift of the goddess is used for evil instead of good, it will twist and mangle your soul until nothing of your true self remains. For your own good, you must guard against your anger, rid yourself of it if you can. Power like yours can't afford the luxury of hatred."

Father Dorsey looked away. "I understand, Your Majesty." But Robrek feared he did nothing of the kind. He'd have to take the priest aside, as Holy Writ had done with him, but first he needed answers to the terrible evil. He felt Dorsey's exhaustion and dismissed him to rest. When the young priest had disappeared, Robrek stood unmoving.

"You don't trust Father Dorsey, do you?"

Robrek started when young Artan uttered such a perceptive statement. He looked down at the boy, who was staring at him in awe.

"He is very powerful and very angry. But at one time, so was I."

Father Loman shifted in his seat; Robrek looked his way to see the old priest smiling. "You will do, Your Majesty. You will certainly do."

Robrek wasn't quite sure what the librarian meant, but he let it go. He looked back at Artan. "You should go rest, too."

"I'm not at all tired," the boy protested. "Please, Your Majesty, can't I. . . can't I help you?"

He's probably afraid Faolan will beat him again, and he may have cause to fear. "You can stay," Robrek said. He sat at the table with Father Loman. Eolande and Artan took up seats as well. Together the three of them told the librarian everything they knew or had guessed. "I'd like any information you could find for me on Armunn and the ancient evil or anything else that might explain the curse on that village and what we all felt last night."

"I'll get right on it, Your Majesty. Armunn would be over in the legends' section. I'm sure Your Majesty knows many don't believe he ever existed."

"I believe they're wrong," Robrek said.

"And Bardic magic, Your Majesty," Eolande interjected. "You said perhaps we could find something."

The priest raised an eyebrow. "Bardic magic? There's been no true Bard in Korthlundia for centuries. The word has been degraded to mean no more than a singer of tales."

Robrek nodded toward Eolande. "Korthlundia has a true Bard now, and I hope you'll give her any assistance you can in understanding her gift. While you're digging up information, I'll have Artan here take me to the stillroom to make that joint cream and liver tonic."

* * *

Accompanied by his guards, Robrek, along with Artan, traveled through the corridors of the temple. Brendan kept his hand on the hilt of his sword. Artan drew closer and closer to Robrek, almost as if he were trying to wrap the king around him like a protective cloak.

"Is something wrong?" Robrek asked.

Artan shook his head. "I've never been allowed in the stillroom before, but if Your Majesty's with me, I'm sure it will be okay."

Robrek breathed deeply to calm himself. "I thought novices started learning how to make remedies at a younger age than you."

Artan nodded. "Most of them do."

But not those whose blood is mixed.

When they reached the stillroom, they found two priests and four novices busily making potions and ointments of various kinds. All six of them gasped and bowed deeply when they saw who entered.

Robrek acknowledged them with a nod. "Artan is going to assist me in making a couple of potions."

One of the priests came scurrying forward, followed by the other. "Of course, Your Majesty. I'm Father Piseag, and this is Father Arabus." He didn't introduce the novices. "Your Majesty, may, of course, do as you like, but I feel I must inform you Artan doesn't know even the most basic rudiments of potion making. I'm afraid he isn't very bright."

Artan turned a brilliant shade of red and looked like he either wanted to punch the priest or melt through the floor. Robrek put his hand on the boy's shoulder. "I doubt that very much."

The priests looked skeptical but didn't seem to dare contradict him. Despite its difficulties, there were advantages to being king. "Of course, Your Majesty," Father Piseag said. "How else may we be of assistance?"

Robrek looked around the room. In the middle ran two large counters at which the novices had been chopping herbs. A fireplace stood at each end. Along the side of the room were shelves and shelves of bottles, boxes, and bundles of different herbs; more hung from drying racks in the ceiling.

"I need a place to work and a cauldron. I could also use the assistance of a novice for help in locating the various items I need. The rest of you, please carry on with what you were doing."

"Of course, Your Majesty. Beynon!" Father Piseag signaled the largest of the novices. Robrek couldn't judge his age. He was taller than Robrek and had a few hairs sprouting from his chin. But his face had the rounded appearance of a small child. He smiled smugly as he came forward and looked down at Artan. Artan moved closer to Robrek, trembling. *Bully and victim?*

The other priest and the two other novices had already begun clearing a space on the counter for him to work. The smallest was a boy of about eight with strawberry blonde hair sticking out in all directions; there were bits of herbs in it, which reminded Robrek of Vaughan. "No, I wouldn't want to take your best helper. The small blond boy will be more than enough." Robrek pointed toward the child; his eyes grew round, and he immediately dropped the bowl he was holding. Fortunately, the bowl was stone and didn't break. Still, the child blushed deeply as he bent down to pick it up.

"Rab? Your Majesty, but surely—"

Robrek cut the priest off. "Surely, you have no objection to Rab helping me?"

"Oh, no, certainly not, Your Majesty, but if Your Majesty finds himself in need of more competent assistance, I assure you Beynon would be more than happy to join you."

"I'll bear that in mind." Robrek walked over to the area that had been cleared for his use. Rab stood there with big eyes and seemed hardly to dare to breathe.

Robrek squatted down so he could look the boy in the eye. He whispered so the others couldn't hear. "Rab, I would very much like your assistance. You seemed the one with the readiest eye and the quickest hand." The boy flushed with pleasure. "I won't make you if you feel uncomfortable."

"Your Majesty, it would be an honor to be of assistance." The boy smiled widely and puffed his chest out.

"Good, let's get to work, then." Artan crept up behind him, and now that Rab had been reassured, the boy was bouncing up and down on the balls of his feet. He seemed the type of child who had difficulty remaining still. "We're going to make a cream for Father Loman's joints," Robrek told them. "You and Artan put some oil in the cauldron over the fire and then gather aloe vera, arnica, beeswax, comfrey, ginger, juniper berry, rosemary, thyme, *and* yarrow."

As the boys helped him chop and grind the ingredients, Robrek explained the use of each one and why he'd chosen them for this particular cream. The two boys drank in his words, and Robrek found himself both liking the boys and his own role as teacher. Robrek had the novices add the herbs to the oil, and as it was simmering, he had the boys gather the ingredients for Father Loman's liver tonic.

They chopped and ground, smiling and laughing. Artan said little, but Rab's mouth seemed to move as fast as his feet, telling Robrek all about his life at the Temple of the Mother's Love, his father, and the temple's cat Wenda, who'd just had kittens. "Their eyes aren't even open yet. Would you like to see them?"

Robrek assured the boy that if he had time, he'd love to see the kittens.

"I like animals, Your Majesty. You always know if they really like you or not. They don't pretend to like you because your father's an important banker or because your mother's the most beautiful woman in the entire capital." The boy's eyes grew both dreamy and sad as he spoke of his parents. "Of course, they're very busy. My parents, I mean, not the animals. I couldn't expect them to have much time to visit me."

By this time, Father Loman's joint medicine was nearly ready. Robrek called Artan over to the fire. Rab followed. "By itself this cream would do Father Loman some good, but now I'm going to add the final ingredient that will make it extremely powerful. I want you to watch what I'm doing—not with your eyes, but with your healing senses. It will probably help if you closed your eyes and touched me while I do it." Artan nodded and put his hand on Robrek's arm.

"Your Majesty, how can he watch with his eyes closed?" Rab asked.

"Magic isn't something you can see with your eyes, so your eyes can distract you."

"Can I touch you, too, Your Majesty?" Rab asked. "I've never seen magic, and Father Faolan told my father I had strong healing magic when he made me a novice."

The king looked down at the small boy and wondered how to break it to him gently. "You know how you just mentioned that sometimes people tell you things because your father's an important banker?"

Rab nodded so enthusiastically Robrek was afraid his head might fly off. "People do that all the time, Your Majesty." Abruptly, he stopped nodding. "Oh, you mean Father Faolan lied to my father. He would do that. I could tell he wanted my father's money."

Robrek patted the boy lightly on the shoulder. "Father Faolan doesn't have any magic himself, so he's unable to tell who does and who doesn't. You see, magic requires mixed blood." Robrek heard a gasp from the other side of the stillroom, but he ignored the priests. They didn't dare say anything to the king, especially with his guards close by.

Rab was still nodding. "Well, if you have to have mixed blood to have magic, I can't have any. My father's always going on and on about how pure our blood is." Rab didn't seem terribly upset by this discovery.

Robrek turned back to Artan. "Watch now." Robrek closed his own eyes and felt pleasure as his magic flowed into the mixture. Artan made a small noise, almost a whimper. Robrek opened his eyes to see Artan shaking. "What's wrong?"

"I don't have that kind of power, Your Majesty. I know I don't."

"No, you don't, Artan. Yours is weaker than mine, but it can still make your potions more powerful than those without magic. I'll let you try on the next one."

But by the time they finished the potion, Artan, like Father Dorsey earlier, looked like he was about to fall asleep on his feet. In his exhaustion, he couldn't manage the concentration necessary to magically enhance the remedy. "It's all right," Robrek reassured the boy. "Just try again when you've had a chance to rest. Why don't you go to bed now?"

Artan's eyes went wide with fear. "Please, Your Majesty, can't I stay with you?"

Robrek wondered if the novice was truly in danger in his own quarters. "I'm about to return to the library. I can have a cot brought there if you'd prefer."

* * *

Robrek saw that Artan was tucked into a cot in front of the library fireplace. The king paused for a moment to brush the hair back from Artan's forehead, and then he turned to face Father Loman and Eolande, who were gazing at him from behind a tall pile of books.

There was a twinkle in the old librarian's eyes. "It was kind to allow him to stay, Your Majesty."

"It is hard to grow up without love." Robrek shook himself and took a seat across from the priest. "I don't suppose you have already found the answer."

The librarian laughed his hearty belly laugh. "I don't know about *the* answer, Your Majesty, but I have found a thing or two. This book here"—he pushed one over to Robrek—"discusses the ritual of the priestesses your novice mentioned. On the night of each full moon the female priestesses go into the woods, and I hear—although this part may simply be rumor; I pray that it is—they dance around without a stitch of clothing on. They say they are holding some ancient evil in check."

"Ancient evil?" *There's that term again.*

"The Soul Stone, Your Majesty. Nothing more is said about it, except that if a sufficient number of priestesses fail to perform the ritual on schedule, the ancient evil will be loosed to again ravage the land. They've been doing this ritual for centuries. I've always thought it was foolish, but perhaps I was the fool."

Robrek read the passages Father Loman had found, but they added little to what he'd already known or guessed. He turned to Eolande. "Was Father Loman able to help you find anything about Bards?"

Eolande smiled. "Quite a lot, actually, although I've barely had time to touch it. There is a book on Bards I thought you might find of interest."

She handed him an open book, and Robrek read the first paragraph:

Beware! Beware! All ye who doubt the power of the Bard! Beware! The very soul of man is mine to command! Beware! Reverence the Bard! Bring your gifts and holy offerings to the Bard! Place the Bard in your heart next to the goddess herself! Love the Bard or you grow to fear the Bard! Beware! Beware!

"Awfully fond of 'beware,' isn't he?" Robrek said.

"Yes, a bit overly dramatic, but the book talks about draining life energy, even the soul itself, to fuel the Bard's power. The draining of energy seems very like what happened to the Korthian village." Eolande pointed out the passages.

"You're saying we may be dealing with a Bard?"

"Except, of course, a single Bard could do nothing on this scale. Your Majesty, the books talk about a person being made up of two parts—the body and the soul, the physical and the spiritual. While the healer's power affects the body, the Bard's touches the soul. We can make others feel the emotions of our songs—because emotions are of the soul, not of the body. I think maybe the ancient evil, the Soul Stone, uses a Bard-like power to drain the soul, and the body can't live without the soul. That's why Oriana, who's a healer, not a bard, could find nothing wrong with the people of her village, though they still weakened and died."

Robrek collapsed into a chair. "Holy Sulis! How will we stop this? Could *you* cure somebody affected?"

Eolande shook her head. "I don't know, Your Majesty. The ancient evil is said to be powerful. How could one untrained Bard combat it?"

"Study more, and see if you can come up with anything else, especially how we can hope to destroy it." He turned to Father Loman. "Any assistance you could give Eolande will be most appreciated."

The priest smiled widely. "I'd walk through fire for one who made me feel this good."

"I won't ask you that, but please, look after young Artan."

"With pleasure, King Young Buck, with pleasure." The priest laughed his hearty belly laugh.

* * *

Robrek was in a hurry to get back to the palace, but he stopped by Father Hafghan's office. The high priest greeted him in an overly jovial manner, and Robrek fully appreciated Rab's remarks about knowing what animals think about people. When Robrek had been a peasant, he knew what people thought of him—it usually wasn't good, but it wasn't a mystery. Now he had no idea where he stood with the high priest. He sat in a chair on one side of the desk; Father Hafghan sat on the other.

"Tomorrow I want both Father Dorsey and Artan sent to Father Leigh for training," Robrek said without preamble.

Father Hafghan picked up a mug of *bhat* from his desk and drank to disguise the emotion on his face, but he wasn't quick enough to conceal his surprise. "I will take that under advisement. You are aware, of course, that the crown has no jurisdiction over the internal workings of the church, and the novices are under Father Faolan's authority, not mine."

Robrek leaned across Father Hafghan's desk. "Faolan's been here, hasn't he? What did he say to you?"

Hafghan cleared his throat. "He merely reminded me that he is in charge of novice discipline."

"That's all?" Robrek didn't try to hide his skepticism.

Hafghan sighed and fiddled with a figurine of the goddess on his desk. "If you must know, Your Majesty, he was furious over what he called your interference, and he indicated I wouldn't be high priest for long if I bowed to any sort of pressure from the crown. And he wasn't the only one who came to me. Father Piseag insisted you were spreading heresy among the novices." He replaced the figurine and sighed.

Robrek laughed bitterly. "Heresy, is it? I can't help it if it's true that mixed blood is required for magical talent." He picked up the figurine and held it out to Hafghan. "The goddess created the laws of magic, not me, and with its preaching on the purity of blood, the church is doing its best to make sure magic is completely obliterated. We are in a crisis here." He told Father Hafghan about the evil Robrek and the others had felt. "Artan and Dorsey were the only two who reported feeling something the night before last. Do you understand the significance of this? They are probably the only two true healers in the largest shrine in the capital, and they are both of mixed blood. Korthlundia cannot afford this continued prejudice against mixed blood."

Father Hafghan didn't meet his eyes. "If Your Majesty's absolutely certain that mixed blood is required for healing magic, it is decidedly inconvenient."

"The laws of magic can't be changed to suit human convenience. Artan and Father Dorsey are either going to Father Leigh tomorrow, or they're coming with me now. I can't afford to have them destroyed, no matter how inconvenient it may be to you."

Father Hafghan sighed again. "Your Majesty, my power base within the church is far from secure. There's a strong contingency that wanted me to denounce Her Majesty's marriage because of Your Majesty's mixed blood. The church has been teaching for centuries that the mixture of blood is an abomination to the goddess. If I instead claim Sulis allows only those of mixed blood to perform her healing magic, I will have a mutiny on my hands."

Robrek leaned closer to the high priest. "As you know the truth about magic, it is your responsibility to bring it to the people, regardless of the consequences to yourself."

Father Hafghan shook his head. "If the Holy Mother has chosen me to be her champion, she has chosen an awfully weak vessel." He sighed yet again and met Robrek's eyes. "But I will send Dorsey and Artan to Father Leigh."

* * *

With Samantha asleep beside him, Robrek sat in bed, reading the Armunn ballads Eolande had copied out for him. The ballads defined the ancient evil in wildly contradictory ways. But none of them talked of how Armunn had stopped the evil, just that he went into the cave, did battle with it, and never returned.

He tossed the ballads aside. "Sulis, if you chose me to solve this problem, you had better give me more information."

* * *

Father Hafghan tried to remain calm as Father Faolan loomed over his desk, spittle flying from his mouth. "You sent Dorsey and Artan to that cothla pretense of a priest? I won't stand for it! The church won't stand for it! Cothlas are an abomination! Even you should know Sulis wouldn't bless them with her holy magic while withholding it from her pure children!"

Hafghan rose to his feet and pointed a finger at the other priest. "You seem to have forgotten who the clergy anointed to be their high priest."

Faolan's voice went deadly quiet. "You think you are fooling anyone? Our cothla king put you up to this! You are allowing the monarchy to interfere in the workings of Sulis's holy church. You are allowing it to spread the lies that magic comes from contamination. Recall Dorsey and Artan to the Temple of the Mother's Love, or face the consequences!"

Hafghan puffed out his chest. "You will not tell me what to do. I am your superior."

"If you persist in this, you won't be for long." Faolan turned and left, slamming the door behind him.

* * *

Mother Venetia shook with exhaustion as she collapsed around the fire with the others combating the curse; they'd been fleeing the sudden expansion of the Dead Lands and had finally reached an area of safety. Despair nearly overcame her as she looked around. Out of all the priestesses and novices who had answered Mother Bensaggyrt's call, only five remained. *What can we do now? Is there any hope?*

* * *

In the late afternoon, Captain Hawk paced Samantha's reception room like an enraged panther. He'd just arrived, and he looked like he been travelling for days without rest. "This Alvabane sang, and I could feel the evil pour forth from her voice. Your Majesty, my men all died without even being able to draw their swords—all one hundred men in a matter of minutes! She claimed she controlled something called the Soul Stone, channeling its power through her voice. She claims she will destroy Murtaghan itself if you don't give into her demands."

"Holy Sulis!" Samantha sank into a chair. "How can such a thing be fought?"

"'Beware!'" Robbie whispered beside her. "'Reverence the Bard!'"

Samantha jerked her head toward him, afraid he'd gone mad. "What are you talking about?"

Robbie's eyes shone as if he'd solved a particularly difficult problem. "I need a map."

Samantha fought off the feelings of impeding doom. *Please, Sulis, let him know what to do—because I don't.* She rang for a page to fetch a map. When it arrived, Robbie spread it on the table. "Where are Duke Torin's estates?" Robbie asked. Samantha pointed to a spot in central Lundia, nestled up against the mountains that separated Korth and Lundia. "And where is Balley Beg, Oriana's village?"

Samantha pointed to a spot directly on the other side of the mountain. "No!" she cried. "It *is* the ancient evil!"

Robbie nodded. "This Alvabane must be a Bard. The ancient evil, the Soul Stone—she must be able to access it from Torin's estate. It has been draining souls on the north side of the mountains in Korth." Robbie pointed to the area around Oriana's village. "The Bard has now used it to steal the souls of the Royal Guard."

The effects of Robbie's tea chose that moment to wear off, and Samantha put her hand to her belly at the horrifying thought. "Could we use Eolande to counter it?"

Robbie's face fell. "I doubt she has anywhere near enough power."

"If the Soul Stone's inside Torin's estate, what can we do? Sending more men would be simply throwing away their lives."

"I know." Robbie's hand shook slightly as he pointed again to Balley Beg. "The cave Oriana spoke of must also give access to the Stone. Maybe, I have to go there. Maybe, I have to do what Armunn did."

Samantha grabbed Robbie's hand and jerked it off the map. "No! I won't allow you to simply ride to your death as he did! If you're going to confront this thing, you need a better plan. The goddess didn't chose you only to have you destroy yourself!"

* * *

Sulis, isn't there a way I can stop this thing without sacrificing my life?

Robrek gathered the healers and Eolande to his rooms and told them what he had learned. Oriana's forehead wrinkled, making her look much like an adult.

"We could give Eolande more power, Your Majesty. We could share our power with her."

"That can be done?"

Oriana put her hands on her hips. "You've never shared power, Your Majesty? How do you think healers less powerful than you heal a great illness? I often leant my power to my mistress when hers alone wasn't enough."

Holy Sulis, how much more is there about magic I don't know? Why didn't Myst or Holy Writ teach me this? How can I ever hope to do what Armunn did? "How is this done?"

Oriana smiled, as if relishing the idea she had something to teach the king. "It's not difficult, Your Majesty. First, we must both enter a healing trance and merge our shields. I'll show you."

They both sat down in the middle of the room, and Oriana reached out for his hands. They closed their eyes. He felt his shields touching hers; hers shimmered weak and feeble compared to his. Robrek concentrated, and their shields merged. As she'd said, it wasn't difficult.

Oriana's voice came as if from far away. "Now open yourself to my power." He felt something pushing against the core of his being, as annoying as a gnat fluttering around his face. Reflexively, his power reached out and swatted it. Oriana screamed, and her hands were torn out of his, her body flung across the room.

"Oriana!" He jolted himself back into full awareness and rushed toward her. The young novice was cradling her hands and crying in pain.

"You blocked me!" she cried.

Robrek took her hands. They were red and blistering. "I'm sorry. I didn't mean to. I'll fix this." He closed his eyes, entered a trance, and healed her hands.

When he opened his eyes, she'd stopped crying, but she scowled at him. "Let's try that again, Your Majesty, and this time don't block me." She said this as if lecturing a simple-minded child.

Robrek helped Oriana to her feet. They went back to the middle of the room and sat down again. Oriana, still the stern taskmaster, met his eyes. "This time, try to see my power as a drink you're thirsty for. All you have to do is receive it. I'll only give you a little."

They again closed their eyes, entered trances, and joined their shields. Robrek breathed deeply, steadying himself to receive the coming power. He felt it coming toward him and felt himself reaching to swat it again. Instead, he did as Oriana instructed and reached for the promised drink. He felt her power dribbling into him, adding to his own.

"It worked." Oriana smiled happily.

They practiced until they had it down, and then they taught Leigh, Dorsey, and Artan. As Oriana said, it wasn't difficult. Finally, they made their attempt to share the power with Eolande.

* * *

Eolande and the healers formed a circle, holding hands. The king and young Oriana were next to her. The healers closed their eyes, and she began to sing. The power rushed into her, and it was as if she'd grown to gigantic size. The power of her voice could reach to the ends of the earth. She was the goddess herself. She could create or destroy at will. She laughed with delight.

All too soon, the king opened his eyes, and the power flow stopped. Suddenly, it was gone, and she felt herself shrinking. She became nothing but a singer of tales. *No! Give it back to me!* She nearly broke down in sobs. Slowly, the other healers opened their eyes. *Sweet Sulis, give me this power, and I'll do anything you want.*

* * *

Pacing her reception room, Robbie told Samantha what he'd learned about sharing power. "It provides Eolande a lot more power than she'd otherwise have, but I doubt it's enough to counter the Bard and the Soul Stone. If this doesn't work, we'll die right along with the villagers. If the goddess chose me to solve this problem, she'd better tell me how."

Samantha grabbed Robbie's hand and pulled him down beside her. "Have you asked her?"

Robbie closed his eyes and leaned his head back. "I haven't been on those kind of terms with the goddess."

"Perhaps you need to be."

CHAPTER 22

Riding toward Gloine Torr to seek the goddess in her most sacred shrine, Robrek kept Wild Thing to a slow pace. *If I never get there, maybe I can make it not true. Maybe I can make it so I don't have to be the second Armunn. Oh, Holy Sulis, you can't have chosen me only to die. You can't be so cruel.*

Despite his pace, he eventually reached the monument. He left Wild Thing at the base with two of his guards, and, fighting the wind, he climbed the long staircase with the other four. The snow swirled through the air, and he shivered against the cold.

At the top of the obsidian monument, a shrine, bigger than the one in Valley Fair, overlooked the plains below. There was a refectory, cells for pilgrims and a few priests, and a large sanctuary.

Robrek entered the sanctuary alone, leaving his guards outside to make sure he wasn't interrupted. He went to the altar and stared at the bigger than human-sized statue of Sulis that rose behind it. As was typical of statues of the Holy Mother, Sulis's hair was confined in hundreds of braids woven through with flowers. The goddess looked down at him with a kindly expression. "They say you're the Mother of us all," he said, closing his eyes and fighting tears. "They say you love us as parents love their children. Have you really chosen me only to sacrifice my life for those who call me a demon?" Again feeling the despair he'd experienced when Eolande sang Armunn's ballad, he wanted to fall at the altar and weep.

Instead, he paced, waiting for Sulis to tell him he was wrong, that there was a simple solution to the problem. But she was silent. "Armunn was older than I am," he muttered, mostly to himself; Sulis didn't seem to be listening. "He was fully trained in his sorcery. How can I do what he did?"

A sudden weariness overcoming him, he sank to the floor of the shrine. "I love her, Sulis. I love her and my child. I don't want to leave them, to never hold my daughter in my arms." He wrapped his arms around his knees and rested his head on them, thinking of Samantha and the small life growing inside her. He sat that way for quite some time. He raised his head and looked at the goddess again. "What if I refuse? What if I won't do it?"

Suddenly, something enveloped him in warmth and light; he fell flat to the ground in awe of the goddess's presence. All of creation spread out before him—people, animals, plants, the earth itself. He felt overwhelmed with love for everything from a single blade of grass to the tallest of mountains, from the beetle to the most exalted person. Nothing escaped his attention or his love. He wanted to embrace everything and everyone. He wanted all to live, to thrive, to be happy, and to fulfill the purpose of creation. A part of Robrek knew the love he felt was the goddess's and not his own, but the thought of any portion of that creation suffering tore into him.

A voice penetrated to his core. It was both the most gentle and the most powerful, the most loving and the most terrible, the strongest and the most mild. It was all and everything, and it was nothing at all. :*All this beauty I created for my children. I gave them love, harmony, and peace.*:

His vision narrowed to Korth, and he spotted the darkness at the heart of the land—the deadness that was slowly creeping forward, killing everything in its path. Creation in all its varieties suffered and died. Robrek wept as he had never wept before, with a sorrow greater and more awful than any he'd ever imagined. Again, he knew the emotions were more the goddess's than his own, but that didn't make his sorrow any less acute. "Why?" he cried out. "Why have you allowed this to happen? If you are so powerful and so good, how can evil like this exist?"

Again, he heard the voice. :*I have given my children free will, without which they'd be nothing more than my playthings. In every generation, some will choose evil over good, hate over love, discord over harmony. Sometimes, their choices threaten the very balance of creation itself. So it was a thousand years ago. So it is today. At such times, I must have a champion who will choose the right path and restore harmony. Doing so myself would violate my children's will.*:

"But what if I don't want to be that champion? What if I want to live? Don't I get free will, as well?"

Robrek felt his suffering tearing into the goddess. The Holy Mother of us all wept for his pain, and Robrek knew the goddess would not condemn him for choosing his own life. He could choose to walk away.

But he also knew Samantha wouldn't walk away. She would stay and do everything in her power to help her people, even if it meant marrying Torin, a man she despised and allowing him to take her to his bed.

The enveloping warmth overcame him again, and to his horror, he saw Samantha's sacrifice wouldn't help. The Bard might be the one threatening Lundia, but the Bard could no more stop the death creeping through Korth than a man could hold back the tide. It was too strong, far beyond her power. The Bard wasn't truly the enemy, but the Stone itself. The Soul Stone had to be destroyed, and he was the only one alive who stood a chance of doing so.

If he refused to be the goddess's champion, the Soul Stone would continue its deadly work until the goddess could raise up a new champion. This could take years, if not generations. He told himself he would gladly die to prevent the disaster, but he knew this was a lie—he didn't want to die. He knew Samantha would have a hard time bearing his loss. "She's already lost so many, Sulis. Does she have to lose me as well?"

Again the presence swept over him. Samantha and he strode hand in hand through a lush field filled with flowers more beautiful than words can describe. Above them, the sky was blue and cloudless, and a soft, gentle breeze ruffled their hair. He realized he was not seeing them together in this world, but Beyond the Far Mountain. :*Any separation would be but for a few moments.*:

With those words, a calmness settled over him. What was death but a change to a new plane of existence—one in which Samantha and he would be together forever? "So there's no hope for us in this life? I'm going to die as Armunn did?"

His entire head pounded with a voice too big to fit inside, but one that didn't make a sound. :*Canst thou do what Armunn couldst not? Art thou stronger than he?*:

"Surely you know his power better than I do."

:It is not thy power that is in question, but thy heart. Is thy heart strong enough to face this and live? Armunn's was not.:

Robrek shook his head. *How can I even begin to compete with Armunn—whose legend has survived nearly a thousand years?* Surely he would die, but as Sulis had shown him, death wasn't the end. "Where must I go? What must I do?"

In his mind he saw the route he must take across the joined kingdoms and into Korth. He saw the one pass still free of snow. He saw his descent to the other side and his short journey through Korth to what had to be Oriana's village. He also felt the need for haste, which meant he needed to go alone. Wild Thing was far faster and had greater endurance than a regular horse. If he allowed others to accompany him, even his personal guards, they would slow him down. "But what must I do when I get there? How can I destroy this evil?"

:If thy heart is strong enough, thou wilst know.:

* * *

When Robrek rode into the palace stables, he found Vaughan waiting for him. "Where were you today?" Vaughan demanded. Robrek looked at him blankly, and the boy sighed. "It was our training time."

Robrek dismounted. "I'm sorry. I forgot."

"It doesn't matter." The boy kicked at the stable floor. "I'm sure you have a lot on your mind."

"If you only knew." Robrek blinked back tears. "Vaughan, I need your help."

The boy beamed. "Of course, Your Majesty."

At Vaughan's smile, Robrek nearly lost his composure. It was Vaughan who'd first told him that Samantha loved him. It was Vaughan who'd been his squire and carried his flag when he'd climbed Gloine Torr, and Vaughan's was another life he'd save by giving his own.

Robrek waved his guards away so they wouldn't hear him. "You can tell no one, and I can't give you any details, but I need to leave before morning."

"Are you going to fight the evil?" Vaughan asked.

Robrek's head jerked backward in surprise. "How do you know about that?"

Vaughan shrugged. "A hundred members of the Royal Guard don't die without word getting around. I'm going with you "

Robrek yearned to take him, but he had no choice. "No, I have to go alone." The boy's expression drooped at his words, and Robrek put his hand on Vaughan's shoulder and squeezed. "Wild Thing's the only horse fast enough to get there in time."

Vaughan kicked at the stall. "That's okay, Your Majesty, I understand."

"But you have a very important part to play. I'll be busy tonight, and I won't have time to gather supplies. I need you to pack for me, only the essentials." Robrek rattled off a list of items he knew he would need. "And peasant clothing, too—nothing to show I'm the king. Leave everything in Wild Thing's stall."

Vaughan beamed again. "You can count on me, Your Majesty."

"That's why I asked you." Robrek prayed to the goddess to keep the boy well. He took the boy by the shoulders, noticing that Vaughan had grown as tall as he. "This is very important, Vaughan. You can't let anyone know what you're doing. You can't tell anyone what I plan to do until after I've left. Then it won't matter."

Vaughan gulped and nodded solemnly. "Your Majesty, I swear by the goddess and on my mother's grave that no one will find out anything from me."

"Thank you, Vaughan." Robrek pulled Vaughan into a hug—something he'd never done before. He pressed the boy to him and fought against tears.

* * *

Samantha trembled as Robbie told her what he'd learned atop Gloine Torr. "Eolande and the others have to go to Reidhlean and slow the Bard down. I must go to the cave and confront the evil at its source."

Samantha stalked to her window seat and glowered at the palace grounds. "I can't let you go. What if you don't come back?" *Please, Sulis, don't take him from me.*

Robbie approached her and put his arms around her. She fought back her tears. *It will be okay. It has to be okay.* She turned to face him. "Of course your heart will be strong enough. Nothing is stronger than your heart."

He kissed her. "I hope so, Sam. I must leave first thing in the morning."

Not so soon, Sulis. Let me have him just a few days more. In case. . . She couldn't finish the thought. She grabbed him and held him to her, reveling in the warmth of his body against hers. How could she lose this love now that she'd found it?

But she couldn't be a woman moping after a man. *You are queen, Samantha. Thousands of lives are at stake.* She broke away. "How large an escort should we send with you and which of the healers?"

Robbie turned away, not meeting her eyes. "A small escort will make traveling faster, but the other healers must stay with Eolande to counter the Bard if I don't make it in time."

Samantha wanted to send an entire army with him. *If only this evil could be fought with swords.* But it was magic that was needed. "Your personal guard should be sufficient. But you must take at least one of the other healers with you. Leigh, I think, would be best." He didn't answer; she grabbed his shoulder and turned him to face her. "Robbie, I insist! Leigh saved your life once. He might well do it again."

Robbie nodded. He drew her close again, and she pressed herself to him.

"It's settled. We give the orders, and then. . ."

He touched her lips with his finger, stopping the flow of her words. "And then I need you, Sam."

* * *

The firelight gleamed on Samantha's skin as she lay sleeping beside him. He had made love to her long and slow, taking time to imprint every detail of her on his mind. He stared at her now, trying to memorize the freckles on her face, the smallness of her ears, the gleam of her auburn hair, the curve of her breast. It hurt to know this could be the last time he ever saw her. He put his hand on her abdomen and felt the life of their daughter within. It pained him to think he might never hold her. But perhaps, he could reach out to her from Beyond the Far Mountain, as his mother had reached out to him. *Mother, watch over them if I cannot.* He bent and kissed Samantha's brow. She stirred and smiled in her sleep—not the court smile she gave everyone else, but a smile of true love and contentment. She'd given him the love he'd thought he'd never have. Surely she was right. His heart would be strong enough. But if it wasn't, he'd gladly give his life to save Samantha and their child. He just didn't want to think of the pain this would cause Samantha. She'd already lost so many. "Keep her strong, Holy Mother," he whispered, "if she has to lose me, too."

He knew leaving wasn't going to get any easier if he waited, so Robrek slipped from underneath the bedcovering, picked up his clothes, and headed to Samantha's reception room. It was cold, but he didn't chance stirring up the fire: Samantha might awake and try to stop him. He lit a candle and dressed quickly, wrapping his cloak tightly around him. He sat down at her desk and took up paper and a quill. First, he wrote a letter to Samantha telling her how much he loved her and pleading with her to understand why he had to leave as he had. The depth of his love for her was difficult to put into words, so the note was rather brief. Only a short time before he'd let her know with his body everything he felt. He wrote an even shorter note to his uncle, thanking him for everything and wishing him all happiness. He paused before the final and most important letter—the one to the daughter he might never meet. Surely she would hear stories, ballads, and legends about him, but he wanted her to know him as he was. He struggled through the writing of it, tears blurring his vision. Sulis had refused to promise him life, so he wrote all that he could think to tell his daughter, all the lessons his life had taught him. When he'd finished, he sealed all three notes.

He left two of them on the desk while he took the third back into Samantha's bedchamber. He nearly faltered when he saw her sleeping so peacefully. *How can I ever leave you?* But if she was to survive, he could wait no longer. Dawn would arrive soon, and he had to be gone before the palace started to wake. He set the note he'd written her on the bedside table, brushed the hair back from her forehead, and kissed her one last time and hurried from the room. He picked up the other two notes and left Samantha's quarters, using his magic so his guards didn't see him go.

Robrek slipped silently and invisibly through the palace until he came to the rooms Leigh had been given. He knocked on the door, and after a moment Leigh answered it, wiping the sleep from his eyes. "Robrek. . . I mean, Your Majesty, have I overslept? I thought we weren't leaving for a couple of hours." Leigh stepped aside to let him enter.

"You don't need to call me that. I was simply a farmer's son when we met."

Leigh shrugged. "You were never 'simply' anything."

Robrek brushed by him and began pacing the room. He wanted to crawl back into bed with Samantha. "I have several favors to ask of you before I leave."

"Certainly, Your. . . Robrek, but I thought I was going with you."

Robrek shook his head. "I'm leaving alone. There is nothing anyone can do to help me."

Leigh grabbed Robrek's shoulder, stopping his pacing. "No!" Leigh said, shaking his head. "No! You think you're going to die, don't you?"

Robrek turned away, pulling free his arm. "I will do everything I can to survive, but Armunn couldn't face this evil and live. Am I stronger than he?"

Robrek felt Leigh's eyes boring into his back. "But surely if I and the others went with you, we could help in some way."

Robrek turned and looked Leigh in the eyes. "Don't make this any harder than it already is. You and the others must help me by stalling the Bard. You can't save me this time." The image came into his mind of Leigh unlocking his shackles as the mob outside howled for his blood.

Leigh nodded. "You are the eagle. Tell me what you need me to do."

"Thank you." Robrek resumed his pacing. "First, I want you to promise to do everything in your power to safeguard both Samantha and my daughter."

"You know I will."

Robrek took the two letters out and handed them to Leigh. "Deliver these. The first one is for my uncle. I'd like to take leave of him, but I can't afford the time." Leigh nodded and looked at the second, far thicker letter. "That one"—Robrek's finger trembled as he touched the letter—"is for my daughter. If I come back, you can simply return the letter to me. But if I do not. . ." Robrek struggled for control. "Keep it, and when my daughter is old enough to read and understand it, give it to her. Samantha knows nothing of this, and I don't want her to. It would hurt her too much."

Leigh grabbed him into an embrace. "The goddess protect you, my friend. The eagle may well be stronger than Armunn. There is no doubt your heart is."

My heart? How could he know the goddess's words? Sulis bless Leigh was right. He pulled back from Leigh's hug and grasped him by the arm. "Good bye, my friend, and thank you for everything."

He hurried from the room.

* * *

When Robrek reached the stables, he found Vaughan asleep on top of the clothing and supplies he'd acquired. Wild Thing neighed a welcome, waking the boy. Vaughan jumped to his feet and jutted out his chin. "I'm not going to let you do it, Your Majesty."

"Do what?" Robrek pulled off the shirt of the king and put on one of rough homespun, such as he'd grown up wearing.

"I figured out why you hugged me yesterday. You think you're going to die like Armunn." Vaughan glared accusingly.

Robrek took off his boots and trousers. He paused, but after all Vaughan had been through with him, he deserved the truth. "I have no wish to die, and I pray I might find a way to stop this thing and survive. But if I can't, I want those I care about to remember how I feel about them."

Vaughan's face brightened at being named among those Robrek cared for, but it darkened quickly. "I won't let you face this alone, Your Majesty."

Robrek pulled on the peasant trousers. Everything fit perfectly. He guessed that now he and Vaughan were nearly the same size, it hadn't been hard for the boy to choose clothes for him "I'm sorry, Vaughan, but I can't let you. Wild Thing is the only horse with enough speed."

Wild Thing nickered. *:Much faster than stupid white horse.:*

Robrek reached up and scratched her neck.

Vaughan crossed his arms across his chest and stood in the stall doorway. "A squire doesn't allow his knight to go into danger alone. One way or another, I'm going with you, even if I have to wake up the entire stables, so it's impossible for you to sneak out without your escort."

Robrek paused, not wanting the last encounter between him and the boy to be hostile. But he knew the child would follow through on his threat. There was only one answer. He touched Vaughan on the shoulder and sent him into a deep sleep.

* * *

In the early morning hours, Samantha turned on the bed and moved over to snuggle against Robbie. She reached out her arm, but all she found was an empty pillow. Her eyes flew open. It was still dark outside, but by the light of the fire, she could see he wasn't there. "No!" she cried. "He didn't! He couldn't have!" She sat up. There, propped against her tea cup on the table beside the bed was a note with her name written in Robbie's nearly illegible scrawl. She snatched up the note. "No, please, Sulis," she whispered. "Don't let him have gone alone." With her hands shaking, she lit a candle so she could read.

My dearest Sam,

I hope you'll forgive me for doing what I know must be done. If my guards or Leigh might have in any way made a difference, I would have taken them with me. I am not eager to die, but they can do nothing against the magic I'll have to face. The longer it takes me to get there, the more difficult stopping the Stone will be.

Sam, I love you with all of my heart, all of my soul. I've loved you since the first day I saw you at the Horse Fair. For a long time I ached with the knowledge that I could never have you. That night when we were hand-fasted beside the river was an impossible dream come true. Your love and our child have been the greatest gifts of my life. I wouldn't change anything I had with you.

The goddess has given me some hope that there might be a way to live through this. I promise I will do everything in my power to survive and return to you. But if I have to sacrifice my life to keep you and our daughter safe, know that I do so willingly. Sulis has shown me we will be together again Beyond the Far Mountain. I'll be waiting for you there.

In case I do not return, I have made Leigh vow to make sure you and our child are safe through the delivery. For my sake, please allow him to do so.

Don't send anyone after me. It will be impossible to catch me.

Take care, my love. Tell our daughter about me. Tell her how much I loved her and her mother. Let me live in her memory if I can't live in her life. I love you, Sam, and I always will.

With all of my heart,
Robbie

Samantha stared at the note, too stunned, too hurt, to even weep. She cried out for her guards. Bearach and Conroy burst into the room, swords drawn. "Find Father Leigh and bring him to me now!" she ordered.

* * *

Leigh bowed as he entered the queen's reception room, pained to see the devastation on her face. *Holy Sulis, please bring him back to her!*

The queen sat in a plush, green chair next to the fire. She didn't ask him to be seated. "You let your king go alone to his death. Tell me how you have not committed treason."

Leigh felt a chill of fear. This was his friend's wife, but a vast gulf separated them. "I have obeyed my king. If you find treason in this, I have no defense."

Her voice clipped and harsh, she said, "You knew he planned to leave alone, yet you told no one."

Leigh stood in the middle of the rug in front of her chair. "He made me promise not to. I know it hurts you to hear this, Your Majesty, but I believe he was right. I have felt the evil. He is the only one who can stop it. The rest of us would have only slowed him down."

The queen rose to her feet and struck him across the face. "You will not make excuses for your cowardice!"

Leigh put a hand to his cheek. He briefly closed his eyes and prayed for the right words to make her understand. "Your Majesty, I am no coward. I gave up everything I ever wanted in life to save him when he was a stranger. I would gladly face all seven of the hells to protect him. But he is the one the goddess has chosen for this task, and only he is fit to face it."

Samantha raised her hand to strike him again, then dropped it, the life seeming to drain out of her face. "Get out of my sight!"

Leigh wanted to put his arm around her, to comfort her, but knew she wouldn't allow such familiarity, especially now. "Yes, Your Majesty. His Majesty made me vow to look after the health of you and your child. I pray you will allow me to keep that vow."

The queen's eyes flashed with rage, and Leigh wouldn't have been surprised if she'd ordered one of her guards to run him through.

* * *

Samantha stared after Leigh as he left her chambers. All hope had left the room with him. She'd wanted him to tell her that what she feared wasn't true, but he'd confirmed everything.

"Your Majesty," Bearach said, but she didn't want to listen to him defend Leigh. She waved abruptly at him, dismissing both of her guards.

She sank back into her chair as the door closed behind them. She'd grown up with the knowledge that she couldn't marry for love. But the goddess had sent her Robbie, and for a few brief, wonderful weeks she'd had what she'd never dreamed possible. She'd shared her life, her throne, and her bed with a man she loved. *How dare you, Sulis! How dare you give him to me only to tear him away! If he doesn't return, Holy Mother, I will never forgive you!*

* * *

Vaughan awoke on the ground in Wild Thing's stall with a blanket over him. "Sulis curse His Majesty!" He added a couple of stronger phrases. The king had used his magic and left him behind. *Well, he's not getting away with it!* Vaughan saddled Thunder Storm and took off after the king as fast as the horse could go.

* * *

Dead inside, Samantha sat at the head of the council table and explained what Captain Hawk had reported and what Robbie had done in response. The councilors responded with stunned silence.

"Will the king be able to stop this thing?" Baron Gwawl finally asked.

Samantha wanted to wail or to deny the danger. *Of course! He has to!* Instead, she clamped a court mask firmly over her features. "I don't know. We must prepare for his failure."

"What can *we* do?" Baron Arawn said. "No army can stand against that."

"Do you suggest we do nothing?" Baron Gwawl demanded.

"Get Captain Darhour back here," Sheen said. "He killed Duke Argblutal; he can do the same to Torin and his Bard."

Samantha fought to keep the emotion off her face. "If I knew where he was, I'd have done that. Do you know of another assassin capable of doing the job?"

No one had any useful candidates or alternatives to suggest. In the end, it was decided that a note would be sent, asking Torin to come to Murtaghan to discuss a marriage contract. No one thought he'd agree, but it might buy them time.

* * *

"You want me to do what?" Father Hafghan fumed, unable to believe his ears.

Father Faolan leaned across the desk. "You will nullify the queen's marriage to the sorcerer, making the child she carries illegitimate and, therefore, unable to take the throne."

Hafghan jumped to his feet and jabbed a finger at the younger priest. "You speak of treason! You think the queen will just sit back and take such an insult?"

Faolan crossed his arms and looked smug. "She will have no choice. If she objects, you will excommunicate her, relieving the populace of their loyalty to the throne."

Hafghan gaped, unable to believe Faolan would suggest so drastic a step; it would be tantamount to declaring war on the crown, a war they couldn't win. "I will do nothing of the kind! The queen is popular with the people. They won't so easily set aside their loyalty."

"They will when their fellow countrymen begin to die. Don't think that cothla sorcerer can stop the curse!" Spittle flew from Faolan's mouth as he spoke. "She needs to be free to marry Duke Torin and put a proper child of the goddess on the throne. You will act, or you leave me with no choice but to call for a vote of no confidence and remove you from the high priesthood. It was a narrow margin that put you there, and that was before you revealed your true colors as a friend of abominations! Cothlas must be purged from the priesthood, purged from the entire land, if we are to see the goddess's blessing upon us!" Faolan whirled and left, slamming the door behind him.

CHAPTER 23

Torin paced the altar room in Alvabane's quarters while his no-longer-old nurse sat impassively in her throne-like chair. The chair was covered with red-velvet and the arms were gilt. She never used to sit in his presence. Now she did without being invited.

"I don't think we should have demanded the sorcerer's head," he ranted. "The bastard's in love with him. I don't think she'll give him up."

Alvabane shrugged. "It matters not."

Torin stopped and stared at her, but quickly looked away. He found her youth and attractiveness offensive. "Of course it matters! I think we would have a better chance of getting her to agree if we instead allowed her to exile the sorcerer. I don't want to go down in history as King Torin the Butcher."

Alvabane stood and walked to the altar, which contained the same grotesque gods as the one at the bottom of the tower. She stroked one of the statues lovingly. "You don't yet understand. The slaughter will happen no matter the bastard's answer. I will drive all the invaders from the land of my people."

"What invaders?"

Alvabane whirled, knocking over the statue she'd been fondling. It crashed to the carpet unharmed. "How dare you, a child of infidels and thieves, ask that question? Are you so ignorant of your history? Do you truly consider this land yours? Your forbearers called forth the demon Armunn to drive out its rightful inhabitants! Did you really think we'd given up on reclaiming what is rightfully ours?"

The witch had lost her mind. "Armunn is nothing more than a myth."

Alvabane's eyes narrowed, her voice shrill. "The suffering of my people—a myth! Armunn is no more myth than the power of the Soul Stone, which he cut off from my people and I have now reclaimed in their name! You have no idea what I and my people have suffered to make this triumph possible. Over the centuries, Bard after Bard has left the land of our exile to reclaim our power and our home. All have failed to return. When it became my turn, I willingly left my babe and the husband I loved for the greater good of my people. It was my duty."

Alvabane laughed a mad laugh. Torin backed away. "Oh, the ignorance of youth!" she snarled. "The folly of it! I was a princess among my people, and so I presented myself at your king's court. I was considered fair among my people, and I naively believed I would have no difficulty bending your father to my will, for I needed to be at his estate to have the Stone at my command. He was attracted to my charms, as I intended, and I believed I could get him to put aside his wife and take me in her place. But you infidels give nothing. You take whatever you want."

Torin had had enough of this nonsense. "You're claiming my father raped you?"

"Yes, and you are the child of that rape." Alvabane cuddled her arms as if holding a baby.

Torin eased his way toward the door. "You aren't my mother."

Alvabane's smile chilled him worse than the cold outside. "Oh, but I am! Your father's wife took compassion on me. Poor naïve Liddy. She nursed me back to health, and soon we discovered we were both with child by the same man. Oh, how I hated her! She expected me to be grateful to her. She expected me—the chosen of my people, the gift of the gods—to cater to her out of servile gratitude. A Bard serves no one except the gods, as she learned when I stuck a knife into her newly delivered womb, ensuring that she would bleed out her last without rising from the childbed."

"You killed my mother!" Torin grabbed hold of the door handle and flung it open. "Guards!" he called to the two men at the end of the hallway.

Alvabane came closer. "Poor Liddy was not your mother. As it happened, we gave birth on the same day. I strangled her babe with my bare hands and substituted mine. I pretended to mourn the tragic death of my own child. You look so much like your father, no one suspected. I admit I had moments of weakness, when I felt a womanly affection for the babe that pulled at my breast. Despite everything I suffered, I have never been able to entirely quash my affection for that child." Alvabane looked at him with a tenderness more frightening than her rage. "But I never let that affection interfere with my duty, and I will not do so now. Can you even begin to understand my heartbreak when I found the Soul Stone completely cold and unresponsive? For years I believed I had failed, as all those had before me. But the Stone sparked to life again! And now that the power is mine, the infidels will pay for their sins against me and my people! You, the son of my breast and of my womb, will help make them pay!" She settled back in her chair. "Or you will die with them. I care not which."

The guards came up, their eyes briefly flickering to Alvabane. "Arrest her!" Torin cried. "Throw her in the dungeon!"

Alvabane laughed and began to sing in her strange language. Before Torin could move, the two guards were dead at his feet. "You can't stop me!" she whispered.

Torin gaped at the witch. All these years he'd believed she'd loved him like a mother. He'd thought all her plotting and plans had been for his benefit.

All these years, she'd been insane and out of his control. *Holy Sulis, what kind of monster have I let loose upon my own people?*

* * *

"Is he mad? He thinks to force me to marry a traitor and repudiate my own child?" Samantha stared aghast at the high priest. *Don't I have enough problems? Haven't I sacrificed enough?* "Does he have any chance of removing you?"

Father Hafghan nodded grimly. "I'm afraid he might. His Majesty's claim that mixed blood is required for healing magic may well have tipped the issue over a precipice. I'm not sure what I can do to stop it."

Samantha got to her feet and worked hard to keep contempt out of her voice. "In that case, *I'll* stop it!"

"How, Your Majesty?"

She couldn't resist the urge to pace. "Under my father, the crown never interfered with the affairs of the church. But also under my father, the church didn't try to interfere in the affairs of the crown." Samantha stopped and faced the high priest. "If the church tries to nullify my marriage and turn my heir into a bastard, it is treason and will be treated as such." She pointed a finger at Hafghan. "And you will remain high priest, no matter how many priests I have to hang to ensure it."

* * *

Mother Venetia and Awena sat staring at each other across the fire. Refugees from the Dead Lands sat at other fires nearby, but they were now the only two healers left. All the rest had been lost fighting the curse.

"What do we do now?" Awena poked at the fire with a stick; she looked as if a slight breath might shatter her.

No child should experience so much hopeless death. Mother Venetia scooted around the fire and put her arm around the child. "I'm afraid there is only one hope—the sorcerer who would be king. If he is not another Armunn, we are all doomed. We'll leave tomorrow and try to fetch him."

Awena didn't lean against her for comfort as she once would have. "But how can he cross the Dead Lands? They spread nearly fifty miles."

"I'll give him my power as Mother Bensaggyrt gave Mother Aeronwen."

Awena grabbed Venetia's hand. "But Mother Bensaggyrt died!"

Venetia kissed the top of the child's head, but Awena pulled away from her. "That she did. I might die as well, though I'm not as old as she was."

"I thought you said it was a vile thing to do! I thought you said it risked both life and sanity!"

Venetia smoothed Awena's hair back from her forehead. "It does, my child, but what other hope is there?"

A look of resolve passed over the child's face. "I'll give him mine as well!"

Venetia's heart felt heavy within her. "No, my child. You are young. You do not know what it would mean to live your entire life without magic."

Awena jutted out her chin. "Are you sure your power alone will be enough?"

Venetia looked away. She couldn't lie to the child. "No, my child, I'm not."

"Then it is as you said—what other hope is there?"

* * *

The ground was frozen solid, but there was little snow, and Robrek made rapid progress—so rapid it was only mid-morning when he reached the outskirts of Valley Fair. He paused as he reached the road that led to his father's farm, only a short detour from the path he had to take. He was uncomfortable with how he'd left things with his father, but he was in a hurry. He almost continued on his way when he heard a voice, or had a feeling; he wasn't sure which. *:A heart full of regrets is weakened when it fights evil.:* He had to make time for his father.

When Robrek reached the farm yard, no one was in sight, but the place looked as if it were being properly cared for. He stopped Wild Thing by the horse trough, dismounted, and drew a bucket of water up from the well for her.

He heard a snort behind him. Filthy and reeking of drink, his father stood there unsteadily. He eyed the peasant clothing Robrek wore. "I thought you were going to be king. What happened? Did the queen throw you out?"

"No, I'm still king. I was passing through. May I come in?"

"Certainly, Your Majesty." Angus bowed mockingly toward the house. Robrek entered to find the inside clean and tidy. Cara and Dillion were doing what he'd hired them to do. "Where's your entourage?" Angus asked, gesturing toward a chair.

But Robrek couldn't sit still at the moment. He began pacing the room. "I left them at the palace. I've come to tell you about your grandchild. Her Majesty is pregnant with my daughter."

"You dress up like a peasant, ride all this way alone, just to tell me this?" Angus raised a brow skeptically.

Robrek ignored the question and took a seat beside his father. "I know things have never been easy between us, but I want my daughter to know her grandfather."

Angus snorted and grabbed a jug from the table. He took a long pull. "After the way I treated you?"

Robrek wanted to snatch the jug away. "Holy Writ made me experience what you went through when my mother died. You never got over her death."

Angus looked away. "What could you know about losing the woman you love?"

As he thought of Samantha lying where he'd left her, Robrek struggled to conceal his emotions. "I'm finding out."

Angus whirled to face him. "You don't think your wife will die in childbirth too, do you? Not with your power."

Robrek shook his head, thinking of the cinnamon scent of her hair. "I guess it's more like she's losing me. Do you know the story of Armunn?"

Angus grunted. "Of course, it's told at half the festivals in the village." Festivals Robrek had been excluded from.

Robrek put his hand on Angus's arm. "Armunn's evil has returned."

Angus stared at Robrek uncomprehendingly. "Armunn's evil? But surely that's only a legend?"

Robrek shook his head. "I wish it were. I have to stop it or hundreds, even thousands, will die."

Angus paused, apparently absorbing the information. Comprehension dawned on his face. He grabbed Robrek's shoulder. "But Robbie, surely you don't believe you're going to die!"

Robrek shrugged. "Armunn did."

Angus opened his mouth to say something more, then closed it. They sat in silence for a few moments. Angus lifted the jug to drink again, but Robrek put out a hand to stop him. "Haven't you suffered enough? Do you have to continue punishing yourself?"

Angus jerked the jug away from Robrek and took another pull. "Someone should. I'm a failure as a father, a failure in all things that matter. Boyden despises me, and you. . ." Angus's voice trailed off.

Robrek leaned forward. "What about me? I'm here, aren't I? Yes, you treated me badly. But that doesn't change the fact that you are my father, and I am your son. It doesn't make you any less my daughter's grandfather."

Angus set the jug down. "Do you mean it, son?" He spoke barely above a whisper, his voice breaking on the word "son." "Can you truly hold no grudge against me?"

Robrek put his hand on his father's arm. "None at all. I want you to pull yourself together, and when my daughter is old enough, I want her to visit the farm where her father grew up. I want her to know her grandfather, especially if she never has a chance to know me." Robrek paused, thinking of the letter he'd written her. He struggled to control his voice. "You gave me little as a child. I'm asking you to give me this now."

There were tears in Angus's eyes when he looked at Robrek. "But Robbie, surely you'll survive. Surely you'll beat this thing."

Robrek shook his head. "I don't know. Is my heart stronger than Armunn's?"

Angus grasped Robrek's hand. "If your heart is strong enough to forgive the way I treated you, it is strong enough for anything. I'll be expecting you to stop back here on your return to the palace."

Robrek blinked back his tears. "But if I don't, will. . .?" He looked away, unable to complete the sentence.

Angus gently squeezed his hand. "I swear, your daughter will know her grandfather."

Robrek put his hand over his father's. "Thank you."

Angus shook his head. "You owe me no gratitude. I'm proud of you, son. I never thought I could be as proud of a child as I am of you at this moment."

It was what Robrek had so badly desired to hear as a child. He opened his arms and embraced his father.

* * *

Father Hafghan glanced around at the assembled priests and then turned his attention to Father Faolan, who shared the dais with him. This assembly would decide Hafghan's fate and with it the fate of the church. Hafghan pitched his voice so that only Faolan could hear. "Her Majesty has made it clear that she will act against the church if the church acts against her or her child. She has promised me the support of the crown in retaining the high priesthood. Go ahead with your plan, and she'll stretch your neck."

Faolan smiled the self-assured smile of the fanatic. "Let Her Majesty try to fight against Sulis, and we shall see who comes off as victor."

Faolan got to his feet and addressed the crowd. "Her Majesty has no respect for the goddess. She is a bastard and an infidel. The cothla she has taken to her bed seeks to pollute the very blood of the clergy. Together they have conceived a being who will fight against the goddess herself. Join me, and we will ensure the monstrosity the queen carries never sits on the throne of this land." The room erupted in both cheers and boos.

Are they for me or against me? Hafghan shivered, remembering the coldness on the queen's face when they'd spoken. *This has to go my way. It will be a blood bath if we challenge the queen.*

Hafghan rose from his chair. "At this very moment, our king rides to fight against the greatest evil that has threatened this people since the time of Armunn. How can you think to act against Her Majesty now? Her Majesty has always been a friend to the people, a faithful daughter of the goddess. We owe her our support and our prayers at this time of crisis, not disloyalty. Not only is it wrong, there is no profit in opposing Her Majesty. Do you think she will sit idly by if we threaten her child? Do you think she will continue to allow the church its independence if we threaten her throne and those she loves? We cannot win if we pit ourselves against the crown."

Again, the room erupted in noise, and Hafghan had difficulty quieting them. He opened the meeting to comment, and priest after priest came forward. For every one who supported the queen, it seemed another condemned her. *Can't they see what they're doing?* But they hadn't seen the expression on the queen's face.

After hours of debate, Hafghan rose again, trying to project a confidence he didn't feel. He called for a vote and prayed while the votes were tallied. By a mere two votes, the vote came down in his and the queen's favor. Hafghan breathed a sigh of relief, hoping that would be the end of it.

Faolan, however, grew red in the face and took the stand. "You are cowards! Infidels! Every bit as much as is our queen! As the church no longer speaks for Sulis, I no longer intend to remain in an organization that owes its allegiance to the seven hells and worldly authorities! I intend to leave this nest of vipers and reestablish Sulis's true church with me as the high priest, as Sulis intended! I invite all those who fear the goddess more than the crown to follow me!"

Faolan stepped down from the dais, and the crowd parted to allow him through. As he walked out the door, nearly half those present followed in his wake. Hafghan could only watch.

* * *

Samantha watched from her window seat as the troops she'd sent to evacuate the village of Reidhlean rode out the palace gates, the healers and the Bard with them. The messenger to Torin had already departed. He would no doubt refuse her offer, and she had to prepare to lead her people through the coming crisis. *What I need is another Darhour.* Assassination was a distasteful business, but if Robbie failed, how else could Torin and his Bard be stopped? Her mind refused to function. *How can I go on if Robbie dies?*

She put her hand on her womb. *He won't die! Sulis won't allow it!*

Blaine entered and told her Father Hafghan was requesting an audience. She squeezed her eyes tight, tried to squeeze all emotion out of herself. She rose and put on a court mask.

Father Hafghan bowed as he was shown into the room, followed by her guards. "Your Majesty, thank you for seeing me."

The queen sat and offered him a seat. "What news of Faolan's challenge?"

The high priest avoided her eyes. "Your Majesty, I have good news, and I have bad news. The good news is the vote came narrowly down in our favor."

Samantha felt a rising nausea and prayed she wouldn't vomit. Leigh had prepared her the tea, but she had thrown it in the fire. She realized it was foolish, but all she could think of was how Leigh had allowed Robbie to face the danger alone. "And the bad news?"

Hafghan heaved a sigh; he looked as if he'd aged ten years in a day. "Faolan has split with the church. He's taken over the Shrine of the True Believer and is setting up what he has called the 'True Church of Sulis.'"

"That's the second largest shrine in the capital," Samantha breathed.

"Yes, Your Majesty. Nearly half the clergy in Murtaghan have followed him. I don't know what will happen in the rest of Lundia."

Samantha's thoughts suddenly flashed to Caedmon; she damned him for betraying her when she needed his wisdom. "Does Faolan intend to continue to fight my marriage and delegitimatize my child?"

Hafghan nodded. "The man is a fanatic."

"What will you do?"

Hafghan cleared his throat. "I will excommunicate Faolan and all those who follow him, but I don't expect that to have much effect. I can do nothing else."

"Thank you for bringing this news to me. Keep me advised." Samantha dismissed the high priest and began pacing her chamber. "What am I supposed to do, Sulis?" Her stomach tied itself into knots, and she found herself bending over the basin on the sideboard, vomiting violently. *Why, Sulis? Why must women go through this in order to bring forth life?* Part of her wanted to give up, to abdicate and leave all her problems behind. If Robbie didn't survive, she didn't want to go on living anyway.

She straightened. She was her father's daughter and could never make such an irresponsible choice. She was the only one who could hold the joined kingdoms together, and by Sulis, she'd do it, even if she became nothing but an empty shell.

Abruptly, she left her rooms and went to the Royal Galleries. Her father's pictures lined the walls. Surely, seated with him, she could figure out what to do about this latest challenge.

But as she sat staring at the portrait of her parents, no insight was forthcoming. Baroness Glynnis arrived. "I saw you pass. Your Majesty. I've wanted a chance to speak with you. Are you well?"

"I'm fine," she started to say, but instead she shook her head. "I'm alone, Baroness, and I have more problems than I can solve."

The baroness sat beside her and patted her knee. "Please call me Glynnis, and tell me about these problems."

Samantha wanted to sob in Glynnis's arms as she'd done on the previous occasion, but crying would do nothing to ease the crisis. Instead, she looked away from the baroness. "There's nothing you can do to help."

"Maybe not, but sometimes a listening ear is all it takes."

Samantha got up and touched the frame of her parents' portrait. "My father was a wise man. He would have known what to do about the schism in the church." Samantha told Glynnis what she'd learned from Father Hafghan. "My father insisted the church and state must remain separate for the good of each, but this 'True Church of Sulis' seeks to undermine my rule and bastardize my daughter."

Glynnis gasped. "How could this Father Faolan be so brazen? Your Majesty, there is only one real answer. What he speaks is treason, and treason is one thing the great Solar never tolerated."

Samantha felt sick again, and she leaned against the wall. The baroness was right. She couldn't allow this treason to grow.

She straightened and faced Glynnis. "Another public execution. Am I becoming a tyrant?"

The baroness squeezed Samantha's shoulder. "No, you're becoming your father's daughter. He would have been proud of you."

CHAPTER 24

Robrek's next two days of travel were as uneventful as they were miserable. It grew warmer, and a light drizzle began to fall, just enough to make sure he always stayed damp.

At mid-morning on the third day, he and Wild Thing broke through the cover of a small forest and reached the edge of a great plain. While the Korthian mountains loomed to the north, in front of them lay nothing but miles upon miles of grass without a single tree. Robrek had heard of the Reidhlean Plains, but he'd never imagined such openness.

But the plains weren't empty. Spread out before them was an entire herd of Horsetads, at least a hundred strong.

Wild Thing stopped and stared. *:Pretty horses. Like Wild Thing.:*

Robrek urged her in the direction of the herd. One of the Horsetads caught sight of them and sent up a neigh. Looking far more like an army of a hostile nation than wild animals, the herd quickly rearranged itself with military precision. The lead stallions moved forward to meet him. Soon Robrek found himself surrounded by at least twenty. From their size, Robrek decided Wild Thing must be some kind of runt among Horsetads, as he was among humans.

:Why other Wild Things angry? What Wild Thing do wrong?:

"I think it's me they're angry with, my girl, not you." Robrek looked the lead stallion in the eye and addressed him. "Greetings, Milord. I mean no harm. I simply ask to pass through your territory." He reached out with his power to soothe the big stallion and convince him of the truthfulness of his words. His power struck something—an invisible shield—and recoiled so powerfully it threw him off Wild Thing's back and onto the grass. The wind was knocked out of him, and if the ground hadn't been so soft from the recent thaw, it might well have broken his back. He hadn't known any creature could block his magic. Wild Thing never had.

As Robrek struggled to breathe, the stallions surrounding him reared and snorted. If Wild Thing hadn't leapt to cover him, putting her body between him and the herd, they would have trampled him. *:Stop, mean bully horses. No hurt Robbie. Wild Thing not let.:*

:You protect the one who made slave of you? Out of the way, and we rid you of him.:

Wild Thing neighed a challenge to the huge horse, who was at least three hands taller than she. It was the sound stallions often made before fighting for dominance or over a mare. *:Back off, bully horse. No hurt Robbie.:*

Robrek struggled to his feet. "Wild Thing is not my slave. She is my friend, my family." He didn't attempt to use his power again. Instead, he stayed close to Wild Thing.

The stallion ignored Robrek and directed his gaze to Wild Thing. *:Allow self to be ridden by mere human? Willingly submit to that?:* The stallion tossed his head in Robrek's direction.

:Wild Thing no submit. Wild Thing friend. Robbie Wild Thing family.:

:Horsetads cannot allow. Human must die. Move aside, and submit to the will of the herd:

"If you'd allow me to speak, Milord, I can explain," Robrek said, but the huge stallion ignored him in much the same way a human would ignore the yapping of a small dog.

Wild Thing's eyes narrowed. *:No hurt Robbie. Wild Thing protect.:* She didn't seem at all intimidated by either the number or the size of those facing her.

A large mare moved through the ring of stallions to stand by the head stallion. *:You cannot risk injuring the mare. She is young and could bear many foals.:*

:No mere human is allowed to ride us. We are not their servants.:

:One human has before, and another is prophesied. 'In their darkest hour, Midnight's Child shall come among them. He will have the power of the Fiery One and the heart of the mountain. He will come to the Council of the Rock and tell his story. The mares will weep for his sorrow. The stallions will cheer his valor. He will rid the land of evil.' Is it not our darkest hour? Do our mares not die giving birth to dead foals? Is he not the color of midnight?:

312

The stallion snorted, and the mare nudged the stallion affectionately with her nose. *:Don't be rash, Autumn Storm. Let him come to Council of the Rock.:*

The stallion flared his nostrils. *:Tell story at Council of Rock. Mares no weep, kill him then.:* The stallion turned to Wild Thing, still ignoring Robrek. *:Bring human to Council of Rock. There abide by judgment of the herd.:*

Wild Thing stamped a hoof. *:Wild Thing no listen to big bully horse.:*

Robrek reached out to calm her. "Let's go with them to their Rock. We can't fight our way through them."

Wild Thing acquiesced, and Robrek walked beside her out of respect to the herd. He reached the Rock—a big block of limestone that jutted five feet high from the otherwise flat plain—where the entire herd awaited him. The head stallion again addressed Wild Thing. *:Tell the human to stand upon the Rock and tell his story.:*

:Robbie not deaf. Robbie hear mean bully horse just fine.:

Robrek smiled as he climbed up on the top of the Rock.

The head stallion turned his way with seeming reluctance. *:If you truly can hear, human, speak your story from beginning. We'll see if mares weep.:*

A sadness descended on Robrek as he settled himself on the Rock. What had his life been? A few small islands of happiness in an ocean of sadness and pain.

He told them everything; as he did so, images flashed into his mind. He again lay across the dining room table, pain searing through his bare back, struggling—and failing—not to scream as the strap hit again and again. He knelt by the bloody corpse of the Horsetad mare killed by a panther, her foal whinnying not far off—half-mad with hunger and fear. With his power, Robrek calmed the hours-old foal, led her back to the barn, named her Wild Thing, and fed her from a bottle, saving her life. He gasped in awe when he first caught sight of Milady at the horse fair. His entire body pounded with pain as his brother Boyden beat him brutally. He begged his brother to stop and crawled to Boyden's feet and licked the blood from his boots.

He woke up in front of Myst's fireplace to the sound of Milady's laugh. She kissed him passionately running her hand up his thigh. He trembled in the fields as he heard the horrible noise of the beasts that had destroyed his father's field. His sword flashed in the moonlight as Brazen taught him how to fight. Fancy Man whined until Robrek agreed to learn table manners and dancing. He sat bound and gagged in the chair in the village shrine while Father Gildas pronounced him guilty of trafficking in demons and sentenced him to burn at the stake. He stumbled out of Murtaghan's square where he'd learned Milady was truly the Crown Princess Samantha. Holy Writ taught him what it meant to forgive, and he again felt the joyous release of his anger.

He donned the mysterious armor and struggled up Gloine Torr on each of the three horses. He lay the three golden apples at King Solar's feet and asked Samantha to be his bride. He awoke in the darkness of the dungeon to find himself confined with the princess's guards. The prison door flew open, and Samantha stood there, dazzling in her beauty, blood dripping from her sword. He sat by the stream and told the princess the story of his life and was then, in a moment of pure joy, handfasted to her. She took him to her tent and made love to him. He rode beside her as they retook the palace from Argblutal.

Restrained by Samantha's hand, he sat and watched Count Nola bleed to death. The scorpion stung his leg as somebody in the palace tried to kill him. He ran his hand over the silky smoothness of the princess's skin. He gave the blind man sight, giving the lie to the notion that he was the butcher of Valley Fair. His skin tingled as he felt the small life that was his daughter moving under his hand. He gasped for breath as the traitor's sword thrust through his lungs. He dreamed of the sinister red lake; the shadows beckoned him to join them. He walked down the aisle hand-in-hand with Samantha and made the vows that joined them as one. He knelt, and he, the despised youngest son of a peasant farmer, became king. He awoke with horror, evil crawling across his skin. Fear chilled him as he learned of Armunn and the Soul Stone. He again climbed Gloine Torr, and Sulis told him what he must do to save his people and the woman he loved.

He made love to Samantha one last time, and he sat in the cold and wrote letters to her and to the daughter he might never meet. *Oh, Samantha, Sulis keep you safe. You and our child.* His voice broke as he spoke of his last sight of Samantha, sleeping in the firelight with his daughter growing inside her—a child who would never know her father unless his heart proved stronger than Armunn's. In the darkness before dawn, he and Wild Thing rode alone from the palace to confront the evil that had killed the greatest hero in Korthlundian history. He burst through the trees and saw the herd of Horsetads spread out before them. Wild Thing celebrated seeing those of her kind. He sat on the hard Rock and told the story of his life.

The Horsetads listened with rapt attention. The mares wept. The little ones pushed to the front of the crowd in order to see and hear better. Robrek was surprised to see they numbered less than a half dozen. A race with so few children had little hope for a future. As the mare had said, this was truly the Horsetads' darkest hour.

When he brought the story to a close, the large mare stepped forward. *:I am Bright Eyes, First Mare of the Horsetads. Can any mare hear this tale and not weep? I say, it is not possible.:* The mare turned to face Robrek. *:Midnight's Child, I name you, Savior of Horsetads.:*

The head stallion took his place unhesitatingly beside Bright Eyes. *:I am Autumn Storm, First Stallion of the Horsetads. Can any stallion among us not cheer the valor of this man? Even though a mere human, he willingly goes to sacrifice his life for the benefit of all.:* Autumn Storm turned toward Robrek. *:Autumn Storm wrong to try kill. Autumn Storm, too, names you Midnight's Child, Savior of Horsetads.:*

Autumn Storm lowered his head and backed into a low bow before Robrek. The stallion was followed by every member of the herd. They'd seen him as a beast needing to be destroyed, and now as a near-god worthy of worship. So it had been his entire life. He was not now, nor ever had been, viewed as normal.

:Robbie, Savior of the Horsetad: Wild Thing beamed proudly. *:Wild Thing carry him beyond mountain. Wild Thing hero, too.:*

Bright Eyes shook her head sadly. *:No, young one, that cannot be. We have felt this evil. Danger is great. Wild Thing young. Can bear many strong foals. Herd need foals. Herd have many strong stallions. Few mares. Strong stallion carry Midnight's Child beyond the mountain.:*

Wild Thing reared and snorted. *:No, no, no! Robbie and Wild Thing family. Robbie no face danger without Wild Thing. Wild Thing protect Robbie. Wild Thing stomp evil into mash. Wild Thing never let anything hurt Robbie ever again.:*

Robrek had thought his heart couldn't break any more, but the herd was right. Risking his own life was one thing. Risking that of his oldest friend was quite another. The Horsetads offered him a way to fulfill his quest while making sure Wild Thing was safe, but it was a way that would tear both of them in two.

Robrek got down from the rock and wrapped his arms around the only friend of his childhood. "I love you, my girl. You've been with me through everything. Saved my life more than once. It isn't possible for anyone to have a greater friend than you have been to me. But Bright Eyes is right. Wild Thing has no foal. Apple Lady is carrying my foal. If I die, part of me will live on. Don't you want that for yourself, my girl? A strong stallion and a little Wild Thing?"

Wild Thing hesitated as her eyes roamed around the stallions in the herd. Robrek could feel her longing. She'd never before exhibited any interest in any stallion other than Fancy Man. Robrek could feel the stallions posing for her benefit. Wild Thing's eyes strayed to the young foals, and Robrek felt her longing increase. Yes, Wild Thing very much wanted a mate and a foal, but abruptly, she snapped the doors of that longing closed. She reared. *:Wild Thing no want stupid bully stallion. Wild Thing no want foal. Foals too much trouble. Robbie Wild Thing family.:*

Robrek felt the pressure of Wild Thing's two desires tearing her apart. He wished he could make it easier for her. Wild Thing had been the one constant in his life. But he realized now that it had truly been his life they both were living. He owed her a life of her own. "Please, my girl, stay safe with the herd."

:Wild Thing no want safe. Wild Thing want Robbie. Stallions not Robbie's family. How can Robbie not want Wild thing?: Wild Thing turned and galloped off.

He tried to call after her. He couldn't let her think he didn't want her. But she was gone. Bright Eyes came up next to him. *:Midnight's Child do right thing. Wild Thing will understand. Doing right thing not always easy. Not always make happy.:*

He nodded and turned away so she wouldn't see the tears in his eyes. He couldn't remember if doing the right thing had ever made him happy.

Autumn Storm approached him, followed by four of the younger stallions. *:Midnight's Child, I explained the danger to my stallions. Asked for volunteers. These four are all eager to accompany. Autumn Storm say Midnight's Child choose.:*

The four stallions snorted and pawed the ground. They all had the beautiful Horsetad coat and the stars on their foreheads and chests, but none of them were Wild Thing. "You choose, Autumn Storm. You know them better than I."

He turned and walked off into the darkness in the direction Wild Thing had taken.

* * *

As the sun rose, Robrek stood beside the Rock. He hadn't been able to find Wild Thing last night, and she wasn't among those gathered to see him and Unrelenting Valor off. Autumn Storm had held some kind of contest to see who got the privilege of accompanying him, and apparently, Valor won. Robrek hadn't asked for the details; he didn't care. The one thing he knew about Valor was that he wasn't Wild Thing.

Robrek realized he could wait no longer for his oldest friend. *Sulis bless I'm making the right choice in leaving her.*

He hung the saddle bags from Valor's neck. The stallion was huge, at least two hands taller than Wild Thing. Wild Thing's saddle wouldn't fit, so he'd have to ride bareback. He didn't consider that much of a problem; he'd frequently ridden Wild Thing that way. The only difficulty was mounting the stallion without the aid of stirrups. Robrek climbed onto the Rock to reach the stallion's back. They'd always need a rock when he needed to mount. Robrek glanced toward the huge and imposing Korthian Mountains; that probably wouldn't be difficult.

Autumn Storm made some kind of speech, but Robrek, scanning for Wild Thing, wasn't listening. A cheer went up from the Horsetads, which Robrek took to mean that the speech was over. Robrek said a few kingly words about honor and sacrifice. He mounted Valor, and they took off with his back to the rising sun.

They hadn't gone far when Robrek heard a sorrow-filled neigh behind him. He looked back to see Wild Thing rearing with the sunrise at her back. She'd never looked more majestic. *Goodbye, my girl*, he spoke to her mind. *I will always love you.* He raised his hand in farewell. Without responding, Wild Thing ran off to join the herd.

:*Mare better with the herd. With foals. We stallions fight.*:

Robrek well knew what Samantha would think of a comment like that, but he couldn't bother arguing with the stallion. Part of him felt he'd already died.

* * *

Wild Thing had been fast, but Valor, with his longer legs and stronger muscles, practically flew over the ground. Robrek, however, felt little of the pleasure he'd felt riding Wild Thing. He and the mare had moved as one, the slightest pressure of his knees getting her to turn one way or another. Valor ignored all of Robrek's signals and picked his own trail. Robrek wasn't truly riding the stallion, but being carried by him.

Valor tried to engage him in conversation throughout the day, but Robrek's heart wasn't in it. He mumbled one-word replies, and Valor gave up and concentrated on running. By nightfall they'd reached the foothills surrounding the pass into Korth.

Robrek built a fire and made a hot stew from the dried meat in his saddle bags. Without Wild Thing's love, he needed the light and the warmth to remind him he was still alive. Valor grazed nearby, but didn't move far, evidently, he took his charge to protect Robrek seriously.

"Who is this Fiery One Bright Eyes spoke of?" he asked the stallion, in an attempt to take his mind off his own loneliness.

Valor snorted his disgust. :*The last male to ride a Horsetad. But he was no friend of the herd.*:

"Why was he allowed to ride? I thought no one could ride a Horsetad against their will."

:*The Fiery One not like Midnight's Child. Not hear the voice of the herd. But he had powerful magic. Came to the herd and tried to steal one of us. Thought us mere horses.*: Valor snorted again. :*Thought because human need he could take without asking. But head stallion and head mare had felt the evil that Fiery One chased. Evil that threatened Horsetads too if not stopped. Human created the evil. Horsetads could not defeat. Back then, evil made mares die in having dead foals. It happens again. Magic usually not touch Horsetads, except when very young or when weakened from foal-bearing. Evil magic threatened future of herd. Valiant Heart volunteered to let Fiery One catch and help destroy evil. Valiant Heart very brave. Greatest hero of the Horsetads. Unrelenting Valor like Valiant Heart. Unrelenting Valor be great hero.*:

The Fiery One was obviously Armunn, and Robrek found it odd to find the legendary hero spoken of this way. Four stallions had competed for the honor of carrying him. Did that mean his heart was stronger than Armunn's? "What happened to Valiant Heart?"

:*Evil go away. Mares bear living foals, but Valiant Heart not return. Herd think he die with Fiery One.*:

"Does it frighten you that you could be carrying both of us to our deaths?"

The stallion snorted as if offended. *:Unrelenting Valor fear nothing.:*

"Maybe you should." Robrek had finished eating, so he rolled himself up in his blanket and turned away from the stallion. *Midnight's Child very afraid.*

* * *

Alvabane sat on her throne-like chair; the son of her breast stood beside her. The messenger of the invaders' queen was shown in. He frowned in confusion at the seated woman, and his eyes went to Duke Torin. He bowed. "Your Grace, Her Majesty, Queen Samantha sends this message." He held out a scroll toward Torin.

"You will address me!" Alvabane said.

The messenger blinked and turned to face her. "Who are you?"

"Alvabane, queen of Lundia. Your queen has no right to this land."

The messenger gaped for a moment and then recovered himself. "You would dare speak such treason?"

Alvabane signaled to the guards in attendance. They ripped the scroll from him and pulled his arms behind his back when he struggled. One of them brought the scroll to Alvabane. The brief message from the false queen requested that Torin come to Murtaghan to discuss a marriage contract. Alvabane ripped the scroll in two, the subterfuge only too apparent. Alvabane asked the only question that mattered. "Has she sent the sorcerer's head?"

The messenger struggled uselessly against his captors. "I am authorized to say nothing but relay my queen's message."

Alvabane got to her feet and approached the messenger. She sang a few notes to call on the power of the Stone. She touched the messenger's face, and he screamed. Only the support of the guards kept him on his feet. She listened for a moment to the sweet music of her enemy's pain. She withdrew her hand. The messenger hung limply between his captors whimpering. "I ask again. Has she sent the sorcerer's head?"

"Please, I'm not authorized to answer any questions. I'm—" His voice broke into a scream as she touched him again.

It took two more times, but the messenger eventually answered, "King Robrek fled the moment Captain Hawk relayed your demands. Nobody knows where he is."

"You lie." She touched him again and relished the sound.

"Please, I can only tell you what my queen—"

"The dark gods do not like liars." She clamped her hand on his throat, and he had no air to scream. She released him and asked the question again.

"He's left the palace. I don't know where he went. I swear I don't know more."

She tortured him until she was certain he had nothing more to tell her. Then she began to sing his soul out of his body as she had so many before him.

"By Sulis, you can't!" The son of her breast called on the name of the infidels' god as he approached her. He dared to lay a hand on her arm. "All laws of diplomacy prohibit the killing of messengers! Release him immediately!"

Alvabane shrugged off his hand and completed her song. The guards released the messenger, and he slumped to the ground. Alvabane turned to Torin. "The laws of diplomacy matter not. You will not question me again." She grabbed him by the wrist and sent pain into him as she had into the messenger. He fell to his knees howling, and she let go. "Am I understood?"

"Yes," he gasped.

She reached toward him, her hand hovering above his arm. "Yes, what?"

"Yes, Your Majesty."

She dropped her hand. "I will make you king of Korth, but Lundia belongs to me and my people."

Torin got to his feet, white and trembling from the pain. "What about the sorcerer?"

"Even if he knows the location of the cave, he cannot harm us. The Dead Lands have spread too far for him to have hope of reaching the cave alive. There will be no second Armunn."

* * *

Father Faolan stood at the top of the steps of the Shrine of the True Believer. He smiled widely and spread his arms to welcome an audience too large to fit inside. That was only right. The True Church of Sulis would soon be the only church.

Faolan lifted his hands for silence, and slowly the crowd quieted. Obviously, none wanted to miss a word from Sulis's holy mouthpiece. "The queen's child will be the cothla child of a cothla! Such impurity can't stain the throne of this great land!"

He heard the jangle of arms, and a detachment of the Royal Guard entered the square. "Cease speaking immediately!" the officer in charge ordered.

Faolan raised his voice; he wouldn't be silenced by the lackeys of a queen who had polluted her bed. "The people of Sulis must be led by all that is pure!"

As Faolan continued to pour forth Sulis's holy message, the Royal Guard forced their way through the crowd, pushing aside Sulis's true children and nearly trampling them in their hurry to silence him.

"Arrest him!" the officer shouted, and his men surged up the steps and dared to place their unholy hands on Sulis's mouthpiece.

* * *

Captain Hawk reported Faolan's arrest and confinement in the dungeon, thus solving Samantha's lesser problem. That of the Soul Stone still loomed. She was queen; she had to face the possibility that Robbie might fail. She fought to keep all emotion out of her voice. "You've seen the layout of Duke Torin's castle and his defenses. Do you think it possible an assassin could sneak through them and kill Torin and this Alvabane before she realized the danger and could call upon the power of the Stone?" she asked him.

Hawk stood at parade rest with his hands behind his back; his eyes narrowed at the mention of an assassin. "I have never had dealings with assassins"—he said the word with distaste—"but I could try to locate one if it is Your Majesty's will."

She nodded. "It will be a few more days until we know if His Majesty succeeds. If he fails, I want an alternate plan in place."

CHAPTER 25

The road over the pass was bitter cold, but it was nearly clear of snow. When he reached the top of the pass, Robrek paused to take in his first sight of Korth. Next to the trail, a magnificent waterfall crashed into the river far below. A huge cliff rose into the clouds on one side of the narrow trail, and a steep drop off over a thousand feet met the other side. Despite his mood, the view was magnificent. He wished he could enjoy it, better yet, enjoy it with Samantha at his side.

As he and Valor headed down, the trail was so narrow a misstep could send them both plummeting to their deaths. Robrek wasn't worried, though. Valor was surefooted. They hadn't been traveling downward long when Valor's ears shifted forward, and he snorted a warning. :*Someone coming. Two someones.*:

The tiny figures down below came briefly into view before a bend in the trail took them out of sight. When the travelers again appeared, Robrek could see they were leading their horses, a sensible precaution considering the trail's width. They came closer, an old woman and a young girl, probably Oriana's age, their hair gathered in the hundreds of small braids common to the Northern priestesses and wearing robes of rough, undyed wool.

Robrek dismounted when they reached speaking distance. Their eyes widened as they took in Robrek and the Horsetad behind him. They fell to their knees. "Your Majesty, you've come!" the old priestess declared, voice trembling. "Has the goddess sent you to fight the ancient evil? Please tell me you are the next Armunn."

As he thought of Samantha and his child, Robrek had to blink tears out of his eyes. "Since Armunn died, I hope not. But I'm here to fight the Soul Stone."

The priestess bowed until her forehead touched the trail, and the novice followed suit. "The goddess be praised! You are our last hope." Embarrassed by their abasement, Robrek held out his hand and helped the woman to her feet.

"Your Majesty, this is my novice Awena, and I'm Mother Venetia."

"Oriana's mentor?" Robrek asked.

The old priestess started. "You know my Oriana? Is she well?"

"Yes, but tell me of the curse. Has it spread?"

The priestess laughed, a touch hysterically. "Your Majesty, the Dead Lands now stretch for more than fifty miles to the north, east, and west of Balley Beg. Nothing can live on the land. Not people. Not animals. Not even insects or plants. The earth itself is bereft of life. Your Majesty, please, there is not a moment to waste. If you will, let me explain as we travel."

They started back down the mountainside, and she told him all she and the other priestesses had done to stop the evil and how they had failed and died.

Robrek felt a sickness roil his gut. *How can I hope to succeed when so many have failed?* "I have learned all I could about Armunn, but I could find him only in the ballads of bards. Do you know of anything that will help me do what Armunn did?"

She shook her head sadly. "What Armunn did can't be repeated."

"Why not?"

"Armunn used his magic to separate his soul from his body and created a shield out of his soul to block the power. But even such a shield couldn't hold so strong an evil for long. For centuries, we priestesses have continually strengthened this shield. But no longer are there enough of us to do so. You can't contain the evil as Armunn did, Your Majesty. You must destroy it."

Robrek staggered, his trembling legs forcing him to sit on a boulder at the side of the trail. He put his head in his hands. "You mean to tell me this evil has already killed all the healers in Korth, and somehow I'm supposed to cross fifty miles of dead land that kills all who enters it, find this cave, and still have enough strength left to destroy this thing without any idea how to do so?" He looked up at the old woman.

The priestess looked down at her feet. "If that is the goddess's will."

Robrek stood and stalked off down the path. Thoughts of the magical horses scorched his mind. Where were Brazen, Fancy Man, and Holy Writ? Why would they take him to the top of Gloine Torr and then leave him before he faced the *real* challenge? When he died and came face to face with the goddess, he was going to tell her exactly what he thought of her priorities.

Mother Venetia hurried to him. "We have a plan to help you cross the Dead Lands, Your Majesty. We will give you our power." Venetia explained what Bensaggyrt and Aeronwen had done and the difference between the sharing and the taking of power. "You can carve the power out of us to sustain your life."

"Are you mad? That's monstrous!" He remembered the horrible nothingness he'd felt when he first learned to shield. He couldn't imagine condemning another to a lifetime of that. It would be worse than dying.

Venetia closed her eyes and breathed deeply, as if trying to contain her emotion. "There is no other choice, and I can feel the strength of your magic. Surely, you can handle the extra power."

"No! I won't deprive you of your magic! That could kill a person!"

Mother Venetia put her hand protectively on Awena's shoulder, but she looked resolved. "It killed Mother Bensaggyrt, but Your Majesty, I'm willing to give all to fight this evil, and so is Awena. You have no choice. If you fail, all life in Korth may be lost, maybe in all of the joined kingdoms. I appreciate that you don't like the idea, but you will take our power."

"I will find another way." Robrek turned his back on her and strode off.

* * *

Eolande looked around as the troop of Royal Guards rode into Reidhlean. The village had a population of no more than five hundred, but all five hundred men, women, and children would soon be dead if they couldn't get out in time. Duke Torin's deadline would arrive tomorrow morning, at which time his Bard was supposed to sing their deaths. *Will I be able to do anything to stop it?*

Lieutenant Agatone, leader of the troop, called for the villagers to assemble. As he told them of their danger and the need to evacuate, the villagers' eyes widened with horror, and they uttered moans of disbelief. "Gather your things immediately, only the most important," Agatone said. "We must leave in one hour in order to be far enough away by sundown."

The problem was, no one knew how far away was safe. *Just how great a range does Torin's Bard have?*

"But when will we be able to return?" one of the villagers asked. "What about our stock?"

That was another question no one could truly answer. *If the king fails, will it ever be safe for them to return?* Agatone turned to the speaker. "You'll have to leave the animals. We can't travel fast enough with them. Hopefully, you won't have to be gone long." Agatone failed to tell them their animals would likely die from the Bard's song. Oriana's brother claimed the ancient evil affected even the cockroaches and vegetation. Even if these people were able to return, they'd be in for a hard winter.

"Where will we go?" asked another.

"For today," Agatone said, "we just need to get some distance from the village. If the king succeeds, you'll return here. If he fails, Her Majesty has promised she will find you a more permanent refuge."

"But what about—" another started to say.

But Agatone put up his hand. "No more questions. We leave in one hour. All not ready to travel at that time will be left behind."

The people scattered, and Eolande sent up a prayer to Sulis for the king's success—and for his life.

* * *

Samantha sat on her throne, the members of the Royal Council arrayed behind her. Even Sheen was there, although most likely he still didn't mean her well. He was an old man, and she could only hope he would soon die and trouble her no more. Otherwise, she would have to act. She just didn't know how.

She looked over the vast crowd of courtiers and clergy who'd come to see her pronounce judgment. Tomorrow was the deadline Duke Torin had set, and even now the Royal Guard would be evacuating the village of Reidhlean. She didn't want to think of what else might be happening or the whereabouts of the man she loved. Had Robbie reached the cave? Did he even now do battle against an evil the hero Armunn couldn't destroy? *Sulis, bring him back to me! You owe me his life for the lives of all those you've taken!* She put her hand on her abdomen. *My love, you will not grow up without a father! And you will reign as queen!*

She signaled to Blaine, and Father Faolan was brought into the room. Despite his chains, he walked with the haughty confidence of the fanatic. When he reached the dais, his guards forced him to his knees. He knelt with a straight back and glared a challenge at her. Samantha pitched her voice so that it would carry throughout the vast room. She deliberately didn't use his honorific title. "Faolan, you have been charged with treason. How plead you?"

The priest met her eyes and also pitched his voice to carry. "I refuse to answer a charge from someone who has no right to the throne on which she sits, a bastard who would further pollute the crown with the production of a cothla child—an abomination to the goddess and all right-thinking people."

Samantha gripped the arms of the throne to maintain royal dignity. "Need we hear more? Even now treason flows from his lips!" She looked to the right and the left; all the members of the Royal Council nodded their agreement. She faced the priest. "Faolan, your own words have convicted you. We find you guilty of treason and hereby sentence you to death by hanging, to be carried out on the morrow."

She prayed that, with his death, the Church of the True Believer would fade into nonexistence.

* * *

Robrek rode with the priestesses toward the Dead Lands without further discussion of Mother Venetia's plan. About sundown, they approached a large encampment of some two hundred people.

"Who are they?" Robrek asked Mother Venetia.

"Refugees from the Dead Lands, those who have survived. They have nowhere to go. If they can't go home, few will survive the winter."

Someone from the encampment caught sight of them, and a cry went up. Soon, the people were pouring out of their tents and makeshift shelters. There were few children and no old people. "Yes, it is him!" someone cried out. "I see his Horsetad's stars! He's with Mother Venetia and Awena! They found him!" They crowded around him, trying to touch him, tears streaming down many faces.

"Your Majesty's come!"

"Sulis be praised!"

"We knew the goddess would not desert us."

"Will you fight the evil?"

"Will you destroy it?"

"Are you the second Armunn?"

Overwhelmed by the people's emotions, Robrek wanted to shrink away, but he needed to speak. Still, his insides squirmed, and he damned the fact he didn't have Samantha's ease in speaking to crowds. He held up his hand for silence. The refugees quieted, expectation on their faces. What could he say to them? The truth would sound arrogant, but it was the truth. "My people," he began, as he'd heard Samantha address the crowds in Murtaghar. "Sulis has sent me to fight this ancient evil. With her blessing, I plan to destroy it. Pray to Sulis to give me strength."

Though he hadn't meant his words to be taken literally, as one, the refugees fell to their knees. Two hundred tongues offered up their hearts to Sulis on his behalf. *Sulis, give me the strength to succeed. These people have faith in you.*

After several minutes, the refugees got to their feet, and a man in his fifties came forward. "I am Zethar. I was mayor of Nios Mo. Since no other mayor has survived the evil, I guess I'm in charge here. We welcome Your Majesty. Will you come and dine with us? We don't have much, but we'll gladly share what we have."

Robrek opened his mouth to refuse. He didn't want to take these people's food, but when he saw the expectant joy on their faces, he couldn't refuse. "I'd be honored," he said, dismounting Valor.

He patted Valor and followed Zethar into the encampment. The people parted to allow him through, but many reached out to touch him. He clasped and released hands as he passed. In the center of the encampment, a fire stood burning, a large pot of stew bubbling over it. Zethar led him to a log near the fire. "It is a far cry from a throne," Zethar said. "But it is the only chair we have to offer."

Feeling self-conscious, Robrek sat on the log, Venetia and Awena beside him. The people began serving up the stew. Zethar brought him a large bowl and a full loaf of bread. Awena and Mother Venetia were given slightly smaller portions and the rest of the people even smaller ones. Few of them had any bread. Robrek wanted to share, but he feared offending those who honored him. He ate in silence for a few moments, the people sitting on the ground and smiling at him from all around the fire.

When he'd eaten, Zethar addressed him. "We have heard rumors and bard's tales, Your Majesty, of your courtship with our great queen. We'd be most honored if you would share your story with us."

Robrek was tired and wanted to sleep, but he looked around the fire at the eager faces and knew he had no choice. Again, he told the story of Brazen, Fancy Man, and Holy Writ. Again, he wondered why they were not here. The people listened in rapt attention as he spoke of his life and of his love for the queen. There was hardly a dry eye in the encampment when he related leaving the queen with his child growing inside her.

When he'd finished, Zethar cleared his throat. "Such love must survive. Sulis would never decree otherwise. I have no doubt you will return victorious to your queen and ours." There was a general chorus of agreement.

After the people drifted away to go to sleep, Mother Venetia touched his arm. "Now do you understand why we must give our power to allow you to accomplish this thing? If you don't, these people will die, and thousands more like them."

Robrek nodded. Awena and Mother Venetia had been battling this evil for months, evacuating village after village. They'd seen the old ones and the children succumbing to the curse. Only the strong and healthy had survived this long. For the sake of the refugees and the rest of the inhabitants of the joined kingdoms—for them and for Samantha—he would do what was otherwise a vile act.

* * *

The next morning Robrek, Mother Venetia, and Awena bid the refugees good-bye and set out for the Dead Lands. After a couple of miles, Valor suddenly reared, neighing and pawing the air. Nearby, a rattlesnake lay coiled, shaking its rattle. Robrek quickly dismounted. He approached the snake slowly and opened his shields to it. "It's okay. Run along now. We won't hurt you."

The snake stopped its feeble rattling, but made no move to leave. Robrek stumbled with almost overwhelmingly lethargy, and he wanted to lay down and take a nap. But the lethargy, he realized, was the snake's: it was too weak to move. Robrek sent out waves of calmness, dismounted, and touched the snake. He sensed no illness or injury. It merely seemed as if its life was being drained.

Robrek lowered his shields completely and almost fainted. He put his hand out to the ground to steady himself, but that intensified the sensation. A land of dead or dying things stretched to the north and south of him as far as his healing senses could reach. Snakes and mice, birds and rabbits, squirrels, chipmunks, deer, a wolf, insects by the thousands, lizards, rats, bats—hundreds upon thousands of lives were being taken. Even the vegetation was yellowing and dying.

He reached out to the west and came to the end of the Dying Lands to find what could only be the Dead Lands themselves. There, nothing lived. No matter how far he searched he couldn't detect the smallest sign of life. Even the earth itself felt dead. He trembled and retched. "Your Majesty," Mother Venetia said, as if from far away. "We must retreat."

Robrek nodded, and they backed up until they were no longer in the Dying Lands. They dismounted. Robrek sat on the ground, Mother Venetia and Awena on either side of him. "How do we do this?" he asked.

Mother Venetia explained the process of severing their power and taking it for his own. "You will be our Dead Lands. We will never again know magic."

He retched again, and Mother Venetia touched his arm. "It is the only way." Robrek nodded numbly. "We should do it now. The Dead Lands grow every minute."

Clenching his fists against the inevitable, Robrek muttered, "Know that if there was another way, I'd never consent to this."

Mother Venetia nodded. "You are a good man. A good king."

Never having felt less like a good man, he joined hands with Mother Venetia and Awena. They joined shields, as Oriana had taught him. He concentrated first on Mother Venetia. She guided him to the heart of her being, to the very source of her magic. Forming his magic into a knife, he tore into her soul and severed her magic from her. The rush of pleasure when her power poured into him dwarfed by far the ecstasy he felt while healing. Every fiber of his being pulsed with it. The power was exquisite, utterly delicious.

He dove into the precious nectar. *Yes, this is what life should be like!* He was a god. Nothing could stop him. Greedy for more, he turned to Awena and, with her help, severed the power within her. Her power dwarfed even Mother Venetia's. If she had grown up, she would have been very powerful.

He threw his head back and howled with laughter. *I can take on the goddess herself!*

He opened his eyes; his very skin glowed with energy. Both Mother Venetia and Awena were lying in the dirt, shaking. Awena was crying. "It's gone, Mother! Everything is gone!" She stared at Robrek, her face contorted. "How can you laugh in the face of what you have done?"

Mother Venetia put her hand on Awena. "My child, it was a sacrifice we had to make." As she turned to Robrek, her voice was hoarse and weak. "Go, and make our sacrifice worthwhile."

A tiny voice of guilt cried out to him as he imagined the horrible nothingness he had reduced the two healers to, but it was drowned out by the utter euphoria that roared through him. "I'll use your power well. I will destroy this thing."

He vaulted onto Valor's back and patted the Horsetad's neck. "Okay, Valor, I need all the speed you can give me. The quicker we get across, the more magic will remain." He touched Valor with his heels, and the Horsetad took off.

Within seconds they had again reached the edge of the Dying Lands. To protect himself, Robrek snapped his shields completely closed and felt as if all life suddenly ceased to exist. *Holy Sulis, to live like this!* But he laughed as the power surged through him, beating back the guilt.

As he entered the Dying Lands, he saw birds and small animals stirring weakly in the dying grass. He felt the subtle pull against his shields. Those Who Were were draining his magic. He grabbed it more closely about himself. *No, it is mine! Mine!*

* * *

As Robrek and Valor crossed the Dying Lands to the lands already dead, they passed mile after mile of dead vegetation. The bodies of animals lay where they had fallen, strangely horrifying to see. They had begun rotting and then stopped mid-process, and the bodies had none of the terrible odor that usually surrounded the dead. Since there were no scavengers to scatter their bones, the bodies were all intact. No insects or maggots ate their flesh. The bodies couldn't be returned to the earth to create new life. In these lands the dead gave nothing back.

About noon they reached the first village. Robrek found dead animals—mice, rabbits, dogs, cats, horses, cows, pigs—in the same half-decayed state. Then Robrek saw his first human corpses. A man knelt in a vegetable garden between rows of dead carrots. A woman leaned against the wall of the nearby house with an infant at her breast. A toddler lay with his head resting on the woman's knee. On the other knee was the head of the family dog. Curled up next to the small boy was a tortoiseshell cat. It was a grotesque parody of the happy family.

The mother, father, and two children were the only human bodies in the open, but Robrek wondered how many lay dead in the houses that lined the village square. *This has to be stopped!* "Get us out of here, Valor," Robrek urged the horse, who resumed his former speed.

They skirted the other villages they came to, but still they came across an occasional farmer in a field of dead grain or a traveler who had not made it to safety. And everywhere they looked were dead animals. He shook with anger far stronger than he'd believed he was still capable of feeling. How could he forgive such slaughter? Those Who Were and the Bard would pay for what they had done!

* * *

As he raced across the Dead Lands, a small trickle of power leaked out of him, reducing his euphoria and stoking his anger. But he still glowed with more power than he'd ever had before. *Surely, it is enough.* To take his thoughts off the fear that it might not be, he called to mind a time when he felt truly happy: meeting Samantha at the Coan Horse Fair. Her auburn hair sparkled in the sunlight, and her smile lit her entire face. Freckles dotted her nose and cheeks. He'd never seen a more beautiful woman. To his shock and surprise, she sought him out, moved close to him, and started a conversation about horses. She touched his leg with hers. She took his hand and wandered the stalls with him. She tried on ridiculous hats, and they laughed. She bought him a green ribbon to tie back his hair, saying its color brought out his emerald eyes—a ribbon that even now he wore around his neck. He whirled and laughed with her on the fair's dance floor of rough-hewn planks, proving to her that he hadn't lied when he said he couldn't dance—

Suddenly, he hit the ground with a jarring thud. From far away, his arm screamed in pain.

Valor wheeled around and neighed in his face. Robrek struggled to sit up, but couldn't. His shields had fallen, and the Dead Lands were draining his life. "No," he whispered.

:Get up!: Valor commanded; as a creature of magic, the Dead Lands had not affect him. *:We are less than five miles from the village.:*

Robrek clawed at the ground, trying to get up, but he lacked the strength. "Can't."

From far away, he heard Valor's mind voice. *:Take my power. Finish this.:* But the Horsetad was a creature of magic. Without its power, it would be nothing but an ordinary horse. It'd lose his intelligence and sense of self.

"I can't do that to you."

:You cannot die. The herd needs you. Valor will sacrifice all for the herd. If you die, the evil lives on.:

Robrek cried out. Valor's words were true. He grabbed Valor's leg. "I'm sorry, my friend. If there was another way, I would take it." He closed his eyes and cut the cord of the horse's power with the knife of his magic. This time, the power rush was even stronger. He screamed with agony, grief, and pleasure as he came back from the edge of death. His body seemed to burst, spilling the excess energy into the ground beneath him. When he became aware of his surroundings again, he was lying on a square of green grass bursting with flowers in a riot of colors. Valor stood cropping flowers beside him.

He asked Valor if he was all right, but all he got in reply was an image of how delicious the flowers were. The mind of the Horsetad was gone.

There was only one thing to do. One thing that would make the sacrifices of the others worthwhile.

He turned west and ran with Valor's speed and energy.

* * *

Despite being exhausted from the flight from Reidhlean, Leigh couldn't sleep. Their camp was a mere ten miles from the village, and tomorrow the Bard would sing its death. They surely hadn't made it far enough away for safety.

Father Dorsey, lying near Leigh in their tent, clambered to his feet. "This won't work!"

"We must have faith in the goddess and the king." But Leigh feared that at the moment his own faith was shaky.

"I have neither, and I won't wait around to be slaughtered with the rest of you." Dorsey pulled on his robes and started gathering his belongings.

Leigh hurried to his feet. "You can't mean to leave! You're the strongest among us! We haven't a chance without you!"

"We haven't a chance, period, and if you had any sense you'd leave, too." Dorsey headed for the opening of the tent, and Leigh caught his arm.

"Please! You must stay! No place will be safe if we don't stop this!"

Father Dorsey whirled, his fist catching Leigh in the jaw and knocking him to the ground. "Don't try to stop me. I'm not going to die for those who consider me a cothla."

* * *

"Can't you at least sing him to sleep first?" the son of her breast objected.

Alvabane continued to make the first cut on the naked servant she had tied to the altar. The servant made frantic guttural sounds, she had already cut his tongue out. "The sacrifice will be more powerful if I don't. The pain helps to feed the dark gods."

Torin's voice trembled. "Do you really have to go through with *any* of this? There are women and children among the villagers."

Alvabane cupped Torin's face lovingly with the hand that wasn't holding the knife. He had to be taught a lesson. She sent a jolt of power into him. He screamed. "No more of your squeamishness. Interrupt again, and you will be next on the altar."

"You wouldn't!" Torin tried to back away, but he couldn't escape her grip.

"My son, there is nothing I wouldn't do to please the dark gods."

She released the son of her breast, and he stumbled. He backed up until he was against the wall, and he said no more as she completed the sacrifice.

The last of the blood was drained from the servant. She was nearly ready to sing the death of Reidhlean, but first she'd have to locate the villagers. Torin's spies had reported the Royal Guard evacuating the village, as Alvabane had expected, but that many people, especially the children, the sick, and the elderly, couldn't travel far. Surely they were still within range of the Stone's power. She began to hum to draw power from the Stone. She closed her eyes and reached out in search of the people her song would soon kill. With their deaths, she'd gain the power to reach farther and farther until, eventually, she could sing the death of Murtaghan and the queen herself.

* * *

Eolande was dozing when she felt a tug of evil against her awareness. She shot to her feet, as she realized what it must be. She shook Oriana awake. "It's the Bard. She's found us. We need the others. Fetch them." Terror clutched at Eolande's heart. The king must have failed, and now it was up to her.

Oriana returned quickly with Father Leigh and Artan, but not Father Dorsey. "He left," Leigh reported. "He was afraid." Tears stung the corners of Eolande's eyes. Without Dorsey, their slim chance of success had been reduced to near zero.

"What can we do?" Artan asked, his eyes wide. Oriana trembled as she took Eolande's hand.

Eolande squeezed Oriana's hand and fought to keep her voice from shaking. "We do exactly as practiced. If we can't stop her, we can at least slow her down and give the others time to flee."

"And then we die?" Oriana asked.

Eolande closed her eyes and sent up a brief prayer to Sulis. "If the king has failed, we die."

Eolande sent Artan to fetch Lieutenant Agatone, and she told Agatone that the Bard had found them. "We will try to contain her while you move the villagers." He left immediately to get the villagers to safety, if that were even possible.

Father Leigh, Artan, and Oriana sat in a circle around her. They linked their power and fed it to her as they had practiced in the palace. But without the king and Father Dorsey, the power felt like a weak gruel compared to the banquet she'd experienced before. It wasn't going to be enough, not nearly enough. Still, she began to sing.

* * *

Alvabane began to sing. Immediately, she felt the power of another Bard opposing her. Alvabane laughed in contempt. None could stand against her; she had the power of the Stone. She would crush the other Bard like a cockroach.

CHAPTER 26

Winded when he reached the outskirts of Balley Beg, Robrek slowed. Ahead of him lay the same horrifying sight of half-decayed corpses of people and animals littering the streets.

In his head, Those Who Were cried, *:Yes! Come to us! Free us from the Witch Alvabane, and together we can be more powerful than ever before. You can restore life to the lands. It is the Bard who is killing them, not us. We only wish to do good, to heal, to end poverty and pain.:* Their words were seductive, but they were untrue. The souls of Those Who Were had been driven mad by so long a separation from their bodies. They needed the body of a healer to become whole again, and they wanted his. The Bard could only make them her servants.

Robrek tried to shut out their voices as he jogged through the village toward the shrine at the head of the main street. As Mother Venetia had said, the shrine was built right into the mountain, the entrance to the cave under its altar.

:Don't be a fool. Even Armunn knew the Soul Stone can't be destroyed. It can only be claimed. But the Witch has stolen it through sacrifice and blood; its power is a healer's by right. We seek only to be one with you, to serve you, and to feel your pleasure. Your battle must be against the Bard, not the Stone. You have felt her evil. Do you know what uses she would put us to?:

Robrek reached the door of the shrine and opened it. It creaked eerily in the stillness. He stepped inside into the darkness, found a candle, and lit it. At the far end of the small chapel stood the altar.

:She talks to us. She tells us what she plans. You need us to keep Samantha safe.:

Robrek froze at the thought of any danger to Samantha. He sensed their pleasure at his hesitation. He made his way to the altar.

:Yes, Samantha carries your child. Join with us to keep them safe.:

He set the candle down on the altar, closed his eyes, and breathed deeply to calm himself. *Are they right? How can I hope to destroy the Stone if Armunn could not?* Pushing his doubts aside, he bent down to release the mechanism Mother Venetia told him would move the altar aside, revealing the tunnel beneath. His skin tingled with the remembrance of the smoothness of Samantha's skin as she joined with him and made him whole for the first time in his life. He remembered the movements of the small life that would be his daughter. But good couldn't possibly come from such evil as Those Who Were promised.

:The Bard sees Sam as the descendent of those who drove her people out.:

No one but me ever calls her that! How dare they use my name for her! Robrek released the mechanism and pushed the altar back to reveal a ladder leading into the blackness below. He grabbed the candle and began his descent.

:The Bard has told us her plans for your beloved. Would you like us to share them with you?:

No! Robrek tried to shut the voices out as he scrambled down the long ladder. The ladder seemed to have no end, and when he tried to shine the light of the candle below him, he saw nothing but darkness. The hole under the altar was now only a small window above him.

:Your beloved Sam and your child will not find a quick death. No, your queen will suffer for months at the Bard's hand. She will beg for death, but not receive it until she has borne your child.:

Robrek stumbled, his foot landing on solid rock instead of another step of the ladder. He fell to his knees and doubled up with nausea. The evil in the cave tingled against his skin, but worse were the words of Those Who Were. *Samantha and my daughter in the hands of that vile woman! No, I won't allow it!*

Those Who Were recognized his emotion, and he felt their glee. Robrek tried to shut them out again. He got to his feet. An ancient torch rested in a bracket on the wall. He took it down and used his candle to light it. He blew out the candle and tucked it in his belt. Under the brighter light of the torch, he examined his surroundings.

He stood in a round chamber with a single passageway leading from it. He gasped at the sight of the walls opposite the ladder. The rock from the ground to three feet above his head was a carved mural of both intense beauty and utter depravity. The carvings were inlayed with gold, silver, and precious gems and painted in vibrant colors that had somehow survived the centuries. Life and death surrounded him and filled him with their power. The pictures were intertwined with each other in a grotesque fashion. Underneath a tree of beautiful spring flowers lay an altar topped by a victim with a hole in his chest where his heart should have been. A priestess offered the heart to two lovers walking hand in hand and staring into each other's eyes. They walked through a river full of fish savaging their legs. The river went over a waterfall into a beautiful pool surrounded by green trees bursting with the fruit of summer. Children laughed and splashed each other in the sunlight. On the far side of the pool a naked woman was being held to the ground by one man while another rutted between her thighs. Her mouth was opened in a scream of agony, disgorging a flock of beautiful birds in all the colors of the rainbow.

All along the passageway, the murals covered the walls, the beautiful continually morphing into the ugly and innocence giving way to depravity only to return again to beautiful innocence.

:Two sides of the same power. We can give life, or we can give death. We can give love, or we can give hate. It is for you to choose how to use us. We are not evil.:

He tore his eyes away from the carvings and broke into a jog. The corridor was clearly not natural, for it proceeded in a straight line. The floor remained smooth, and the ceiling remained a consistent distance above his head. Robrek wondered what kind of magic could have created such a place.

* * *

Samantha stood in the city square. Before her loomed the gallows built to hang the treasonous priest. The crowd filled the square and overflowed into the side street. It was in an ugly mood. Some clamored for the priest's blood while others stood in stony silence. Faolan clearly had support among the people. But so did she.

The cage containing the priest rolled into the square. Some tried to throw rotten fruit at the priest, but the silent ones stood in the way, protecting the priest with their bodies. The cage stopped at the stairs to the platform, and two members of the Royal Guard opened it. Faolan stepped out with his head held high and a smile on his face. He didn't look like a man about to die. He spoke a single word.

"Now!"

The silent ones broke into a shout and surged forward as one, drawing clubs from under their cloaks. They quickly overwhelmed the Royal Guard, who'd been stretched thin with the one hundred dead and others gone to evacuate Reidhlean.

"Stop them!" Samantha shouted, but her six personal guards and the remaining Royal Guardsmen weren't enough to fight their way through the fifty or so wielding clubs. Father Faolan had faded into the crowd and was gone, but the ones with clubs didn't back down with Faolan's escape. Instead they pressed on toward the queen, knocking aside all who stood in their way. Her personal guards drew their swords and formed a protective circle around her. The ones who had helped Faolan escape stopped just out of reach of the swords. A priest stepped out from somewhere holding a cup. He had the hood of his cloak up, so she couldn't see his face. "Her Majesty will drink this," he said. "It will rid her womb of the abomination she carries."

Samantha's eyes narrowed with rage. "How dare you threaten my child! You speak treason against the heir to the throne!"

The priest's hand didn't waver. "I speak Sulis's will. You will drink this willingly, or we will force it upon you."

Samantha drew her sword. "Leave this square immediately! My men and I will fight to the last drop of our blood to protect my heir."

"So be it." The priest stepped back. "Take her."

The men wielding clubs surged forward.

* * *

Visions filled Robrek's head of sorcerer after sorcerer entering this very tunnel throughout the ages. He saw them die horribly in their attempt to destroy the Stone, and he saw their agonized souls become part of the blood red lake. :*If you try to destroy the Stone, you will fail, as all those who tried before you have failed. Do you really think your magic stronger than theirs? Because no one in the joined kingdoms today can match you, you've grown arrogant. But if you are to defeat the Bard and keep Sam and your little one safe, you need us.:*

The farther down the tunnel he walked, the more the voices pounded in his head until he was no longer sure which thoughts were his own and which were the doubts and fears Those Who Were poured into him. *:How can you deny you are one of us? Don't fight us; join us. To fight us is to fight yourself. Think of what your principles will cost those you love. Think of your Sam being tortured for months until finally being granted the death she begs for. Hundreds of other men will know her as now only you do.:*

Robrek's stomach clenched with nausea. A vision of Samantha held down on a table by the hands of filthy men filled his head. "No! No!" Robrek tried to tear himself away, but the vision held him. He grabbed the wall. When he looked at his hand, he saw himself touching a naked young woman screaming in agony as she was being sodomized by demons. The woman had auburn hair. Robrek jerked his hand away from the wall as if it had been burned. "No!" he whispered. "No!"

:Your child will be the daughter of an aurora and a healer. Have you ever thought about the potential of such mixed blood? The Bard has. Alvabane has plans for her.:

"Don't torment me with your lies!" But panic rushed through him as he realized they might indeed be showing him the truth. He broke into a run.

:Wouldn't you do anything necessary to protect them? Will you die attempting the impossible and leave them in the Bard's hands?:

Tears streamed down Robrek's face, and the voices tore at his mind. He could barely see. *Where am I? What is it I'm supposed to do?*

Abruptly the tunnel came to an end, and Robrek found himself in a vast cavern. In the middle of the cavern was the blood-red lake of his dreams, and in the middle of the lake was the Soul Stone, a large column of what appeared to be a blood-red ruby. Pulsing with energy and light, the Stone reached from the cavern's floor up to the roof far above. If legend were correct, it stretched all the way through the surface and into a room in the base of a castle. From this room, the woman who would torture his family controlled the Stone.

No! He wouldn't allow the Bard that power!

* * *

Each of Samantha's guards was fighting at least two opponents, and as soon as one went down, another took his place. It wasn't long before the platform became slick with blood. Findley took a blow to the arm, then was felled by a blow to the head, opening a gap in the defense. A man with his club held high rushed toward her, but she stepped to the side and slashed the man across the gut; another took his place and then another. Her guards tried to keep them off, but gaps in the circle kept appearing as Guthrie lost his footing and was trampled, and Rian went down under repeated blows. Before too long, she was fighting alongside Conroy and Bearach only. Rage flared through her. *Robbie is risking his life to protect these people, and they're trying to kill his child, kill my child.* She feared they would succeed.

But soon Samantha became aware they weren't fighting alone. Her supporters among the crowd had also surged into action. The club wielders were grabbed from behind, and supporters of the queen took up the clubs of the fallen.

"We need to get you to the palace," Conroy said. "To me!" he yelled, and men with clubs and other crude weapons circled them. Bearach and some of her other supporters took the rear.

They fought their way through the crowd, but it was impossible to tell which club wielders were her supporters. The rioters were in a frenzy, their original purpose lost in the collective urge to destroy. Windows were broken all around the square; fires burned in several of the shops, and smoke billowed into the air. Samantha's sword dripped with blood.

* * *

The blood-red lake whirled and swirled as Robrek approached. He couldn't see the tortured souls as he had in his dreams, but he could feel them. He couldn't hear the shrieks and moans that had reverberated in his dreams, but somehow the looming silence was even more disturbing—a silence thick with a pain that had no way to express itself. Finally, he reached the edge of the lake. He could feel the anticipation of Those Who Were. They thought they had him, and maybe they were right. Maybe he'd have to risk taking on their evil to protect Sam and his daughter.

At the edge of the lake he bent down and touched the red substance. He had no words to describe the sensation. It was both freezing cold and blistering hot. Both pleasure and pain. As viscous as liquid and ethereal as gas, and somehow neither. He swirled his hand in it as if it was water, but no droplets fell when he withdrew it.

:Come to us. Be one with us. Together we will destroy the witch.:

Robrek stood up and began to tear off his clothing. He needed the lake to be in contact with his body, as it had been in his dreams. He dropped the last of his clothing on the cavern floor and lay his sword on top of it. The only thing he wore as he stepped in was Samantha's ribbon around his neck.

Stepping into the lake sent a shock through his body. The rush of power nearly caused him to lose consciousness before he could raise his shields tightly enough to dampen the effect. But he couldn't shut it out completely, and half of him didn't want to. Here was power the likes of which he'd never dreamed. It felt like a natural part of him, like a missing limb regained or an extra, yet necessary eye. At the same time, he felt nearly crushed under the torment and despair of the thousands of souls trapped by the Stone. A cacophony of voices filled his head. Some begged and pleaded with him to release them. Some had lost all trace of sanity and raved. How could he ever imagine using such evil? How could he even entertain the idea such power could be used for good?

Still, he trembled at how much he wanted to. He could only imagine how good it would feel. It was like paipin, a thousand fold— a drug that would produce a craving that could never be satisfied.

* * *

Alvabane hesitated in her song as she heard Father Gildas's voice. :*He's here. The demon child is here.*:

The sorcerer had somehow found the cave. He was at the base of the Soul Stone itself, and he planned to steal it from her. *No, he will not take the power of my people! The power is mine!*

But the gnat-like irritation of the other Bard tugged at her, making it harder to concentrate on the threat below.

* * *

As Eolande sang, sweat poured off her brow, running into her eyes and blinding her. The other Bard pressed against her, crushing her mind, like a giant stepping on an insect. She might be able to sting the giant's foot before she died, but die she would and all those with her. She only prayed the villagers could make it to safety. *Please, Sulis, I'll give my life to stop this evil, but let my death have meaning.*

Suddenly, the giant's foot reduced in size to that of a small child. Could it be possible? Had the king come at last?

* * *

As Robrek moved forward through the lake, he struggled to keep his thoughts his own. But too many voices filled his head. Too much pain. Too much suffering. Too much ecstasy. His mind writhed as if taking a beating as brutal as the one Boyden had given his body. His body had barely survived that beating, and his mind couldn't survive this one. *I am Robrek Angusstamm!* he cried. Then he was not; he was the sorcerer Duarcan linking himself to the Stone's power through the rape and torture of young women. He was the maid Imogen screaming in agony that didn't end when her soul left her body. He was King Eamonne sodomizing a little boy over the table in the room above. At the moment of his release, he slit the boy's throat. He was the horrified mother who tracked down her son only to join him in death.

He both committed and suffered every depraved act imaginable. One moment he was in the throes of ecstasy, the next in unbearable agony. He laughed in triumph, then fell to his knees in panic and pain. *Who am I? What am I doing here?* He clung desperately to the ribbon around his neck, forcing himself to think of Samantha, laughing with him as they danced on the day they met. He grabbed that image and the memory of his unborn child moving within her. The voices continued to bombard him, but he clung to the ribbon and pressed steadily toward the Stone.

After hours, or perhaps mere minutes, Robrek reached the Stone and laid his hands upon it. The sensations that exploded through his body and his mind made those from the lake feel like the drops of a gentle rain. His laughter echoed through the cavern, joined by the laughter of Those Who Were. "All of this power is mine! Mine!"

But the power of the Stone wasn't his alone. Two other presences were fighting him for control. He snarled as he recognized the first as Father Gildas, who'd made his childhood a living hell, who'd wanted him dead since he was a mere infant. All the hatred he'd once felt for the priest came rushing back, amplified a thousand times by the power of the Stone. He laughed as he realized Father Gildas was no longer alive, but merely another trapped soul. Father Gildas wasn't the true threat; the priest merely served as a conduit to give the Bard access to the power of the Stone. He raged at the sacrilege; this power was a healer's power! This power belonged to him, not a Bard!

He would take it from her, and he would destroy all who dared to challenge him!

Somewhere in the depths of his mind, a faint voice cried out that this was not who he was. But the memory of torturing the young women, sodomizing the little boy, and committing thousands of other evil acts proved the voice wrong. If he'd done those things, what depravity was he not capable of? Yet the silk of the ribbon rubbed against his chest, and for brief moments he was aware the memories weren't his.

He felt himself weakening; the Bard was using the power of the Stone to drain his life and his soul. He snatched at the power, but Father Gildas had linked her more tightly to the Stone than Robrek was. She had control of its power in ways he did not.

Those Who Were cried out in panic. *:Take us! Take us into you! Now, before it is too late!:*

If he did, his mind would be completely lost. He would no longer be the man he'd been, but part of a much larger whole that reveled in the pain and suffering of others. But if he refused what they offered, it would be mere moments before he too was dead and his soul trapped along with theirs. His purpose in coming here would be lost.

The image of what Alvabane had planned for Sam filled his mind again. He wouldn't let that happen. He dropped his shields completely and allowed Those Who Were inside. He writhed and laughed as they poured into him. He was not one now, but many. *:Yes, We are powerful now! The Bard is no match for Us!:*

They pressed Their hands into the Stone and raged at the Bard. "We are more powerful than you!" The Bard's panic was intoxicating. The Bard shed more blood upon the Stone, strengthening her control. "You know that won't be enough. It's only a matter of time now before both you and the Stone are Ours!" More and more blood poured into the Stone, and They relished it. In the end, it would only add to Their power. They crept slowly through the death and blood closer and closer to the Bard herself. Soon They would have her.

Somewhere within Their mind, They again felt the ribbon. The ribbon was important, They knew. The ribbon meant something, but what? Words the goddess had spoken atop Gloine Torr flashed into Their mind: *Is thy heart strong enough to face this and live?* They hadn't understood what she meant then, but—

Robrek knew. If his capacity for love was stronger than his ability to hate, he could ensure that neither he nor the Bard won control of the Stone.

At last, he knew what he had to do.

He focused all his thoughts on Samantha and his daughter. He gathered that love and used it as a barrier between himself and Those Who Were. Instead of fighting the Bard for power, he began pouring all of his own energy into the Stone and sending it toward her. He doubted he would survive, but he'd take the Stone with him.

* * *

Killing Torin's guards on the altar, Alvabane fought for control of the Stone. But the annoying Bard's voice continued to pull at her attention.

Suddenly, the Stone's power rushed toward her like a torrential river of molten lava. *No, it would destroy her!* She tried to snatch her hands from the Stone, but she had tied herself too closely to it. It had her now. The sorcerer king had her now.

The molten lava of power rushed inside her, filled her, burned her from the inside out. She screamed as her flesh began to boil.

* * *

Those Who Were screamed in delight, but the sorcerer didn't stop with the destruction of the Bard. :*Stop! Stop! The Stone cannot take any more power! Stop! You will destroy it and kill us all!*:

"You are already dead, and I'll die if I must."

Those Who Were tried to fight him, but it was too late. The barrier of love protected him from their attempts to seize his mind, and he continued to pour more and more power into the Stone. He felt his own life, his own energy fading, but it didn't matter now. He'd done enough. The Stone and the cavern trembled and in a deafening crash exploded outward. Robrek was flung into the far wall of the cavern. Pain ripped through him, and his flesh burned. But as his world went dark, he smiled.

He had won.

* * *

Torin watched in horror as Alvabane's flesh began to melt. The Stone glowed brighter and brighter, and Torin ran for the door. But as he reached it, the cavern exploded in a hail of stones.

* * *

Eolande's mind rocked with the power of the explosion, but she laughed with delight. No longer could she feel the presence of the Stone. The king had won.

Everything went dark.

* * *

Samantha and her guards fought their way out of the square and toward the palace gates. Trumpets sounded from the castle's battlements, and within moments guards surged out from behind the gates. They helped fight to clear a path to safety. Other guards at the palace gates tried to stop the rioters from entering the palace grounds.

By the time the gates were finally closed after her and her defenders, her arms were trembling and her hands slick with blood. She fell to her knees in exhaustion and put a hand against her abdomen; her child was safe. Sulis bless its father was as well.

CHAPTER 27

Vaughan had to maintain a slower pace. He'd been riding at top speed for five days, and both he and Thunder Storm were exhausted. He should have known that catching up with the king would be futile.

Suddenly, the mountain, still some distance before him, exploded with a deafening crash, rocking the ground and nearly jolting him off his horse. Boulders rained down from the mountain, and dust filled the air.

"The King!" he cried, coughing. "We have to get there, Thunder Storm! He may be hurt!" *Or dead. No, not the King. He's the goddess's choice.* He urged the horse to a faster speed, and Thunder Storm startled him by responding eagerly. Vaughan, too, realized that his fatigue had fled, and energy flowed through him. All of a sudden, the ground all around him burst into green, covered with flowers in the riotous colors of spring. "He's done it! The King's done it!" Vaughan cried to the horse.

Resting only when Thunder Storm absolutely had to, Vaughan flew through a sea of flowers for two days. Ahead of him, he spotted Wild Thing. He rode closer and was about to hail her, but stopped himself. The Horsetad was too big to be Wild Thing. The horse also drooped rather than frolicked about as Wild Thing would have. Vaughan rode closer. He dismounted, and to his shock, the Horsetad allowed him to approach, rather than shying away from him as he'd expected. "What are you doing here?" he asked, stroking the Horsetad's nose. "Don't you belong on the Reidhlean Plains? Where's Wild Thing and the King?"

The Horsetad merely snorted in answer and went back to eating flowers. Perplexed, Vaughan remounted. After another five miles, he reached the ruins of a small village, mostly buried in boulders from the explosion. It had to be Oriana's village of Balley Beg. Was the king buried under all that rock? In the spaces between the rocks, flowers bloomed. A thick stench filled the air, as if the boulders concealed a vast graveyard of rotting corpses. Vaughan realized they probably did.

Vaughan dismounted and picked his way between the rubble, not even knowing where to begin looking. Nestled against the mountain, he came to a ruined shrine. The walls were gone, and the altar was covered in dust and small stones. The altar was pushed aside to reveal a ladder reaching deep into the ground. Rocks and boulders littered the ground, but somehow the hole itself remained free of clutter, as if the goddess herself was pointing the way to the king. "He's down there. I just know he is," Vaughan told Thunder Storm.

The horse neighed in what Vaughan took to be agreement. He fetched a candle from his saddle bags, lit it, and started down into in the dark hole. Darkness closed in around him, the candle a feeble ward against it.

After what seemed like an hour, he reached the bottom. He gasped as he caught sight of the walls. They were covered with melted silver, gold, gems and running paint. They seemed to have once been pictures, but were now utterly ruined. A tunnel stretched out in front of him, again, miraculously free of rubble, another clear direction from the goddess.

Vaughan started down the tunnel, his footsteps echoing hollowly off the walls; there was no other sound. After a long way he entered a cavern, far bigger than the Temple of the Mother's Love. In the middle, a pile of red stones littered the ground, shattered like glass. Near it lay a badly burned body. Vaughan rushed to it.

A green ribbon lay unburned around the man's neck! The king! "Holy Sulis," Vaughan whispered. "Don't be dead! You can't be dead!"

With a trembling hand, he touched the king's neck. A faint pulse beat under his fingertips. The king, the most powerful healer in the history of the joined kingdoms, was alive. Surely he could recover from even this.

EPILOGUE

In Robbie's sickroom, tears filled Samantha's eyes as she looked down at the badly burned body of the man she loved. An exhausted Vaughan had brought him in yesterday and told a harrowing story of finding Robbie. Fearful of hurting Robbie more, she touched his fingers gently. With her other hand, she fingered the miraculously unburned ribbon around his neck. This symbol of their love had survived. Surely, Robbie would, too. "Will he be all right?" she asked, as Father Leigh came out of his healing trance.

The priest straightened from his ministration. "He's still alive, Your Majesty. That's what matters." He didn't look at her directly.

"Yes, that's what matters," she told herself. As long as Robbie lived and breathed, everything else would be all right. It had to be.

Samantha left Robbie's sickroom and climbed to the palace battlements. Father Faolan had not surfaced, but the Church of the True Believer still flourished, and Samantha was certain Faolan was running it from wherever he had hidden. The priests of the new faith were careful not to say anything directly against the queen, but they still preached mixed blood as an abomination. Robbie's heroic victory against the dark evil had cut deeply into their numbers, and Samantha hoped they would simply fade away.

As she looked down at her kingdom, she felt something move inside her for the first time. She put her hand to her belly, and she felt love burst inside her for her unborn child and for her child's father. Yes, everything would be all right.

If you enjoyed the novel, please leave a review on Amazon or Goodreads.

To follow learn where Darhour has been all this time, read *The Ghost in Exile*. I have an excerpt below. If you enjoy it, the novel can be purchased on Amazon

Also, subscribe to my mailing list to
get monthly updates on my writing, specials,
and advanced news on upcoming releases.
You will also received a free ecopy of my short story collection,
Blood Cursed and Other Tales of the Fantastic.
http://jamie-marchant.com/newsletter/

THE GHOST IN EXILE
(EXCERPT)

A Korthlundian Kronicle

By Jamie Marchant

CHAPTER 1

The Ghost sat in the temple district of Argos staring at the Temple of Ares, the god of war and of killers. Due to the disguise he now wore, people passed without exhibiting the fear that his own features usually invoked. With the aid of wax and cosmetics, he'd hidden his numerous scars and remade his face in the image of a Saloynan mercenary, a persona he'd never thought to assume again. He pulled his cloak more tightly around him to protect against the chill. It was mild for mid-winter, but still the cold was biting. Ares's temple looming in front of him deepened the cold. It was constructed of black marble and decorated in blood-red stone with sharp lines and geometric shapes, conjuring images of the horrors of the battlefield. He looked from the red and black temple to his fingernails. During the three-month crossing from Korthlundia to Saloyna—the rough winter sea making the crossing take longer than usual—he'd succeeded in scrubbing the blood out from under his nails, but it hadn't been easy. When he'd been the world's most notorious assassin, he'd owned a brush specifically for that purpose. But after he'd knelt at Sulis's holy altar and made the vow never to kill again, he'd thrown that brush away. He guessed he'd need to find a new one.

The Ghost rose abruptly. There was no point in delaying any longer. He'd broken his vow, and it was past time to admit that making it had been foolish to begin with, as if such a small act could cleanse his blood-drenched soul. He'd long ago earned his place in the seven hells. Now, he must embrace the fact that he had one skill and one purpose—to kill those who needed to die. For a brief time he'd tried to forget that, and because he hesitated to kill a monster, the man had nearly destroyed his homeland and his daughter. Some people's deaths were a thing to be celebrated rather than mourned, and because he was forever tainted, forever a killer, he should be the one to kill them. He hoped the high priest had an appropriate target for him. Zotico was a ghoul, but he'd always been reliable in ferreting out the fiends whose deaths were most needed.

As The Ghost entered Ares's temple, an oppressive presence settled over him. He seemed to be alone in the huge sanctuary, but he knew the acolytes of Ares watched through hidden panels. Rumors claimed they waited for someone with signs of weakness to enter. Then they would pour forth, seize the unfortunate, and sacrifice him to their god. The Ghost had found no evidence to support such rumors, but he knew that animals and criminals were regularly sacrificed on Ares's altar, bleeding out their lives into the bowl at the foot of his statue. It was a hard death, both the blood and the pain feeding the magic of Ares's priests.

The Ghost knelt at Ares's feet, where the stench of blood was nearly overpowering. The altar was stained with it, and the bowl at the god's feet was full from a fresh sacrifice. The power present in this place was undeniable—dark and forbidding, far from the peace and serenity in Sulis's temples. But he was no longer worthy of Sulis's blessing. The Ghost drew his dagger, held his left forearm over the sacrificial bowl, and sliced a new cut alongside his numerous scars. As he bled into the bowl, he felt the magic of the place coalesce around him. His blood sizzled as it hit the bowl, and the wound on his arm healed instantly, signaling that The Ghost truly belonged to the Saloynan god.

A door opened behind him; he stood and faced the high priest. Zotico was completely bald and looked no older than he had when The Ghost had first met him ten long years ago. He had small, beady eyes and a typical Saloynan narrow nose. "Pandaros! How wonderful!" the priest beamed, calling The Ghost a name he'd decided he must take up again. He could no longer be either "Ahearn" or "Darhour"; they were both dead. "Rumors said you were no longer among the living. Come in, come in." Zotico gestured toward the doorway. "I can't tell you how happy I am to see you."

Zotico's enthusiasm seemed excessive even for him. Warily, The Ghost followed Zotico down the corridor to the high priest's office. It was large, the walls covered with instruments of war—swords, shields, battle axes, and plaques ornamented with what looked suspiciously like human ears. The ears were new. Zotico caught The Ghost looking at them and swept his hand over a plaque that contained five ears nailed side by side. "Do you like the new decor? Sacrifices, all of them. I had them moved from our private sanctuary so I could better remember the devotion demanded by the god I serve."

Zotico may not appear to age, but his ghoulishness grew with each passing year. The Ghost carefully schooled his features to avoid betraying any sign of revulsion.

In the center of the office was a large desk with one chair behind it and two large, comfortable chairs facing it. Zotico gestured The Ghost into one of the facing chairs. The Ghost sat, and the high priest offered him a glass of oenomel, a sweet mixture of honey and wine. Zotico poured himself a glass from the same pitcher and sat behind the desk. "Pandaros, my friend. Why have you neglected your obligations to Ares?"

The Ghost waited for Zotico to take a sip of his drink, then took one of his own. It was cloying in its sweetness. "I've been distracted."

Zotico smiled sadly. "A true tragedy. There's no one better with a blade." The priest mimed drawing a knife across his own throat. "I've had acolytes scouring the city more than once looking for you, but I gave up years ago when not the slightest sign of your whereabouts could be found. Tell me, my son, where have you been?"

"Away." The Ghost had no intention of ever letting Zotico learn anything about Samantha, who was both his daughter and his queen. Because of his careful disguise, Zotico believed The Ghost was a Saloynan.

Zotico laughed. "Long have I wished for the power of Delphi to penetrate your secrets. Is there a person in the world who knows even half of them?" Zotico looked expectantly at him, but The Ghost didn't answer. "I see my curiosity shall have to be contained. Ares is a harsh master and not attentive to trifles. Still, I can't tell you how happy I am that you have now returned to his fold. His temple has truly felt your absence."

The Ghost grunted, "Do you have a job for me?"

Zotico's eyes gleamed. "Do I ever! I'd nearly despaired of finding a capable assassin, but your fortunate arrival proves that Ares will never fail those who serve his name."

"Who do you want dead?"

"I think it would be best explained by the one in need of Ares's assistance, but I assure you it is your sort of kill. May I tell the client you'll meet?"

The Ghost nodded.

Zotico's entire body relaxed. "Good, good. The client would prefer not to be seen here. I've an arrangement with the high priestess of Aphrodite. The two gods were lovers, after all. Enter the goddess's temple tomorrow morning and choose the acolyte wearing the pendant of a vulture." Zotico smiled broadly. "Pandaros, my friend, it is a great day for you to have returned."

"You are not my friend." The Ghost left with Zotico's laughter ringing in his ears.

* * *

Desperately needing the distraction, The Ghost went for a walk after his supper at the Green Sandpiper, an inn that catered to mercenaries and other unsavory types. The falling of night deepened the cold, but he didn't cut short his walk. He wandered the filthy streets of the poorer section of the city, thinking about past kills—those in the distant past, not those connected with his daughter. He couldn't think of her ever again. The few short years he'd spent with her had been the best in his life, but he hadn't deserved them. The only thing he deserved was to rot in the seven hells. He wondered how many had died at his hands. Two hundred? Three? More? He'd never kept count.

Few of the street lights were lit in this part of town, but that was no hindrance to The Ghost. When he'd been the Saloynan king's personal assassin, he'd had an enchantment performed on his eyes, giving him the ability to see in the dark, even the complete darkness of a cave.

Passing an alley, he heard a commotion. He turned to see a young woman pleading with two men. "Don't make me go with him," she begged. "He hurts me." The Ghost recoiled when he heard her Massossinan accent. He hated Massossinans.

The first man slapped her across the face, and The Ghost saw the iron slave collar around the woman's neck. Her red hair confirmed her nationality. She wore a low-cut, red bodice trimmed with black lace and an extremely short red skirt. She had to be freezing in this weather. "You'll do as you're told and like it, or . . ." He drew a knife and ran it across her right breast, drawing a thin line of blood.

The second man grabbed the woman. "You know you like it rough." He too drew a knife. "Maybe I'll slice you open when I'm through with you."

"That will cost you extra," the first man warned.

The second man shrugged. "I'm good for it."

He imagined his daughter being similarly assaulted. He stepped into the alley. "Let her go."

The man pulled the woman closer to him. "You can have a turn when I'm done with her." He grabbed the woman's breast, and she tried to squirm away. She looked older than he'd thought at first, nearly thirty—old for a whore. Most didn't live that long.

The Ghost drew his sword and stepped forward. "I said let her go."

The woman's master stepped between The Ghost and the other man. "Mister, you have no right to interfere with lawful commerce. She's mine, and I'll do with her as I see fit."

"Not tonight you won't. Move aside."

It must have been too dark for the man to see the menace in The Ghost's eyes. Few men dared stand up to him after they'd gotten a good look at the coldness he held there. The slave owner, however, crossed his arms. "Go away."

The Ghost raised his sword and struck the man on the head with the flat of his blade. He went down, and The Ghost stepped over him and addressed the customer. "I said let her go."

The man placed his knife at the woman's throat. "She's mine, or she's no one's."

The Ghost surreptitiously palmed a knife with his left hand while he continued holding his sword with his right. Even more than he hated Massossinans, he hated those who preyed on women's flesh. He looked at the woman. "Your choice. Does he live or die?"

* * *

For an instant, Brigitta was too shocked by the stranger's actions to answer. Saloynans were nothing but godless barbarians. She'd once been raped in the street, and not a single Saloynan had done anything to help her. The few men who had even deigned to notice merely did so to applaud her rapist and to vilify her homeland. Still, if he was offering help, she wasn't about to turn him down.

"Kill him," she hissed. Antero would not use her again.

She never saw the stranger move, but Antero toppled over, taking her down with him. He rolled off her, screaming and clutching at his face. She barely had time to notice the knife in his eye socket before the stranger had moved again and plunged his sword through Antero's throat. *Frigg preserve me!*

Fearfully, she scrambled to her feet and glanced in her rescuer's direction, but she was too late to call out a warning before her master hit the stranger from behind with a rusty pipe. She cried out as the stranger fell to his knees, dropping his sword. After Damien killed the stranger, he would punish her horribly. She looked around for a place to run, but she knew it was useless. There was nowhere in this savage land that her master couldn't find her.

To her relief, the stranger survived the blow, and he somehow had another knife in his hand. He twisted, and before she'd realized what was happening, Damien was on the ground as well, his entrails exposed to the night air. The stranger's sword was next to her foot. She grabbed the heavy sword with both hands and rushed the man who'd made her life a living hell. Her rescuer rolled aside and allowed her access to the ogre. She raised the sword over her head.

Damien flung up an arm. "No, please!"

"You kidnapped me!" she screamed, as she rammed the sword into his heart. She raised the sword and plunged it over and over again. "You raped me! You made me a whore! You left my children motherless!"

The stranger grabbed her arm. "Enough. He's dead." He took the sword from her and wiped it on her dead master's clothes.

He stumbled as he slid it into its scabbard and put his hand to the back of his head where Damien had hit him with a pipe. His fingers came away bloody. He tore off Damien's shirt and pressed it against his scalp. "Damned fool!" he muttered, seemingly to himself.

Brigitta thought she should offer her rescuer assistance, but she looked down and saw her master's blood covering her legs. Her legs buckled, and she sank to the alley floor. Slaves who killed their masters were subjected to the cruelest deaths. "I killed him," she whispered. "I killed the bastard. Dear gods, what will they do to me?"

Her rescuer threw her master's shirt aside and held out his hand. "Come with me."

She scrambled away from him and grabbed the knife from Antero's eye. She pointed it at the stranger. "Stay away from me. Before you people made me a whore, I was an honorable wife and mother. I'll die before being used again."

The stranger dropped his arm. "I don't intend to use you."

But Brigitta knew better. Saloynans were worse than the trolls that peopled the bard's tales of her land. She got to her feet, her trembling hand holding the knife. "I'm leaving now. Going home to my little ones. Move out of the way."

She knew the situation was hopeless. She'd tried to fight when Damien's squad had invaded her hut, but it had done nothing to stop them from raping her in front of her children. She was certain that this stranger could disarm her without even trying.

"I can't do that," he hissed through his teeth as if trying to convince himself of something. "You're covered in blood. You're collared. You're dressed like a whore. You'll never make it out of the city on your own, probably not even out of this neighborhood. They'll capture you and torture you to death. I can't let that happen. I'll find a way to get you home, and I won't touch you without your permission. I give you my word."

Brigitta laughed. "And a Saloynan's word is worth ever so much."

Brigitta's mouth dropped open as the stranger switched from Saloynan to her own language. "I'm not Saloynan." The light was poor, and the stranger was wearing a large hood. Was it possible that one of her countrymen was here in the heart of the enemy's capital? Was there hope for her after all?

Her entire body trembled as she lowered the knife and answered him in the language she'd despaired of ever speaking again. "Do you swear on Frigg that you'll do as you promised?"

"You have my word. I'll get you home."

"May Frigg curse you with barrenness if you lie."

The stranger took off his cloak and draped it around her shoulders. She wrapped it tightly around her, grateful for the added warmth.

* * *

The Ghost looked down at the Massossinan woman sleeping in his bed. *What in Sulis's name have I gotten myself into it?* He'd been able to break into a blacksmith shop and use his tools to remove the slave collar from the woman's neck. He'd sneaked her up the rear staircase of the Green Sandpiper, but she'd hardly stayed awake long enough to wash off her master's blood. She was still dressed as a whore and unmistakably Massossinan. For Sulis's sake, the very sound of a Massossinan accent made his stomach heave. Without provocation, he'd come close to stabbing the Massossinan prince who had courted his daughter. He rubbed his arms. They felt as if insects swarmed over them. While he served in the Saloynan army, a Massossinan officer had tortured The Ghost, coated him in honey, and staked him over an ant hill. That same officer had eaten Phelix's heart.

And he'd promised this woman to take her home to her husband? Had he lost his mind? He'd come to Saloyna to be a killer again because it was the only thing he'd ever really been good at. He'd barely set foot in the country, and he was already acting like a knight in shining armor from the worst of the bards' tales, rescuing damsels in distress. Just how was he going to keep his promise to both Zotico and this woman? He should know better than to get involved in things like this. He was not a good man.

He groaned and collapsed on the chair in front of the mirror. He picked up a poultice of crushed cabbage leaves and parsley he'd made in the inn's kitchen and held it to the back of his head. Phelix would probably have had better advice on what to use to treat the ridiculous injury. No, Phelix would have cursed him for being a brainless twit for allowing an enemy to get behind him. He'd lost his edge.

He threw down the poultice and turned to the mirror to remove the wax and cosmetics from his face. As he did so, he revealed the extent of his facial scarring, horizontal lines carved every inch from his forehead to his chin. The scars gave him a fearsome look, one that Samantha said could make men piss themselves if he so much as glanced in their direction. They also made him look far older than forty as did his gray hair and beard. He wondered what the woman would do when she saw the scars. Perhaps she'd run screaming from the room and relieve him of his responsibility to her.

When he'd cleaned his face, he looked back at the bed. The woman slept exactly in the middle, leaving no room for him on either side, and he was sure the woman wouldn't welcome his company. He arranged his weapons and settled down on the floor in front of the door with the poultice. He stared at the wall for a long time, holding the poultice to his head and reminding himself that he was a killer, not some knight errant hero.

* * *

Brigitta woke in a panic, at first not remembering where she was. The weak light of early dawn streamed through the window, and a male voice muttered in his sleep in a language she'd never heard. She sat up and noticed that the weight of her slave collar was missing. She put her hand to her neck, and the entire horrible memory came back to her. She'd killed her master. If she was found, she'd be tortured to death. Her children would grow up without a mother's love, and she knew how little they could count on their father's. Worse yet, the man who rescued her seemed to have lied to her about being a countryman. She couldn't see him well in the thin light, but the language he was speaking was certainly not Massossinan. If he'd lied to her about that, what else had he lied about? She heard her husband's voice telling her how stupid she was, and it was true. Only a true idiot would have gone with a man that had proven himself to be as good at killing as the stranger obviously was.

To make things worse, he was sleeping in front of the door, evidently to stop her escaping, but his sword rested on the floor near his hand. If she could get his weapon, maybe she could force him to let her go. If not, well, she'd already killed one man. She'd kill another if that's what it took to get back to her children.

She slipped silently from the bed, trying to move across the floor without sound, but the boards creaked under her weight. She froze, but the stranger continued to mutter without waking. She crept forward more carefully. The stranger stopped muttering, but he remained still and didn't seem to be awake. Not even daring to breathe, she took the last few steps and put her hands on the sword. She tried to draw it from its sheath, but she'd forgotten how heavy it was. Before she'd cleared it more than an inch, the stranger's hands grabbed hers. How had he moved so fast?

"Let's put that away before someone gets hurt," the stranger said.

As she pulled her hands free from the stranger's grasp, Brigitta wanted to cry. She was certainly no match for this barbarian. The sun's light streamed more brightly though the window, and she gasped at the sight of the stranger's face. Someone had carved it into mincemeat. She backed away from the nightmare. "You're not Massossinan. What kind of monster are you?"

Brigitta expected the stranger to sneer at her stupidity in believing him, but instead, he stretched, as if shaking off the last of his sleep. "The worst kind of monster." He got up from the floor and towered over her. She'd always been small, and this man was huge. "I'm also Korthlundian."

She wondered if this were some kind of demon she'd never heard of. "What's that supposed to mean?"

The stranger leaned against the wall, keeping his distance from her. "Korthlundia's a small country, a great distance from here."

Brigitta decided that where he was from didn't matter. What mattered was that he was standing between her and the door.

"I won't hurt you," he said in a gentle voice completely at odds with his appearance. "I haven't even tried to touch you."

Brigitta had to admit this was true. If he was going to do something to her, why had he slept on the floor? Still, she shuddered at the horrible scarring. "Let me go." She was ashamed that her voice trembled.

For a moment, the stranger looked like he was considering stepping aside, but then he shook his head. "You don't need to be afraid of me. Despite how I look, I'm a man of my word. If you trust me, I'll get you home." He left his place by the door and sat at the vanity in front of the mirror. He picked up some wax and began spreading it over his scars. She inched her way toward the door, not believing he would truly let her go. But he ignored her movements and continued to work on his face.

She opened the door, and he still did nothing to stop her. She heard male voices speaking Saloynan coming from the common room below. She closed her eyes and imagined what would happen if she walked into that room alone, dressed as she was. She closed the door and looked back at the stranger, who was applying cosmetics. He didn't look quite as frightening now, but how could she trust a man who killed so easily?

"Who are you?"

He shrugged. "It doesn't matter." He said nothing more as he continued his transformation. She stared as the scarred monster became a normal looking Saloynan man, just like the hundreds who had used her against her will.

The stranger stood, got out his purse, and handed her some coins. Her eyes widened as she saw the glint of gold among them. It would take half a year on her back to earn this much for her master. If the man had this much money, what was he doing staying in a dive like this?

"I have an appointment to keep. If you truly think you're better off on your own, leave when I'm gone. But if you have any sense, you'll still be here when I get back. I'll bring you some new clothes, and we can make plans." He buckled on his sword and stowed his knives all over his body. She couldn't see a one of them when he was finished.

When he was gone, she sank onto the bed. *Please, Frigg, what should I do?* she prayed. *My children need me.* She thought of the huge smile that had appeared on Elva's face every morning when she woke and caught sight of her mother. That smile had brightened Brigitta's entire world. But Elva had run to her and hid her face in Brigitta's skirts when her father came home drunk. *Dear Frigg, protect Elva and little Vigi until I can get back to them.* She curled up in a ball, clutching the coins in her fist and hugging the pillow to her. She was so tired of trying to be strong.

* * *

The Ghost rubbed the back of his head as he went down the back steps of the Green Sandpiper. It still hurt, but not too badly, making it clear that he'd suffered no serious injury. Still, what had he gotten himself into with the woman? *I tried to reform; it didn't work. I'm a murderer. Nothing more.* He had no idea what he would tell Zotico about the job they'd discussed. If it truly was his type of kill, should he turn it down to help a woman whose name he didn't even know? He saw Samantha's face. He knew what his daughter would expect, but she'd never known the murderous depth of his soul.

He blocked her out of his mind and focused on his surroundings instead. Five years had dulled his memory of the horrors of the Saloynan capital. Beggars were everywhere—young children and old men and women, emaciated and covered in running sores. In the poorer sections of the city, sewage ran down the middle of the streets. Whores, far younger than his daughter, plied their trade, and a few bodies of those who'd frozen in the night hadn't yet been gathered up. The capital of Korthlundia was not without problems, but poverty was nowhere near this widespread or abject. In Saloyna, King Salome, like his father before him, cared nothing about his people. They starved while he lived in luxury that would empty the Korthlundian treasury.

The Ghost was relieved to reach the temple complex, which was kept clean and free of beggars. In sharp contrast to Ares's temple, Aphrodite's shone a brilliant white with carvings of lovers frolicking in every imaginable position. While The Ghost had seen Aphrodite's temple every time he visited Ares's, he had never been inside. The only thing a woman's love had ever done for him was ruin his life and send him into exile when he had been only eighteen years old.

When he entered the temple, he was greeted by soft music and delicate perfume. Young women and men—acolytes of Aphrodite— in sheer robes that concealed nothing, danced in celebration of the goddess. Worshipers watched the dance until they found an acolyte to their liking. They gave the priestess the proper donation and disappeared with the acolyte into one of the private rooms that lined one wall of the temple, where they worshiped the goddess in a more intimate manner. Some of the acolytes danced near him. He examined their necks until he saw the one wearing a vulture pendant. He took the young woman's arm and led her to the priestess. "I'll take this one," he told her.

The priestess looked him over and nodded. "Chrysante, make sure this gentleman receives our special treatment."

Chrysante led him toward the rear of the temple. She opened a door, and they entered a room with nothing other than an altar. Climbing onto the altar, Chrysante purred, "Would you like to take your pleasure on Aphrodite's altar before meeting your guests? Ares's high priest said you might, and it will bring you luck with the young woman who accompanies him." Chrysante arched her back, making her breasts stand out beneath the sheer fabric.

Embarrassed, The Ghost felt himself harden. "I would not," he snapped.

The acolyte paled and jumped off the altar. *Sulis curse it! It isn't her fault the Saloynan gods are twisted.*

"Right this way, sir." She scrambled to the door on the opposite side of the altar and opened it. Following her, The Ghost entered a corridor. She took him to the end of the corridor and stopped before another door. "They await you in there. I'll leave you now." She fled back down the corridor. He must have sounded even harsher than he thought.

When the acolyte had disappeared, The Ghost knocked on the door, and Zotico's voice bid him enter. Zotico luxuriated on a sofa decorated with nymphs doing things The Ghost would rather not imagine. Two easy chairs flanked the sofa, and a table in the middle of the room was covered in breakfast food. A woman stood on the opposite side of the room with her back to him. She was studying a tapestry. "Do you think this is even possible?" she asked of the act the tapestry depicted.

Zotico waved his hand dismissively. "I'm sure it is. Those who worship Aphrodite are quite talented." The priest looked at The Ghost. "But considering how quickly you arrived, I take it you didn't avail yourself of their expertise. I assure you, young Chrysante can—"

"I didn't come here to 'avail' myself," he snarled. "I came to tell you I may not be able to take the job after all."

"You what?" The young woman whirled around. The Ghost gasped and hurriedly bowed. Last time The Ghost had seen her, Princess Acantha had been a gangly girl of fourteen with a fondness for horses. Now, she'd filled in her womanly shape. She was tall, with dark hair flowing around her head, deep set eyes, and an extremely narrow nose. "You would refuse to do a service for your queen?"

The Ghost blinked. "I hadn't heard of your father's death."

"He's not dead yet," Zotico answered for her. "But I'm sure shortly you will help spread the good news. The monster has ruled for far too long, and at the rate he's going, he soon won't have any heirs left. He had the last of his sons executed just last month."

The princess glared at The Ghost. "How long before he decides I, too, am a threat?"

"A true lover of his country wouldn't let such atrocities continue," Zotico said. "Besides our land will be plunged into chaos if he dies without an heir. We'd be completely vulnerable to those heart-eating fiends."

The Ghost sickened as he remembered the sound of the Massossinan officer taking a bite out of Phelix's heart. But it wasn't the thought of the Massossinan menace that moved him. He thought of the children starving in the streets and of the Salome he'd known when he worked as his father's assassin.

You could tell a lot about a person by the way they treated animals. When The Ghost had been the king's assassin, his cover was as assistant master of the horse. Salome had been brutal to his horses. The Ghost had spent countless hours doctoring the injuries the prince inflicted on his beasts and in calming their agitation after he'd ridden them. But his most vivid memory of Salome involved the young stable boy, Paulos.

Paulos hadn't been quite right in the head. He was slow catching onto things and needed any order explained slowly and carefully before he was sure what to do. But once he understood, he was reliable, and he was always smiling. The Ghost had never known how the lad had gotten a place in the king's stables, but he assumed he was the bastard of someone important.

The Ghost had been on an errand for the king and had just finished cleaning the blood from under his fingernails. As he was returning to the stables, Prince Salome and some of his hanger-ons— Salome didn't have any true friends—were leaving. Salome had laughed. "That will teach him to obey his lord and master."

The Ghost had assumed the prince was referring to his stallion, who had developed an intense fear of Salome and resisted all of Salome's attempts to control him. But when The Ghost entered the stables, it wasn't Aquafire the others were gathered around. The Ghost pushed through the stable hands to find Paulos staring sightlessly at the ceiling with bloody stumps where his hands and feet used to be. Blood dripped onto Paulos's face, and The Ghost looked up. The missing appendages hung above him.

"Dear Gods, what happened?" he asked.

One of the stable hands lifted his head from the carnage. His face was white, and his entire body shook. "You know Paulos. He didn't get the prince's horse saddled fast enough."

The Ghost had wanted to kill Salome then and there, and he should have. Frare had been a horrible tyrant, but Salome made his father look like a saint. He clenched his fists. *Damn all of Massossina to the seven hells! I don't owe her anything.*

He berated himself for his initial hesitation to take the job. He'd hesitated when he should have killed his daughter's enemy, and he couldn't bear to think of the pain that had caused. He wouldn't fail another young woman who should be sitting on a throne. He'd keep his promise to the Massossinan woman, but she could wait a day or so. And who knew, maybe he'd be lucky, and she wouldn't be there when he got back.

"When do you want it done?"

"As soon as possible."

"Tell me your father's habits, as thoroughly as you can."

Zotico gestured to the table. "Please, let us do this over breakfast."

The Ghost and Acantha seated themselves in the easy chairs on opposite sides of the breakfast table. Princess Acantha poured herself a glass of wine and sipped it as she detailed her father's routine. She ate nothing. "He has everything tasted before he eats or drinks. He wears amulets protecting him for all kinds of magic, and he has guards with him constantly, except at night when he sleeps with two large boarhounds. They'd tear a man to shreds at the slightest provocation."

Excitement built in The Ghost as he continued to ask questions and a plan formed in his mind. "I'll need the livery of a palace servant," he said. He closed his eyes and savored the rush. If he was destined to be a killer, he might as well enjoy it.

* * *

After leaving the temple district, The Ghost went to a nearby apothecary. The man behind the counter looked at his weapons warily. "Can I help you?"

The Ghost nodded and rattled off a list of ingredients.

The man frowned. "There's only one thing you could be making with that lot—Uttvos serum." Uttvos serum was a powerful sleeping potion, one The Ghost had made frequent use of. He preferred to kill no one but the target.

The Ghost put menace in his eyes. "Is that any concern of yours?"

The man shrugged. "No, but I could save you the trouble. I have some already made up." The man took out a vial containing a thick liquid. "First class quality. Knock out your strongest stallion so you can castrate it without the least fuss."

The Ghost nodded in acknowledgment. "I prefer to make my own." Only in that way could he ensure the proper strength.

The man shrugged and assembled the ingredients.

Next, The Ghost went to a second-hand clothier and bought two gowns for Brigitta. He thought he could guess her size, but he was unsure what colors and style to choose. Just what class had Brigitta been in before she'd been enslaved? He settled on two wool dresses—one a midnight blue and the other an emerald green, both with minimal embroidery. He also bought a black cloak with a large hood and a veil like those worn by all respectable women in Saloyna. He hoped Brigitta liked his choices. He'd never purchased clothing for a woman before.

When he returned to the Green Sandpiper, the Massossinan woman was asleep in the bed. He set the package containing his purchases beside her and quietly began making the serum over the fireplace. He made it extra strong on account of the boarhounds. As he stirred, he played over in his mind his intended trek through the palace and King Salome's death at his hand. Part of him thrilled at the idea of Salome's life in his hands. The rest of him knew his excitement meant his soul was forever lost.

He'd come back to Saloyna to take up his former profession because it was the country that had turned a simple stable groom into an assassin whose reputation spanned the world. Still, he wondered, *Holy Sulis, Mother of us all, could Ahearn have taken a path that didn't leave a pile of corpses in his wake? Or was the choice taken from him when a naïve young queen chose him as her lover?*

CHAPTER 2

Ahearn sat at a table in the back of the king's stable eating porridge with his fellow stable grooms, Gille and Jowan. The three of them had grown up together, first as stable boys, now as grooms. The king's stable was huge, housing more than a hundred horses. A cool morning breeze was blowing in through the open door, so it wasn't as unbearably hot as it would be at midday. He struggled not to smile. Today it was his turn to accompany the queen on her ride. He couldn't let his friends suspect that he no longer dreaded his turn as they did theirs.

"I'm glad I got two more days until I have to do it again," Gille said, scratching at his sorry excuse for a beard. "You better pray she's in a better mood than she was yesterday, and make sure you clean her saddle, her horse, everything until they sparkle, and I mean shiny. You know how prissy she is. Yesterday she found a speck of dirt on her saddle and yelled about me to Eamon for nearly fifteen minutes. I thought she was going to order me flogged."

Ahearn rubbed his much fuller beard, which Fenella said made him look manly. She also said its auburn color enhanced his masculinity further. Ahearn wasn't sure why, but who was he to question the queen?

The Master of the Horse came up behind them. "See that you do, Ahearn," Eamon said. "I do not want to get another earful today. If it'd been you that left the speck, I have no doubt she would have ordered at least ten lashes. Not that she likes any of us, but she especially seems to have it in for you."

"Yes, sir," Ahearn answered, struggling to keep his smile suppressed. Their plan was working. No one seemed to have the slightest suspicion of what they were up to.

"Can't you talk to the king, sir?" Jowan asked. "Get her bodyguards back on her at least. Then there'd be witnesses if she said we did anything wrong. I don't want to hang because she got her monthlies or something."

"I tried, boys, but His Majesty says the queen is insistent in not wanting bodyguards following her around, and he still won't allow her to ride unaccompanied. Someone needs to be near in case of an accident." Ahearn couldn't tell them about the tantrum Fenella had had to throw to get His Majesty to dismiss her bodyguards or her reason for wanting them gone. "Just keep at a respectful distance, and you needn't worry overly much. The king knows what she's like, and he'd never order you hanged on her word alone. A thorough flogging is probably the worse you have to fear."

"A flogging's the worst?" Gille said. "I saw Calder's back after he was flogged. I might rather hang."

Eamon put his hands on Ahearn's shoulders and squeezed them in a manner that reminded Ahearn of his dead uncle, who had been Eamon's best friend. "You know I'll always do my best for you boys, and it might well be that your fear of the queen is exaggerated. She's only a girl, after all." Jowan and Gille both scoffed loudly. Eamon patted Ahearn's shoulder. "All the same, do make sure everything is perfect. You better get a move on it, so you have plenty of time."

"Yes, sir." Ahearn jumped to his feet.

Ahearn grabbed an apple from the barrel and headed for Alita's stall near the front of the stables, next to the king's own gelding. The queen's white mare nickered at the sight of him. He held out the apple and scratched her neck in the way she liked. "You like me almost as much as your mistress does, don't you?" he whispered, as he began brushing the coat she always managed to dirty. "She could have had almost anybody, but she chose me. For a bastard son of a whore, I don't think I've done too badly for myself." The truth was he never would have gotten this job if it hadn't been for his uncle. He almost started whistling, but he heard someone coming and stopped himself. He shouldn't seem happy.

Gille stopped in front of Alita's stall. "I have just the thing to cheer you up. Jowan just found out from Dewin who found out from

Laoch that there's going to be a dance tonight at the weaver's guild hall. You remember how fine the girls were last time."

A few months ago Ahearn wouldn't have hesitated, but Fenella would throw a fit if he danced with another girl. "I'm a little worn out. Go without me."

"Not that excuse again!" Jowan joined them. "You need a new girl. Stop moaning over Sorcha. You know she's doing it with Gradh now."

"As if I care who that kitchen slut fucks," Ahearn scowled. A few months ago he'd cared a great deal. He'd lost his virginity to Sorcha, but it hadn't taken her long to decide she preferred the uniform of the Royal Guard to the stink of the stables. Gille and Jowan locked at each other with raised eyebrows. Gille shook his head, and Jowan shrugged. If they thought he wasn't over Sorcha, they'd never guess what he was really up to.

"I'll go get Hellfire ready for you," Jowan said, as Ahearn got down Alita's saddle. Hellfire was a jet-black gelding with a personality that matched his name. The queen always insisted whoever accompanied her ride him because he provided the perfect contrast for her mare.

When the horses were groomed and saddled, Ahearn and Jowan led them toward the stable door. Eamon stopped them and looked the horses over. "Just want to be sure the queen has nothing to complain about."

When Eamon was satisfied, they led the horses out to the mounting blocks. Ahearn handed Alita's reins to Gille, so he could be ready to assist the queen in mounting.

The side palace door opened, and a woman emerged. Ahearn couldn't see her well from this distance, but he had no doubt it was the queen. Jowan let out a whistle as she got close enough for them to see the way her riding dress clung to her curves. Her long blond hair was tied back in a braid. "Her Majesty is certainly easy on the eyes," Gille said. "If she weren't such a bitch, I'd almost pity her for being married to a man old enough to be her grandfather."

"Try great-grandfather," Jowan said. "His Majesty is over seventy, and the queen just turned fifteen."

"Maybe that's why she acts the way she does," Ahearn said, before he could stop himself. They didn't understand how awful it had been for her when her father sold her to the king.

Gille nodded. "You have a point. But I hear His Majesty's tiring of her. He spends far more time with his mistress."

The queen was getting close enough she might overhear, so they stopped talking and waited at respectful attention. They all bowed when she reached the mounting blocks.

"You again?" The queen looked at Ahearn like he was a piece of horse shit.

"If you'd prefer, Your Majesty, someone else could accompany you."

"What I prefer is to ride alone." She accepted Ahearn's assistance in mounting. It was hard to make his body behave when she was close.

"I'm sorry, Your Majesty, but His Majesty's orders are that you are to be accompanied."

"Just keep your distance," she said, and took off.

As he hurriedly mounted Hellfire, Ahearn rolled his eyes, and his friends gave him sympathetic looks.

From behind, he watched the queen riding sidesaddle and couldn't believe he'd soon hold those buttocks in his hands. As soon as they were out of sight of the stables, he caught up with her. She gave him her most radiant smile. "They still don't suspect anything, do they?"

"No, Your Majesty, but could you maybe be a little nicer to them? I don't like the things they say about you."

"I told you not to call me 'Your Majesty' when no one's around. You know why I have to act like I do. We can't afford anyone getting the slightest suspicion about us. I couldn't bear it if His Sulis-cursed Majesty hurt you in any way."

Ahearn grinned at her continued demonstration of how much she cared about him.

"I promise I'll make up for my rudeness," she said in that throaty voice that drove him wild. "Race you to the stream!" She touched her heels to her horse, leaving him behind.

As Ahearn took off after her, he felt a tightening in his groin. *Holy Sulis, how did I get so lucky that a woman like her wants a nobody like me?* Even though Hellfire could easily outdistance her mare, he stayed behind her, enjoying the view. Besides, she got huffy when she lost, and he definitely didn't want that.

Fenella laughed as her horse's feet splashed into the edge of the stream. Ahearn had never heard anything quite so musical. He jumped off Hellfire, looped the reins around a branch, took a blanket off the saddle, and laid it on the ground. He hurried to help Fenella dismount. She slid down the full length of his body as he lowered her into the stream. She turned her face up to his, and he kissed her deeply. Without warning, she wrapped her leg around his and jerked him off balance, falling on top of him into the stream. They came up together, laughing and dripping wet. Her dress clung to her body, leaving little to the imagination. He grabbed the dress around her waist and pulled it up over her head; she wore nothing underneath. He cupped her ivory breasts and found her lips again. He moved his hands down her body until they found the smooth firmness of her buttocks. She was so small he had no difficulty boosting her against him and carrying her to the shore. He lay her on the blanket, quickly tore off his own clothes, and lay down beside her.

"Oh, Hearn," she whispered. "Make love to me."

He readied her as quickly as he could and slipped himself slowly inside her. He hadn't gotten deep yet when he heard the crunch of a footstep behind him and felt the cold sharp point of a sword on his back.

"I think you've done enough, you rutting swine," a harsh voice commanded. "Stand up and turn around. Slowly." Certain he was about to die, Ahearn eased himself out of the queen and stood.

He turned to find Lord Caedmon holding the sword on him. Behind Caedmon, Duke Connor, the king's chancellor, approached, accompanied by two vicious dogs. "You should have let him finish, son," Duke Connor said. "It isn't good for a man's health to be left in that condition."

"His health is of little concern now that he's completed his service to his country," Caedmon grunted.

Ahearn didn't understand what they were talking about. He wanted to fall to his knees and beg for mercy. But why humiliate himself when he had no hope for leniency? He licked his lips and looked at Fenella, who'd wrapped the blanket around herself. She looked far more angry than frightened. Maybe she didn't understand the consequences of what they'd just been caught doing. "Don't hurt her, please," he whispered.

Duke Connor laughed. "Hurt Her Majesty? I wouldn't think of it. She is carrying Korthlundia's future—His Majesty's long-awaited heir."

"Like hell I am." Fenella jumped to her feet. "Solar is a wrinkled old man. He hasn't been able to do it in months. This baby,"—she touched her stomach, still smooth and flat—"isn't his."

Ahearn stared at the queen. "You're pregnant, Fen?"

Duke Connor smiled nastily. "The continued stability of the joined kingdoms requires that Solar have an heir. Since he's unable to beget his own, he needed someone to do it for him. I've informed His Majesty of your vigorous efforts on his behalf." Ahearn stared at the duke, mortified at the thought of the fifty-year-old pervert looking on and evaluating his performance. "Now that you've done your part, I've been ordered to 'take care' of you."

Ahearn dropped to his knees, afraid he was either going to faint or vomit. *His Majesty set me up! Holy Sulis, how could I have been so stupid to think no one knew?*

"No!" Fenella screamed, seeming to understand for the first time how bad the situation was. "Don't hurt him! It's all my fault! I just wanted . . . I just wanted . . ."

"Wanted what, Your Majesty?" Duke Connor asked, as if what she wanted was of no concern.

Fenella's words cut like the sharpest sword. "You smug bastard! No one knows better than you what I wanted! I told you I wouldn't be given to an old man to be used as a brood mare! But nobody listened! Not you! Not my father! And not His Sulis-damned Majesty! But I've had my revenge! I got a stable groom with shit on his boots to do what the great Solar couldn't!"

Ahearn felt like he'd been kicked in the gut. "Fen, you can't mean that. I thought . . ."

"I'm afraid thinking played little part in your activities," the duke sneered. He nodded, and Ahearn felt something smash into the back of his head. He fell to the ground, his skull erupting in pain. He tried to move, but was struck again. As if from a great distance, he heard the noblemen talking.

"This is a waste of effort and money," Caedmon complained. "We should just kill him here and dump him in the harbor. The rutting swine's only a stable groom, and he'll be a liability as long as he's alive. We both know what His Majesty meant by taking care of him."

"Enough!" the duke snapped. "We've been over this. He's just a lad. I'm chancellor, and you'd do well to remember that. Now, take him as we've arranged."

"Fine," Caedmon snapped, and Ahearn was kicked in the head.

* * *

When Ahearn woke, he found himself, still naked, in a small, dark place, lying on bare boards. From the way the floor moved under him, he knew he was on a ship. His head pounded abominably. He curled up into a ball, shaking with cold and fear. *Holy Suis, Mother of us all, what are they going to do to me?* He thought he knew the answer. They couldn't hang him if they wanted the affair to remain a secret, so they were going to take him out to sea and throw him overboard. He couldn't swim, and the thought of drowning terrified him more than the thought of a noose. Maybe he could fight them and make them kill him before they threw him over.

For a long time, no one came, and over and over again he replayed the scene by the river and heard Fenella's mocking voice. *It isn't true. She couldn't have just been using me. She told me she loved me.* He remembered the first time they'd made love. It had been just after her bodyguards had been dismissed, and it had been his turn to accompany her riding. She stopped at the edge of the stream. She'd said she wanted to watch the fish for a while, so he'd helped her dismount. She sat at the edge of the stream while he stood at a respectful distance.

After a few minutes, he noticed her shoulders shaking and heard her sobbing, her head buried in her arms. At first this surprised him. He'd never consider royalty to be like real people with real emotions. Still, as a servant, he knew he should pretend not to notice. But she sounded so sad he couldn't just stand there. He'd knelt near her. "Can I fetch someone for you, Your Majesty?"

She shook her head without looking up. "Nobody here cares about me. They all think I'm just a foolish girl."

"I'm sure that's not true, Your Majesty," he said, even though he knew it was. Most of the nobility never seemed to see stable hands, so they talked freely in front of them. "Foolish" was one of the nicer words they used to describe her.

"Of course it is," she sobbed. "They see me as nothing but the *great* Solar's brood mare. I hate him. I wish he'd just die."

Ahearn froze. He couldn't begin to count the number of things wrong with her talking to him like this. Queens didn't talk to servants, except to give orders, and what she was saying was close to treason. He tried to tell himself to just walk back to the horses and remain properly oblivious to the actions of his betters. But her sorrow tugged at him, and instead, he found himself asking, "Can I do anything for you, Your Majesty?"

"I feel so alone, Ahearn." The queen met his eyes, her face streaked with tears. He was surprised she knew his name; she'd never used it before. He couldn't remember any of the nobility ever doing so. "Could you . . . could you hold me? Just for a little while?" The sane part of his brain told him to run away as fast as possible. This was the queen! If anyone saw, he'd hang. She noticed his hesitation, and her eyes welled up with tears. She looked so young and vulnerable. "Please. Nobody will ever know, and I need someone."

He swallowed the lump in his throat and sat next to her. "If you want me to, Your Majesty." She threw herself against his chest. He put his arms around her, his heart pounding in terror. She clung to him and sobbed on his shoulder. Her hands started wandering, and she nibbled slowly up his neck, searching for his lips. Before he could think about it, he was kissing her. It felt so right, so natural that it wasn't long before kissing wasn't all they were doing.

"I love you," she'd whispered, as they lay together afterward. "You're always so kind, so gentle with the horses despite how strong you are." She caressed the muscles in his arms. He'd believed her love then, and the hundred other times she'd told him since. Because of that love, he'd been willing to risk his life to comfort her.

But as he heard her voice again, shouting at the nobleman about the shit on his boots, he knew it had all been a lie. She'd chosen him because his place at the bottom of the social ladder would amplify the insult to the king. He also realized her revenge would be meaningless if the king was ignorant of the affair. *Holy Sulis, she'd wanted us caught. She threw my life away. How could I have been so stupid?*

Now, he sat in the darkness, waiting to die. At last he heard footsteps. Two men opened the door. One of them held a sword while the other brought in food, water, and a bucket. They said nothing to him, met all of his questions with silence, and left him in darkness again.

* * *

The darkness allowed Ahearn no way to keep track of the days and nights. Food and water were brought at regular intervals, and the contents of his bucket emptied. But no one explained what was being done to him. If they were going to kill him, he could see no reason for them to wait this long. His best guess now was that he was to be sold as a slave.

After what seemed like months, Ahearn felt the ship stop moving and heard the bustle of noise that told him they'd made port. Still, it was hours before anyone came for him. When they did, it was the same two men he'd always seen. One of them threw him a pile of clothes and finally spoke, "Get dressed."

Ahearn did as ordered. They directed him up the ladder onto the deck. Ahearn blinked as his eyes adjusted to the light after so long in darkness. He was indeed in a harbor, one nearly three times the size of Murtaghan's. Hundreds of ships were lined up on either side of his, flying flags of all nations, some Ahearn had never seen before. A huge city crawled up from the edge of the water into the surrounding hills. It gleamed white and pink in the late afternoon sun.

The men led him to the gangway where others were unloading the cargo. "You're free to go," one of them said. "Don't come back."

Ahearn started down the gangway, not quite believing he'd be allowed to simply walk away. He expected a knife in the back at any moment. But he reached the dock without incident, and when he looked back at the ship, he couldn't see either of the two men. No one paid any attention to him as he blended with the people that thronged the busy harbor. *Where am I?* As he moved away from the docks, olive-skinned, thin-nosed people filled the city's streets. He'd seen Saloynan ambassadors and envoys at the palace, so he knew what they looked like, but he knew next to nothing about the country.

His stomach rumbled, and he stopped abruptly as he came to fully realize his predicament. He couldn't speak the language. He had no money, no food, nothing at all but the clothes he was wearing. *Holy Sulis, what in the seven hells am I supposed to do now?*

ABOUT THE AUTHOR

Jamie began writing stories about the man from Mars when she was six, and she never remembers wanting to be anything other than a writer. Everyone told her she needed a back up plan, so she pursued a Ph.D. in American literature, which she received in 1998. She started teaching writing and literature at Auburn University. One day in the midst of writing a piece of literary criticism, she realized she'd put her true passion on the backburner and neglected her muse. The literary article went into the trash, and she began the book that was to become *The Goddess's Choice*, which was published in April 2012. Her other novels include *The Soul Stone* and *The Ghost in Exile*. In addition, she has published a novella, *Demons in the Big Easy*, and a collection of short stories, *Blood Cursed and Other Tales of the Fantastic*. Her short fiction has also appeared in the anthologies--*Urban Fantasy* and *Of Dragons & Magic: Tales of the Lost Worlds*—and in *Bards & Sages*, *The World of Myth*, *A Writer's Haven*, and *Short-story.me*. She claims she writes about the fantastic. . . and the tortured soul. Her poor characters have hard lives. She lives in Auburn, Alabama, with her husband and four cats, which (or so she's been told) officially makes her a cat lady. She still teaches writing and literature at Auburn University. She is the mother of a grown son, who is a fantastic young man.

OTHER BOOKS BY JAMIE MARCHANT

The Kronicles of Korthlundia

> *The Goddess's Choice*, expanded edition (2017)
>   original edition (2012)
> *The Soul Stone* (2015)
> *The Ghost in Exile* (2016)

The Bull Riding Witch (2017)
Blood Cursed and Other Tales of the Fantastic (2016)--short story collection
Demons in the Big Easy: A Novella (2013)

Story Collections including her work
>   *Waiting for a Kiss: A Princess Fairy Tale Anthology* (2017)
>   *Of Dragons & Magic: Tales of Lost Worlds* (2014)
>   *Urban Fantasy* (2013)
>   *Best Genre Short Stories Anthology #2: Short-Story.Me!*
>   *(Volume 2)* (2010)

www.ingramcontent.com/pod-product-compliance
Lightning Source LLC
Chambersburg PA
CBHW030248270626
47156CB00021B/202